The Tiler of Althurst

LEO BLACK

Cover image by Blake Sullivan

For C for her patience, and O for his lack of it.

'Alas! the grim legion…they must be suffered to slumber, or we perish.'

EDGAR ALLAN POE, *The Premature Burial*

PROLOGUE

Althurst Abbey, Hampshire – 1171

The interior of the cell was cool and grey, its corners hidden in shadow - even on this bright spring morning, and even before the men had begun the slow work of walling her up inside.

Sister Merwinna stood very still for a moment, breathing deeply, allowing her heartbeat to slow, and letting her eyes adjust to the reduced light. Then she reached out a hand, and gently ran the tips of her fingers along the section of wall nearest to her, tracing the outlines of the stones. Every tiny crack or blemish, every slight rise or fall in their surfaces would, she supposed, become familiar. The stones were cool to touch. The warmth of the sunshine outside had not reached them. Apart from the area opposite the small window to the world beyond, it never would.

She smiled to herself. She was glad now that Father Jerome had insisted upon her spending some time inside this place prior to today. That way, the priest had told her, the impact of the change when it became permanent would not be quite such a shock, and quite so overwhelming for her. Sister Merwinna was glad, and she would not deny it. But not glad for the reasons that the priest had suggested. Father Jerome had been worried that the immediate effect of so drastic an alteration in the way she would experience the world from here on would threaten to undermine her resolve. It was no small thing, he said, to choose the life of an anchoress. To be walled up inside a cell for the rest of your days, even if it was by choice, in order to be free from worldly distraction, and therefore to be brought nearer to God. In fact, Merwinna had not been worried about that at all. She was glad to have prior experience of these new surroundings because she wanted as little as possible that

1

could divert her attention from the joyful prayers of thanks that she intended to be the focus of the first few days of her new life – prayers she hoped would set the pattern for the rest of her time on earth, before she was gathered unto the Lord completely, and for good.

Behind her, Merwinna heard the Bishop begin to read the order of the dead. "Dead," she whispered the word to herself. Strange to have that term applied to oneself and yet still be alive to hear it said. She gave the merest of shrugs. It held no terrors for her. It was simply how she would be as far as her old life was concerned. Gone from it, and gone forever. It was her new life that mattered now: the fulfilment of her desire to become an anchoress, and all that entailed. There were some, she knew, would mourn for her. She, Merwinna, would rejoice.

Outside, the Bishop's voice now had to compete with the sounds made by the mason and his men as they began the task of setting in place the first of the stones that would seal up for good the last remaining way to leave this small space. When that work was complete, the only openings would be the three small windows: one in the wall the cell shared with the Abbey Church, through which Merwinna could hear the mass, take communion, and make confession; another out into the Abbey grounds, covered in a translucent cloth to keep out the cold when the seasons changed, but allowing in sufficient sunlight by which she could read and, perhaps, write, if she were so inspired; and a final gap – not really a window – close to the ground, where those whose task it would be to see to her less spiritual needs could pass her food and water, and remove her earthly body's waste products. She did not like to think about, let alone look at this last gap; it reminded her of all she wished to leave behind her but, no matter how apart from the world she set herself, never quite could. Not yet, anyway. She was a young woman still, but that time would come.

When first asked, the men now placing the final stones

had refused to perform the work. They, like many living in and around Althurst Abbey, had known Merwinna from a child and said they did not want to be responsible for such a deed. It was only when Abbess Claire had rebuked them for a lack of faith, asking how they dared put their personal affections for the girl before a calling she had received from God Himself, that they had agreed. Even so, they had looked pale and uncomfortable when she greeted them that morning. "Do your work well, and do it with a full heart," she had said to Big Peter, the master mason as she passed him. He had not spoken in reply, merely nodded, and looked down at the ground in front of him.

Merwinna knew Big Peter and his men were not alone in having doubts about her choice. Even among the other nuns of the Abbey there had been whisperings. Some of her fellow sisters worried she may have misinterpreted the signs, misunderstanding what it was that God wished from her. Others, she was sure, had been less charitable, accusing the young nun of the sin of pride. Her actions might well appear driven by humility and self-effacement - denying as much as it was possible of her own earthly wants and needs, without actually committing the sin of self-murder - but could not that be done just as well within the broader walls of the Abbey? Why was so dramatic an act as having oneself walled up within the confines of a tiny cell required? Wasn't she, quite literally, singling herself out as being special, and by implication, chosen above all others? But then, the doubts and disapproval of other people was just one of the many tests Merwinna knew she must undergo, and she was more than prepared for it. Without question, there would be far more difficult things ahead of her in the coming days.

Only the thought of Garrick's suffering on his learning of her decision had her caused Merwinna any real misgivings. She and Garrick had both grown up in Althurst. Merwinna an orphan in the care of the sisters at the Abbey, Garrick the son of a potter in the town. They had played together as children, and always been close. Unfortunately for Garrick, while his affection for Merwinna grew from being a child's friendship into an adult's love, her love for him had been more like that of a sister for a brother, and had never grown beyond that. The great love of Merwinna's life had always been God, and Garrick ought to have known that. Even so, it had nearly destroyed him when she took holy orders. He had moved away from Althurst in the hope of forgetting her – taking work as a potter in another town - but had been forced to return when his father grew too ill to support Garrick's mother and younger sisters. He took over his father's business and, eventually, married a girl from the town whom, Merwinna feared, he might never truly love. Still, knowing Garrick for the good and kind man he was, she knew he would never mistreat his bride. After that, Merwinna did not see him as often. When she did, he never spoke, and avoided making eye contact with her. But she knew he saw her, and that just being close to her caused him pain. What would he feel when he learned – as she knew he must – of her decision to become an anchoress? How would it be for him knowing that, every Sunday, when he and the rest of the town gathered to worship at the church, she would be only a few yards away, listening to the priest saying the same mass as he, Garrick, was hearing, yet shut alone in her cell, walled up in what some whose faith was not so pure and so strong as her own, considered a living death? She imagined the scene, felt a brief pang of guilt and pity for poor Garrick, and then quickly dismissed it as irrelevant, temporary. Garrick's reaction had worried her to begin with, it was true. Eventually, however, Merwinna had reasoned that he would grow used to his pain; much as she would grow used to her new situation and its privations. She told herself that he would, one day, come to be grateful to her. His suffering, he would come to realise, was transitory. The kind of love that currently tormented him, and bounded his every action – much as the walls of her cell bounded hers – though it seemed otherwise to him now, was in fact a selfish love. He wanted her for himself, and would keep her from God. He wanted her flesh for himself. But, as his own flesh withered with age, and desire lost its shameful influence upon him, Garrick would see that Merwinna had been right all along. He would be thankful to her; he had but to wait. As he grew older and wiser, he too would reach the sort of understanding that she had been blessed with reaching at so early an age.

So enraptured was Merwinna by her thoughts, it was only gradually that she became aware that someone was singing outside. Was it a child's voice? No, a woman's. One of the sisters who gathered to say their goodbyes, perhaps? Surely now it was a male voice? Father Jerome's, then? No, it would not be him. Who did it belong to, then? Definitely not the Bishop's. Big Peter? Or one of his men. Had to be. Could only be. There was no one else.

Something brushed against her face. She flinched, and then, almost immediately, smiled to herself. A mayfly, of course. Up from the river. It was that time of year, after all. She hadn't seen it, but what else could it be? Her smile broadened. Even inside her cell there were some aspects of God's glorious creation that would still be available to her.

The singing caught her attention again. The melody was sweet, if a little mournful. Even though she could not make out the words, she could tell it spoke of a loss so painful it could almost not be endured. *Garrick*? Please, no. Don't let it be Garrick!

Foolishness! It couldn't be him. He, like the rest of the townsfolk, had been ordered to stay away. Although, he might have ignored the command, of course. Then again, she had not known Garrick to be much of singer, happy or sad. She shook her head. What did it matter who it was? She tried not to listen. She took a deep breath, clearing her mind of it. But the sound kept finding its way in, interrupting her thoughts. The melody had changed now. It was no longer sad at all. It grew much louder, and the tempo increased. This was no pious, Christian song. It was secular, bawdy in style and content. Even before she was able to pick out the lyrics, she knew they would be unworthy. When, finally, as the volume rose, they became clear to her, they were so unpleasant and degraded they made her put her hands over her ears.

In the song it was May Day. A young man was singing of his intentions towards a young woman. Horrible, horrible things. How could the Bishop be allowing this? It was not fitting for her special day. Why on earth was the singer not made to stop? More and more descriptions of his lustful intentions. And the name of the girl to whom these intentions were devoted? It was hers. Merwinna. Disgusting to taunt her in this way on such a day as this. Again, she wondered why nobody was doing anything to make the singer stop. May God forgive them for it. How long before that last brick was in place and the sound at least muffled, if not shut out entirely.

Then the singing stopped.

Sighing with relief, Merwinna allowed herself to take her hands from her ears, and open her eyes.

The cell was much darker now. She had her back to the men walling her up, and saw in front of her that the rectangle of daylight shining through from the entrance was almost gone, reduced now to a small bright patch on the opposite wall. Without thinking, she turned, and saw the sad eyes of Big Peter looking in at her through the remaining gap. They made eye contact for an instant, and then the big man's ashen face moved away. The next moment he was putting the last stone in place, shutting her in, and most of the daylight out. She felt sure he had said something as he did it. Almost under his breath. Not quite. A prayer, perhaps? No, something else. What had it been?

"May God forgive me, sister." That was it.

Poor Peter. He just didn't seem to understand. There was nothing to be forgiven.

She had a sudden doubt. Something troubled her. Was that *really* what Peter had whispered to her? She tried to remember.

Had he actually said…? No, it was unthinkable. Why would he say such a thing? But that *was* how it sounded now, as it echoed in her memory. "May God forgive you, sister." May God forgive *you*.

She had a sudden urge to push out the last brick before the mortar set. Not to escape, only so she could call Peter back while there was still time, and ask him what he had said. And, if he had said what she now thought he had, what he had meant by it.

She shook her head, and turned her back on the newly filled in wall. It was foolishness, she told herself. Peter might have said it, or he might not. Even if he had, Peter himself might not know exactly why, and what he had meant by it. What she was doing confused many people. It seemed to make some of them angry, as well as sad. Not everyone was as strong as she was, or possessed her level of faith, that was all.

Looking around, she took a deep breath. So, this was it. This was to be her world from now on. This perpetual half-light. A living nightmare to most people, but a rare and wonderful gift to Merwinna, because she knew a day would come when the shadows evaporated, and all would be brilliance. Eternal, heavenly, brilliance. And she would be suitably prepared for it. In fact, she would begin that preparation right now, with a prayer of thanks. She knelt down, hands pressed together, and head bowed.

To her dismay and frustration, the awful singing started up almost the same moment she closed her eyes. Nearer now, but strangely muted - almost as if the singer had his hand over his mouth.

The unseen mayfly flitted past her face again. She brushed it away.

Then, whoever was singing must have taken his hand away

from his mouth because she could hear it so loudly and clearly it was as if he were crouched right behind her, his mouth against her ear.

Merwinna cried out in shock. She raised her hands - at first with the intention of pressing them to her ears. Instead, she clasped them back together in front of herself once more, and began to pray as fervently as she was able.

******

CHAPTER 1

Althurst Abbey – 1307

Will Tiler was sitting on a bench against a wall of the antechamber to the Abbess's receiving room. It might only have been the antechamber, but it was a far larger and far grander room than most ordinary people – like the majority of those who lived in the town beyond the Abbey walls, where Will was lodging - were ever likely to see in their entire lifetime. Even so, it was nothing compared to many of the other buildings in the Abbey complex. Particularly the huge Abbey Church itself, with its long knave and high tower making it easily the largest building for many miles. Although Will's work making and laying tiles had taken him to many similar places in the past, he had never lost his astonishment at the wealth it must require on the part of the religious communities they housed to create and maintain them. And, of more interest to Will, the skill of the men who built them.

The antechamber walls were of dressed stone, with a single glazed window at the centre of the wall on the side of the room that looked out over the Abbey herb gardens. This window was a relatively small one when compared to some of those Will's craftsman's eye had already noticed in the Abbey Church itself, but it was impressive, nonetheless. The time was around midday, and the June sun was high in the sky above Hampshire, shining down through the window onto the stone floor in a gradually elongating trapezium, with patches of all the colours of the glass it had passed through contained within the shadows of the surrounding tracery.

Despite the heat outside, the air in the antechamber was cool – even to the point of being slightly chilly – which made Will suspect incipient dampness in the walls or in the flagstones underfoot. In other circumstances this coolness might have come as a relief on such an otherwise stiflingly hot day, but Will was nervous, and cold tremors ran up and down his back. Worse, the palms of hands had developed a cold clamminess, forcing him to repeatedly rub them on his tunic. The cool of the surrounding air did nothing to alleviate his discomfort, and he found himself longing to be back outside in the warmth, out from this uncomfortable chamber, and getting on with the work he understood and was good at.

Opposite him, on the other side of the window, sat a young woman whose clothing seemed to mark her out as a member of the Abbey community, although maybe not yet of the order. She must still be a novice, Will decided, with her final vows yet to be taken. From the paleness of her features, the distracted way her eyes darted about the room, and the anxious way she was rocking back and forth, with her hands clasped between her knees, she seemed even more nervous than Will. He guessed she was in some sort of trouble, and was about to confront the displeasure of the Abbess as a result. A novice, but possibly not a terribly obedient one. Will wondered what the nature of her transgression could have been. She looked so young and, in his eyes at least, innocent. Whatever it was, she would have to wait until Will had had his own audience with the Abbess before she would learn what the punishment for it was going to be.

Will could hear the voice of the Bishop in the next room. He was letting Abbess Rhoswen know more of the detail of his intentions for the tiled floor Will was to create in the new chapel dedicated to St Merwinna. The matter was already settled in the Bishop's mind, despite the many objections the Abbess had raised in recent communications. The reason for Will's presence here today was merely for him to be introduced as the man Bishop Baldwin had chosen to be the instrument of those intentions, and for the Abbess to be reminded to co-operate as Will carried them out. This, the

Bishop had explained to Will, had become something of regular requirement, ever since he had announced the decision to build a small chapel on the spot where what remained of the saint's cell stood. On learning of it, the Abbess had been outraged, claiming that such a thing was in direct opposition to the example of humility and disavowal of earthly vanities that Merwinna, as an anchoress, had set. It was, the Abbess claimed, not fitting. These objections notwithstanding, work on the building had gone ahead as the Bishop had ordered. The masons had been busy, and the major structural work was complete. The interior decoration was now underway; the floor Will was to create being the next stage in that process.

Since the saint's mysterious death, her crumbling cell had become a shrine. Pilgrims came from all over England to kneel before the darkness beyond the hole in the wall where once her everyday needs had been attended to. The inescapably unsavoury nature of what some of those needs were was rarely mentioned, although they cannot have failed to cross the minds of many of the pilgrims who knelt there. Even so, the ruined cell was considered a sacred place, and many miracles had since been attributed to the prayers given there in Saint Merwinna's name. And so, from the moment the first mason had set the first stone of the new chapel in place, Abbess Rhoswen had gone out of her way to interfere with, and hinder the work. Eventually, tales of her interference had reached the ears of the Bishop, and it seemed the only way for this troublesome little woman – as the Bishop candidly, but privately, described her to Will – to be kept in her place was to be regularly reminded of it by visits, like this one, from the Bishop himself.

What bothered the Bishop most, he had said, was the narrow-minded woman's wilful refusal to appreciate that, as things stood, the walls of Merwinna's cell would have been nothing but rubble in a very few years. The new chapel had been built with the intention of preventing that from happening. Due to the careful planning by the master mason in charge of the renovation, what remained of the cell walls had not been destroyed at all. The exact opposite was true. They had been preserved, and incorporated into the new, much stronger walls of the chapel. When the work was complete, pilgrims would no longer have to crouch down in the mud and grass, screwing up their eyes to look into the gloom of a hole where the saint's shit bucket had once travelled back and forth. *That* was what was not fitting. When the chapel was complete, visitors could walk right inside, kneel, pray before an altar, and give their thanks in appropriately magnificent surroundings. Surroundings that befitted the shrine of a saint. And no small part of the splendour of those surroundings would be the floor of tiles that Will would make and lay. The Bishop's plan was for the preservation and enhancement of the saint's reputation, not the diminishment of it. It was just the stubbornness of the Abbess that prevented her from acknowledging that fact. Hers was the sin of pride, not the Bishop's.

Will had merely nodded when Bishop Baldwin had explained all this to him. Although he could not help reflecting on the one point the Bishop had been careful to avoid touching upon. That being the fact that, as a Bishop, Baldwin was not, in fact, a member of the Benedictine Order. Ordinarily, he could expect to have no say in what did or did not get built at Althurst Abbey. What gave him a say on this particular issue was the will of the King. And that was never going to be something Abbess Rhoswen, or any of her order, could choose to ignore.

If ever it was spoken of, the circumstance for the involvement of the King in the matter of the chapel was usually referred to by the Bishop as the 'conversation'. It seemed that King Edward had, in conversation with Abbot Stephen - a high ranking member of the Benedictines - heard the story of the miracles attributed to Saint Merwinna and her, now crumbling, chapel. Impressed by what he heard;

King Edward had expressed a wish do something to honour the saint. It was at this point that Bishop Baldwin, also present at this conversation, had suggested rebuilding the chapel. It was also at this point that Abbot Stephen had made the mistake of baulking at the idea. Not, as Abbess Rhoswen would later, due to its not being fitting, but due to the potential costs involved. This had provided Baldwin with the opportunity of offering to finance the building from Church funds, given that the Benedictines themselves were refusing to pay for it. So flagrant a piece of one-upmanship made it difficult for many - Will included - not to suspect that it had, in truth, been Bishop Baldwin and not Abbot Stephen who introduced the subject of the Saint's chapel with that very outcome in mind. The apparently casual 'conversation' he referred to might actually have been a deliberately planned raising of a subject with a particular motive behind it.

Generally, Will did not trouble himself much with such things. The role God had picked out for him was that of a craftsman, and his craft was making tiles. If it was God's will that the floor be laid, it would be. The King, it seemed to Will, was more powerful than Bishop Baldwin or Abbess Rhoswen, so if God had put it into King Edward's head that the chapel should be built, then it would be. It must, therefore, be God's plan. And that was sufficient justification for Will to carry out his work with a clear conscience.

Nonetheless, Will reflected, whatever it was the unhappy young woman sitting opposite him right now might be accused of having done, it was very likely the Abbess would be far more displeased with Bishop Baldwin and, through him, with Will, than she would be with this novice. Unfortunately for the girl, however, whilst Abbess Rhoswen might stress her objections very strongly, it was not, and never had been, within her power to prevent the Bishop from having almost his every wish for the new chapel carried out. That included Will's floor, so there was every chance she would end up taking out her frustration on the unfortunate novice.

When she was not looking, Will took a minute to study the young woman. Her expression - a mixture of anxiety and resentment - reminded him a little of how his own daughter, Sarah, used to look when, as a child, she knew she was about to receive a scolding from her mother, Will's late wife. And it was true that, more often than not, it was his wife, not Will himself, who did the scolding. In fact, it was a frequent complaint of his wife's that Will was too soft on the girl. On reflection, Will now felt she had probably been right about that, God rest her soul.

He glanced at the novice again. Odd, these nuns were all someone's daughter once. He supposed they still were, but it no longer seemed appropriate to think of them in those terms. For once, he was glad his Sarah was married, even if it was to the workshy Hamo. Better that by far, than shut away in a place like this. Married to God? Wasn't that what they said? Or was it to Jesus? Well, it was something like that anyway. Will was only glad his own daughter would never be enclosed by stone walls like these, no matter how grand they might be.

Just at that moment, the girl looked up, inadvertently meeting his eyes. She had a nice face, thought Will. Not perhaps truly beautiful as the conventions for such things would have it, but pretty and pleasant in its own way. The anxious frown that sat upon it at present was out of place on such a face. Will smiled, but she looked away, embarrassed, and clearly more than a little irritated. Will shook his head, smiled again, only this time to himself. Like Sarah in more than just the way she looked, then. That same stubbornness and pride. It made sense for a girl like that to be in trouble with the Abbess.

When the oak door of the next room finally opened, the face that peered around it was not, as Will had expected it would be, that of Father Hugh – an elderly priest, long-time friend and, these days, personal assistant to the Bishop, who accompanied him almost everywhere that he went – but, to Will's surprise, it was that of the Bishop himself. Will immediately stood up. The young nun, clearly a little dumbfounded to see the Bishop standing there, was about to do the same, but the prelate raised a pudgy hand and gestured for her to remain seated.

"No, no, my dear child. You stay as you are. You look so very… comfortable."

She is anything but that, thought Will.

The Bishop turned to him with a barely concealed smile, clearly enjoying the novelty of having opened the door himself, and the shock it had caused. "Come, Master Tiler, join us," he said.

Up until now, the Bishop's manner towards Will had not been as unfriendly or as remote as it might have been expected to be, given the difference in status between them. This should not, perhaps, have surprised Will; the prelate had a reputation for fairness and openness compared to others of similar rank when it came to his interactions with those around him. Even so, such affability from someone so high in the Church had, at first, been almost as uncomfortable as the usual aloofness that Will had come to anticipate when, and if, they chose to address him. He had found it difficult not suspect it was all simply an act put on by the Bishop in order to maintain his reputation for Christian warmth and kindness. After all, such a reputation made it difficult for anyone who opposed him not to seem, almost necessarily, in the wrong, simply by going up against the will of such an apparently warm, godly man – a true Christian if ever there was one. There were times when it served Baldwin better than an army when it came to getting his way. However, the more times Will met with the Bishop, the more he came to think that it might not be an act after all. Well, not entirely, at any rate. He had soon found that, despite his reservations, he had warmed to this apparently genial man of God. This *fat* man of God.

Fat Bishops. Baldwin was the very epitome of the overweight, over-fed member of the clergy that was so often grumbled about. Will knew full well that the diet that had fuelled the creation of that vast, round belly and those double chins was a sign of the wealth of the Church that many in the land resented – although few would ever express it in public – and he was not immune to a touch of that resentment himself. However, that diet seemed to be where Baldwin's self-interest ended. The food at his table aside, he gave the impression of genuinely wanting to use the wealth of the Church for the glory of God. Better if all of that wealth were to be used to clothe the naked and feed the starving, some said. Yet when had that ever happened? It never had, and it never would. Human nature being what it was, that *some* of it *some*times would be was most likely the best anyone could expect. Besides, Will was not blind to the fact that it was the wealth of the Church that provided him with his own livelihood. The poor could not afford tiles for their lowly dwellings, could they? Without the patronage of the Church, Will himself would starve, and join them in their poverty. It did not do to dwell too much on the rights and wrongs of such things. Whereas the big sins could be avoided, the little ones were part of day to day living. Nothing could be done about them in this life. As for reward or punishment, that came later. Looked at like that, Bishop Baldwin was far from the worst of men. Why should Will not like him a little? And take his money, too.

All the same, the tone with which the Bishop now spoke to him was more than merely cordial. It was that of one old friend speaking to another. He had never been quite *this* friendly before, and this, Will knew immediately, *was* an act. It disappointed him. Baldwin wanted the Abbess to see just how friendly with someone of low birth he was capable of being; just how humble and free of airs he was. How could she stand in the way of such a man? How could she dare say he did not understand the legacy of Saint Merwinna? Was not the Saint's humility embodied in this man of God who stood before her now?

"Join us," repeated the Bishop, and then, detecting Will's reticence, backed this up with a reassuring nod of his head. "Come in, William. Come in."

William. Even in their most informal discussions – usually those concerning the problem of the Abbess's objections to the building of the chapel – he had, until now, always been *Master Tiler.* Today he was *William*?

Will nervously wiped his palms on his tunic again, ran a hand through his hair, and then followed the Bishop into the next room. The Bishop had waited just inside in the doorway, one arm outstretched towards Will who, for one uncomfortable moment, thought the cleric might even be intending to put that arm around his shoulder in a fatherly manner. Thankfully, Bishop Baldwin had not gone quite that far in his display of affability towards the tiler. He had, however, gone as far as putting a friendly hand on Will's shoulder, and steering him towards a large oak table, behind which sat a woman whose face displayed suspicion and irritation in equal parts, and made no attempt whatsoever to hide it. It was an expression as calculated in its show of displeasure at meeting Will as was the Bishop's in its show of pleasure. So, this was Abbess Rhoswen. It seemed to be Will's day to irritate the women of Althurst Abbey.

Although from this first impression the Abbess was clearly every bit as determined and formidable as the Bishop had described her, what surprised Will was that she was only in her middle years. In fact, she was probably not very much older than Will was himself. From the Bishop's description of her, Will had imagined someone much older, similar in age to the Bishop. And, now Will saw her, he realised he had also imagined someone heavier. Someone large, and broad of girth like the Bishop - Baldwin's mirror in all but gender. Instead, the woman before him did not need to stand for Will to see that, in reality, she was not only very slight of build, she was also unusually short. From a distance she might easily be taken for a child. It made Will feel oddly self-conscious about his own height; he was a tall, well-built man. He suddenly remembered something the Bishop had once said of Abbess Rhoswen. He had called her '*a little woman in a role far too big for her.*' At the time Will had not understood that the insult was almost as much literal as it was figurative. What the Bishop had followed this statement up with also made more sense to Will now. He had said, "*I caution you not to let that fool you, Master Tiler. The vipers that glide through our own meadows on a summer day may not be as large as those I have heard tell of living in the Moorish lands, but they still have a venomous bite of which you must beware.*" The Bishop had then formed a beak shape with his pudgy thumb and forefinger, and pinched at the air, laughing at his own words.

Now the eyes of that viper were fixed upon Will. As was the custom on meeting such people, Will knelt, his own eyes to the floor. "My Lady."

"You will address me as Reverend Mother, for that is who I am. Your lack of knowledge surprises me. I cannot be the first of my kind you have had occasion to meet, given the nature of the trade you are in. If I am, the men of the Bishop's party should have better prepared you." It was not clear what, if any, of this had been put as a question, and Will was uncertain if a reply was required. He decided to hold his tongue, and remained kneeling, waiting for permission to stand. There followed a long pause during which the Abbess fell silent, and Will could not help thinking she was enjoying prolonging his embarrassment.

"*Reverend Mother.* Yes…indeed you are," agreed the Bishop, after a moment, his tone expertly judged to be as close to mocking as was possible without actually being so. "I wonder…might not permission now be given for…" The sensation of a fleeting breeze above his head suggested to Will that the Bishop had made some gesture in his direction.

"You may rise, man," said the Abbess at last.

"William, you must do as the Reverend Mother bids," said the Bishop, his tone still bordering on the sardonic. It was an unnecessary instruction, as William was already in the process of getting to his feet. But now he wondered if it might be better to appear to respond to a command that came from Abbess Rhoswen, rather than from the Bishop, given that it was her receiving room they were in. He hesitated, in an uncomfortable half-crouch, uncertain what to do.

"*Rise*, man," repeated the Abbess, her tone one of undisguised irritation. The question being how much of it was with Will for not having immediately responded to her instruction, and how much at the Bishop's derisive manner towards her.

William looked up. The Abbess glanced down, very briefly met William's eyes, and then gestured impatiently for him to get to his feet. Before Will had risen she had already turned back to the Bishop. "This irresolute fellow is the tiler you recommend," she said. It was more statement than question. The Bishop answered it nonetheless.

"This is the man upon whom I insist, yes. This is William. William Tiler. I have seen his work," said the Bishop. "It is of the highest quality. We must have nothing but the best for our saint. You will do your best work for Saint Merwinna, will you not William? William…?"

Will did not answer. Now he had had a moment to take in his surroundings, he had been distracted by them. The difference between this room and the antechamber where he had just been waiting was not only in size. Whilst the latter had been impressive enough by most people's standards, this new room easily surpassed it. What contributed to this most was the painting that took up almost the entirety of the wall behind the high table at which the Abbess was sitting. It was among the most striking Will had ever seen, and he prided himself on having an eye for these things. Much of his work was on the floors, steps, and stairways of ecclesiastical buildings, so he had the opportunity to see more of such paintings than most people.

What made this particular painting so striking was the central figure. It was obviously meant to be Saint Merwinna. She was shown enclosed within the walls of her cell, beyond which, and much smaller in scale, was depicted a group of buildings, the tallest of which bore a reasonable enough resemblance to the Abbey Church with its high tower that Will had seen as he entered the through the Abbey gates, to make it clear that they were meant to be the buildings here at Althurst. Inside Merwinna's cell all was darkness - the effect created by enclosing her within a background of black paint, somewhat faded now with age, but still sufficient to make the bright pigments used to colour the saint herself seem to glow in contrast, and lend her an almost ethereal appearance. But it was not only that aspect of the painting that made the image so striking. What else was it then? It took Will a few seconds more to realise, and when he finally understood, he felt ashamed. This Saint Merwinna was attractive. Attractive in the way that real women were. The effect of the bright colours was only the initial impression. Once yours eyes had grown more accustomed, you were able to look upon how Merwinna had been portrayed. And the more you looked, the more she seemed anything but ethereal or saintly. Hers was very much the beauty of a woman of this world. More than that, she was alluring, sensual. Her eyes – wide, with long lashes – looked directly at the viewer, with a look that was at once challenging and inviting. Her lips – redder and fuller than they ought to be – were bisected horizontally by a broad brushstroke of a deep purple shade that suggested they were very slightly parted, as if she were about to speak or – and though he tried, Will could not dismiss the idea – open them in a lover's kiss. In addition, her figure was the full figure of a real woman. It had none of not the demure, occasionally boyish, flatness that was usually considered fitting for the depiction of female saints and martyrs. The expertly painted light and shade of the folds of her gown only accentuated, rather than concealed her curves. Where the saint's hips and breasts were, there were fewer folds, which gave the impression that the material there was pulled more tightly, stretching against the contours of the flesh beneath.

What then, if that gown were to fall open? Would the saint invite you to join her within its folds? Or would she strike you blind for even daring to look? Either way, such eroticism seemed out of place, and certainly inappropriate for the depiction of a saint.

"William? *William*," said the Bishop again.

Will turned from the painting, looked into the face of the Bishop. He felt as if he had been caught in the act of spying on the saint. Like the paint on the wall, his sinful thoughts must surely be written upon his on his face. He half expected the Bishop to admonish him for his lewd behaviour. Instead the Bishop merely smiled. "Ah, I see your attention has been caught by the painting. Much as I had expected it would be, to tell you the truth." The Bishop stepped across, stood next to Will, making a show of joining him in inspecting the painting. Far from reassuring Will that he was not being prurient, this had the opposite effect. The Bishop glanced at Will, and must have seen some of his discomfort because he chuckled and said, "No need to be self-conscious, man. We are not the elders, and she is not Susanna." He chuckled again, nudging Will. "For it is surely *we* who are helpless."

Will struggled unsuccessfully to recall the story to which the Bishop must be alluding. It might have been in some sermon he had heard once heard. He was not certain.

After a moment the Bishop lifted his hand and, once again, rested it on Will's shoulder. "So, tell me, William, what do you make of her?"

"Her?" asked Will, experiencing a frisson of confusion and alarm when he thought for a moment the Bishop might be asking him to pass comment on the Abbess in her presence.

He realised, almost immediately, that the notion was a ridiculous one but, before he could stop himself, he found he had already pulled away slightly from the Bishop's grip.

The Bishop reached out a little further, gently returning his hand to Will's shoulder, and saying, with the merest hint of a knowing smile, "The painting. What do you make of the painting? It is a fine piece of work, is it not? As a craftsman, you, of all people, must have a particular appreciation of the quality of such a thing. The work that goes into it, I mean. The time it takes. The great skill required..." The Bishop left the slightest of pauses before adding, "And, of course, the very great expense incurred for a piece of work such as this." By now, although supposedly still addressing Will, the Bishop was not looking at him or even up at the painting. He was looking directly at Abbess Rhoswen – any attempt at subtlety now abandoned. "This painting... you recognise the subject, do you not, William?"

Of course Will did. He was not a fool, damn it! All the same, he was unsure if it would be politic to say so. Before Will could make up his mind, the Bishop provided the answer to his own question. "I know you will recognise that it depicts our saint. Saint Merwinna. A painting in her honour. Much as the new chapel has, *similarly*, been built to honour her."

Abbess Rhoswen would not react to the blatant provocation. Instead, she also addressed her comments to Will.

"It is wondrous what the Good Lord will allow us to create. Is it not, Master Tiler?"

Increasingly uncomfortable, and not wishing to be seen to have taken a side, because he might have to answer to either one of these people in the future, Will merely nodded in reply. The Abbess waited a moment to see if he would actually say anything, and gave a very audible sigh of frustration when he did not. "You *do* agree with me, then?" she pressed.

Will shrugged. Knowing he had no choice but to answer he said carefully, "I do. I must."

The Abbess turned her head a little to one side, with exaggerated confusion. "You *must?*"

"As you say, Reverend Mother, it is the Good Lord puts the skill into a man's hands," replied Will, still carefully, but glad that this was a question to which he had given thought in the past, and felt he could safely provide an answer. "It is only required of the man that he discover that skill, and make the best and proper use of it."

"Really, Master Tiler, I must admit that is a more considered answer than I had expected. That said, please, tell me, I am curious. How does someone such as yourself know what the *proper* use is?"

Will found he was becoming angry. Did the woman really imagine a person could spend their entire life carrying out the work associated with his particular trade and not give any thought to such matters? It made him bolder than he would otherwise have been with such people. "I myself would never pretend to know that, my lady. I am employed by those who do. That knowledge and understanding is given to them, not to me. I am not educated in such matters, and so must trust in the decisions of those who are." He shrugged, and then added, "I will do as I am bid… one way… or the other… You two must reach that decision yourselves," and immediately regretted it. It might easily have been a step too far.

There followed a pause, when neither the Bishop nor the Abbess spoke. Will had resented being involved in their power play, and had hoped to withdraw without seeming to favour either party. The danger now was that he might only have succeeded in coming across as impertinent, satisfying neither and angering both. He was not usually so lacking in prudence; he knew his place, particularly when it came to those who paid him for his labour. He should have moderated his tone, and tempered his comments with more of a show of deference. His only hope now was that their current focus on the issue of the chapel, and the obvious animosity they bore towards one another would distract them, and prevent them from paying particular attention to the tone of voice employed by a mere craftsman. He looked anxiously from the Abbess to the Bishop, trying to gauge their reactions from the expressions on their faces, both of which remained unnervingly free of any sign as to the owner's feelings.

The silence seemed to expand and deepen until, finally, the Bishop smiled again, and said, "Well done, William. You know how to walk the middle path." He looked at the Abbess. "Oh dear, am I being indelicate?"

"Not at all, my lord Bishop," replied Abbess Rhoswen indifferently. "Not at all. We two do not agree on the matter of the chapel. It is a fact. It cannot be avoided. In wishing to disentangle himself from the webs we weave between us, Master Tiler here has exposed us for the schemers and manipulators we are." She turned to William and, with a touch more warmth in her tone than previously, she said, "I should ask your pardon. You are quite right. It is not your place to decide where your craft should be employed."

Almost as soon as the Abbess had finished speaking, Will felt the Bishop's hand resting on his shoulder once more. Unlike the Abbess, however, the Bishop did not apologise. He simply smiled again, gently squeezed Will's shoulder, and nodded towards the door. As Will bowed to the Bishop and the Abbess, Brother Hugh, who had been so silent up until that moment that Will had almost forgotten he was present, now stepped out from the shadows of the corner where he had been waiting, and opened the door.

As Will turned to leave the room, he could still feel where the Bishop's pudgy hand had rested, and he wondered if the squeeze it had given had really been intended to be as gentle. Or was it only that it was weak? If so, was that only because the hand that had done the squeezing had been an old one, or was it also because it had never developed the strength it might have gained through honest physical labour? Then again, there was undeniable power in that smallest of nods. It had indicated that Will should leave the room, and he had done so, obeying without question or hesitation. He was at the door when the Abbess called him back.

"Master Tiler."

Will turned back. "Yes, my lady… Reverend Mother."

"In response to the point about the painting the Bishop has been at pains to make…though his words danced about the question without ever quite putting it."

"Oh, come now …" said the Bishop, waving a hand dismissively. But his protest was perfunctory, deliberately half-hearted. He knew exactly what she meant, and was scarcely embarrassed about it. He had succeeded in making the Abbess uncomfortable enough about the issue that she was unable to let it go, and he was enjoying this fact as much as she disliked it.

"In answer to the question," continued the Abbess, "the painting was commissioned by one of my predecessors…nobody can say which of them… and carried out before I was ever born."

"Oh, yes, I knew that," replied Will.

"*You knew it?*" exclaimed the Abbess, as if such a thing were impossible.

Now it was Will's turn to rise to the bait. "Yes. My eyes told me so. Long before you were born, if I am any judge."

The Bishop let out a small grunt which Will, at first, took to be a stifled cough. However, after glancing in the Bishop's direction, Will quickly understood that he was making a deliberate show of attempting to suppress a chuckle. He followed this up with a loud clearing of his throat, and said, "You presume to judge the Abbess's age, Will? I confess I am at a loss for words. I do not know what to say."

Oh, I'm sure you do, thought Will. Then again, unlike the Bishop, he was not immune to embarrassment. Nor could he, in his position, risk causing offence, so he looked at the ground, and said, "No, my Lord, I do not. Forgive me. It is the age of the *painting* I guess at." *As we both know you know.*

The Bishop smiled a beneficent smile. Will knew the smile was as counterfeit as the man's apparent attempts to suppress his amusement. "Come now, William, it is not *me* but the Reverend Mother whose forgiveness you should be seeking," said the Bishop.

Abbess Rhoswen shook her head and raised a hand in the Bishop's direction to suggest the matter was unimportant. "The age of the painting…what informs your guess, I wonder?" she asked, pointedly addressing Will only.

Will looked up, a little uncertain.

"I am interested to know upon what it is you are founding your guesswork," explained the Abbess.

Will nodded. He thought for a moment, attempting to compose his response. When he spoke, his words were measured and careful. He wanted to avoid further mistakes that might risk insulting the Abbess, but he also wanted to do justice to his own knowledge, and the skill of whoever it was had created the painting in front of him. Like Will, they had been a craftsman, and he respected that. "The style of it tells me it is not so new," he said. The Abbess nodded, indicating she was listening with interest. So Will went on, "The images…they are heavy, if you take my meaning. It is that which shows their age. I do not mean they are clumsy," he added, "for in my view they are impressive…But compared to those being made these days they are…well… heavy is the best way I can put it, I think. And that is no longer the style. In the wealthy church buildings at any rate. The poorer village buildings, where the newer style is not yet known or the skill not as yet available among the local craftsman, and therefore required to be brought in, making it too costly, they do still commission such work, it is true. Not a place such as this, though. Not here. If this were a recent work, in a place such as Althurst Abbey, I would expect it to be much less blocky…more…" Will struggled for the right word, almost said curvy, but quickly dismissed the idea. There were curves present in the painting, but they were somehow unnerving, and suggestive in a way to which he knew it would not be prudent to refer.

"Fluid?" suggested the Abbess. The way she had been able to come up with the adjective so quickly made Will think this was perhaps not the first time she had given thought to the question.

"If that means the flow of the lines is less awkward, then yes. More *fluid* in its lines. It is the fashion these days. Come over the sea… all the way from France, so they say." This last was said with an edge of regret. France was an almost constant thorn in the side of the English craftsman. Much as the innovations made across the Channel were much admired, they were equally as much resented.

"You do indeed have an eye for such things, it would seem," observed the Abbess.

Will bobbed his head in grateful acknowledgment of the complement. "It is my trade…or linked to it, at least. A tiler, like any craftsman, needs to know what the fashion is if he is not to be outdone by his competitors. Changes in the one thing may lead to changes in another. If the paintings and the carvings in a place are done in some such way, then so must the tiles be. They must not go against what surrounds them. They must match…not be in contest… if you take my meaning? Besides, the paintwork itself tells me this is not so recent. It is a little faded in places. A child could…" Will stopped himself going further with the comment.

"The child of a man such as you, perhaps. One skilled in what you yourself are skilled in," said the Abbess. "What would you say, Master Tiler, if I told you that the story goes the man who painted this actually saw her, hmm? Saw the saint, I mean. It is from the life."

"*Saw* her?"

"That is correct. If so, then this may be something of a

genuine likeness. Personally, I doubt it. I doubt it very much. I cannot imagine our Lord would have placed the qualities of saintliness into one so..." Now it was Abbess Rhoswen's turn to search for the right word.

"*Comely*?" offered the Bishop. The slight turn of his head suggested to Will that he had attempted to meet his eye. Thankfully, from where the Bishop stood, it had not been possible. Perhaps he had intended a conspiratorial acknowledgement of what a red-blooded man might see when he looked upon the image. After all, the supposed celibacy of the clergy was at best doubtful. Then again, was it, in fact, a test to ensure that Will did not see it or, at least, acknowledge it? Either way, Will was glad not to have had to choose.

"Beguiling," corrected the Abbess. "Even were she not, I would still not have allowed such a thing to be created in this, my private receiving room. Such things should be created for the lessons they teach, and the examples that they set. For that to happen they need to be seen by the many, not hidden away for the eyes of the few. To have this here, it is... vanity. That is why I have had another created in the church where all can see it. One, however, that is less...specific, in its depiction. That is what I believe Saint Merwinna would have wanted."

The Bishop's head cocked. "Then why have you not destroyed this one, Reverend Mother? If its very nature is so questionable, that would seem the obvious thing to do. If you feel it is not proper, it would seem to me you must be rid of it. After all, does not your Rule of Saint Benedict...the Rule by which you live...say that an Abbess should...now, how does he put it?...*Labour effectually that her deeds be according to her name*?"

Abbess Rhoswen showed obvious displeasure at the Bishop's quoting of the Rule. Will suspected it was a quote Baldwin had been saving for just such a moment, and he imagined the Abbess probably thought the same thing.

"I think you know the matter is not so simple, my Lord Bishop," snapped the Abbess. "For all I myself might find the painting objectionable and dearly wish it gone, I cannot in all right and conscience simply have it removed. That, too, would be wrong."

"Oh?" asked the Bishop. "Why such scruples, I wonder?"

"It is art in honour of the Saint, and it is not for me to destroy what has been created for that purpose. I do not know for certain what was in the mind or heart of whomever of my predecessors had this done. I cannot possibly know that. There is no way that I can."

The Bishop had placed his hands together, steepled his fingers, and now held them under his chin. It was a posture Will had seen him adopt before. It was not a pose that flattered the man; his heavy jowls sagged down over his fingertips, accentuating the fleshiness of his features, and yet it had a disconcerting effect on most people, being suggestive of deep thought while, at the same time, suggestive of prayer. The whole impact naturally heightened by his being a man of the cloth. Confronted with it, you felt as if you were being judged. And not by Bishop Baldwin alone, but also, through association, by God Himself. The pose was almost certainly deliberate, calculated to put those in his presence at a disadvantage. If so, it had no such effect on Abbess Rhoswen. She straightened her back, rose to what little height she possessed, and looked up into the Bishop's eyes, challenging this unspoken claim to authority.

"You disagree, Bishop? You imagine we…you…*can* know what was on my forebear's mind?"

Baldwin shrugged. "Not on their mind…not that…" He slowly took one hand out from under his chin, placed it gently, almost tenderly, upon his chest. "In their *heart*, perhaps? I believe 'vanity' was the word that you yourself used but a moment ago."

Her eyes blazed with anger, but the Abbess said nothing.

"That *is* correct, is it not, Abbess?" asked Baldwin,

obviously stressing her title to remind her that, however much she might resent it, in the eyes of the Church he was senior to her.

When, at last, she answered, Abbess Rhoswen's response was clipped, her voice tight, and her rage barely contained. "As I have said, *I* cannot know that."

Noting that, despite her attempts to conceal it, Abbess Rhoswen was becoming flustered, Bishop Baldwin pressed his advantage.

"Oh? Only moments ago, you claimed to know what the *saint herself* would wish. Now you tell us that you cannot know what a mere...forgive me... abbess wished?" Once more, he placed a stress on the title. "Are we to infer from this that abbesses are more mysterious than saints? These are fine words indeed to come from one who is herself an abbess. In whose breast does vanity dwell now, I wonder?"

"I am sure you are fully aware that that was not my intended meaning," protested Abbess Rhoswen, clearly struggling to resist the urge to raise her voice.

Uneasy at the prospect of witnessing any more of what was now becoming a heated exchange between these two high ranking members of the clergy, and very aware that it could well compromise any later working relationship he might have with either one of them, Will looked at Father Hugh, hoping he would help him to make his escape. But the old priest was once more making use of his ability to become almost invisible to those whom he served. He seemed to Will to have frozen in place where he stood, his eyes fixed upon the floor, no more capable of movement than the figure of the saint painted on the wall. Will was forced to employ the not very subtle technique of loudly clearing his throat to remind them that he was still present.

"Ah, yes, Will. Still here. You may leave us now," said the Bishop.

Will gave a slight bow. "Very good, my Lord." He turned, and bowed to the Abbess. "My Lady..."

Abbess Rhoswen, her face now flushed as red as Will imagined his own was, barely glanced at him. She raised a hand in an unnecessary gesture of dismissal, given that the Bishop had already told Will to leave. "Yes, go now, Master Tiler. Thanks to my Lord Bishop, I will be seeing more of you in the future. I have no doubt of it."

Doubly dismissed, Will was relieved when the door closed behind him. Shaking his head, he expelled air from his nose and smiled humourlessly to himself. Abbess Rhoswen was right, of course. She *would* be seeing more of him. Bishop Baldwin would inevitably have his way regarding the new chapel for the saint, and the tiled floor he planned for it, no matter how strongly the Abbess might protest. All the same, it would have been far better for all concerned if the two had been able to agree. The Abbess was clearly not one to give up without a fight, no matter how hopeless the cause, and Will was likely to find himself a pawn in the strategies of both sides of the argument.

Looking up he saw that the young nun waiting in the antechamber earlier had now been joined by another, older looking, sister. The mixture of exasperation and concern on the older woman's face suggested she was probably the mistress of novices. Both women looked up, and Will saw that the younger one had been crying. He attempted a reassuring smile. As she had before, the young woman looked away.

******

When he saw them approaching, Swire put down the cold mutton bone he had been gnawing away at all that morning, wiped his hands, and stood up ready to receive them. As they drew nearer, he cursed under his breath. It was not difficult to see what they were: more pilgrims come to worship at the cell where Saint Merwinna had spent her final days before being gathered unto God, which meant more pilgrims he was going to have to disappoint. The cell was not available to be visited these days, and until the chapel being built around its shell was complete it would remain that way. Why couldn't people learn? Surely it had been long enough now for the message to have spread? Yet still they kept coming: pilgrims from all over the country. Even one or two from across the sea. All of them to be disappointed by the news that he, as gatekeeper – or Allard, when Swire was off duty – had been instructed to give them. The Abbey would feed them, accommodate them for one night, and then they must be on their way. One night, and one night only. There were very few exceptions to that rule, and absolutely none to the rule that no one was permitted access to the chapel. They would have to make do with the painting of the saint in the church building. And no miracles had ever been ascribed to that. Perhaps, if they were in luck, Father Thomas, the Abbey Priest, might be available to lead them in a brief prayer, but this was small compensation for what they had journeyed for so long to see and were being denied. Swire could not get used to the look of disappointment that crossed their dusty faces as he broke the bad news. Nor could he get used to the frequent tirades to which he was subjected after it had sunk in.

He felt bad for some of them, of course he did. Particularly those who had come in hope of a cure for whatever ailment it was had blighted their lives. He saw how close to despairing many of them were. The problem was that there was nothing he could do to help them. Obviously, they were welcome to return in a few months when the chapel would, hopefully, be complete. But for many that was not possible; theirs had been a once in a lifetime journey they could not afford to make again. For others - those with the most severe illnesses - it would simply be too late. Although, Swire often thought to himself, it was extremely unlikely to make a difference anyway. It was true that, on occasion, a sickly pilgrim had been known to recover, and much was made of these miracles. It was equally true, however, that the saint was sparing in how she gave out her favours. There was no telling who would be judged deserving of a cure and who would not. What *was* clear was that, for those who were not, there was now the added grief of knowing they had not been considered fit for one, and the worry that this was a reflection of how they would be treated come the day of judgement. Better not to know in Swire's opinion. Though that was an opinion he knew to keep to himself.

This latest party of pilgrims was of the worst kind to be faced with. They were on foot, their clothes ragged and dusty, and their expressions that mix of desperation and hope Swire had seen so many times before. Worse, he now saw, they pulled a litter behind them. Which could only mean they hoped for a cure for its occupant. The more wealthy pilgrims might be more likely to rant and rave and demand to see the Abbess – a demand nearly always denied unless, of course, they were of noble birth – but their anger, although unpleasant, was still easier to endure than the tears and cries of despair from the more deserving. The wealthy ones usually arrived in carriages, carts, or on horseback. Sometimes, however, they walked the final stage of the journey as was befitting a pilgrimage. Swire could always spot them, though. They were never so tired or dirty from the roads and tracks as they would have been had they truly made the journey on foot.

This current group stopped a few yards from the gate. They conferred for a few moments before one of them walked over to where Swire, his heart now sinking at the prospect, waited to greet him with the bad news.

******

CHAPTER 2

Sister Euphemia supressed a yawn. Although no one would blame her for being tired at such a late hour – especially a woman of her advanced years - it didn't alter the fact that it always felt wrong to her to yawn in performance of her duties; and in the Abbey Church even more so. It seemed to show a lack of respect and, perhaps worse, a lack of gratitude. Making preparations for the Matins service was as much an honour as it was a chore. Euphemia always tried to remember that, no matter how tired or cold she might be, or how tedious carrying out the same tasks, night after night, sometimes became. Or even how unwell she might be. She had rarely missed her duties – maybe three or four times in all the years since she had been appointed Sacrist here at Althurst. She took the role seriously. Even to the point of being chided by Abbess Rhoswen for risking her health by carrying on with the tasks on days when it was plain for all to see she was not really well enough. There were others who could step in while she recovered her strength, the Abbess had often insisted. Sister Euphemia was an old woman, so there was no shame in her taking advantage of the help of the younger nuns who could, temporarily, take her place.

As she made her way down the nave, Sister Euphemia huffed contemptuously to herself at the very thought. Others who could take her place indeed! If by that the Abbess meant the likes of the feckless Sister Marigold, Euphemia would do all in her power to avoid them taking it. Even the more dedicated ones like Sister Winifred could not be wholly trusted to do things properly, if the truth were told. No, the only person Sister Euphemia really trusted to carry out the tasks of the Sacrist was the Sacrist herself, Sister Euphemia. That was not pride; that was plain fact. The others played a part, and she would never say they didn't. There was a difference, however, between having a part to play and actually overseeing the task. Sister Marigold in particular was a worry. Euphemia was not unaware that the younger woman was a possibility as her successor in the role of Sacrist, but the girl was far from ready. Very far, in fact. Tonight was a good example. Not for the first time, she was late. Frequent reprimands and the occasional mild disciplinary measure seemed to do no good. The girl would simply accept the punishment, and then carry on exactly as she had before. She treated the experience like one might treat a Sheriff's fine. Once paid, all forgotten. That was most definitely not how it was meant. Such penance was supposed to be as much a lesson as it was a punishment. If anything, the instances of tardiness had been on the increase of late. She would have to take it up with the Abbess again.

The ceiling of the Abbey Church was far higher than that of any of the other buildings in the Abbey grounds. Entering the south transept, Sister Euphemia sensed, rather than saw, the space in the darkness above her becoming higher still where the great tower rose above the crossing.

She paused, listening.

Had something up there made a sound? A scuffing of feet upon stone?

She huffed again, only this time at her own lack of good sense. How could there possibly be anyone up there? With an effort of will, she held her candle up into the darkness to prove this to herself. She moved the flame around, blinking a little as she tried to follow the lambent circle of light, and smiling to herself as it spread over the reassuring image of Saint Merwinna. This more recent painting was not as grand as the one in the Abbess's house. It was not so finely executed, so those who claimed to understand such things said. Well, Sister Euphemia made no such claims to that understanding for herself but, even if they were right to say it, at least this painting was more as such a painting should be - as far as she was concerned, at any rate. There was none of that disquieting and, quite frankly, highly unsuitable sensuality to this image that, in her humble opinion, tainted the other one.

Her gaze now dropped to the area of wall below the image, and to the dark, slightly uneven, rectangle created by the window from the saint's cell. Bigger than it had been in the saint's day - the stone lintel having been damaged in the past, and long since fallen away – and temporarily boarded up while the work went on beyond it.

Sister Euphemia crossed herself. This was the very window from which the blessed saint herself had once looked out from her cell, made confession, and participated in the mass all those years ago. Although what sins one such a she could possibly have to confess was a mystery.

Inside, it was no longer a cell, of course; it was a chapel, or it soon would be. There was work to be done yet before it was complete. There was talk of a fine stained-glass window to be installed; a door of oak to be built; and a tiled floor, specially made, to be laid. She had seen the tiler arrive that very morning. The poor man would not be made welcome by Abbess Rhoswen; her opposition to the project was well known. Still, Euphemia could not help feeling that the work so far had been very fine. The master mason and his men had created a wonderful space. Was the Abbess right to say it was not as fitting as the, quite honestly, crumbling shell that it had replaced? But then, she herself made no claims to any knowledge on such matters.

Lost in these thoughts as she continued on, lighting the candles as she went, Sister Euphemia yawned again. Immediately she felt a flush of shame. There she was ruminating on the failings of Sister Marigold, when she herself behaved in a way that was less than correct. Although she would include it in her next confession, that was not enough. She must remember to set an example. Suppose Sister Marigold or Sister Winifred had witnessed it? What model of behaviour would that provide?

Just as she always did, when she entered the ambulatory - the long passage that ran around the east end of the building – Sister Euphemia kept her head bent forward, her eyes down, fixed on the flagstones in front of her, and the flickering shadows there, cast by the flame she carried. High above her, at the top of the nearest pillar, lodged in the capital there like some terrible bird of prey looking out from its nesting place, she knew the Imp, with his horns and that peculiarly twisted beak would be gazing down at her with those terrible stone eyes of his. Just as he always did. It was night, so he would be concealed within the shadows – even if she were to lift her flame, look directly up at him, she would not see him – but he would be there, nonetheless. And he could see her, even if she could not see him. She felt his cold, forbidding gaze on her hunched shoulders even now.

Old fool, she scolded herself. *He cannot see you.* How often must she remind herself? Eyes of stone can see nothing at all. And whilst they may, for all the world, seem to convey hatred, they were no more capable of actually feeling it than was any other block or pillar or carving in the rest of the building. *Only stone*, she told herself, as she had on so many nights previously. *Only stone.* Terrible eyes they may be, but they are only the eyes of a carving in stone. *Remember that.* They were not created by God. Nor were they, as was sometimes speculated by others, and Sister Euphemia herself also occasionally feared, crafted by the Devil. They were long ago fashioned in stone by the hands of a man, nothing more than that. A carving by some stonemason whose motives for doing so were long since forgotten.

She stopped. Perhaps tonight she would finally find the courage to look up, stare back into the darkness at what she so feared dwelt within it. Her head, still tilted downward, rose up just a little, and then remained where it was. Perhaps not. No, tonight would not be that night after all. Those eyes, and their dreadful expression; she could not find the courage to face them. Not tonight. Maybe never. Not that expression, so hateful, contemptuous and, above all, threatening - suggesting all the Imp would do to her if only he were able to take on corporeal form, become living flesh instead of shaped stone, and pull himself away from the wall where, like Prometheus, he was held fast. Not for the first time, Sister Euphemia wondered at the decision of the original builders of the Abbey to include such a dreadful thing inside the house of God. Whilst she knew the horrid gargoyles and corbels gazing out from the walls outside were there to frighten away demons, why this thing was inside remained a mystery. Why had it been allowed? What could its purpose be? Nobody now knew. If the original sisters had had their reasons, they had not seen fit to pass the knowledge down. Or it had been lost long ago.

She had rounded a corner when she came to a halt. Up ahead, candles were already burning. How could that be? Sister Winifred? Impossible, she was nowhere near this part of the building. Right now, she was at the far end, over to the west door – Sister Euphemia could hear the soft padding of her feet on the flagstones over there even now. She would have to have lit these few candles and then run back to the other end of the building the moment she had done it. Why on earth would she do such an odd thing? Was it possible she herself had lit them, then? After all, she had been lost in her thoughts only moments earlier; it would not be the first time she had done something and not remembered having done it. The shadow of approaching old age and the possibility of senility that came with it fell over her as it had been liable to do quite often of late. Any small mistake or failure of memory now struck her as somehow significant – a portent of things to come. Sister Euphemia shook her head. No, she would not entertain such thoughts. Perhaps she had lit the candles in her reverie, what of it? Everyone did that sort of thing once in a while. Youth was not a defence against mistakes. Sister Marigold was evidence of that much. So, yes, she herself must have lit the candles without thinking, and no, she need not give the matter too much thought.

But there was something else. Something she had not taken in at first. The candles had been moved. Instead of being placed evenly every few paces along the wall as usual, they had been gathered together in a line, forming a barrier across the width of the ambulatory. To have done that she would have had to lift the heavy iron candleholders - a feat which, on her own, she doubted she could have managed. And even if she could have done so, it was not something one could do without paying attention. It was something she would, without question, have remembered doing. The next thought was as unwelcome as it was inevitable. Someone else – not her or Sister Winifred - had done it. Sister Marigold? No, she was slack in her duties, but not wilfully disruptive. Someone else had done this. Someone who had no business being in the Abbey Church at all at this hour of the night.

Sister Euphemia shivered. It had grown colder. She parted her lips to ask who was there, and then thought better of it. Although she had not spoken, she saw her breath condense in the air in front of her. She shuddered, hunching her shoulders against the chill, and the growing fear inside her. A thought struck her then, and she looked anxiously back over her shoulder to see if there was anyone approaching from behind her – someone who might have been concealed in the shadows as she passed them. There was nobody there. She peered forward now, straining her eyes to see if anyone waited within the darkness beyond the light of the flames. Again, she saw no one. *Enough of this,* she told herself. To investigate further alone would be folly. She would gather Sister Winifred and Sister Marigold, if the girl had arrived, and inform them they must leave immediately. Intruders in the church were not for them to deal with. She turned to leave.

Before she could hurry away, she heard a whisper from beyond the candlelight. Too soft to know if was male or female, but without question a voice. There was no mistaking it. Nothing else it could be. On this summer night the air was quite still, with not even the mildest of breezes outside to be mistaken for a human cry or the sibilance of speech. It came again. Plaintive. Soft. Not, however, too soft to hear what it had said this time. It had said her name.

"Who's there?" asked Sister Euphemia.

"It's only me," said a voice so full of sadness it made her own heart ache, and a gasp catch and shudder in her throat.

"Who is it?" she asked.

"Please help me," the voice said, still not much more than a whisper.

Sister Euphemia took a step forward, and then held back. She tilted her head to one side, suddenly suspicious. "Why will you not tell me your name?"

"*Please*, Sister Euphemia. I need your help."

"Yes, but who are you?"

"Come here. Help me." The voice sounded slightly different this time. Less sad. Almost amused.

Sister Euphemia was caught between the desire to turn and leave, to escape any possible threat, and the desire not to abandon someone who might genuinely be in need of her help. Although her heart raced, her old legs felt even weaker than they normally did. Could she even run if she chose to? "I can't see you…the flames…" she said, more afraid now, and struggling to keep her voice calm. "Please…come out from beyond the flames, so that I may see you better. That is all I ask. Do that, and I will help you if it is in my power. Please… come out…"

"You would bargain with me?" the voice said, the amusement unmistakable now. "As you wish. I shall do what you ask of me."

Sister Euphemia squinted. In the darkness beyond the shimmering line of candlelight she thought she saw a heavier, even blacker darkness begin to take shape. This new darkness moved. It came forward, towards, and then through, the candle flames, yet without seeming to disturb them.

Inexplicably, despite them now being in the light, where she ought to have been able to see them far more clearly, whoever it was still remained in complete darkness, as if the darkness was something solid that hung about them, something they brought with them. It made no sense. It was impossible. Sister Euphemia had a momentary awareness of the warmth of her own urine as it ran down her legs. She whimpered, fear and shame mingling. Then she screamed, or thought she did. Some of it might have been in her mind alone because at that same moment something dark, possibly a huge hand, had wrapped around her face so quickly and so firmly that the scream she made might never have fully escaped her mouth. She was briefly aware of a smell like putrefaction in her nostrils before they were crushed shut under the pressure of the grip, the cartilage of her nose clicking and breaking with the force of it, her ceaseless high-pitched squealing stifled by the rough palm that pressed against her lips. She gagged, but the vomit that came into her mouth could not escape, she was forced to swallow it back, and she began to choke on it.

Squeezed more tightly now, she felt herself jerked up into the air. The sudden strain on her jaw and neck was immense. She heard a ripping, and felt a rush of chill air as her habit and all beneath it were torn away. The brief sense of outrage and humiliation the old nun felt was quickly replaced by a greater feeling of confusion, and increased pain. The indignity of her nakedness was nothing compared to the agonized throbbing of her face and jaw. She felt a jarring click as something splintered and sinews stretched and shredded. Then came an unnaturally loud crack as something – her jawbone? - finally snapped under the pressure of the grip. The sound of it, and her own muffled screaming, echoed back to her from the stone of the surrounding walls and pillars. Then, in spite of the pain that seared through her face and neck, Euphemia was half aware of a different sound that followed on from this. More ripping. A sucking and tearing, accompanied by the sound of something splashing onto the flags below her weakly kicking feet. For a moment she did not understand. Her clothing had already been shamefully torn from her. What now remained? Then came the sickly-sweet smell of the slaughterhouse, and with it, a final, dreadful understanding. An instant later, as if brought by that understanding, the pain of what was being done to her became unbearable.

In her final torments she attempted to pray to God for the end to come swiftly, but the pain was too intense to allow her to focus on anything else, and the words would not come to her spinning, howling mind. Everything then, even prayer, had been taken from her. All she wanted now was an end to herself. An end to all things, if that was what it took to put a stop to her unbearable pain.

******

She was walking far too fast, as usual. The flame she carried fluttered obliquely, and then threatened to go out entirely. If it did, it would not be the first time she was reprimanded for allowing her haste to extinguish her candle. Sister Marigold forced herself to stop for a moment, take a calming breath, and continue on her way more slowly along the passage from the dormitory that led to a door into the nave of the church. She might still be in trouble if she were late for her duties, of course. Better, though, to be in trouble for one thing only rather than two.

As Succentrix, her role of assisting the Sacrist to prepare the church for services was considered an honour. After all, it was potentially a preparation for the more senior role of Precentrix and, you never knew, perhaps even Sacrist one day. Unfortunately, it also meant Sister Marigold had to rise before the other nuns for the Matins service at two in the morning, and was among the last to return to her bed when the service was over. She sometimes felt that there was a fine line between honour and exploitation. It never caused her to question her faith. There were times, though, when she questioned her ambition. There were those nuns who never rose to any rank at Althurst. Perhaps theirs was the easier life? Moreover, shouldn't humility be high among the qualities of the truly devout? And didn't ambition run contrary to that?

Was it simply that she was tired tonight?

Well, at least it was the middle of the year. The summer months were always the best. The shifting of the schedule of worship in the winter months might make better use of the limited daylight hours, but it did nothing to make the stone passages and rooms of the abbey buildings any warmer. In winter you could often see your own breath, even in the church itself. At least tonight it was warm. There would be no need for hunching her shoulders against the cold, tucking her chin down inside her woollen habit, and pulling her wimple down extra tightly – something else that had got her into trouble in the past. Only the novice, Ingrith, seemed to get into more trouble than she did.

When she reached the door to the nave, Sister Marigold paused for a second time; taking another breath, and readying herself for the scolding for tardiness she was likely to receive from Sister Winifred, the Precentrix. It would come from her, rather than Sister Euphemia, the Sacrist. Old Sister Euphemia might show her displeasure more subtly with a reproachful look or gentle sigh, but she nearly always left the actual business of delivering the reprimand to Sister Winifred. Whether Sister Euphemia considered her age and status meant she was above much involvement in such petty issues or whether she merely found them distasteful, Marigold was not sure. All she knew was that Sister Winifred was not troubled by any such scruple. That woman always made the most of any opportunity to lecture the less senior sisters about any perceived shortcomings in their behaviour.

Sister Marigold was not very late, so it was unlikely there would be any punishment prescribed beyond some minor act of penance and a reminder to mention it in her next confession. Although, it would not be because the Precentrix did not wish it. Sister Marigold was sure the punishments meted out by Sister Winifred would be more severe were she not bound by the standards imposed by Abbess Rhoswen. The Reverend Mother was a just woman, not a cruel one. Which, in Sister Marigold's opinion, was more than could be said for Sister Winifred.

Sister Marigold immediately reproached herself for the thought. It was unfair and it was unworthy. Sister Winifred was not cruel. Her fault, if it she had one, was only that she was not a woman possessed of much imagination. Her interpretation of the standards by which the sisters were required to live their lives was an extremely straightforward one. The occasional foibles that, in Sister Marigold's opinion at least, simply made the sisters human, and more often than not deserving of forgiveness, were to Sister Winifred nothing more than failings to be overcome if their foremost duty, the duty to serve God, were to be carried out as it should be. In fact, her punishments might be seen as kindnesses.

Or they might not.

Uncertain of the answer, Sister Marigold braced herself, and then opened the door.

Inside the church, many of the candles were already burning brightly, throwing light onto some parts of the stonework and decorations, deepening the shadows around others. Sister Marigold glanced about, looking for either the Sacrist or the Precentrix. Obviously, someone was here because they had already lit the candles. She groaned to herself; helping to light them was supposed to be one of her duties.

She closed the door behind herself, and walked over into the side aisle, looking in both directions as she went. There was no one near the west door, so she turned and went east, in the direction of the chancel. It was there where the majority of the candles were burning. Her own candle fluttered again. Frustrating and a bit odd, since she was being particularly careful not to walk too fast. At the same moment, it seemed as if something flew past her face. An insect of some kind. Probably a large moth. She brushed it away, and then stood still for a moment, allowing the candle flame to settle. Then she continued forward, very slowly, the flame cupped closely in her hand.

As she walked, she startled herself by shivering slightly. There was a slight chill to the air, which struck Sister Marigold as peculiar on such an otherwise warm night. And there was something else about the air: it smelled different from usual. The customary, comforting smells of dust, mild damp, stale incense, and freshly lit candles were intermingled with something else. It was something at once familiar, and foreign to her. She screwed up her face and sniffed, trying to identify it. All that came to mind was a butcher's stall on market days, which could not possibly be right.

When she reached the start of the ambulatory she stopped. A voice had whispered her name from somewhere close by.

"Hello?" she replied, careful to keep her voice low. Speaking too loudly – particularly in church - would be another source of annoyance for Sister Winifred.

She flinched as the moth, or whatever it was, brushed past her face again.

Then she heard her name whispered a second time.

"Sister?" she asked. "Who is there? I cannot see you. Where…"

A hand reached forward and grabbed her roughly by the wrist, pulling her into the shadows behind a pillar. She shrieked, but another hand was swiftly clamped over her mouth. From the darkness a familiar face appeared, very close to her own.

Sister Winifred looked pale, terrified.

Sister Marigold tried to speak, but Sister Winifred clamped

her hand even more tightly over her mouth. She lifted a finger to her lips, and shook her head. Sister Marigold nodded her understanding, and Sister Winifred removed her hand.

Without actually speaking, Sister Marigold mouthed the words, "*What is it?*"

In response, Sister Winifred pointed a trembling finger down the ambulatory. Marigold saw nothing at first, and looked questioningly back at Winifred. The other nun pointed again, with more emphasis, and this time Marigold followed the direction of her gesture more carefully. She was pointing downwards, towards the floor. Again, Marigold saw nothing. She shook her head. Frustrated, Sister Winifred crouched down, leaned forward, and gestured more frantically to the far end, where the passage disappeared around a corner into the area beyond the high altar.

Marigold understood now. She gasped. A patch of shadow on the flagstones was moving, expanding, as if whatever were creating it was itself slowly moving forward and would, at any moment, appear around the bend in the passage. Marigold took an involuntary step back, but never took her eyes off the slowly growing patch of darkness on the floor of the passage up ahead. The more she studied it, the less like shadow it appeared. Then she realised it was, in reality, a gradually spreading pool of some dark liquid. Too thick to be spilled wine. Oil, perhaps? No. It did not take much imagination to guess that it was blood, and that the source must lie just around the stone pillar, at the corner of the ambulatory.

Still only mouthing the words, Marigold asked, "*Euphemia?*"

Winifred nodded, her eyes glistening with terror.

"*Dead?*"

Winifred shrugged.

Marigold looked again. Then, confused, she looked back at Winifred. Why had she not gone to the aid of her fellow sister? Well, if she would not go, Marigold would! As soon as she began to move forward, however, the older woman, with a strength that surprised Marigold, grabbed her and pulled her back again, pushing her against the wall. Then Winifred raised a hand. For a instant Marigold thought she would strike her. Instead, she reached up and pulled Marigold's head down closer to her own so she could put her mouth to her ear, and whisper something.

Marigold could not quite make out the words.

"I don't understand," she whispered back.

Winifred pulled her closer still, cupping her hands around the younger woman's ear. Pressing her lips to Marigold's wimple, she spoke more slowly this time, emphasising each word.

"There... is... some...thing... with... her!"

Marigold pulled away, staring in disbelief at the other woman. Winifred was nodding emphatically. Her choice of words had seemed very deliberate. Some*thing* rather than some*one*. Marigold felt herself shudder.

"What is it that is with her?"

In her shock, Marigold had spoken out loud rather than whispered. Sister Winifred glanced around, terrified, and gestured frantically for her to keep silent. At that moment, all the candles in the church guttered. Marigold cried out. The last thing she saw before the candles went out entirely was Sister Winifred's frightened face. In the darkness that enveloped them, the two women clung to one another. Marigold felt Sister Winifred's light frame against her own. Like Marigold, she was shaking.

From somewhere high above them, in the pitch-black spaces of the vaulted ceiling, came a sound that might be laughter.

******

Will Tiler heard all about it from his assistant, Silas. They were in a corner of the Abbey grounds, digging the trench that would form the basis of the furnace chamber of the kiln in which the tiles would be fired. Will had yet to form them from the clay that had been left to weather in a heap over the winter months, and was now ready for use, and he was uneasy about which design he should use. Besides that, it was a baking hot day, and the ground was hard, the digging difficult. Will felt a little like a tile in a kiln himself. He was in no mood for the old man's gossip.

"They say one of 'em is dead, Will. *Murdered,*" said Silas in his broad Hampshire accent, and then added, too salaciously for Will's liking, *"Raped* and murdered." He paused for effect before asking, "What d'ya say to *that* then?"

Exasperated, Will only offered a grunt in response.

Undeterred, Silas went on, "Her body so torn up as they could hardly know which one of 'em she was at first…Like a hen after the fox has been at it, so I heard,"

Finally, Will glanced up at his assistant. "Is that so?"

Beyond Silas, Will saw the high walls of the Abbey Church, the buttresses creating thin strips of shade that ran perpendicularly up its sides. Above the walls, rose the tower. And above the tower the summer sun sat in a blue, cloudless sky. The sun made him blink. He looked away - back down at the church. Nestled between two of those buttresses, just east of the south transept, he could see the dark rectangle of the doorway to the new chapel of Saint Merwinna. He wiped his brow, frowned. It was too hot to work *and* talk. The problem was he knew Silas well enough to know the old fool would not be satisfied unless he had had the opportunity to tell his tale in full. He would be ill-tempered for the rest of the day if it was denied him. Will looked Silas in the face and said, as seriously as he could manage. "So, you're telling me one of the nuns has been killed by a fox?"

Silas appeared puzzled for a moment, and then chuckled. "No, it's how they says she looked when they found her."

"Do they?" asked Will, his accent also a Hampshire one,

but nowhere near as thick as that of his assistant.

Will had, in fact, already heard that a nun was dead. He let Silas go on with his story all the same, as he knew he must if he were to get any peace. When Will had been told of the tragedy by Father Thomas, the nuns' priest, there had been no mention of rape. That, he guessed, was an unnecessary and unpleasant detail, invented either by Silas or by whomever it was had told the story to him.

"They do," Silas replied, acting shocked and solemn. "And they say one of the other two who was with her when it happened is a raving madwoman."

"Do they?"

"So scared she was, she has taken leave of all her wits they say." Silas lolled his head and crossed his eyes in an attempt to convey madness.

"*Do they*?" Will said again. He gave a sly wink to Alf, his young apprentice, who he noticed had just returned from their cart with an armful of the old waste tiles and bricks that would be used as the main building materials for the kiln when the trench was finally dug. Alf smiled, and put down his load next to the heap he was building before immediately heading back to the cart for another.

Finally, it seemed, Silas had picked up on the sardonic tone in Will's voice. "Well…yes…that's what I heard, anyway," he said, a little affronted.

"From?" asked Will.

"What's that?"

"From who? Who did you hear it from? Who told you all this that is *said*?"

"Do you really want to know, or is this more of your fuckin' mockery?"

Will raised a conciliatory hand. "Forgive me, Silas. Yes, I really do want to know, as it happens. Where *did* you hear all this?"

"Right," said Silas, still not entirely sure he believed Will was sincere, but enjoying telling his tale so much that he was willing to take the risk. "I heard it from one of the servants. Woman in the kitchen. Nice girl…Big set of teats on her."

Will shot Silas a warning glance, then nodded in the direction of Alf who was only a few yards away, his arms laden with more old tiles.

Silas shrugged. "Anyway, this girl…she says all the sisters are real shook up about it. They was all there, you see. All goin' into Matins." Silas pronounced it *Mat'ns*. "So they was all there when they was found. The dead one and the other two. In the dark they were. No candles burnin'. Not a one. Huddled up together, shiverin' an' whimperin' like a pair of scrawny dogs afraid of a beatin', they were."

Against his better judgement, Will found he was becoming more interested. "What was it they were so afraid of?" he asked.

"Well," said Silas, puffing up, pleased now he saw he had Will's full attention. "That's just it, Will. Nobody can say. They is both driven so mad with fear that, whatever it were, they can't get it out of 'em. Tis' all very strange, if you ask me."

"Strange," agreed Will. He didn't bother to point out that only minutes before, according to Silas, there had only been one nun driven mad. No doubt, given time, the story would be embellished to include both of them having been raped as well.

Alf had reached them by now, and was setting the broken tiles down in the heap with the others. "Thanks lad," said Will. "Time for you to take a breather, eh? Have some water. It's hot today. You must have a rare old thirst on you by now, I reckon. Well, there's a water butt over by there…You see it? Rainwater. I'm told it should be safe enough."

"Good to know that," said Silas. "Don't wanna end up with the boilin' shits. My sister's husband shat himself into an early grave, he did. Looked like he was made of twigs before the end."

Alf giggled. But Silas saw the irritation in Will's expression and muttered, "Can't say anything right for sayin' somethin' wrong it seems to me sometimes. The boy's heard worse than that before now, I can tell you that. It's done him no harm."

Will ignored Silas. Turning instead to Alf, he smiled conspiratorially, inclined his head slightly in Silas's direction, and raised his eyebrows. He was pleased to see Alf smiling back. In Will's opinion Alf occasionally had a tendency to be too serious for a boy of his age. Will also knew that Silas was right; of course the boy had heard far worse things before now. Still, given Alf's background, Will could not help but be a little over-protective towards the boy sometimes.

"Well, now," said Will, "you getting us that water I spoke of or not?"

As Will knew he would, the boy chose to nod rather than actually speak in reply. He could talk, only was made shy of doing so by a bad stammer. Will had been a close friend of Alf's father, and had agreed to take his son on as his apprentice. He did not regret it. The boy showed promise. He was hard-working, attentive, and could already lay tiles almost as well as Silas, who would never be more than an assistant, and did not aspire to be. In Will's view, Alf could be more than that. He had the potential to become a master tiler, if only he could also master his stammer. Or at least his fear of speaking with it. There was more to being a tiler than just laying tiles. There were many people you needed to communicate with – from patrons to suppliers of tools and materials. If Alf could not manage his stammer, he would not reach his full potential. Many times Will had told him not to worry about how he sounded. There were plenty of people who sounded far worse and had done well enough for themselves.

Alf absentmindedly lifted his hand to his face, running a finger along a broad scar that curved up from his left temple and into his hairline. The finger was dirty with the dust of old tiles, and it left a red-brown mark on his face. It reminded Will of the crescent moons he had seen on Moorish designs brought over in the ships docking at Portsmouth and Lyme. He considered mentioning this to Alf, but changed his mind; the boy would be embarrassed. Will hoped Silas had not noticed because he would not be so tactful.

"Off you go then," Will said. "And bring Silas and me a jug back when you are done. There's a good lad."

Alf nodded, and then turned to go.

Will had a sudden thought. "Oh, and splash your face with it…give it a really good rub all over with the water… cool yourself down more that way, trust me." Alf ran off in the direction of the water butt. "Hot as the flames of perdition, and still he runs like that," said Will, amused. "I wouldn't have it in me most days, let alone on a day like this. Would you, old man?"

Silas did not answer Will's question. His thoughts had already returned to their previous conversation. "Whatever the truth of it. Someone did for the other nun, that's for certain. Cruelly done to death she was. She's in the 'firmary as we speak."

"I thought you said she was dead?" asked Will.

"Aye, that she is, Will. That she is."

"Well, if she's been taken to the infirmary, they must believe they can cure her of it."

Silas looked dumbfounded for a moment. "She's *dead*, Will?" Then, realising Will was joking, he began to laugh, his mouth opening wide to reveal the few teeth he still had.

"You seem to enjoy your work very much," observed a voice behind them.

Will turned around and, to his consternation, saw the small figure of Abbess Rhoswen, and another of the sisters, standing only a few feet away. Will glanced back at Silas to give him a warning look, and was dismayed to see the old man had his hand to his mouth in a childlike *I hope they didn't hear us* gesture. He frowned at Silas, and turned back to the Abbess.

"Good morning to you, Reverend Mother," he said,

removing his linen cap and touching his finger to his forehead. Behind him, Silas did the same.

"I'm afraid it is not such a good morning for us here at Althurst today," replied Rhoswen. "Last night one of our most dearly loved sisters was gathered unto God. It was much before her time. And, I regret to say, it was violently done."

"Yes, so I heard. I am very sorry for your loss. We both are." Will gestured towards Silas, who nodded his agreement.

Rhoswen pursed her lips for a few seconds as if thinking something over. "I am curious," she asked eventually. "You have heard of this already, you say? Of our grief... here at Althurst Abbey? Our sad loss?"

"We have, Reverend Mother," said Will, not unaware of the trap into which he was being made to walk, but not able to see how it could be avoided.

Rhoswen paused again deliberately, before adding, "And yet I find you and this fellow laughing? Such levity...laughter... I would have thought was... inappropriate...unsuitable... on such a day as this... don't you think? I know I do. Or possibly you disagree?"

"Oh, no, no. Indeed it is out of place, Reverend Mother. Please forgive us. We were not thinking. No disrespect was intended, I promise you. None at all."

"No, that it wasn't, Good Mother," added Silas, fervently shaking his head in a clumsy attempt to emphasise his sincerity. Will gave thought to giving the damn fool another warning look, then saw that the Abbess had not even glanced in the old man's direction.

"Master Tiler," she said, still looking directly at Will. "You know my views on this enterprise. This chapel of Saint Merwinna...it has been built against my wishes."

Will said nothing.

"Well," continued Rhoswen, "given that I had no choice in the matter, I have made it my business to see to it that it is done well at every stage. The stage we have now reached is your floor. I would have that done well also."

"I will do all I can to…" began Will, only to have the Abbess speak over him.

"My duties as Abbess occupy much of my time. I am a busy woman. I cannot be constantly here to keep a watchful eye over your progress, much as I would wish to. That being so, I have allotted the task of being my eyes to young Ingrith here."

For the first time Will looked past the Abbess towards the other woman. Only now did he recognise the novice he had seen in the antechamber to the Abbess's receiving room. She did not look much happier now than she had back then. She certainly looked no happier to see Will. He nodded to her. "Good morning to you… Ingrith, was it?"

"Master Tiler," replied Ingrith, flatly.

"You are very welcome here," lied Will.

"Oh, I doubt that," said Rhoswen, humourlessly. "Welcome or not, you must learn to accept her presence. It is an arrangement that should benefit you as well as me."

"How so?" asked Will, and immediately regretted asking what he realised was an impertinent question.

Luckily for him, Rhoswen chose to ignore it. "Ingrith will not get in your way, I assure you. She will merely observe. And then she shall report what she has observed to me, of course." She paused, appeared to be about to say something more, and then changed her mind. Finally, she said, "Well, that is all. Good morning to you," and walked away.

Will was about to introduce Ingrith to Silas when he saw the Abbess had turned around, and was walking back.

"Master Tiler," she began as soon as she reached them. "I am sure from your point of view you are simply doing your work as best you know how, and as you have been instructed by My Lord the Bishop. That is fitting. Therefore, I do not doubt you find me an irritation…unwelcoming… mistrustful. Ingrith's presence must seem to attest to the latter. Let me say this much. I do not mistrust you personally, or your good intentions. Nor do I doubt your skill. It is not you I dislike. It is the task you have been set which vexes me. So, in answer to your question, trust me when I tell you that this *will* be of benefit to you if it prevents you from going too far in the wrong direction with your labours, and in so doing prevents you and me from falling out. You would not wish for that, I am sure."

Will shook his head. "No, Reverent Mother, I would not."

"Good. Then let us hope it does not come that. My intention is that this arrangement be of benefit to *all* parties involved." The slightest movement of the Abbess's eyes in the direction of Ingrith suggested that this last comment was intended as much for her as for Will. "That is all," she said. "Please, continue with whatever it is that are doing there in that ditch."

"It is a kiln. The beginnings of one anyway," explained Will.

"Oh, …I see," replied Rhoswen indifferently, and then, without another word, she walked away. In doing so she passed Alf, who had returned unnoticed from fetching water. He had hung back when he saw the Abbess and Ingrith talking to Will. A small incline of her head suggested to Will that the Abbess had greeted, perhaps even blessed, the boy, but Alf only looked anxious, and remained predictably silent.

"Alf lad, I hope you weren't bothering the Reverend Mother with all your talk," teased Silas when the boy came up to them. If Alf heard, he showed no sign of it. He was staring at Ingrith.

"Hello," said the novice.

Alf blushed, and looked down.

"What do they call you?"

Still Alf would not look up.

"That's Alf," said Will. "It's not personal. He doesn't say much to anyone. What was it your Abbess said? He doesn't mistrust you personally?" Will took the water jug from Alf, drank half, and then passed the rest to Silas who drank greedily.

"I see," said Ingrith. "I am glad to meet you, Alfred. Will you not you say hello back to me?"

"Oh, he won't talk unless he has to," explained Silas, water dripping from his grizzled beard. "On account of his trouble with words. They come out all j- j- jerky like a stack of tiles slowly collapsing. And it's not Alfred, just Alf. Ain't that right, boy?"

Ingrith frowned. "Oh, dear. Well, Alf, I had a cousin who had difficulty with some of his words. Yet he is a Baron now."

He was always going to be a Baron, speech problems or not, thought Will. Then again, at least this young woman's intentions towards Alf seemed good, even if she did remain cold towards Will himself.

"I saw you once before, sister," he said.

"Oh, yes, that's right. I remember it now," replied Ingrith. In fact, she had recognised the tall man in front of her immediately they were introduced.

"You do?"

"Yes, I do," she said, in tones that made it clear she thought it of no consequence.

Will decided to give up the attempt at pleasantness; the girl seemed determined to be distant. "Well, I must be getting on with things. This kiln won't dig itself, eh? You must choose where you want to be. But if you want my advice, I'd stand over there in the shadow of that yew tree. It's going to get much hotter before this day is out. Make use of the shade while it's there."

"And I will be out of your way over there too, I suppose?"

Yes, that, too, thought Will. *That, too.*

******

CHAPTER 3

From the windows of her receiving room Abbess Rhoswen watched as one of the sisters gathered newly opened Chamomile flowers from the abbey herb garden. She allowed herself a faint smile; Chamomile infusions were good at easing flatulence. This probably meant poor Sister Lorica was suffering from her unfortunate complaint again. Then Rhoswen's smile quickly faded as she recalled that the plant was also good for calming the nerves. She reproached herself and asked God for his forgiveness. More than likely the infusion was for poor Sister Winifred. Neither she nor Sister Marigold had fully recovered from whatever they had witnessed on the night Sister Euphemia had been found dead. But it was Sister Winifred's nerves that had suffered the most. Young Marigold, at least, was well enough to talk with some degree of lucidity about what had happened. In fact, it was Sister Marigold she was waiting for right now. Sister Helewise, the Infirmaress, had come to Rhoswen earlier that morning and said that, in her opinion, the young woman was now strong enough to talk about what she had seen. So Rhoswen had requested she be brought to her after the Prime service was over. It might have been kinder to allow her to stay where she was in the comfort of the infirmary. Regrettably, Rhoswen felt this was a conversation best had out of the hearing of the rest of the Abbey.

When, a few minutes later, Sister Elisabeth, an assistant to Sister Helewise, brought Sister Marigold to her, Rhoswen was shocked to see how pale the girl was. She glanced questioningly at Sister Elisabeth. Sister Marigold must have seen the glance because she said, "Oh, no. It is all right, Reverend Mother. I promise you I am content to talk about it." She paused, and then added more softly, "Though I do not know what I can tell you that will make any sense."

"I understand. Sit down, my child, and tell me what you can. Let us see if we cannot make sense of it together?"

For a moment, once Marigold was seated, she gave the impression that she had become lost in her thoughts. She was staring down at her hands, which she had folded in her lap.

"Sister Marigold?" prompted Rhoswen.

When Marigold looked up, she had tears in her eyes. "Oh, it's all so terrible, Reverend Mother. I fear some dreadful wickedness has been visited upon us."

"Of that there is no question," agreed Rhoswen. "What I wish to learn is in what form."

"I wish I could say. Although I know Sister Winifred believes she saw the Devil himself."

"And you? What do *you* think you saw?" asked Rhoswen, careful to keep her voice and expression as calm as possible. From the corner of her eye she saw Sister Elisabeth had begun repeatedly crossing herself. "You may leave us, Sister Elisabeth," she said firmly.

"But Sister Helewise told me to…"

"I will bring Sister Marigold back to the infirmary when we are done. She will be safe with me in the meantime." When she saw Sister Elisabeth still looked doubtful, Rhoswen snapped at her, "I am the Abbess and perfectly capable of taking care of one of my daughters."

Looking away from the flustered Sister Elisabeth, Rhoswen smiled down at Sister Marigold, attempting to reassure her. At the same time, she wondered about her choice of words. *She will be safe.* Why had she said that? Was there any possibility that she would not have been?

Sister Elisabeth was still hovering at the door indecisively. "Yes, Reverend Mother, I understand that. It is only that Sister Helewise will…"

"Understand as well," interrupted Rhoswen. "She will understand that I gave you no choice. Thank you, Sister Elisabeth. Off you go now," said Rhoswen, with more kindness in her voice than before, but no less firmly.

When, at last, they were alone, Rhoswen crouched down in front of Sister Marigold, and repeated her question from before. "So ... tell me...what is it that you think you saw?"

Sister Marigold stared into the distance at nothing. "I cannot truly say I *saw* anything. I was late for my duties and..." She stopped, looked up anxiously.

Rhoswen, guessing she was worried by this admission of tardiness in front of her Abbess said, "Never mind that. Go on..."

"At first, when I entered the church, it seemed nobody was there. It was odd. A lot of the candles were already burning, but there was no movement. I couldn't see Sister Winifred or Sister Euphemia. And then I came across Sister Winifred. She was hiding behind a pillar in the ambulatory. She looked so frightened, Reverend Mother. All I actually saw after that was something...a shadow, maybe...maybe not. There was blood, you see...poor Euphemia was lying there. I wondered why we were not going to help her. Then all the candles went out." Sister Marigold clapped her hands together. "Just like that. It was complete darkness. I could see nothing more after that. Although I did hear..."

Still crouching, Rhoswen leaned forward. "What? What did you hear?"

Sister Marigold passed a hand in front of her face as if brushing away an insect or cobweb. Rhoswen could see neither.

"What did you hear, Sister Marigold? Tell me what you heard."

"Sister Winifred started to scream...So did I, I think. Before that..."

"Yes? Before that...?"

Sister Marigold's eyes grew wide. "There was laughter. Horrid, scornful laughter."

Rhoswen sat back. "A man's or a woman's?"

"I can't say. It was shallow, breathy..."

Rhoswen frowned, asked, "From where did it come?"

"That's what is so strange. It seemed to come from above us. It moved about. But always it was from above. Sometimes high in the nave. Sometimes closer. Oh, Reverend Mother, it was so horrible. So frightening."

"This voice that laughed, did it say anything?"

"No…I don't think so. Maybe. It might have…One thing. A single word."

"What was the word?"

"It sounded like '*Bartholomew*.'"

Rhoswen failed to prevent the shock from registering on her face.

"What is it, Reverend Mother?" asked Sister Marigold, growing anxious.

"Oh, nothing, nothing. Did it say anything else this voice?"

"No. I don't think so. Mostly it was laughter. So full of bitterness and cruelty. The more we screamed, the more it laughed."

"What happened after that?"

"Nothing more. The door from the dormitory passage opened, and we heard you and the sisters entering. Then you found us. You and the other sisters."

Rhoswen stood up, walked to a window, glanced up at the cloudless summer sky, and then turned back. "The candles were all burning when we entered. How do you explain that?"

Sister Marigold looked confused. "No…Were they?" She thought back for a moment. "You hadn't re-lit them?"

"No, my child, they were burning bright and steady when we entered. The melt of the wax suggested they had been burning for some time. We heard your screams and rushed in. All was bright inside. It did not take us long to find you both. And, sadly, poor Sister Euphemia."

Sister Marigold started to speak, then stopped.

"What is it, my child?" asked Rhoswen.

"How? How did she die? Sister Euphemia…How did she

die? I saw much blood. I did not see her."

"I don't understand. You say you did not see her?"

"She was out of view…beyond the altar. I never got close enough to see where she lay. Sister Winifred stopped me. I saw only the blood that came from her. There was so much of it…. yet we did not…I did not…"

"Help her? You worry that you did not go to her aid?"

"Yes. I did not go to her. I was afraid. That is not justification enough, is it?" Sister Marigold forced herself to look her Abbess in the eyes. "It isn't, is it, Reverend Mother?"

Sister Marigold was becoming agitated. Rhoswen began to question the wisdom of talking with her about the events in the church quite so soon. Sister Helewise had been mistaken; the young woman was not yet ready. Rhoswen also regretted her decision to dismiss Sister Elisabeth. Getting Marigold back to the infirmary unassisted might prove harder than she had anticipated. She took Sister Marigold's hands in her own.

"Calm yourself, daughter. Fear can make us someone other than we are. Someone other than who we might wish to be. It robs a person, not only of courage, also of judgement."

"But I did not always like her!" Marigold cried. "I thought her unnecessarily harsh at times. She seemed to me to look for…"

"That's enough, sister!" said Rhoswen, a little shocked at the honesty of the statement. She found, also, that she was a little irritated by it. To her shame, this was not because it was unkind and unnecessary; it was because she knew it to contain some truth. Sister Euphemia's zeal for her duties could be irksome. Sister Marigold was not alone in that view. There were times when Rhoswen herself shared it. Right now, however, the subject was not relevant. It would do nothing to help the situation. There was enough to deal with as it was. "This is not the time," she told the younger nun.

"Still, it is the truth. She… and Sister Winifred…they were

always displeased with some aspect of my performance. Why, I do not know."

"I have said that is enough!" said Rhoswen firmly. Then, in a more sympathetic tone, she added, "Really, you will regret saying such things. I know you do not mean them." She looked to the window once more, and said, "It is such a beautiful morning. I think you and I should walk a while together outside. Nothing aids clear thought better than the combination of a mild breeze and sunlight on one's face. Don't you agree?"

"There is no breeze," said Sister Marigold softly.

Once outside, the two women walked in silence for a while. There were too many inquisitive glances from the other sisters in the cloister, so Rhoswen led Sister Marigold further out, into the grounds of the Abbey. They continued to walk in silence for some time. All the while, Rhoswen noticed, Sister Marigold was chewing her bottom lip. At last she turned, and said imploringly, "What must I do, Reverend Mother?"

Rhoswen frowned. "*Do?*"

"About my feelings towards Sister Euphemia. I regret they were not always charitable. Only moments before…before what happened… I was thinking badly of her. There must be some penance…?" pleaded Sister Marigold.

Rhoswen felt genuine pity for the younger woman. "That is between you and your next confessor. Until then, you must ask God for his forgiveness in your private thoughts and prayers. I caution you, however, do not allow it to eat away at you too much. That guilt in itself will likely be your hardest penance."

Sister Marigold nodded, although it was plain she was not entirely satisfied.

After a moment, Rhoswen added, "I believe it is important that you understand… understand *and accept* …that you could not have helped Sister Euphemia even had you tried. Nobody could. Her injuries where such that…well…I doubt there was life remaining in her when you arrived."

"She could not have survived?" asked Sister Marigold.

"No. Nor, I think, would she have wished to. There would have been much pain."

"How did she…?" Unable to finish the sentence, Sister Marigold looked away.

"Die?" asked Rhoswen.

Her head still turned from Rhoswen, Sister Marigold nodded.

Rhoswen considered this question for a moment. Knowing the answer would be hard for the girl. But imagining might be worse. "I tell you now only because you will hear it from someone else eventually."

Sister Marigold turned to face Rhoswen, who took a breath before saying, as steadily as she could, "Sister Euphemia was flayed alive."

Marigold cried out. "Oh! Oh, no! How unspeakable." Then she gasped, and covered her mouth with her hand, as she realised what the Abbess already had. "*Bartholomew!*" she mumbled from behind her fingers. When she removed her hand from her mouth her voice came in a panicked staccato, between gasps. "Her skin cut from her body… Like the saint…. Like Saint Bartholomew! Oh, Reverend Mother… It is too wicked. So cruel a jest. Wicked… wicked… wicked." She looked directly at Rhoswen. "Perhaps Sister Winifred was right? Perhaps this can only be the work of the Devil himself?"

Sister Marigold staggered a little, looking almost as if she might faint. Rhoswen stepped forward and clasped her by the shoulders in an attempt to steady her, and guide her to the ground if she did lose consciousness. Instead of fainting, Sister Marigold pulled away, and began to turn frantically about, pushing out at the air with her hands as if attempting to keep some invisible assailant at bay. She was becoming hysterical, and Rhoswen's lack of height made it difficult for her to maintain any sort of control of the taller woman. She called for help.

******

"What's going on over there, I wonder?" asked Silas when they heard the Abbess's cries for help. "Looks like they ran into a fuckin' wasp nest or some such thing."

"Whatever it is, I think we'd better go see," replied Will, dropping his spade and climbing out of the nearly completed kiln trench. "Come on, old man."

When Alf made to follow the two men, Will waved him back. "You stay where you are for now, boy. I'll call if I need you."

Will broke into a run, and reached Sister Marigold and the Abbess ahead of Silas. "What's wrong with her?" he asked.

"You take her," barked Rhoswen, ignoring the question. "I can't hold her much longer. I fear she may injure herself if she is not restrained until this has passed."

Will stepped up behind Sister Marigold and wrapped his arms around her, clamping her arms to her sides. He leaned his head over her shoulder and spoke gently into her ear. "There now, sister. Just you calm down now. The Reverend Mother is right; we can't have you doing yourself a harm." To the obvious chagrin of the Abbess, Sister Marigold complied almost immediately, slumping back into Will's arms.

"The idea was to stop her hurting herself. I hope you have not been too clumsy, and squeezed too hard," said Rhoswen.

"No, she's not hurt. Not fainted either. A touch tired, that's all. Isn't that right, girl?" Sister Marigold managed a slight nod of her head, and Will lowered her gently to the ground, where she sat with her head in her hands. "There now," said Will. "Whatever it was, it has left her."

"I can see that," replied Rhoswen, brusquely. "You may leave us."

"Do you not require help getting her inside? I'd be happy

to…"

"No. Ingrith can assist me. That is all the help I will need."

Will turned and saw the young novice standing next to Silas, who was leaning forward, hands on his knees, getting his breath back after having run. Will had not been aware of either of them until now. Despite his struggles to regain his breath, Silas was looking on with undisguised inquisitiveness; this would be his main topic of conversation for some time to come. Ingrith, on the other hand, looked uneasy. It struck Will that, for some reason, the girl was embarrassed. She was looking at the ground, and there was a definite colour in her cheeks.

"Come, Ingrith," said Rhoswen.

Ingrith looked up. "Reverend Mother?"

Rhoswen, looked down at Sister Marigold, swallowed, and then said, "Help me get her up. We'll take her back to Sister Helewise." She crouched down in front of Sister Marigold. "Can you stand for me, sister? If you can get to your feet…if you feel ready… we will walk alongside you. We'll take you back to Helewise…to the infirmary… She can give you the care you need. More than anything, I suspect that should include rest. You must forgive me if I have been instrumental in overtaxing you. Can you rise?"

Sister Marigold nodded. Despite this, she seemed to be having difficulty getting to her feet. When Will stepped forward to offer assistance again, the Abbess shook her head. "No," she snapped. "We are fine now. Go back to your labours. Ingrith and I will attend to our sister."

Will clapped Silas on the back. "Come on, old man. We're not wanted here."

As the two men began to walk away, Rhoswen called them back. Still supporting Sister Marigold on one side, while Ingrith held the young nun on the other, Rhoswen fixed Will and Silas with a stare for a few seconds. Will stood still. Silas shifted his weight from foot to foot. Finally, Rhoswen said, "No doubt you will chatter about this amongst yourselves the moment you have the opportunity to do so. I suppose that cannot be prevented. Nonetheless, you are to speak of this with nobody else, is that clear? I shall hear of it if you have, believe me."

"Why does that little woman always have something else to add?" asked Silas, when they were sufficiently out of earshot. "Seems to me the talking is never quite done with her, is it? There's always another bit to be said."

Will shrugged. "People like that have a lot going on in their heads, I suppose. They think they've got rid of all the cracked tiles in the stack, and then another one shows up."

"It was that young nun whose tiles were cracked, if you ask me," said Silas. "What was going on with her? Did she have the fitting disease like old Winchester Jack, d'ya think?"

Will thought for a moment. "No, I don't reckon so. She was not trembling and twisting as Jack did."

"Lost her wits, then? Ah, that'll be something to do with what happened last night, won't it?" A thought occurred to Silas, and his face brightened with the excitement of it. "Hey now, maybe she was one of the nuns who was in the church when it happened. That's it! She's the one gone mad, Will. She's the one gone mad."

"Or just very upset about it. Whatever 'it' was."

"Murder and rape," I heard.

"You said that before about the rape."

"It's what they say."

"Well, it's what they always say. Doesn't make it true. And you don't have to keep saying it, truth or not. Especially not in front of young Alf."

"The boy has got to learn about such things from somewhere sometime," sniffed Silas. "He might as well hear it from us."

"True. Or maybe he already knows about such things. Some of it, at least. You know he does. Either way, it doesn't do him any good to keep hearing it. Besides, like I told you, it's more than likely not true about that part. The woman is dead, I grant you that. As for the rest, you don't know. Nor do I. Nor do I care to, for that matter. Nor do I care to."

******

When she returned sometime later, Ingrith stopped a few yards away from them. Will saw her from the corner of his eye, but said nothing. After a minute, she came over and stood by them. "Master Tiler. Please know that I, for one, am very sorry."

"Whatever for, girl?" asked Silas. "We knew where you was. You was with the Good Mother… and the mad nun. And… not to be rude or nothing like that… but it isn't as if you help us any when are here. You just watches."

Despite herself, Ingrith half-smiled at the remark. "No, it's not about that. I have no illusions that my presence is in any way essential to your work. I am not so foolish as that."

Will looked up from his work, curious. It was the first time the girl had spoken to them with anything in her voice other than mild disdain. "What is it about, then?" he asked.

"About the Reverend Mother," said Ingrith, awkwardly.

Will stared at the girl for a moment. He noticed she found it difficult to look him in the eye. "The Abbess? Go on. What about her?"

For the second time that morning Ingrith felt the sensation of heat in her cheeks that she knew meant she was blushing. The injustice of it made her want to stamp her feet. Other people – Abbess Rhoswen for one – seemed able to say what they liked, how they liked, and to almost anyone. And to say it without the slightest trace of the self-consciousness that always threatened to undermine Ingrith. It was so unfair that she was the one to whom the task of saying what she felt must be said to this man had fallen, even though for her it would be far more difficult than it would be for the Abbess, who really ought to be the one to say it.

Ingrith barely knew William Tiler, or any of his kind, for

that matter. Nor did she know if she would like him if she did know him better. All the same, she had felt keenly the unfairness of the way in which the Abbess had spoken to the man earlier. He had helped her. He had stopped what he was doing, and gone over to help when Marigold had had her fit, or whatever it was she was having. Had he not been the Good Samaritan? Had he not acted as the Bible taught you should act? Yet how had the Abbess treated him? Almost with scorn. Certainly with ingratitude. Ingrith was no fool; she understood the social divide between a craftsman like William Tiler and an Abbess. Nonetheless, Abbess Rhoswen had owed the man at least some slight recognition for his kindness. He was certainly not owed the churlishness that the Reverend Mother had displayed. Despite the nobility of Ingrith's own birth, from an early age she had followed the example of her father, Baron Edgar. He was a proud and distant man who, nonetheless, made sure to acknowledge the deeds of those below him - if only once in a while. It was God's will that there was structure to the way the world was, and it could not, and *should* not, be avoided, he had explained. Some people were born lower than others, and that was the correct and necessary way of things. Without that structure, all would be chaos. However, although servants, for example, were far lower in rank than a baron such as himself, or the daughter of a baron, such as Ingrith, that did not mean they did not exist and did not have a right to have their existence in this world acknowledged from time to time. Even a horse, he had once told her, gets a pat when it has carried its rider well.

War and the business of the court had kept her father away from home for most of Ingrith's childhood – and she did not always get on with him that well when he was home – but she had learned to respect his wisdom on this particular point.

"I believe we…the Abbey…the Sisters…owe you thanks for your help."

"I am being paid for my work here," said Will. "I do not do this for free, sister."

"You play games with me," said Ingrith, her face feeling hotter still. "You know full well that is not what I am referring to."

"I do, sister. Maybe you feel I am owed thanks for helping that poor girl who lost her wits earlier. And maybe you are right. But I do not expect them. Not from Abbess Rhoswen. She has no love for me."

"She is a representative of God."

"That she is. So…?"

"So, she should have love for everyone. Kindness is her duty. Yet it seems to me she does not show it," insisted Ingrith, and instantly regretted being so vocal in her condemnation of the Abbess's shortcomings. She glanced about herself, worried that one of the other nuns or some of the abbey servants might have been within hearing distance.

"Only us here," reassured Will.

"Nevertheless, I should not have…"

"I will not tell. Neither Will Silas." Silas nodded his agreement, although it seemed to Ingrith he looked a bit disappointed by the command. "As for Alf here," continued Will, "even if he understood…well…you know he has no enthusiasm for it when it comes to talking. Besides, who would he tell? The children of the Abbey school?" Will laughed at the absurdity of the idea. So did Alf, although he did not fully understand what it was he would tell even if he did. "Who would any of us tell?" continued Will. "Worry no more about it, Sister Ingrith."

"Thank you."

"No, it is I who thank you."

"For?"

"For your thanks…the ones the Abbess did not provide. Although I never did expect them. They were kindly meant, I see that."

To Will's slight irritation, Silas laughed. "That completes

the bargain. I swear I cannot follow this tale. Who is thanking who for what?"

"Sometimes I think it would be better for us all if it were you had the stammer, and Alf that spoke more," said Will.

"That's because all the lad would say is 'Yes Will, no Will'," replied Silas. "I keeps you in your place."

"And I keep *you* in bread and ale," replied Will. He turned back to Ingrith. "I suppose we had better be getting on with things, don't you? After all, you'll need something to take back to Abbess Rhoswen at the end of today. Something more than you watched us talking, eh?"

"I am sorry for that too," said Ingrith.

Will leaned on his spade. "I do believe you are, sister. You need not fret so much about it, though. We have had worse task masters than you or your Abbess Rhoswen. You have a job here that you must do, just as we have ours. We won't hold you responsible. The real difference of opinion is between Bishop Baldwin and the Abbess. Neither you nor I can do anything about which master or mistress we must serve. All we can do is get on with the tasks we have been given. Don't you think?"

Ingrith nodded. "I do." She stepped closer. "Still, if I am to take something back to the Abbess, as you say, I would ask what it is you are doing?"

"Diggin' a kiln," said Silas. "Nearly done with the diggin' as it happens. Mind you, it's been a while since we dug one."

"And the broken tiles…the bits of brick…all the pieces of them that Alf has been piling up… are they to form part of it?"

"That they are," said Silas, grinning through his dirty and matted beard.

"They will line it," explained Will, surprised, but not displeased, by Ingrith's interest. "They will make up the floor too. We'll build brick arches over the top of this trench…That's the furnace. Then the kiln itself will be built over it… and there you are. The tiles go in the top, the fire burns fierce in the bottom. We'll put in a stoke hole so we can feed it. Mind you, like Silas says, it has been a while since we had to make one of these. More usual in my father's day."

"You father?"

"Taught me all I know. Lucky for us, that included how to build a kiln. These days we work mostly with tiles that have been made elsewhere…and by other hands. They are brought in, not made on site."

"Not so many people would know how to do it," added Silas, with obvious pride. "Not often we get asked to make the tiles specially these days, is it Will?"

"True. Last time was at…where now?… Romsey Abbey."

"Well, there you have your first compliment from the Abbess," said Ingrith.

"How's that then?"

"Between us, she has already seen some of your work. The very tiles you speak of in fact…at Romsey. She made enquiries about you, and discovered you had worked for the sisters at Romsey. It is only a few days travel, so we went to look. I can tell you, she admired them very much."

"I am glad of it."

"You must never tell her I told you so."

"I will not, you have my word. Tell me, though, why is it we must make the tiles on site? It is rare these days. The ones they make at Alresford say, or just over the border in Dorchester are about as good as I've seen. I can't make better, though I do pride myself the ones I make are as good."

"Ah, but yours will be unique. Exclusive to Althurst. Exclusive to the chapel, in fact."

"You mean by that they will be a one-off set?" asked Will.

"That's correct. Abbess Rhoswen told me that, in her view, if a floor must be laid in Saint Merwinna's cell, then it should be exceptional…unlike any other. That cannot be true if the same design is used elsewhere, now can it? So, you see, this really must be the best you can do."

"I will do my best, as I always do. Still, they could have done such one-offs in Alresford if your Abbess had asked them."

"No, that would not do. It must be matchless. You will be *our* tiler, working on every stage of the production and laying of the tiles. It should be the best work you have *ever* done."

Will's expression darkened. "That is quite some challenge."

"It is, yes."

"I suppose it goes some way to explaining your presence."

"Yes. I suppose it does."

"But…and forgive me Sister Ingrith…it does not explain why you in particular. Why have *you* been given the task? Although I don't doubt your Abbess's choice, I am a bit curious as to what is behind it."

Will was not certain, but he thought Sister Ingrith looked a little pained. "There are two reasons. One is a source of pride. The other a source of shame," she told him.

"Tell me of the one of which you are proud. I need not hear the other."

To her surprise, Ingrith felt she wanted Will to know both reasons. "Unfortunately, I cannot do that if I wish to make you understand fully. What I mean to say is that I think the one is bound up with the other. So, I think you must hear both. Your understanding will be more complete that way."

"If you cannot tell one without telling the other, I am content that you tell me neither if to do so will cause you grief."

"No, I shall tell you. It is right that you should know."

"Is it a long story?" asked Silas.

"You will never know," Will told him. "Sister Ingrith, perhaps you and I should put some distance between ourselves and Silas's leathery old ears." He pointed at a patch of open space between where they were digging the kiln and the walls of the infirmary. "If we step over there a small way, we will still be within sight of some of the sisters, but out of the hearing of Silas. There will be no impropriety."

Silas grunted his annoyance, and got back to his digging. To him, talking with someone of Ingrith's birth and breeding was a novelty he had been enjoying. That Will seemed now to want to enjoy that novelty on his own irked him.

"You feel I have no fondness for you," said Ingrith when she and Will were a sufficient distance from the kiln trench.

Will glanced back, caught sight of Silas and Alf watching them. Alf turned away and made a show of sorting through a heap of broken tiles that Will knew he had already sorted. Silas, on the other hand, made absolutely no attempt to hide the fact that he was watching them. "Perhaps we are not such a likeable bunch," Will said, as much to himself as to Ingrith. "At least not Silas and me, anyway."

Ingrith allowed herself a slight smile. "You might say the same about the sisters here at Althurst."

"I would not."

Ingrith tilted her head. "I fear that is not the truth."

"Well, I might…if I dared," replied Will. As he said it, he was struck by the fact that in saying it he *had* dared. In front of this young woman, at least. He wondered at the wisdom of it; whether he should, in fact, suggest they ought not to be so frank.

"But we should be," said Ingrith. Will gazed at her, wondering if she had somehow read his thoughts.

"What's that?" he asked.

"Likeable," she said. "If nothing else, we should be likeable. Approachable… cordial. Our hearts are meant to be open and warm. We are meant to care. For you and Silas, tiles are your trade. For us…caring should be ours."

"The charity you offer the sick and the needy is…"

"Is something…but what if that is all show…what if…?" Ingrith saw Will was frowning. She stopped herself. "I apologise. I have let my thoughts run on."

"You apologise too much, sister. That you are sorry about something is almost all I hear from you."

"It is because I am uncertain of myself...and of this place..."

Will's frown deepened. "I do not think I am the right person..."

"Yes, yes, forgive me...Oh, there I go again."

Will felt a sudden pity for her. "You're saying you're sorry for saying you're sorry now. Listen. Why not tell what you were going to? Tell me why you have been chosen to watch over me and Silas and Alf."

"Yes, that is why we have stepped away, is it not?"

"It is..." said Will, then waited.

There followed a few moments of silence while Ingrith collected her thoughts. At last she said, "You are comfortable talking to people outside of your own...well, status."

"I needs must be to do my work. Poor people can't afford tiled floors."

"I do not share that ease."

"You are high born, and well bred, I can hear that. I am not. If you prefer, we can limit our conversation to what it is I am doing with the floor. That is fine."

"No, you misunderstand me. I mean more generally. I mean I am not comfortable with people...whatever their background. I am here because my father thought it the best place for me. Out in the world I would not have been a success. I would have not brought pride to the family name. I would not have made a good marriage."

Will disagreed with this – the girl was pretty enough, and quite likeable, once you got past her awkwardness, that was – and he would liked to have told her so, only he was made anxious by Ingrith's sudden candour. "Sister, you must mind you don't say anything you will regret. Remember I am but a tiler. A craftsman...I am not...What I mean to say is that it is not proper for you to talk to me of such things. You may regret..."

"There, you see," said Ingrith. "I say nothing, and then I say too much. I have succeeded only in making you as uncomfortable as I am. My curse is to be ill at ease almost everywhere, and in any situation. Worse, I make other people uncomfortable."

"You were kind to young Alf. He likes you, I can tell."

Ingrith gave a little shrug. "He has an innocence about him that it is easy to be kind to. I doubt many would have difficulty being kind to such as Alf."

"You would be surprised. There is a reason why the boy cannot open his mouth without tripping over his words. He was not always so. But that is a story for another time. You were to tell me why the Abbess chose you."

"My awkwardness has meant I have, on more than one occasion, upset the sisters. I follow the Rule, I really do. Or try to. And still it seems I transgress all the same. Talking when I should not. Failing to communicate when I should. Yet it is not for want of a calling. At least I believe not."

"The Rule. That is like your own special set of commandments, is that not so?"

"I suppose it is, yes. If you want to call it that. Set out for us to follow by the saint."

"Merwinna?" "

"Benedict. Saint Benedict. We are Benedictines you see."

Will slapped his forehead. "Of course. I knew that. For a moment I wondered if this place had its own set of..."

Amused, despite herself, Ingrith smiled. "No, we do not," she said.

Will was surprised by her expression. It was not unwelcome on a face that had, up until now, seemed permanently downcast. He found he, too, was smiling. "Never mind my foolishness, please go on with what you were telling me."

Ingrith's smile quickly faded. "Well, Abbess Rhoswen has had her doubts about me. Not my willingness...I am sure she knows how hard I try... My suitability is what she questions. Since coming to this place, I have always seemed to be explaining myself to her. Why I failed to do some or other thing, complete some or other task in the manner it should be completed."

"Which is what you were doing when first I saw you. In her ante-chamber…waiting for a scolding?"

"Probably. Something of the sort. Perhaps *scolding* is not the best word. But yes, I will not have been in there for any reason for which I would have been proud. However…" Ingrith paused, seemed to be composing herself. Will saw now that, despite the smile of only a few moments earlier, she was now close to tears. "However, there is one area where I have some ability, where I do not always blunder, and my every step is not always a misstep."

"If you are going to tell me you can lay tiles, I will have to tell Silas, despite my earlier undertaking not to," said Will, attempting to lighten the atmosphere.

"No, not that." Ingrith took a moment to recover herself, fought back the urge to cry. "What I am good at…and you must forgive my boastfulness on this one thing….is how things should appear. How they will look their best."

"I am not sure I understand you, sister."

"Ingrith, please call me Ingrith. I am not yet a sister. It is not right to address me as such."

Although Will understood the point that it would be wrong to call this young woman 'sister' given that she was not yet due the respect of that title, it still seemed wrong to use her first name. "Then, perhaps Mistress Ingrith would…?" he offered.

"No, simply Ingrith…It is what I wish." Even as she said it, Ingrith was unsure why she was insisting. Will was right. 'Mistress Ingrith' would have been far more appropriate, and certain members of the community at Althurst would, without doubt, be shocked to hear her addressed by this man as plain Ingrith. But then, perhaps that was why she was insisting upon it?

Looking at her, Will saw he had no choice, and decided not to press the matter. He would, however, be careful to avoid calling her by her first name in the presence of the other sisters, and he would make sure Silas was equally careful. "Very well, Ingrith it is then. Now, please go on with what you were saying. How things should appear…your skill…"

"Oh, yes… What I mean to say is that I have…" Ingrith felt a little ashamed at the immodesty of what she was about to say. Yet it was true, and needed to be said if Will was to understand. "I have a gift…" she said, adding hastily, "Albeit a small one…in as much as I know what is pleasing to the eye. It is natural to me…inborn… I can recognise what is good in matters of style and art. An ability to judge what is suitable…what goes together, and what does not. Forgive me if I sound proud, but my designs for embroidery, although not necessarily exceptionally well executed are always very fine designs. My arrangements of flowers on feast days outshine those of the others…that sort of thing. Oh dear, I really am sounding proud."

"Not if it is true. Your skill is a gift from God. As is mine. To use it well is to honour Him."

Ingrith looked surprised. "Perhaps you are right," she said to Will. But to herself she said, "Still, I must confess this later. Do what penance I am given." Then, to Will again, she said. "The Abbess herself has noticed these things. I only echo her words when I praise them."

"You have a good eye, is what you are saying."

"I have a good eye," said Ingrith, trying out the phrase. "Yes, I like that. I have a good eye."

"And the Abbess wants you to keep that eye on me."

"She does. Oh…not that she does not trust your skill or good intention."

"Just my judgement. It seems to me she and I have had a talk on this very subject before."

"I can imagine you have. That the chapel be fitting is very important to her."

"Fitting. That word again. Everything is about what is

fitting. Still, I suppose it should be. And your Abbess is killing two birds with one stone. She keeps you occupied with something that you might be good at, and through you keeps an eye…a *good* eye…on me."

"Yes, that's it exactly. She believes if I can do something well…*really* well…better than the others could… then it might help reverse the unfortunate tendency in my progress here. This is a bit more than merely arranging flowers, you see."

"You mean it could turn the tide for you?"

"Yes, something like that. I hope you do not object."

"I cannot deny that I did," said Will. "I don't now, though."

It was true. Will found that he really did not object. His only misgiving – and one he did not share with Ingrith – was that, if the chapel floor turned out not to be to Abbess Rhoswen's liking, in spite of Ingrith's attention, it might well be the girl's undoing rather than her salvation. The arrangement might also be a means by which Abbess Rhoswen would have someone upon whom to deflect blame if others in the Order did not like the finished result.

"I wonder if maybe you ought to tell Silas. Explain at least some of it," suggested Ingrith. "Although, maybe not *all* of it. Some of what I have made known to you about my own shortcomings is rather private."

"I'll tell him just enough to stop him scowling," said Will. Ingrith smiled at this, yet Will sensed there was something more she wanted to say. "What is it, sister?"

"Ingrith."

"Right. What is it, Ingrith?"

"I wish to be employed."

"Employed?"

"I wish to be of use. Also, if I am honest…"

"It's always best to be."

"I wish to be occupied. Merely observing is a little…tedious."

"Dreary you mean? Well, I did think watching two men digging a hole for half the day might be. The thing is, I doubt I can find you work. If I did, I could not promise it would not be almost as dull for someone like yourself as just watching has been. The problem is it takes experience to do much of what we do. Those are jobs I could not give to you. You would find yourself doing the work the boy does, and I already have him for that. No, I regret your hands will have to stay idle. Let your eye do your work, eh?"

"If there is no task you will allow me to perform, then I would like to be instructed. I wish to learn what it is you are doing. How you make the tiles...things like that. You teach the boy, do you not?"

It was clear from Will's expression that the request surprised him. He rubbed at his chin as he considered. "Well...as much as I can when there is time for it. I do instruct the boy, yes. You could listen to that, I suppose." A frown crossed Will's face. "What about the Abbess, though? Will she not be angered to find you being made my second apprentice?"

"I will say I insisted. It will be part of my keeping an eye on you. How can I say you are doing the wrong things if I do not understand the processes by which you do them?" Ingrith smiled. "In fact, I *do* insist."

Will was pleased to see the smile again – even if it was a little forced - and worried that if he did not agree it would soon disappear once more. He nodded. "As you wish."

Ingrith clapped her hands. "Good."

"Although, right now, we really *are* only digging a trench. There is no hidden art to it. Sweat and an aching back, that's all. I cannot think you want a lesson in the use of spade, pickaxe and shovel."

"No, not that. I do have a question, however. The first of many, I believe."

"Go on."

"Is it true what the old man...?"

"Silas."

"Silas. Is it true what he says about the kiln? Do fewer people know how to build them than once did?"

"It is. There is less call for it these days. Usually, the only reason to do it is that the job is distant enough from any of the places of manufacture that the cost of making them on site is less than transporting them there. That is how I came to learn to make a kiln. From my father it was. Now, I have a question for you, if I may be so bold."

"You may."

"You must tell me if it is disrespectful. It is not one I would ask Abbess Rhoswen."

Ingrith could not conceal her pleasure. "In which case you must definitely ask me it."

"Very well then. Why would a young woman...one not unlike you, I suppose... why would she do what Saint Merwinna did? Why would she want to have herself walled up like that? Did she hate the world so much? I have heard tell of the miracles that came of it, and I do not doubt them. Yet it still seems…"

"Too great a sacrifice?"

"Something like that, yes."

"Matthew of Bridport is an Anchorite...that is how they are known...or an Anchoress in the case of a female like Saint Merwinna...Well, Matthew is not so very far from here. A few days travel."

"I have heard those terms for such people. And I have heard tell of Matthew of Bridport. My work took me near there a while back. What of him?"

"If you were to go there...to Bridport... and ask the same question of him, I believe he... like Merwinna would have... would tell you he does what he does so he can better serve God. Anchorites devote their lives to His praise, and prayers for all our salvation. They do not hate the world as you say: they have great love for it. A stricter separation from the world, however...the solitude it provides...it allows for more attention to prayer and penance…They are not distracted from their task by unnecessary things."

"Is that not what you and the sisters do here at Althurst?"

"There are still a great many distractions put between us and God."

"You would not want to be shut away from everything?"

"No. That is not the nature of my calling." Ingrith looked downcast again. "Perhaps mine is not as strong as it should be. To hear the Bishop read from the Order of the Dead and to know it was for me he read it…I do not think I could bear it."

"The Order of the Dead?"

"Yes. To this world they are in many ways dead."

"By choice?"

"Yes."

Will looked confused. "Is not self-murder a sin?" he asked.

Ingrith opened her mouth to reply, but found no words. Her heart sank when she realised it was because she did not know how to answer Will's question. She felt that she should have. Somehow, she should have been able to counter his objection, and yet she was unable. If she asked one of the sisters, they might be able to help, although they were sure to see it as just another of her failings.

Misunderstanding her silence, Will asked for her forgiveness. His question, he said, had been disrespectful.

******

CHAPTER 4

Merwinna, 1171

A thought struck Merwinna. She sat down on her stool, pulled off her sandals, and looked down at her feet. She gasped. They looked as if they might belong to one of the destitute she used to see in the streets of Althurst on market days - people so used to indignity that any sense of shame had all but deserted them. How was it possible she had not noticed how filthy her feet had become? The toenails were long and blackened, the pale skin surrounding them crusted with grime and dirt. She grimaced. Then she held her hands in the shaft of light from her one window onto the outside world. They were the same as her feet. They were filthy. And the stronger light showed just how ingrained that filth had become. Now she lifted her hands to her head, and began to slowly trace the contours of her face with her fingertips. Without the aid of that instrument of vanity, a looking glass, it was impossible to know for certain, but her guess was it, too, was badly in need of a wash. This was inexcusable. She must not let it happen again. Maybe the world beyond her cell walls could no longer see the sorry state she had allowed herself to get into; that did not mean God could not.

"*He* sees," she whispered to herself.

She must make mention of this new failing in future prayers for guidance and forgiveness. And in her next confession. Yet one more of so many failings. It could not wait; she must pray right now. Merwinna fell to her knees, the stool tumbling over behind her. Before she could think of the right words to form her prayer, her chest hitched, and she let out a sob. Then, before she could stop herself, Merwinna began to cry uncontrollably.

Minutes passed this way until, suddenly aware of how loud

her crying must be, she bit down on her fist to stifle any further sobs that might come. The world beyond her cell might not be able to see her, but it could still hear her. What if someone were passing the church right now? Worse, what if someone were inside? Father Jerome, perhaps. Or one of the sisters. Her other window – the one that looked into the church – would certainly carry the sound she was making. Crying too loudly was yet another thing she must guard against doing again. She waited a moment, holding her breath, listening. If Father Jerome, or one of the sisters, had heard, they would almost certainly have come to the window to enquire if she were alright. Nobody came. Merwinna breathed a sigh of relief.

Now, she must wash. She scooped a jug full of water from her pail and poured it into a shallow dish which she set down on the floor. Then she pulled the stool upright, sat down again, and lifted one of her feet in order wipe it with a dampened cloth. Then the other foot. That done, she dipped the cloth in the water once more, pulled her habit higher, and began to clean her lower legs.

"What about higher still?" he suggested.

Merwinna ignored him, so he spoke again, as she had known he would. "Higher still and you might enjoy it, eh?"

"Be gone!" hissed Merwinna.

"You could think on Garrick. I'm sure he thinks on you at such times, don't you? Not that plain wife of his. She is all bone. Nothing a man could rest his head on. Nothing to stroke. Nothing to knead. She has none of your curves. Such curves. Wasted, all shut away in this place. God's gift, wasted."

"Be gone! I will not heed you!" Merwinna now did as she always did when he came. She fell to her knees again, and began to pray.

"Your answer to all problems, it seems. Back on your knees. Do you imagine the Almighty really enjoys receiving prayers from people with shit under the nails of the hands they raise to him? That close to your own face they must smell, even to someone whose body is as soiled as yours. Well, I suppose it might help keep your mind off the fine-looking Garrick. Who knows? All those things you imagine doing with him. He might be doing some of them with someone else even now… at this very moment. Think on it. Garrick, at this very moment bedding down with that little slut from the town he married because he couldn't have you. The pair of them making the beast. Grunting. Heaving. Sweating out their animal passions as a temporary diversion from their mutual disappointment. Mind you, although his manhood might be moving up and down inside his helpmeet whore, his thoughts are sure to be with his precious Merwinna. Such a waste, don't you think?"

"Stop it! Such things are unworthy!"

"Oh? I thought you were paying me no heed? Then is that not what you always claim? Well now, as I know you *are* listening, how about your thinking on this. When he cries out at the moment of release, whose face does he see, do you think? Into whose little cunt do you think he pictures spilling his seed?"

"Foul creature! I will not listen to you!" cried Merwinna.

"But you *do*. You *are*."

"Though I cannot help hearing your words, I will not let them reach me. Try as you might."

He chuckled. "I wonder if he ever says your name by mistake. Now wouldn't that be something, eh? How would he explain *that*, hmm? Mind you, he might have a change of heart if he could see how disgusting you were these days…"

Merwinna continued with her prayers. Her hands now clenched so tightly they had begun to ache. "Lord, I beseech you…"

"Little slut of God," he growled. "Tell me, how can you hope to fool Him with all that pleading and whining when you cannot even fool yourself?"

"Unworthy! Unworthy! Unworthy!" screamed Merwinna.

******

Inside the Abbey Church, Father Jerome, the nun's priest, covered his ears, closed his eyes, and prayed for the young woman whose cries he had been unable to avoid overhearing. She would not be the first of her kind whose mind was unable to adjust to the isolation to which she had committed herself, no matter how convinced she had been of her calling to begin with. She had never been a popular member of the Abbey community. The manner in which she indulged in, even flaunted, her piety irritated people. Her certainty that her own faith was stronger than anyone else's made her difficult to like. But surely no one, not even her most heartfelt of detractors, could wish on her the profound suffering he heard in her voice at such times as these? Not even the wife of Garrick the potter.

And yet, whenever Father Jerome went to the small opening in the wall that gave onto Merwinna's cell, and softly enquired after her welfare, he knew she would assure him that all was well; she always did – her tone, at times, verging on the ecstatic. Almost unseemly.

******

CHAPTER 5

Althurst Abbey – 1307

Will stepped out of the summer sun and into the cool of the shade created by the ceiling and walls erected around the previously cracked and crumbling stone of Saint Merwinna's cell. This was far from the first time he had stood in the new chapel but, as he always was, he was again struck by how well the master mason and his men had done their work. He stopped, looked about himself, and then reached forward, tracing the lines of the cool stonework with his fingers. It was just as Bishop Baldwin had claimed it would be. The older stones were incorporated into, not obscured by, the surrounding stonework of the walls that had been created around them. Nothing – or at least very little – of what had previously been there was lost to view. Even so, from her continued hostility to the project, the high quality of the workmanship had not been enough to satisfy Abbess Rhoswen that the chapel should have been built. Will suspected that, even were she to be convinced, she would never admit to it. Not given how badly she had clashed with the Bishop. She had lost considerable face because he had forced her to submit to the building work against her will; she would not wish to lose even more by confessing that she now agreed with his position. Whatever she felt, she would have to live with the chapel, even if she would never accept it. This was a shame, thought Will, because it really was very fine work, and showed a respect for the enterprise – and, therefore for the saint herself - on the part of the builders that surely could not honestly be denied by anyone.

The high quality of the masons' work both motivated and daunted Will in equal measure. Although matching its quality was a challenge he knew in his heart he was capable of meeting, now and again there was still that creeping doubt. The '*what if this time I should fail?*' question that could make his chest tighten. Thankfully, Will knew himself well enough to recognise that he often had such feelings at the beginning of a new job. He had risen this far in his trade without significant disaster. There was no particular reason this time to expect anything more than the minor problems and setbacks that were usually encountered, and always overcome. And yet, there it was again, that doubt, that question.

"Fool," he said to himself out loud. The word resounded unnervingly from the stone walls. He continued under his breath, "Get on with what you came in here to do, man. Measure out the area to be covered."

Will shrugged off a coil of twine he had been carrying looped around his shoulder, and caught it in his hand. Then he squatted down, and began to shuffle along the wall of the chapel; laying the twine around the edges of the rectangle formed by the floor as he went; pushing it flush with the bottom of the stonework; making a mark with a lump of chalk at the points where the corners were; and, finally, cutting it off when it met up with itself at the last corner. He then repeated this process for the smaller area that marked out where the altar would stand. He would have to remember to remove this second area from his final calculations. Other tilers had their own ways of measuring areas to be covered, but marking it out with a piece of twine was the method Will's father had taught him, and it usually served as well as any; particularly when, like this one, the area to be covered was formed by perfect right angles – the high quality of the mason's work again. Things could be a bit more tricky if the area was less regular in shape. At times like that, it was as much to do with the eye as with the measurement. Will made a mental note to show Alf how to use the twine at some point. If he had thought about it, he would have shown him today. The boy was ready, and it would be useful to have a second set of hands and eyes. Silas had never grasped it, and never really wanted to.

Several minutes later, the task all but complete, Will attempted to stand, but found his knees had cramped up from too much kneeling and shuffling. Cursing, he shuffled himself in the direction of a shovel that had been left in one corner, and used it to lean on as he pulled himself up. Another reason to get the boy involved, he thought.

"Is that how it is done then?" a voice said from behind, startling him, so that he came close to losing his balance, and dropping to his knees once more.

Will was close to uttering a curse when it came to him who the voice belonged to, so he spoke more pleasantly in reply than he otherwise might have. "Depends what you mean. Getting up or measuring out?"

"The second," said Ingrith, then followed this up with, "I am sorry if alarmed you."

"Not alarmed, lass. Ashamed."

"Then you should not be, for the fault was all mine. I should have been more careful. Anyone can be taken by surprise."

"Only the ancient of bone are so caught whilst prising themselves up from the floor like some alehouse drunkard."

"Oh now, Master Tiler, you are only a small way into your middle years. It was the position, not your age that caused the stiffness. Only the very young are free of such things. In future you should get the boy involved."

Will grunted, and finished the task of pulling himself up. "Tell that to my knees! Besides, I think you may be applying the years of the clergy to a working man. The two do not tally as well as they might."

Ingrith nodded, aware of the disparity between the two walks of life, and uncomfortable with it. She was silent for a moment. Finally she asked, "Is it?"

"Is it what?"

"How you measure the area."

Will nodded. "To begin with it is…for a rough idea, you understand."

"Why not simply use a tile? Count how many times one goes into the space required?"

"That is another way. And I do sometimes use it. Usually only for the smaller spaces, though. With a length such as this…" Will gestured along the floor of the chapel. "Well, I would be flipping the tile from sunrise to sundown. From…what is it for you Sisters, Lauds to…?"

"Vespers."

"Aye, that sounds about right. So really, you see, a rope serves best in my experience. To start with, anyway."

"To start with," echoed Ingrith, talking more to herself than Will.

"That's half the job…the start. Get it right and you're set for the rest. Get it wrong and…well. Mind you, that Abbess of yours, …she didn't want it started at all. And I think we can say for certain she will not be pleased with whatever we do. I've never seen her but she is frowning. Get stuck that way looking into the wind, did she?"

Against her better judgement, Ingrith laughed a little at this, and then just as quickly, she stopped, and put her hand over her mouth. To her exasperation, if not to her surprise, she felt the warmth of a blush come to her cheeks. She was alarmed by a fleeting sense that it was not only because of what had been said, but also because of who it was had said it that she was blushing. It was only the thought of an instant, but it had been there. Worse, despite Will looking away tactfully when she glanced in his direction, she knew he must have noticed her blushes; it was impossible for him not to have done. By an unfortunate chance, at that moment, she had been standing directly in the light that entered from the, currently doorless, doorway, so even the otherwise subdued light of the chapel would not have helped hide them. She knew, too, that she was blushing even more now due to the very fact of his noticing. Hopefully, he would have assumed it was due to embarrassment at her inappropriate laughter, nothing more than that. It was, after all, almost true. The other thought had been confused and transitory, and surely of no real significance if she herself could not understand it. He could not have read it in her face for it had had no time to register there – had it?

Embarrassed for her, Will gave thought to telling the girl not to worry, and then decided this would only make her feel more awkward still. Instead he steered the conversation in a different direction.

"Well now, I think I have what I need here. Thing to do now is make the templates."

"Do you have designs in mind?" asked Ingrith, glad of the change of subject.

"Not mine to choose. The Bishop had some ideas, and I produced designs based on them. In the end, though, he said the Abbess could have her way on this, if nothing else. All my work for nothing. I'm having to start again in order that I might satisfy Abbess Rhoswen's wishes."

Ingrith was curious. "What did she suggest?"

"Suggest?" said Will with a humourless chuckle. "She didn't *suggest* anything. What she *demanded* is something that is proving to be a bit of a problem."

"Which is?"

"Which is images of the saint herself... in her cell... And of the angel...The one that is said to have come for her. Not that I will not be able, you understand. It will take a bit of work, that's all. It will not be the first time for such a specific request."

"I see. Have you any designs yet?"

"Some ideas...nothing that satisfies so far."

Ingrith looked at floor for a moment, seemed to come to a decision and looked up, directly at Will.

Meeting her eyes this way made Will uncomfortable. Such directness was improper. He had to resist the urge to look away. "Sister? Ingrith? What is it?"

Ingrith took half a step in his direction, hesitated, and then reached out a hand – although she did not actually touch him - as if she thought he might run away when he heard what she said next. "I have something I wish to suggest…to *ask* of you…definitely *not* demand…. You must believe me when I say I have no wish to offend. So please hear me out. Will you do that?"

Will nodded his assent but, without thinking, he also stepped away from her a little.

Ingrith took a step forward, closing the distance Will had opened. "Do you promise not to become angry? I should hate to…"

"Who can promise that before he knows what it is he must consider?" interrupted Will, a touch impatiently.

"You see, I have angered you already."

"No, you have not. Go on," said Will.

Ingrith was careful to resist the urge to put a hand out towards him a second time. "I repeat my request that you trust my intentions."

Will answered with another nod. When Ingrith hesitated he said, "Say your piece. I promise not to think ill of you."

"Let me help you with them…The tile designs, I mean," said Ingrith. The words, when they came, had tumbled out from her. Will looked taken aback. She took a breath and continued. "You must forgive my seeming pride. False modesty is a sin of a kind too, is it not? So I say it as plainly and honestly I as am able. I am skilled at such things. Truly I am. As I made known to you, it is part of Abbess Rhoswen's reason for giving me this duty."

Will cocked his head, studied the young woman in front of him. If she was bothered by how much she was now blushing, this time she did nothing to hide it. She looked directly at him again – an inappropriate display of frankness between a woman such as her and a mere artisan such as Will – but the frankness was genuine. Still he said nothing.

"I am in earnest," said Ingrith. "Forgive me if I make you

uncomfortable. I know no other way to propose this. I wish to be involved in the creation of the floor, and if my abilities can be put to good use, then why not?"

"And the Abbess?" asked Will.

The Abbess. Ingrith realised she had not considered this aspect of her proposal. What she said next came as almost as much of surprise to her as it did to Will. "She need not know of it."

Will looked unconvinced. "I don't think…"

"You tell me what you need, and I will produce it."

"No. I am sorry. You ask too much. It could cost me my livelihood if she were to discover such a thing."

Without knowing exactly why, Ingrith found she wanted to be set the task more than she had wanted anything since coming to Althurst. "Then I will do them in secret…away even from you. You will not be connected with it in any way. If I am discovered, I will swear it was something I did without anyone else knowing. Something I took upon myself unbidden."

"Take care what you swear to, lass," cautioned Will. Despite his words, Ingrith hoped he might now be warming to the idea. She took another step towards him.

"I can create…"

"You can create *nothing*!" snapped Will, the anger in his voice unmistakable. "You mistake what is my livelihood for a girl's fancy. What I do was taught to me by my father. It took time to learn my trade…Years! You may have a woman's eye for pretty things, what of it? It is not the same. Not the same at all. Now, excuse me, I must be about my work." As he stepped past her, he paused. "*My* work," he hissed, and then walked on. But when he reached the doorway he stopped. He shook his head then, and without looking back he said, more softly now, "Forgive me, lass. I cannot agree to what you ask of me. That is how it is. Nothing to be done about it."

"I am sorry. Please, do not be angry," said Ingrith, very

aware that she was apologising to Will yet again.

"It will pass," replied Will, still not looking at her, and then he stepped back into the daylight.

Alone now, in the cool shade of the chapel, Ingrith's chest heaved, and she fought back a sob. She would not cry. She might not be able to prevent the colour that came to her face, but she was determined she would let no tears fall. She had made an error, that was all. She had mistaken the man's kindness for fondness. The two things were not the same. The next thought that came to her made her grimace. Was it kindness or was it pity? One was often the result of the other. If it was pity, she did not want it. Suddenly she felt angry at Will. Who was he to pity such as her? So he knew his trade. It was well that he did. It was *all* he knew. All he *should* know.

Ingrith stamped her foot. It caused a small amount of gritty dust to rise then settle back onto the earth and builder's rubble that currently made up the uneven surface of the chapel floor – the same floor that would eventually be covered by the tiles Will would make, and then set in place. She sobbed again, and felt a tear run down her face. Frustrated at her failure to prevent it coming, she briskly wiped it away.

What should she do? The truth was that Will was right; he would be badly compromised if he were to consent to her request, and then subsequently be discovered to have done so. His anger might be justified in that respect. Then again, she did have something she could offer. What would be the harm? It would not be so difficult to conceal her part in designing the pattern for the tiles.

What should she do?

She knew what the sisters would advise. What they always advised: she should pray. An ironic smile played briefly across her lips. Pray? Why not? After all, she was in a chapel. What better place? She looked down at the floor again. The rubble would be uncomfortable on her knees. Perhaps it should be. A punishment for her silly smile if nothing else.

And maybe for her wish to deceive Abbess Rhoswen. The sisters were right. She should pray. She *must* pray.

Ingrith hitched up the bottom of her habit and knelt. As she had expected, it hurt as small chips of stone were pressed into her flesh. She winced, but accepted and bore the discomfort. After a while, the soreness started to diminish as her flesh numbed, so she rocked herself from side to side, intentionally creating fresh darts of pain that shot through her knees as they were ground into the rough floor. With eyes squeezed shut, and her brow wrinkled in concentration, Ingrith struggled to master her emotions and to find the right words to say to God.

Tell Him the truth. That was always what the sister's counselled. He sees all, so he knows it already - including that which you hide in your heart. When you attempt to deceive God, you merely deceive yourself. Part of the problem, however, was that Ingrith was not certain that she knew the truth. Not entirely. She knew her gift was much more than what Will had so derisively – hurtfully - called an eye for pretty things. It could not be vanity to know that about herself. Not when it was a plain fact. The question she could not answer was whether her desire to use that gift was born out of wish to venerate St Merwinna and, through her, God Himself, or whether it was because she knew she would find it rewarding in a way nothing else in her life was these days?

No, that was not the question. She knew the answer to that: it was a bit of both. The real question was whether or not the pleasure she would get from creating a design for the tiles – the personal satisfaction she would derive from it – was a sin. Everything the sisters at Althurst did seemed to be posited on the idea that a life of devotion should be one with the minimum of earthly pleasure. The righteous path, it always seemed to Ingrith, must be the most difficult. In which case denying herself the pleasure of helping Will would be the path she must take. But if she took it, then the gift God had given her would not be used, and the chapel floor would be the lesser for it.

Another thought came unexpectedly on the back of those that had gone before it. Ingrith's eyes opened wide with the discomfort and shock of it. If God had given her this gift – just as he had given a gift to Will - and if those gifts were used in venerating Him, was God Himself not creating the means of his own veneration? Did it not follow, therefore, that God was guilty of the sin of pride?

Such an appalling thought to have had. Ingrith let out a small cry – partly of disgust, partly of shame. She closed her eyes again, pulled her head back slightly, and brushed a hand at the space in front of her face as if to brush the terrible, unbidden thought away from herself; as if the source had not been her own mind, but rather something external that had planted such a terrible idea inside her head. Immediately she did so, her eyes snapped open again. She could swear her hand had made contact with something. Something small had brushed past her face, and her hand had touched it as it passed.

The thought made solid?

Madness!

An insect. Nothing more.

Ingrith tilted her head sideways, listening for any buzzing. There was nothing. Only…maybe…a whisper!

Ingrith screamed as she was plunged into almost complete darkness.

******

Will was less than two hundred yards away, walking back to where Silas and Alf would be putting the finishing touches to the almost complete kiln, when he heard the first scream. His first thought was of Sister Marigold, the nun whose wits had left her. Well, she could take care of herself this time or, at least, the other nuns could. Will was damned if he would be on the receiving end of Abbess Rhoswen's flinty ingratitude for a second time. Another scream came. This time, Will turned his head, searching out the direction from which it came. It had been lost on the breeze before he had time to place it. He saw two or three of the sisters, and a couple of servants who, like himself, had obviously been interrupted in going about their business by the sound and, like him, were now looking around for the source. It was clear none of them had been the one who screamed. He stood still, his chin lifted, as he listened for further cries. It was not long before another came. This time the direction was unmistakable.

Will ran back in the direction from which he had just come. Up ahead he could see a small group of people beginning to gather at the entrance to the new chapel. Only then did it occur to him that the cries might have come from Ingrith. A momentary fear rose in him that he had somehow been the cause of whatever had taken place to make the young woman scream. But it was not possible; she had been fine when he left her - perhaps a little upset, that was all. He ran over towards the group, but stopped when he was still a few feet away. At the centre of the knot of people, was a short, stocky man Will thought he recognised. Wasn't it Ned, the carpenter from the town? The man tasked with making the door for St Merwinna's chapel. Usually a hearty sort of fellow, right now the man looked pale and anxious, as if he had suffered a shock. Will now saw that the carpenter was, in fact, being restrained by two of the Abbey's male servants. Beyond him, to Will's relief, he saw an embarrassed looking, but safe, Ingrith. She was pushing away the hands of people who sought not to restrain, but to assist her, saying, "I am fine. It was nothing. A misunderstanding. Nothing more. Please, you must release him. It was a misunderstanding. Please, leave me be. I am fine. You must let that man go free, I tell you." One of the sisters leaned in and whispered something in her ear. Ingrith pulled away looking disgusted. "No! No, nothing of that kind. I would say if it were so. He has done nothing. Nothing! Look at me, won't you. I am unharmed."

When Ingrith saw Will, it seemed she guessed his thoughts. She caught his eye and gave a small shake of her head which he hoped he correctly understood to mean that, whatever had happened, it was not any of his doing. All the same, he wanted to be sure, so he resolved to stay until he found out for certain what it was. In the end it was Ned, the carpenter, who explained. When, at last, and at Ingrith's insistence, he was released, the man staggered away from the group, almost knocking into Will as he did so. Will grasped his arm as he passed.

"Hold there a moment, man. It's Ned, is it not? Are you well, master carpenter? What has happened here? Tell me."

The man pulled his arm free and stepped back, fearing he was once again being restrained. Only when he saw the concern on Will's face did he understand.

"It is not me that you should ask. It is that girl."

"Why? What do you mean by that?"

Ned took a moment to catch his breath. "I confess I made a mistake. I don't deny it. Her reaction though…I could not foresee *that*!" Seeing from his expression that Will did not know to what he was referring, Ned explained. "I was merely trying to see how well it fitted…the door, I mean. The frame is in place. I had fitted it there already. I placed the door over the entrance to gauge the fit…make any adjustments that might be needed. You know…shave anything that wasn't flush…that sort of thing."

"Ah," said Will, believing he understood now. "She was inside when you put the door in place?"

The carpenter confirmed this with a nod of his head. "That she was. I suppose the sudden darkness did it… gave her such a fright, I mean. Maybe she thought she was struck blind, I don't know. Whatever it was, the girl let out screams to wake the dead. Naturally, I went in to help her, but she fought me off. Did this…" He raised his arm, and Will saw a deep scratch that ran the length of the man's forearm. "God only knows what might have happened if she had not explained to those people. They acted as if they thought I'd... well...you know...tried to have my way with her. A nun for Jesus' sake. A nun! I'm a carpenter, not some outlaw rogue. I have a wife! I have a family! I would never..."

Will patted the man's shoulder reassuringly. "Well, all is understood now, is it not? The girl saved your good name."

"Aye, that may be...although not before she came close to robbing me of it first! God knows where I would be right now if she had fainted or some such, and not been around to speak up for me. I'd have been locked away somewhere darker than that chapel, that much I know." Ned shuddered at the thought. "What was she thinking? I ask you...screaming like that? What can she have been thinking?"

Will considered patting the man's shoulder again - even raised his arm a little - but found his heart was not in it. For all he sympathised with the man, he was beginning to find him annoying. Instead, he said, "Still, you are walking free in the daylight, and here talking with me. So, all is fine then, eh? As has already been said, it was a simple misunderstanding, no more than that."

"Was it? What I can't understand is why was the girl so damn skittish in the first place? I can understand it made her jump my coming up like that. I can understand that. How she acted, though..."

Will could no longer hide his impatience when he spoke. "Think man! Do you not know what has happened here of late? The death...? The attacks on the sisters?"

Ned put his face in his hands. "Oh, and she thought..."

"Yes," said Will. "She thought..."

"Oh, that would explain it."

"So, you see now, she had reason to be nervous. They all of them do." Even as he said it, Will did not entirely believe it. Ingrith might have had her peculiar fancies about designs for the tiles, but generally the girl had struck him as quite level-headed. More so than most of the sisters, in some ways. Still, it seemed to put the carpenter's mind at ease.

There seemed to Will nothing more to say on the matter. Ned must have felt the same because he bade Will good day, and walked off to retrieve the half-completed door from where he had dropped it earlier, and load it back onto his handcart. Will watched him for a while. The man was evidently still nervous, casting anxious glances towards anyone who drew at all near him, as if they might be about to seize him, and restrain him once again. Will continued watching him until he and his cart moved out of sight around the corner of a building. Then, as he himself was turning to leave, Will noticed Ingrith being led away by one of the nuns. The other woman murmured something to Ingrith, to which she responded with an impatient shake of her head. The girl was proud, thought Will. He couldn't decide if that pride should be counted as her strength or her weakness. Either way, it didn't seem to him worthy of qualifying as a sin in this instance.

*****

Sister Elisabeth was trying not to think about what it was she was getting on her hands as she wrung out the cloth. Thanks to her work assisting Sister Helewise in the infirmary, she had developed a stronger stomach than she once had – not like some of the other sisters: the ones who always seemed to manage to avoid similar duties – but this felt somehow different. For anything else it would have been one of the Abbey servants down on their knees scrubbing away at the stains on the flagstones of the ambulatory. As far as Sister Elisabeth was concerned, it still ought to be. Unfortunately for her, however, that was not what Abbess Rhoswen had thought. In the Reverend Mother's view, the blood of Sister

Euphemia must be shown the same respect as the rest of her mortal remains. The Sacrist had died on this spot, and shed her life blood onto these stones. A holy woman in a holy place. Respect must be shown. There was no getting around the squalidness of the task – scrubbing away at human blood – but it could, if nothing else, be performed by someone other than a mere servant; someone more appropriate; someone who led the same sort of life that Sister Euphemia had led. Obviously, that meant another nun. And the nun the Abbess had seen fit to give the task to had been Sister Elisabeth.

She sat back for a moment, wiped her hands as best she could on a dry cloth, put them her on her hips, and stretched her back. She looked down at her work. The results were not encouraging. The blood had been left for too long. There had been time for the stains to take hold. It was possible that, no matter how much effort was made to erase them, there would always be something there to serve as a reminder to those who knew what had happened. What *had* happened, though? Sister Elisabeth shuddered. Something bad, that much was certain. Exactly what depended on to whom you spoke: human or supernatural cause; murder or rape and murder. There were several differing versions going about. Whatever it had been, everyone was praying for Sister Euphemia's soul. They were also praying that Sister Winifred would recover her wits. If she did, she might have more to tell than the small amount Sister Marigold, the only other witness, had proved able to provide so far. Not that the Abbess was letting people know very much of what that was. Most of what Sister Elisabeth heard was through gossip, hearsay. The Abbess herself had only confirmed that Sister Euphemia had been killed in the church. By whom – she had been careful never to say by *what* – it was unknown. However, whoever they were, they were gone, and the Abbey was safe. Unfortunately, the Abbess had somewhat undermined the sisters' trust in this last claim by adding that they should all, nonetheless, be on their guard against the appearance and activity of any strangers to Althurst Abbey.

Sister Elisabeth ran the back of her wrist over her brow. This was hard work. She reached for the brush, dipped it into the water pail, and then leaned forward and began to scrub once more. For some reason the rhythm of the work suggested an old song from her childhood. Without thinking about it, she began to sing. Under her breath at first, then louder as the melody and the brushing merged, becoming part of the same action. She had only been scrubbing for a few minutes more when she thought she heard voices. She had thought she was alone, and she had not heard the creak or thud of any of the doors being opened or closed. She stopped what she was doing. There it was, that murmur again. She stood up now, peered slowly around the pillar beneath which she had been working, looking back up the ambulatory in the direction of the side aisle.

"What do you think you are doing, daughter?" said a voice from behind her.

Sister Elisabeth cried out, dropping the brush and nearly stumbling over the bucket.

"Oh, Abbess Rhoswen...I did not hear you approach."

"Evidently not, or perhaps you might have curbed your unfortunate desire to sing, hmm?"

"Oh, was I singing? I did not realise."

Rhoswen looked sideways at her. "Oh, I believe you know full well that you were. Do not lie to me, daughter. Do not compound things by adding dishonesty to your list of errors."

"I'm very sorry, Reverend Mother."

"Yes, well..." Rhoswen looked down at the area of floor where Sister Elisabeth had been working. "Tell me, how do you progress?" she asked.

Sister Elisabeth shook her head. "Not well, Reverend Mother. Not well at all. I fear it was left too long. My actions have cleaned away some of it. Much remains, however. I do not think scrubbing alone will remove it."

The frown on Rhoswen's face softened into a look of sadness as she studied the stones. For a moment she seemed about to say something. Instead, she gestured towards the stains. "Do what you can for now, daughter. We will revisit the problem if we must."

"What should I do with the water?" asked Sister Elisabeth.

Rhoswen looked puzzled. "The *water*?"

"The water," said Sister Elisabeth, and nodded towards the bucket, its contents now coloured pink by the blood that had been introduced.

"Oh, yes, I see what you mean," said Rhoswen.

"Should some words be said?"

Rhoswen considered this for a minute. "I think not. Nothing like that. Though, I must say, it was thoughtful of you, daughter. And there is something in what you say, so take care you do not throw it away anywhere inappropriate."

Sister Elisabeth looked puzzled. She did not know where *would* be appropriate. The Abbess must have understood because she said, "The roses outside my house. I know Sister Euphemia enjoyed the blooms there. Pour it there. No words need be said. Simply pour it away there. Pour it. Do not throw it."

"It is tainted. Might it not harm the flowers?" asked Sister Elisabeth, and instantly wished she had not when she saw the displeasure on the Abbess's face.

"Oh, Sister Elisabeth! Now how could it be? Simply water, and a small amount of….No, it is not *tainted*. If anything, it is hallowed. The blood of a bride of Christ does not *taint*!"

Maybe not, but it stains, thought Sister Elisabeth, then immediately felt ashamed of the thought. "Yes, Reverend Mother. I will do as you bid me."

"I know you will," said the Abbess, more kindly.

Sister Elisabeth turned back to her work. She began to scrub, more aggressively than before – partly because she hoped it would be more successful in removing the stains, and partly because the discomfort it generated in her knees and her back seemed to her a fitting act of contrition for her unworthy thought about Sister Euphemia's blood.

Sister Elisabeth had expected the Abbess to leave. However, upon sitting back to study the progress of her efforts, she discovered the woman was still there, gazing down at the rust coloured patch on the stone. It was then that she noticed the tiny points of light from the tears that were starting to form in the older woman's eyes. It occurred to Sister Elisabeth that she should perhaps say something - some words of comfort – but nothing appropriate came to her. Besides, she was not sure such words would be welcome; it might not be her place to offer comfort to the Abbess. So, as an alternative, she turned back to her task with renewed vigour, deciding she would not look up from it until she was absolutely certain the Abbess had gone. This entailed an occasional slight tilt of her head in order to discover if the Reverend Mother was still visible from of the corner of her eye. She lost count of the times she did this, and still the Abbess had not moved. So Sister Elisabeth had no choice but to continue working under the uncomfortable scrutiny of her senior.

Fortunately, she seemed, at last, to be making some progress with her scrubbing. The edges of the stains were beginning to fade. There was still a stubborn area at the centre – perhaps where the blood had been at its thickest – but the edges were most definitely fading.

Suddenly the Abbess gasped. "Get back from it, sister!" she commanded.

Sister Elisabeth did not understand. "I have not yet completed...?"

"Never mind that. Stand up, step away, I say! Immediately. Do as you are instructed!"

Confused, Sister Elisabeth drew herself back, and stood up. She turned to the Abbess for explanation, but Rhoswen did not look at her. She was staring down at the stained area.

Her eyes, now brimming with undisguised tears, were also wide with astonishment. Sister Elisabeth turned and looked down. Her own eyes now grew wide.

The stains, having faded at the edges, now revealed a definite shape. An image. One familiar to both women, and particularly so to Rhoswen. The remaining patch formed the distinct silhouette of a woman. Not any woman, though. This was the exact shape of the depiction of Saint Merwinna that was to be found on the wall of the Abbess's receiving room. It was unmistakable. As they watched, the water that remained on the floor from where Sister Elisabeth had been scrubbing sizzled, steamed, and evaporated in a cloud of vapour, as if the flagstones where it pooled had grown hot. Then the dull matt of the stain started to take on a new lustre as it slowly returned to the original crimson of the fresh blood that had originally created it.

Rhoswen crossed herself. Sister Elisabeth let out a shriek.

"There is nothing to fear," said Rhoswen, in a low voice.

Despite this reassurance from the Abbess, Sister Elisabeth felt a strong desire to run, and would have done so had not Rhoswen taken a firm hold of her arm. Shaking her head, she said, "No, my daughter, we have been chosen for this…It is a great honour. We must bear witness to this miracle."

"A *miracle*, Reverend Mother? You are certain? Not the work of…"

Rhoswen smiled. "No, not the Evil One. Lucifer is not with us. How could he be in such a place as this? No, this is nothing less than the work of the saint herself!" Yet, even as she said this, Rhoswen wondered why the saint had chosen this particular image of herself to manifest her presence. Surely the one close to them right now, the one in the church itself was far more fitting, less provoking. The thought was only a brief one, however, and soon lost in the wonder of what was taking place before her very eyes.

The bright red of the image had started to glisten with points of light far too bright to be reflections of anything present in the church. Then the surface rippled, and rose. It was as if fresh blood were seeping up through the stones beneath it. Before long, there was so much of the red liquid that it seemed it must soon spill out beyond the outline it had formed. Yet it rose higher still. An inch. Almost two. Hovering impossibly for almost a full minute before it finally did begin spreading outwards. Even then, it did not behave like any normal liquid should. It spread evenly in four directions, until it formed a perfect square, perhaps three feet by three. It lingered there for a moment, and then rapidly drained back into the stone, leaving behind the original, rust coloured and shapeless stain that had been left by the blood of Sister Euphemia.

Sister Elisabeth shrieked again. She herself could not have said if it was with ecstasy or with fear. She trusted the Reverend Mother's interpretation of what they were witnessing – she must - and yet there was still something undeniably frightening about being in the presence of the supernatural, even if it was the miraculous manifestation of a saint who sat with God. She felt the Abbess's hand release its hold, then she sensed, rather than saw, the Abbess fall to her knees beside her.

"Pray with me, sister. Pray with me now. We must give thanks," said Rhoswen in a voice tight with emotion. When Sister Elisabeth failed to respond, Rhoswen reached up, took hold of her habit, and tugged. "Pray with me."

Without really thinking about what she was doing, Sister Elisabeth did as the Abbess instructed. She was on her knees before the stain again. Only this time she was not scrubbing but praying. And the small figure of the Abbess was kneeling alongside her.

Even as she prayed, Rhoswen's eyes opened, and once more grew wide as she thought she began to understand the meaning of what she had witnessed, and all the things she must now do because if it. The first of these was to swear Sister Elisabeth to silence. The second was to conceal the stain. For now.

******

CHAPTER 6

The letter had been difficult for Rhoswen to compose. Several times she had had to stop herself from including the barbed comments that had been the mark of recent communications with Bishop Baldwin or – and this was even more difficult - from shying away from acknowledging the full extent of her error in attempting to block the construction of the chapel. Once complete, the letter had sat on her table for nearly an hour. Still, in her heart, she knew it must be sent. She knew now that her objections to the building of the chapel to the saint had been wrong, and it was only proper that she should confess to her error. Once done, it would allow her to take things forward with a clear conscience. All the same, she could not deny that it galled greatly having to express such remorse to the Bishop, of all people. It must be done, nevertheless. That was what Abbess Rhoswen told herself. And kept telling herself once the letter was dispatched and the rider carrying it impossible to call back. Get it done. Clear the way for a fresh approach. It was important the Bishop understood how changed on the matter she now was and, more crucially, that the saint herself understood. The letter to Bishop Baldwin, and the pain it caused her, was Rhoswen's gesture to Saint Merwinna that she now understood her mistake and was prepared to carry out the saint's wishes, no matter what the cost. The next step was to summon William the tiler.

So it was that Will once more found himself sitting on the bench against the wall of the antechamber to the Abbess's receiving room. This time, however, there was no Bishop Baldwin already inside to stand between Will and Rhoswen's ire.

Will – who was still turning over in his mind his earlier exchange with Ingrith - had expected a long wait, and was surprised when the door opened within only a few moments of his having sat down.

"The Reverend Mother wishes you to enter," said a nun, holding the door open.

"Right now?" asked Will.

"Yes, right now," confirmed the nun, a touch impatiently.

In an unconscious repeat of what he had done the last time he had been summoned into this particular room, Will nervously wiped his palms on his tunic, and then ran a hand through his hair. Once inside he knelt, eyes down.

"You wish to see me, Reverend Mother."

"I do. I wish to discuss the design for the tiles for Saint Merwinna's chapel."

Will was confused. No design had been agreed upon, so how then could the Abbess already be objecting. Abbess Rhoswen must have seen the confusion on his face. "I wish to tell you what that design should be," she clarified. "You may rise."

"Thank you," said Will, standing.

"I have the Bishop's approval," Rhoswen lied. It made her uncomfortable, but then this man before her would probably never know the truth. Besides, it was only a small lie. She doubted very much that Bishop Baldwin would even care what the design was, as long as it was appropriate. And what she was going to tell this man came from a higher source than Bishop Baldwin. It was more than appropriate. It came from the saint herself.

"I see," said Will, as if he understood – which he did not. The Bishop and the Abbess had been at constant loggerheads for the duration of the entire business. Why now would Baldwin approve of anything this woman suggested when she had disapproved of almost everything *he* had suggested? It seemed unlikely. Still, Will was in no position to question her about it. If what she said was subsequently proved to be wrong, it was for her to defend it, not Will.

"You were in this room once before, as I recall," said Rhoswen.

Will nodded. "Yes… with the Bishop."

"With the Bishop, that's right. And do you recall the subject of the conversation that was had?"

"I do. The Chapel and the floor were discussed. I was to…am to…make and lay the tiles for it."

"Yes, yes, of course that was discussed. But do you not recall what else came up? Do you not recall discussing this?" She gestured over her shoulder towards the wall behind her.

"The painting? I do remember something was said of it."

"And you remember I told you that the man who created it is said to have seen the saint in the flesh?"

Will thought back for a moment. "Indeed I do… now you remind me of it."

"Well, there you are," said Rhoswen as if it explained everything. When she saw from his face that Will did not understand, she said, "There is your design for the tiles. What could be more fitting than an image of the saint herself? And this is the nearest to a true image that we have. This will be your guide."

Will looked up at the painting. A growing knot of anxiety began to form in his chest. The woman was misguided if she believed that something like that could be reproduced on a tile. It was impossible.

"Well?" asked Rhoswen after a moment.

Will cleared his throat.

"Speak man," she said.

To her irritation, Will only cleared his throat again.

"Must I command you?" she asked.

At last, Will found his courage and, with it, his voice. "Forgive me, Reverend Mother. I do not think that it will be possible. I wish I could tell you differently. But you must understand…a tile is not like a painting. The two colours of a tile allow for only limited images. Not like a painting at all. Besides…the detail… a tile is so much smaller. No imagine upon one could ever capture…"

"Do not be foolish, man," snapped Rhoswen. "Of course

I do not expect you to reproduce this *exactly*. Such a thing would smack of witchcraft. One does not need to be a craftsman to grasp something of the limitations of your particular craft. I only ask for an approximation."

"A what, Reverend Mother? Forgive me… I don't think I follow."

Rhoswen turned to face the painting. With her back to Will, she said, "I wish for something that *suggests* this image. Is *inspired* by it." Turning back, she saw that Will still appeared confused. She thought for a moment, and then said, "If you knew the one, then you would be reminded of it by the other. You understand me now?"

"I think I take your meaning. All the same…"

Becoming more impatient, Rhoswen interrupted, "If you do your best, then I believe your hand will be guided. Trust in that, and it shall be so."

Will felt the knot of anxiety begin to expand into something like panic.

The little woman stepped closer to him, reached up, and put her hand on his shoulder – a gesture that reminded him of the Bishop. She squeezed, and – unlike the Bishop – Will judged there to be some strength in her grip; particularly for one so small and of her sex. It surprised him. He saw from the woman's face that she had seen that, and was pleased.

"Many things we think unlikely can prove to be the case. Not everything is how it appears on first consideration. Tell me, do you trust in God?"

"Yes, of course," Will said, wondering what other answer he could have given.

"You understand what I mean when I talk of faith, then?"

"As we must have in the word of the bible?"

Abbess Rhoswen nodded, pleased. "Just so. Well, master tiler. Have faith in this work. It *will* come to pass. I cannot tell you why. Not yet. All the same, I know it. I know a way will be found. Only do your best, and God will do the rest."

Will stared down at the woman; saw a light in her eyes that

made him believe her. Almost.

"Faith," she said, as if this answered any further questions he might have. "It is all that is required of you. Of any of us."

******

Will knew what faith meant. Like everyone, he believed in the God who watched over people. That He rewarded the good, punished the wicked. How He judged who was which remained a mystery, however. On their way through the woods outside Althurst Will, Silas, and Alf had passed what they had been warned by a fellow traveller was a Leper Hospital. When young Alf had asked what evil the poor people inside could have done to be so punished, Will could not answer the boy. On the other hand, Will had heard tales of other men doing things to their fellow man of such wickedness and cruelty they seemed the work of the Devil himself. And yet many of the men in those stories were prosperous and healthy. Some even members of the country's ruling elite. Why had *they* not been struck down with disease and misery like the unfortunate wretches in the hospital? Priests often said that the wisdom of God was a wisdom hidden from the mind of man, so man, like Job, must continue to seek wisdom by fearing God and avoiding evil doing. How was it, then, that the Abbess felt so sure she could say what it was God wanted when it came to the chapel floor? She had tiptoed carefully around the subject; never quite saying that He had made his wishes known to her. But it was what she was implying. It was what she wanted Will to infer from what she told him.

Whatever the truth of it was, it made no real difference; she had left Will with no choice. He must try to come up with a design for the tiles that conveyed something of the painted image on the wall of Abbess Rhoswen's room. That uncomfortably curvy, almost comely, representation of Saint Merwinna. It was such an odd choice. The Abbess's newfound enthusiasm for the floor the Bishop had commissioned Will to create for the chapel was matched in its strangeness and suddenness by her change in opinion of the painting. When first she talked of it, she had clearly been uncomfortable with the blatant sexuality it conveyed. Now she was saying it should be the image used above all others to represent Saint Merwinna – a woman who died a virgin in the service of God. Will shook his head, walked back towards Silas and Alf.

"What'd the old girl want? Still got your balls have ya?" asked Silas.

"Still got 'em," replied Will. "To tell the truth, it was all a bit strange. You know how she has been against us from the start…?"

"Is that so? Hadn't spotted it," said Silas.

Smiling a little at this sarcasm, Will continued, "Well, she seems to have changed her mind on the matter."

Silas tilted his head, looked sceptical.

"As God is my witness," insisted Will.

"No need for that," said Silas. "Your word will do for me and young Alf."

As if this had served as an invitation, Alf stopped what he was doing, came over, and stood next to Silas. The boy looked up at Will expectantly.

Why not? Thought Will. *The lad might as well hear it.*

Will told Silas and the boy what the Abbess had told him.

******

Ingrith had been adamant that she did not want to be the subject of any unnecessary attention after the incident with the carpenter in the new chapel. What she had wanted was to get straight back to her duties. The problem she faced was that the concerned sisters and servants who had hurried over upon hearing her cries would not be satisfied until she had at least visited the infirmary, and been looked over by Sister

Helewise. Ingrith had kept insisting that she was perfectly well, even though it was not entirely true. She did feel a little shaken, however she was sure it would pass in a while if they would all just leave her be. What she really could not tolerate was being the centre of so much fuss. Aware of so many eyes upon her, she had to resist the urge to shout at them to leave her alone. Appreciating that their concern was genuine, and that they would not be satisfied unless she complied, she had finally agreed to visit the infirmary. Unsurprisingly, the sisters had also insisted that one of them accompany her there. What if she were to faint? They would not be responsible for letting her walk there alone, they said. So, in the end, Ingrith had been forced to walk arm in arm with one of them until she was handed over into the care of Sister Helewise. As she walked, Ingrith had glanced back and seen Will in conversation with the carpenter. That Will should have been witness to any of it troubled her.

Sister Helewise had said Ingrith was suffering from the effects of the shock she had received; even if Ingrith herself did not realise it.

"I don't know what happened to you, but your skin is white as chalk and clammy as a pond frog. Your heart is beating too fast for my liking. You need to rest a while."

"No, I feel perfectly well."

"Even if I believed that…which I don't…you may feel the effects later. Light-headedness or vomiting. They can still come to you quite some time after a shock like you have had. No, I'm afraid you must rest…You may not feel the need of it right now, but you may yet… whatever you feel at the moment."

Ingrith did not bother objecting further. When it came to matters of health, the Infirmaress was the law, and her say was final. On other matters, outside those of the infirmary, she could be as meek and modest as any nun in Althurst. When came to the world of the infirmary, however, there she ruled, and she expected to be obeyed. Even Abbess Rhoswen deferred to her on such things. The old woman had been in her role for so long it would be foolish not to follow her advice. And, as it turned out, she was correct. Once Ingrith had been made to lie back on a bed, she discovered she did feel a strange fatigue coming over her. She may even have slept; she was not certain.

When Sister Helewise returned later with a cup of her camomile infusion, she looked down at Ingrith and smiled a kindly smile.

"You see? Sometimes our bodies get us through by telling us one thing until it is safe to tell us another." She paused. "Just as you may tell us one thing about what happened until you judge it safe to talk about what really took place." She patted Ingrith's wrist. "That will be between you and the Reverend Mother, hmm?"

"*Must* she be told?"

Sister Helewise raised her eyebrows. "Of course she must be told. I'm sorry child, the wellbeing of the sisters is her first concern…and mine. I would be failing in my duties if I did not inform her of this. As it happens, I have already sent word. Besides, do you really think the other sisters will not tittle-tattle about it in her hearing? I'm afraid such gossip is meat and drink to one or two of them. It is not as if…ah…" As she was speaking, something had caught the old Infirmaress's attention. "Here she is," she whispered to Ingrith, and then stood up. "She is over here, Reverend Mother," she called.

Ingrith turned to look. Abbess Rhoswen had obviously paused in the infirmary doorway, allowing her eyes to adjust after the brightness of the day outside. She looked over, nodded, and then began to walk towards them. Ingrith hoped for a moment that Sister Helewise, having got to her feet, would walk over, and meet the Abbess halfway; heading her off, telling her Ingrith was in need of more rest before she spoke to anyone. To her disappointment, Sister Helewise simply remained where she was, waiting for the Abbess to join them.

"So, how is she?" asked Rhoswen as she drew near.

"No physical injuries," replied Sister Helewise.

"But…?"

"More ashamed than she needs to be, less rested than she should be," replied Sister Helewise. "The former I can do nothing about, the latter time will see to." The two women then exchanged a concerned glance that Ingrith guessed she had not been supposed to see. "I will leave you now," said Sister Helewise. "I am serious about the need for rest. Please do not overtax her, Reverend Mother."

Rhoswen was looking at Ingrith when she replied. "I will not. If at any time Ingrith wishes to end our conversation she need only say so. We can continue it some other time." Rhoswen smiled at Ingrith. It was meant to be playfully conspiratorial, mocking the Infirmaress's concern. She noticed, however, that the smile the novice gave in response was weak, and perhaps a little guarded.

"Good," said Sister Helewise, and left them without another word. However, she did not go very far. The old Infirmaress had positioned herself at a nearby table, and was now making a show of being busy, apparently grinding something with a mortar and pestle. Rhoswen knew full well that this was not the place where she unusually did such work, and that whatever work she was doing would last exactly as long as Rhoswen's talk with the novice. She estimated the old woman was out of earshot, so long as they kept their voices down, but she was also easily close enough to see if Ingrith was becoming overstressed. The only other patients in the place were on the far side of the room and, as long as Rhoswen and Ingrith did not raise their voices, there was nobody now to overhear them.

"So, how are you, daughter?" asked Rhoswen.

Ingrith saw the concern in the Reverend Mother's eyes was genuine. She knew it would be. The woman took her duty of care for those under her seriously, and whilst she could be firm when it came to discipline, she was also capable of showing compassion. But Ingrith also knew that she herself was a problem for the Abbess, and this latest incident would only serve to make her seem more so. She must do what she could to play it down. "It really was nothing, Reverend Mother," she insisted. The Abbess said nothing in response, so Ingrith followed this up by adding, "Really it was," and immediately regretted doing so. She was aware how desperate her voice had sounded, and determined to try and sound more matter of fact, less emotional about what had happened. Still the Abbess said nothing. *She wants me to say more, betray myself,* thought Ingrith, so she too fell silent.

Eventually, it was Rhoswen who spoke. "It was nothing, you tell me. And yet the sisters who witnessed it said you screamed. Quite unnervingly so, I was told."

"That's just it, Reverend Mother. Don't you see? They didn't *witness* anything; they only heard my reaction. My overreaction."

"How about you let me be the judge of whether or not it was an overreaction by telling me what did, in fact, happen."

Ingrith had sat up and taken a deep breath, and was about to begin her explanation, when Rhoswen raised a finger in caution. "I know already the business of the carpenter and the door. Do not simply repeat that part alone, and expect me to accept it as everything that happened. Both you and I know you are not such a silly young woman as one or two of the other sisters here can be when the mood takes them… God forgive them for it, and me for indulging them at times. That is not you, though, is it? Something like a suddenly closed door might give you a start…Even make you jump…It would not make you scream. Not that alone. Not you, Ingrith. There was something more to it. We both know it. And I know you are not telling me. If it helps, you may tell me first what it is your fear I will do upon hearing your explanation. That I will punish you for dishonesty, perhaps? Mind you, my child, until I know what it is *did* happen, I cannot promise I will not react in the way you fear. But I can keep it in mind."

Ingrith studied the face of the woman sitting next to her. She meant what she said, it seemed. "Very well, Reverend Mother. I fear you will think I am being fanciful. Not that I am dishonest. If I were lying to you, I would make up something less... strange..."

"But you might want the attention. Being fanciful and outright lying have a grey area between them that the teller of the tale may not even themselves recognise. You would not be the first person to claim to have been spoken to by a saint. Down the years there have been many tales of sisters here, in this very Abbey, who say Merwinna came to them in one guise or another. Some of them in my own time here as Abbess." Rhoswen sighed and shook her head. "Although, none to be believed, I'm afraid. None of the ones whom I myself encountered, at least."

"And that is what you think I am going to give as my explanation?" asked Ingrith.

"It is what I suspect, my child, yes. Am I wrong?"

"You are, Reverend Mother. I wish it were so simple." Ingrith paused, confused. "Why would you think a visitation from our saint would cause me to scream? Surely it would be a gentle, wonderful thing?"

"It could be, yes. But the way of such things is not always...to use your own words... so simple. If people can be beguiled by the charms of the Evil One, might not the opposite be true also? Might they not mistake the wonders of the Lord and His saints as something frightening? God is a power beyond our understanding, His ways as terrible and mysterious as they are wonderful."

Ingrith shook her head. "No, it could not have been..."

"*What* could not have been? We have walked around this particular thicket long enough now. It is time we raised our sticks and flushed out whatever game may be in there, don't you think?"

"It is," Ingrith replied, at the same time thinking, *So that you may shoot at it with your arrows?* When Rhoswen did not say anything more, merely opened her hands in a gesture that she should begin, Ingrith reached for the cup of water Sister Helewise had left on the small stand by her bed, took a sip, and then attempted her explanation. She found, however, that the words did not come as easily as she had hoped.

"What is it, daughter?" asked Rhoswen.

"Where to start. It is difficult…"

"Why not start by explaining how it was you came to be alone inside the chapel to begin with. What was it you were doing in there?"

Ingrith nodded. "Yes…Although, I was not alone at first. I had been in conversation with Will. Then he left. So I took a moment to…"

"*Will?*" interrupted Rhoswen.

Ingrith realised her mistake immediately. "William…The tiler… Master William."

Rhoswen raised her eyebrows. "Am I to understand that the two of you…you and '*Will*'… had been alone together in the chapel?"

Ingrith groaned inwardly; she had made another mistake. "We were in full view of others, Reverend Mother. The doorway was open," she said, trying hard to make it sound a straightforward explanation; she must not seem to be defending her actions because that would be to concede that they were in need of defending. "There was no door to *be* closed," she added, fully realising the irony of what she was saying. Luckily, Rhoswen responded with an equally ironic half-smile, and nodded her understanding. So Ingrith continued, "He was measuring the area his floor…"

"*His* floor?"

"The floor he is making for the chapel. He was measuring the area it must cover, so he might work out the number of tiles required to cover it. I was asking him how he went about it. I told him I wish to understand as much as possible about his working methods so I might better explain them to you. He is not always comfortable with my presence, and I fear this was one of those occasions. I fear I angered him."

"It is not his place to be angry with you. I will talk to him about his manners."

"No, please do not do that..."

Rhoswen frowned. "Why not?"

"I fear...I believe... I may have been deserving," replied Ingrith softly.

"The man is but a craftsman!" snapped Rhoswen, impatiently. "Whatever you may have said to him, it was not for him to question. This is Bishop Baldwin's doing. He has spoilt the man by being overly familiar with him...eschewing the proper distance required by rank and position...and in doing so he has primed him to affront me. Oh, this particular arrow has long been set in the bowstring. I only regret that it has fallen to you to be on the receiving end of something for which I was the intended recipient."

"No, please believe me when I tell you it is not so."

"How is it, then? What prompted such a man to consider himself worthy of expressing his anger with someone of your birth?"

Worried that through her lack of caution she might have got Will into serious trouble, Ingrith struggled to say the right thing to extricate him from it. "Are we not taught that every man...no matter how low born... is at least deserving of...I mean...there must be limits to such things?"

Exasperated, the Abbess saw the direction Ingrith's argument would take, and would have dismissed all she was suggesting, had it not been for the fact that she remembered a time when, as a much younger woman, she too had been moved by inklings of the inequity inherent in the lot of those of lower birth than herself. She counselled herself to patience with this young woman who was, after all, still only a novice, and said quietly, but firmly, "Daughter, this world is as it is because God wills it to be so. A person is born into the role allotted to them. Without that, disorder and confusion would reign. Our maker intended the world to be as it is. Every man has his place, and there are reasons why this is so." Seeing Ingrith about to raise an objection, Rhoswen continued, "It is possible, I suppose, that at each level in that design there are limits to what must be endured…however…"

"I reached those limits where William Tiler was concerned. He did not behave inappropriately. Please, trust me on this, I beg you."

Rhoswen did not appear fully convinced. "I am not at all minded to debate this with you." Even so, she gestured for Ingrith to continue.

Ingrith took another sip of water, buying extra time to collect her thoughts. "After our discussion, William left me. Being in Saint Merwinna's chapel…although I know it is far from complete…I was moved to prayer." Rhoswen indicated her approval with the slightest tilt of her head. Ingrith went on, "So I knelt and attempted to find the right words. I confess I struggle sometimes…"

"As does everyone at times, daughter. Go on."

"It was as I was kneeling there that it happened."

"*What* happened?"

"I heard a voice speaking my name." As she said this, Ingrith saw an expression of frustrated resignation on the Abbess's face. Ingrith waved her hand back and forth. "No, no. I know what you think I am going to say. It was not that. It was not the voice of our saint. I never for one moment thought…"

Rhoswen looked sideways at Ingrith. "Oh? How is it you were so sure? How would you know what Saint Merwinna sounded like?"

"I do not know. I do know she was a young woman, though. And this was not the voice of a woman."

"Oh," said Rhoswen, in a manner that suggested this confirmed a conclusion she had already reached. "It was a man's voice, then. That of the carpenter. It is, is it not, the most logical explanation?"

Yes, and also the most convenient one, thought Ingrith bitterly, realising Abbess Rhoswen had been steering the conversation in this direction all along. Nonetheless, because the suggestion had come from the Abbess herself, and because Ingrith did not want to appear unprepared to consider all possibilities, she was careful to at least seem to give the idea some consideration; although she knew already that it had not been the carpenter. "Perhaps…" she said, and then speedily followed this up with, "But no, I do believe it can have been the carpenter. He had not yet arrived. It was not a man's voice."

"That is not what you said a moment ago. You said it was a man."

"I said it was not the voice of a woman," corrected Ingrith.

Even though a slight hardening of her expression made it plain that the Abbess was vexed by this fine distinction, Ingrith continued, anxious to make her point before the older woman attempted once more to steer her thoughts in a different direction. "It was not female. It could have been male…If such things apply."

"*Apply*? What on earth do you mean by that, girl?"

"It was not human sounding."

"Oh!" said the Abbess. This time the exclamation was not one of recognition, or pleasure at the apparent confirmation of an already reached conclusion. It was one of apprehension. "Please explain what you mean by that."

"It is difficult."

"You must try. Tell me what happened."

"I remember…yes that's right…I remember I had just brushed away a fly or a moth or something of the sort. It fluttered up towards the ceiling.…"

"What is the importance of that detail?"

"The voice it…" Ingrith stopped, attempted to remember. " Yes, it was from that direction the voice came."

"Tell me. This voice you say you heard, are you certain it

was not human…mortal."

"No, not certain. It was whispering."

"What did this voice say to you?"

"What it said made no sense."

"Which was?"

"It said, *Do what you will.*"

"What do you think it meant by that?"

"I cannot tell you." Ingrith looked the Abbess in the eye. "I think you do not believe me."

"I do not know what I believe. I do not yet *dis*believe you, if that helps."

"Not yet? You think you will eventually, then?"

Rhoswen's tone became gentler. "Forgive me, daughter. I do not wish to seem doubting. You must understand that yours is a story to which it is difficult to give credence. As I said, you would not be the first to assert such a thing. Many want to claim contact with the saint. Too many for all the stories to be true. Though some, I do not doubt, are."

"I have said I am not claiming that!"

Rhoswen lifted a hand to calm Ingrith. "And that is the very reason why I am still listening to you. You have not been prone to an overly ecstatic faith in the past…In fact, the opposite has been true…the cause of some of your difficulties here…Yet that is not to your disadvantage on this occasion. There are some…even here, I regret to say… whose willingness to see the Lord's work in so many things renders them blind to its presence when it is truly there to be seen. Do you understand me?"

"I think so."

"You, however, have been a tough stone to crack…"

"Oh, Reverend Mother! You are too unkind!" protested Ingrith, her voice getting louder. "My faith is as strong as that of anyone here!"

Rhoswen glanced over at Sister Helewise. The Infirmaress had put down her pestle, and was no longer making any attempt to conceal the fact that she was watching them. The old woman scowled at the Abbess, and shook her head. Rhoswen - as she often did - found herself half-amused and half-annoyed by the old woman's presumption. She gestured for Sister Helewise to stay where she was. Sister Helewise seemed on the verge of protesting, and then backed down. Although she still did not take her eyes off them or return to her work.

Rhoswen turned back to Ingrith.

"Calm yourself, daughter. Be assured your faith has never once been in question. Never. Do you imagine I would have had you remain here if it were? Yet you have struggled to *see* God's work. There is a difference. For all your belief, you have struggled to find its confirmation in the world around you, have you not? So now, when you, of all the sisters, come to me with this story, I find I must listen. Tough stones sometimes split more fully than softer ones when they do, finally, crack."

Both women now fell silent for almost a full minute; both pondering what their role in events dictated they ought to do next. Ingrith was looking down at the floor when she felt the Abbess's hand upon her shoulder. "I will leave you now, Ingrith. I wish to think on all you have told me."

"Yes, Reverend Mother. I am sorry if I am a burden to you."

"Let us call you a challenge, shall we. Not a burden. Oh, and Ingrith..."

"Yes."

"Do not talk of this to the other sisters. They will be curious. Let us, for now at least, let them think it was simply the poor carpenter giving you a fright."

"But..."

"For *now*."

It was then that something else occurred to Rhoswen. It was something she had meant to ask before, but had been distracted from doing so. "There is one thing. Before I go, can you remember what it was you were praying for? Was there a specific cause? Was it something to which '*do as you will*' might be considered an answer?"

To Rhoswen's surprise, the young novice's eyes suddenly widened. Her hand came to her mouth, and then fell away again.

"What is it?" asked Rhoswen, maintaining a steady voice, but inwardly as curious as she was concerned by this reaction. "Tell me, daughter. What is it?"

"You will be angry... Think me foolish..."

Rhoswen forced a smile. "Now I absolutely *insist* you tell me. I *order* it, in fact."

Ingrith looked up at Rhoswen, and Rhoswen was surprised to see the girl was smiling, almost laughing.

"I see now. Oh, Reverend Mother. I understand. I hope you will not think me haughty...arrogant...It's simply that I *do* see. I *do* understand."

A little taken aback by this sudden change in Ingrith, Rhoswen nodded for her to continue.

"You asked about the nature of my prayers..."

Rhoswen nodded again.

"Guidance! I was praying for guidance."

Rhoswen, restraining her exasperation, nodded yet again. Only a very slight flutter of her eyes gave away anything of her impatience. *Let the girl talk on*, she counselled herself. *Allow her free rein, and we will get there.*

A few minutes later, watching from across the room, Sister Helewise was surprised when Abbess Rhoswen clapped her hands with obvious delight at something the novice must have told her. She was even more surprised when the Reverend Mother leaned forward and embraced the young woman.

******

Bishop Baldwin read the letter for a second time. Then he put it down on the table in front of him, sat back, and smiled.

He was able to smile because, for the moment, there was nobody else in the room with him except his old friend and confidant, Father Hugh. In front of anyone else he would have nodded gravely in his usual, studied manner - a manner designed to give away as little as possible of what he really thought to anyone observing. He was well practised in it, and could receive the best or the worst of news with the same apparent degree of equanimity. With only Father Hugh present, Baldwin was able to be more frank. He even indulged in a satisfied chuckle as he passed the letter across the table to him.

"What do you make of that, old friend? Our diminutive Abbess out at Althurst claims she has finally come around to my way of thinking. She would have me believe she is now all in favour of building the chapel to honour Saint Merwinna." A smile played on Baldwin's lips as he watched the old priest read. When he judged Hugh had studied the letter sufficiently, he said, "You see? She is, it seems, all contrition and pricked conscience for her past attitude towards the idea. *My* idea."

Father Hugh, following the Bishop's lead, allowed himself a brief smile. "So it appears, my Lord."

"*Appears*, that is exactly it. *Appears*."

Father Hugh frowned. "You do not believe her?"

"I most certainly do not!"

Hugh's expression turned to one of confusion. "Forgive me, my lord, then why are you so pleased?"

"I do not believe for a moment that the miniature she-devil has had any sort of change of heart regarding this matter. She may be small, but she has always had the stubbornness of an ox. Whatever she may say, whatever her reasons for saying it, she will not have changed her opinion. She is a strong-willed woman...I admire her for it...I do. It is how she has got to be where she is... despite only being the size of a fat butcher's thumb." He glanced down at his own pudgy hands, chuckled. "Or should I say my own thumb, beneath which she now sits? No matter. What is important is that she has seen fit to agree with me, regardless of what she truly feels. The stubborn ox has turned about and begun to walk in the direction I desire it to walk. It does not matter a bit whether or not it wishes to travel in that direction. It only matters that it does. And so, I have my victory, Hugh. I have won." He chuckled again. "I always knew I would, of course. The fact that a chapel has been built meant my victory was all but complete. This…" He leaned across and flicked at the letter, still held in Father Hugh's hand. "This is the final treaty. She sues for peace. It is gratifying to receive it, even if it was not necessary. Come, old friend," he beamed, "you will share some wine with me. Pass me the letter. I shall read it again while you fill our cups."

******

CHAPTER 7

Merwinna, 1171

Merwinna was dancing. She knew many in the world outside her cell would be surprised if they were to discover it. Some of them would even think it inappropriate behaviour from someone in her position. As long as God understood – as she knew He would - that was all that really mattered. Besides, could it really be called dancing, what she was doing? Simply swaying a little from side to side in time to the melody she was humming to herself? She did not know the complete song, only the main refrain, and it was this that she was humming, over and over. She was trying to remember the words, and where she had last heard them. They were something to do with Spring and how the season reflected a young man's hopes for the future. She seemed to remember a girl was involved. Was the young man in love with her? They usually were in such songs. Did he hope to marry the girl, was that it? Was the song about his plans to propose? He was going to take her to a garden... or was it a clearing in the forest... and ask for her hand. Was that it?

"Oh my!" Merwinna said aloud. She spoke aloud to herself more often these days. She giggled. No, that wasn't it at all. Merwinna giggled. "Not at all." It was definitely springtime, and there was definitely a girl involved. But what the boy planned to do in the forest was anything but make an honest woman of her. "Oh dear, oh dear," said Merwinna and giggled again. A boy and a girl in the forest. Young sinners. But were they? Where was she harm in it? Was their sin really so grievous?

Suddenly Garrick entered her thoughts.

"Go away!" she said, peevishly. "I don't want to think about you. Go away!"

The two of them were walking hand in hand towards a stand of trees. Where they were it was spring, just as it had been in the song, not winter, as it was outside in the Abbey grounds.

"Now, haven't I told you, Garrick. We shouldn't do this again. It's wrong. I have to concentrate on my prayers for all the other sinners of the world. How can my prayers be of any worth if I myself am steeped in sin? I must be righteous. We both know what you want of me is far from that."

"What if I only want to propose…pledge my troth? Oh, but you can't marry me. You are already a Bride of Christ. Still, what he doesn't know will do him no harm."

Merwinna clapped her hands with delight. "True…and it is not a though he ever asks for what it is *you* want of me!"

Merwinna had lifted her arms to clap her hands together for a second time, when she paused in what she was doing, her arms hovering uncertainly in front of her. Instead of clapping, she gasped, and then wrapped her arms around herself; following this up with a great howl of dismay, overcome with remorse at the shamefulness of her thoughts. Led astray once more. How could she have been so weak?

"God forgive me! Oh, dear God, please, *please* forgive me! I am bedevilled…tormented…!"

Merwinna began to look frantically around her cell, but found she needed to wipe away the tears that now filled her eyes in order to see clearly enough to locate what she was looking for. This done, she soon found it. She grabbed the small knife she used to cut her food, and held it out before herself as if it were an offering. "I seek forgiveness, Lord," she said, "and so I offer my pain in expiation." Then she drew back her sleeve and began to cut; the fresh wounds on her forearms joining many older, healed, and partly healed ones.

From the corner of the cell, partially hidden in the shadows there, Garrick chuckled.

"Oh come now, woman. A little puncturing of the skin

will not atone. If you want stabbing, Sister Merwinna, I can offer you a far better tool for the job than that stubby little blade you have in your hand. Better by far. The best thing for piercing flesh is flesh, in my experience. Curl those soiled fingers of yours around this instrument instead. Firm and long it is. Just right for…"

"Enough!" yelled Merwinna, and lunged at Garrick with the knife. In the fraction of a second it took her to reach him he had disappeared, vanished back into the shadows where he came from. Merwinna was not surprised. She knew he would have. She stepped back, glanced down at the knife she held in one hand, and then at the blood running down her forearm and wrist onto the other. She stood there for a time, watching it as it trickled down, drops of it occasionally rolling off and landing on the cell floor where they were absorbed into the dust and grime. After a few minutes, a thought struck her. She turned her hand over so the palm was facing upward. This way some of the blood that ran down her wrist pooled in her palm. When she judged there was sufficient, she lifted the hand and rubbed the contents over her face. Then she bent down, scooped up a handful of dirt from the floor, and rubbed that into her face as well.

"It's no more than you deserve," she whispered to herself. Then, loudly, she called, "Garrick!" She began turning round and round on the same spot. "Garrick! Are you there? Garrick?"

"Yes, I'm here."

"Look at me. Do you see me?"

"Yes, I see."

"I paint myself for you…like Jezebel. Do you see it?"

Garrick laughed. "And will you end like her…food for the dogs?"

Ignoring this, Merwinna continued. "Is this what you want? A painted whore?"

"This catechism of yours grows wearisome."

"Answer me. Is this what you desire?"

"Now we both know that is the wrong question."

Merwinna stopped turning, stood still. "What do you mean by that?"

Garrick did not respond.

"What do you mean? Answer me," insisted Merwinna.

"Oh, now I think you know exactly what I mean. It is not *my* desires that are in question here, is it? I was not the one who was dancing earlier… humming and swaying her hips like a Gomorrah slave girl."

From the corner of her eye Merwinna saw movement in the shadows. Garrick had revealed himself once more. He stepped forward, a knowing grin on his face. She saw to her consternation that he was wearing the habit of a monk.

"Blasphemy!" she hissed.

"You don't approve?" he said in a pretence of innocent surprise. He shrugged. "Oh, well." Still grinning, Garrick pulled the garment over his head. He now stood before her naked.

Merwinna turned away, a hand over her eyes.

"What is it? Frightened you will turn into a pillar of salt?"

With her eyes still firmly shut, Merwinna lunged at Garrick with the knife again. This time she did so with such force that she lost control, pitched forward, stumbled, fell heavily against the wall of her cell, and crumpled to the floor. Not for the first time she had to resist the urge to call out for someone to come and free her from her prison of torment. She rolled over and threw herself prostrate onto the floor, praying desperately for the strength she feared she lacked.

"Oh Lord, I beg of you, do not allow me to grow weak and seek escape from this place. All would be lost. It is in your honour that I have had myself so confined. Give me the strength to remain. Oh, dear Lord, give me the strength to achieve what you would have me achieve. I must not leave. Although I do confess there are times…such as at this moment…when I ache for it with all my heart. And yet I *will not* leave. I will not fail in my task. I will not fail you, dear

God, if you would but give me the strength. He *will not* drive me out, he will not. No matter how hard he tries. He will not make a mockery of what I have done. He will not. He must not. It is he who should be cast out, not I!"

After a few minutes, Merwinna rolled over onto her back, arms thrown out to her sides, and gazed up into the dark shadows at the roof of her cell. Tears streaked the blood and dirt on her face, but she felt calmer. Garrick was gone for the time being. She had no sense of him near her. Although she did not doubt he would return to torment her again when the mood took him. Once her breathing had steadied, she spoke to God again. Only more steadily now, less hurried, and with more composure. Almost a whisper.

"Dear God, who watches over me, hear my prayer. It is the prayer of a sinner who wishes only to serve as I am bid. I do not know if my trials are your doing, or the Devil's. I only know a demon is sent to test me. I will not fail that test. I will not fail it. I will not fail *you*, dear Lord. I will not fail you!"

******

Not for the first time, Father Jerome had been forced to chase away a group of the townspeople he had discovered gathered outside the walls of the anchoress's cell. As usual, they had been drawn there by her cries, and were now listening at the opening to the noises coming from within. A small number had looks of concern on their faces; many more listened with undisguised amusement as they attempted to make out what the poor girl was saying. These days the nuns and servants of Althurst Abbey knew better than to stay and listen. They had been instructed to fetch Father Jerome or one of his assistants if they heard Merwinna in this state, and then to withdraw. Any of the inhabitants of the town who might be in the vicinity, however, were not so easily kept back. There was no disciplinary action that he could take against them. In truth, they had every right to be there. He had no real right in law to move them on; they merely accepted his apparent authority to do so by the sheer weight of his conviction when he railed at them. But the inducement of the anchoress's cries, and the entertainment they provided was a strong one. That the content was at times salacious made it stronger still. Despite the best efforts of the Abbess and Jerome, Merwinna had become the talk of the town – and beyond - for all the wrong reasons. Worse, news of the scandal had now reached the senior figures of the Order.

Satisfied there was now no one but himself within hearing of the young woman's ravings – inside or outside the Abbey Church - Jerome now sank down onto the ground and, as he usually did, closed his eyes, and waited for the wild cries to subside into the unintelligible mumbling that usually followed. The latter, he fervently hoped, being her prayers because, if there was any comfort to be had for the girl, it must surely derive from prayer and the knowledge that the Lord would surely listen to entreaties from one such as her.

Father Jerome resolved to talk with her again - for all the good it would do; he knew any offer of help on his part would be rejected, and he would have no choice other than to respect her wishes when she insisted – as she always did - that she was fine and should be left alone. He did not, however, imagine the same respect would be shown by the senior figures of her Order when they arrived in the next few days. He wondered if he should give Merwinna warning of this when next he spoke to her, but decided against it. If she were forewarned, she might make an extra effort to curb her behaviour, and the visitors might not get to hear just how extreme it could become. It was better that they witnessed it for themselves. That way they might use their influence to ensure the girl got the help she needed. Father Jerome himself did not know exactly what form that help should take. Perhaps these people would have a better understanding of such things, be better able to judge. Wasn't that why they had achieved the levels of power and influence in the Order that they had?

******

CHAPTER 8

Althurst Abbey – 1307

Abbess Rhoswen's change of heart with regard to the Chapel of Saint Merwinna, and the tiled floor it would house, should have been a good thing, and made things that little bit easier for Will. No doubt, in the long run, it would still prove to be. Right now, however, it was giving Will problems. And these were all down to the Abbess's - to Will's mind at least - peculiar insistence that any design for the tiles must take their inspiration from the wall painting in her receiving room. Will had not been prepared for such a request. He had had a few ideas, and sample tiles had already been put before Bishop Baldwin in Winchester, who had indicated that he would be content for any one of them to be used. The Bishop had been in one of his particularly avuncular moods that day and simply said, "You know your business better than I, Master Tiler." On a later occasion, his mood more sombre, he had warned Will that the Abbess would need to be consulted, nonetheless. "That unholy dwarf at Althurst will want her say," he had said. "Better let her have it. Let the choice be hers. But from among the tiles you showed me, mind you. I don't mind what she chooses, so long as it is based on those I myself have seen and approved, you understand me? My say first, and then she gets hers. She gets to exercise her small bit of power, that's all. A token, nothing more."

Things were different now. The Abbess having written to Baldwin to make known to him her newfound enthusiasm for the project, he had obviously been persuaded to surrender some of his control. Will was informed via a messenger from the Bishop that he should now co-operate with all Abbess Rhoswen's wishes on the subject of the tile design. As a result, he was left with no choice but to scrap his previous ideas and begin anew. All jobs had their share of problems – areas of dampness on the floor, poor quality batches of tiles from the manufacturers, and so on - but Will had not foreseen or been prepared for this particular development. In the past he had had to deal with patrons having last minute changes of heart about which pattern of tile should be used. He had even had to request that complete new batches be sent from the tile makers. But to be asked to design and create bespoke tiles from such an extremely specific subject was an entirely new experience for him, and one he did not enjoy. Nor did he approve. He was not a painter of wall paintings. He had an appreciation of the art, it was true. This did not mean he had any particular skill in that area. Nor was it right that he should have. Just as he, Will, had worked for many years to acquire his skills in his own chosen trade, so the painter had spent years acquiring his skills. It seemed somehow disrespectful to the man – whoever he had been – to act as if it were possible to achieve in so short a time what he had achieved through years of effort. Abbess Rhoswen had explained that she did not expect a recreation of the image on her wall, only what she rather obscurely referred to as an *echo* of it. But, if by that echoing, she meant Will to capture what was striking and unique about the image, surely that was where the original creator's art lay?

Quite apart from Will's objections based on principle alone, the change in commission also meant he would now fall behind the rough schedule for the work he had set out and carried in his head. Hopefully, this would only be by a few days. A week at most. The problem was that things had reached a stage where, until the design was finalised, there was very little more for either Alf or Silas to be getting on with. The lad would occupy himself either playing his games or watching Will at his work, so he was not a worry. Silas, on the other hand, was likely to find his way to one of the alehouses in the town. Sometimes this was not a problem either. The difficulty would be if Silas were to fall into one of his melancholies as a result of his drinking. If that were to happen it would most definitely be a problem. These moods encouraged the old fool to drink more than he should. And drinking more than he should encouraged the melancholy within him. There had been times in the past when he had drunk so much that he was of no use to Will for days on end. On these occasions Silas was lucky that Will's affection for him was such that he attempted to help him recover rather than sack him as many in his position would have done. Also, Silas was a good assistant. Finding another would be as time consuming as sorting him out. Either way, it all took time, and caused delays. Will would have to keep an eye on the old man.

While he worked on his design for the tiles, Abbess Rhoswen had little choice but to allow Will access to the room containing the painting - when it was not being used for other business - so that he might study the image. It was there that Ingrith found him.

"How goes it, William?" she said, startling him. He had been sitting on the floor directly beneath the image of the saint, and now leapt to his feet and spun round upon hearing her voice. He was doubly surprised because he had, just at that moment, been thinking about her – at least, somewhere in the back of his mind. His second thought, and his first fear, was that she might be accompanied by the Abbess herself, who might not be too pleased to see him sitting so casually on the floor of her room. Thankfully, Ingrith was only in the company of a young girl that Will recognised as a servant from the kitchens. She could not be much older than Alf.

Seeing Will notice the girl, Ingrith said. "Oh, William...this is Tick, she sometimes assists me...errands...that sort of thing. Today she was helping me look for you. And we have found you."

"Hello, Tick," said Will. "I'm William. Will."

There girl seemed shy, and merely nodded.

"Respond to Will when he greets you," said Ingrith, giving the girl a friendly bump with her shoulder. Tick looked up and opened her mouth to speak, and then lost confidence at the last moment.

"Another quiet one," observed Will. "You should meet our Alf. He holds his tongue more often than wags it. That's fine by me. Still, just you remember, you may speak to me if you wish. I will not reproach you for it. I am no high born lord, so you need not fear me, girl."

"No, indeed he is not. A lord would not be found sitting upon the floor," teased Ingrith, and bumped shoulders with the girl again. This time Will thought he caught a hint of a smile. He smiled back, and then to Ingrith he said, "You wish to speak with me, or is it the room you require? If so, I can leave you be."

Ingrith looked puzzled. "You think my time with you is at an end?"

"Is it not? We have not seen you in some days. I took your absence to mean…"

"Wait a moment, please," said Ingrith. Turning to the girl she said, "You may leave us, Tick. Thank you for your help." When the girl had gone, Ingrith said, "I was somewhat unwell after the incident in the chapel, and then I was away. I went to Romsey Abbey as it happens."

"Oh?"

"To study your work there, Will. Abbess Rhoswen thought it might be useful. Particularly given what I have to tell you. I have news, Will. A wonderful thing." She paused. "Although given our last conversation you may not agree. If so, I hope to convince you otherwise."

"Something tells me I have no choice," said Will, his tone becoming more serious. He had guessed something of what was to come. "Perhaps you should save your words. I will do as I am instructed."

"No, I shall speak my piece. Firstly, you are a skilled man,

Will. Having seen your work at Romsey, there can be no doubting your ability...the gift the Lord has seen fit to place in your hands." Despite their complete sincerity, when she spoke them, her words sounded to Ingrith like blandishments. She wondered if Will had been right. Perhaps she should have saved her words? Right now the man's face was expressionless, so it was impossible to tell how he had taken them. Whatever his reaction, it was too late now. She had begun, and must go on to the end. Not to do so would give the impression that she had lost conviction in what she was saying. Or, worse, that she had never had any to begin with. She hurried on. "When we spoke before, I caused you much offence. That was not my intention. I promise you it was not. If I could only have…"

Will stopped her. "Girl, if you are about to offer another of your many apologies, let me halt you there. I have no need to hear it."

"Please I…"

Will closed his eyes and shook his head. "No. I will not hear it, for it is not required. Not from you, Ingrith. If any request for forgiveness is due on this occasion, it is I should be making it, not you. When we spoke before I was short tempered with you. Needlessly so. It was not justified. My late wife…God rest her…would tell me there were times when I was far too full of self-importance where my work was concerned. Without her steadying words, I fear I can be worse than ever these days. I do not deny I do feel no small amount of pleasure at being good at what I do. Who does not…a craftsman should…But that should not prevent me from being kind. Your offer was no insult, yet I reacted as if it was."

Mention of Will's wife distracted Ingrith for a moment. Her head was suddenly filled with questions about the woman; questions she knew it would be imprudent to ask at any time, let alone right now when it seemed she and Will were bridging the rift that had opened up between them.

Whether he sensed this, or whether he would have been moved to say it anyway, Ingrith would never know, but Will said, "Hildy, that was her name. She was a good woman, and a good wife to me, was Hildy. She provided my children. Two of which lived beyond being babes. A lad and a girl. Younger than you, but old enough to have gone and made their own way in the world."

"Your son did not want to be a tiler?"

Will looked away, seeming to see old events that, from his frown, must have pained him a great deal then, and still did so now. "He did not. He wanted to fight for a living. Heaven knows where he is now, or even if he is alive. Somewhere in the King's army no doubt…If he lives still. It has been years…"

Ingrith noticed Will had not given her his son's name, as if it would have pained him to speak it. "And your daughter?" she asked.

Will looked back at Ingrith. "Sarah? She married a baker's son. Hamo was a good-for-nothing boy in my opinion. Still, the girl had her heart set on him, and my wife said she saw some good in him that I could not, so I let it be. They should be fine, I suppose. His father was teaching him his trade, so they will not starve. Sarah will be stirring flour or some such for the ne'er-do-well in Winchester right at this moment, I don't doubt it. Anyway, I've strayed from my point. What I mean to say is that it is I who am sorry for biting your head off before. I hope we can put it behind us."

"I believe we can," said Ingrith. Then she smiled - a little timidly, it seemed to Will. "Al*though*…" she said, stretching out the second syllable.

Will, narrowed his eyes suspiciously, but he was smiling at the same time. "What? What is it, woman? I have the sense we are returning to a thorny subject. Am I right?"

"You are, I regret to say." Ingrith paused, reconsidered. "No, that is not the truth. I do not regret it. I only regret the annoyance it may cause you."

"My father had a saying at times like this. We are at the river. Time to wade in if you wish to reach the other side. It's the only way. Get your feet wet."

"If the current is too strong, the water too fast?"

"If you mean will I act as I did before, you have my word that I will not."

"I'm glad of it. And so…"

To Will's mild amusement, Ingrith straightened her back, and clasped her hands in front of herself, before she continued. "As you know, the Reverend Mother has had quite the change of heart regarding Saint Merwinna's Chapel. This is because she now believes that it is what the saint herself desires to happen. As do I, in fact. I believe it too."

Will raised his eyebrows. "The Saint *herself*? Well now…"

"It is for that very reason you find yourself in here." Ingrith waved a hand around the room.

"To get ideas from the painting," said Will. "Your Abbess has decided the design must come from it. I have a headache at this very moment from trying to do just that. How is this to do with the wishes of Merwinna?" Even as he said it, Will guessed at the nature of the explanation to follow, if not the details. "Oh," he said, "you're about to tell me your saint spoke to her?"

"I am!" said Ingrith eagerly. "Well, not *spoke*, exactly. More *revealed* herself."

"How did she reveal herself? In what form," asked Will, trying not to sound sceptical.

"I cannot tell you, for I am not permitted to say. Not to anyone. Abbess Rhoswen…and I think rightly…says that such things can cause unnecessary excitement… even feverish behaviour…among the common people if they are not fully understood. That I am permitted to tell you this much took some persuading on my part, I can assure you. Oh…and you cannot reveal this to anyone else. Not anyone!"

"Who would I tell? Silas? Young Alf? The boy would not

understand, and the old man wouldn't care."

"Wouldn't *care?*" asked Ingrith, a little dismayed.

"I chose my words badly. Silas is no heathen. He would be as impressed and pleased as I am to discover he was working according to the saint's will. What I meant to say was that it would not change how hard or well he does that work. Silas always does his best." *When he is not drunk*, thought Will. "He does as I bid him, and he trusts in me to have found us work that is worthy of doing well. You have your Reverend Mother, Silas has me. Not quite the same, but that's how it is. We…the three of us…Silas, Alf, and me…we are our own small community, much as Althurst is yours."

Ingrith smiled at the comparison. "I see."

"What I mean to say is that you need not worry, Ingrith. I shall keep it to myself. Though I admit I am curious about one thing."

Ingrith grinned. "Only one? Which is?"

"Why the saint chose *this* painting above all others. It is, unusually…" Will struggled for the word. The Bishop had called it *comely*, but that word had been chosen with the intention of provoking Abbess Rhoswen. Will did not wish for the same effect where Ingrith was concerned. He seemed to remember the Abbess had offered another word, but he could not recall it.

Seeing his struggle, Ingrith suggested, "Beguiling? I believe that is the word I have heard Abbess Rhoswen use…on more than one occasion… when asked to describe the singular qualities of this image…How, erm… affecting it can be."

"I think I have heard her use it myself," replied Will, relieved. "*Beguiling,*" he repeated to himself.

"I asked the Abbess the exact question you have asked me. Why choose this image?"

"What did she say? What was her answer?"

"She responded by telling me she believes it is the saint's choice because it was painted by someone who actually saw her. Someone who actually saw Merwinna. It has always been rumoured to have been, and this seems to confirm it." Ingrith fell silent for a moment, studying the painting before them. "If it truly is her likeness, how wonderful it is for us to be able to look upon her all these years later."

Will had studied the painting enough for the moment. He was looking at Ingrith, intrigued by the gleam in her eyes.

"So what is this news you wish to tell me, and worry I will not receive well?"

Ingrith turned and looked at him. Had she known he was studying her? Will wasn't sure. "Ah, yes," she said, reminded. "I must tell you, must I not? Here it is. The Abbess has decided that it is *I* who should produce the design for the tiles, not you."

"I see," said Will. "And this is linked to the saint's wishes, is it?"

Ingrith tried to find irony in his tone or anger in his features, but there seemed none to be found. "It is, yes. She says it was no mere coincidence that someone whom she knows to have …abilities…in such things…Oh dear, it appears I am exhibiting pride again…"

"Enough of this," said Will, surprising both Ingrith and himself by briefly touching her on the arm. Ingrith looked down at where his hand had been, involuntarily putting her own hand there afterward.

"Enough of *what?*" she asked. Will seemed unable to reply; too embarrassed at having touched her the way he had. She took her own hand away from the spot, and said, in a deliberately more relaxed way, "Enough of what, Will?"

This seemed to free Will from his discomfort. "We will get nowhere if you do not cease this modesty. Let us have it understood between us both that you thank and give credit to God for the abilities you say He has given you….we both do….You have them, all the same, and there is an end to it. So, tell me, what is it you need from me."

"It is the other way around, Will. I need to know what *you* need from *me*. What should I produce that will translate…transfer…into a design you can put on a tile?"

Will considered a moment. "An image…a shape. Nothing special. If you come up with it, I can make the template. That is not my difficulty. I have struggled to come up with anything. That has been my difficulty. Far from being angered by what you tell me, I am relieved. I am glad you have been handed the task for which I found myself unfit." As if to illustrate his point, Will let out a long, slow breath. "It was tasking me greatly."

"Will you show me then…how you create a tile?"

"We go before our horse to market. We should…Or rather *you* should give me your idea. Have you one?"

"No, not yet. Soon, I hope. I came here because I thought I would find you, it is true. However, I also came here to get a better look at her…Merwinna."

Will looked at the painting, then back at Ingrith. "I will leave the two of you in peace, then."

"Wait, I still do not know what I must produce. Will you not show me examples of what you have used in the past?"

Will chuckled, bemused. "You have seen the tiles at Romsey. You've seen the contents of my cart…such as they are…the sort of thing that the tiles have on them."

"No, I mean the templates, the images…which method did you use to make your starting images?"

Will looked puzzled. "I don't know that I understand what you're getting at. There is no one way. Some are copied from others; I won't deny it…The more usual ones, I mean …the French lily…the fleur-de-lis, as they call it. As for the ones I come up with myself… I just come up with them." Will saw from her face that this was not a sufficient answer as far as Ingrith was concerned. He tried again. "Look, let's say I get an idea…Well, I might scratch it out on a piece of wood, or maybe onto an old slate… so I can remember it. Then I make that shape into a wooden stamp based on the idea. Sometimes I just make the stamp as soon as I get the idea… see how it goes. Listen, you come up with an image in whatever way suits you best, girl, and I'll make the stamp."

"You stamp the tiles?"

"That's how it's done. The red clay is hammered into a wooden mould…that's how you get the basic tile. Then the shape you want is stamped into the clay. A wooden stamp… hammered into it. Fill the depression produced with clay that fires pale, and you get the two-colour design. Yellow set against the clay-red background." Will scratched his head. "Sounds simple put that way, I suppose?"

"Oh, no, I'm sure it is not. I'm sure there is much more to it."

"Oh, there is, believe me. As a real young-un, when first I would watch my father at work, I thought it looked easy. Only when I was old enough to try for myself did I discover the truth of it. My old man would shake his head. 'Have another go, Willy, my boy,' he'd say with a laugh, 'have yourself another go and see if you can't do it properly this time.' What makes it hard is the actual *doing* of it. Understanding the basic method…filing in stamped clay…is easy enough. But doing it…Now there is where it gets to be more thorny. Firstly, you have to prepare the clay…know where to dig it. What to dig. Know when it's ready."

"Ready?"

"Oh yes."

Ingrith found she was moved by Will's obvious pleasure in explaining all this to her. He was in no way boastful; it was simply that he was clearly in love with the processes, and pleased that she was genuinely interested to hear about them.

"Tile making is a seasonal business, you see," he went on. "You have to weather the clay in heaps over the winter months. Then the making and firing is for spring and summer. Mind you, that is not a problem if you bring your tiles in ready made from the centres where they are produced. Only, that's not what we're doing here, though, is it?" Will rolled his eyes in mock frustration. "Making them on site is our task in Althurst. Well, you have your clay, and you have your stamp." Will held out both hands, as if each one contained one of the two things he was talking about. Then he closed one hand upon the other. "You've put the clay in the mould, and now you're ready to stamp it. And that has to be just right. Getting the indented impression you want takes some learning. Too hard with the hammer and it becomes uneven, fat at the sides as the clay tries to escape from the mould. Too soft and the depression won't hold enough of the white clay, and it'll split when fired…fall out like dry skin on an old monk's head."

Ingrith nodded, smiled at the image. "And then…?"

"Then, you have to trim it. Maybe you've stamped it just right, but you still have to trim it to the perfect size. Again, making them all even is something that takes a practiced eye. After that, you have to leave it to dry out. It needs to be harder…although not too hard…about like leather. Once it's right, then you can put in the white clay. Again, this wants experience. Depending on the feel of the red clay, you may want to change the thickness of the white. Sometimes it's best to make it thick and trowel it into the gaps. Then again, there are times when a smoother result is gained by having it runnier…a 'slip'…that can be poured into the spaces. Now comes more trimming and scraping to get rid of the excess white, and reveal the surrounding red. The whole thing needs to be sharp and clear, the one colour against the other."

"And then you can fire them in the kiln…the one you and Silas have built?"

"Not quite yet. You still have to coat the tile in the glaze. That's really what turns the white clay into the yellow, and the surrounding body the rich red-brown." Will's face became serious, and then he smiled, self-consciously. "I've let my mouth have rule, haven't I? I'm sorry."

"No, I want to understand it all," said Ingrith, then added, "You apologise too much, Master Tiler."

******

Ned the carpenter frowned; he really did not want to go back to the unfinished chapel. Although, he knew he must if he wished to keep his reputation as an honest and trustworthy craftsman. He could not abandon a job halfway through completion, and then still expect others to employ him having gained a name for unreliability. The problem was that he had allowed himself to brood upon what had happened the last time he went there to measure the door before final fitting. That screaming girl and the restraining hands of the crowd that gathered. He could not shake the feeling that something similarly bad – or even worse - would befall him if he returned there. It was nonsense, of course. His wife said he was a fool to let it play on his mind the way it did, and he agreed with her. Only she had not been there, had she? She had not experienced those angry faces and grabbing hands. Those people would have gladly hanged him from the Abbey gates if they had been allowed – with or without absolute proof of his guilt. And now he was expected to happily push his cart back through those same gates, and finish the task their eagerness to see him punished had prevented him from completing. It was not so simple as all that. He would do it. He must. But it was not so simple.

As he neared the Abbey Gatehouse, Ned found he could go no further. His legs and feet felt as if they were made of the same heavy mud that clumped and rutted the track to the Abbey beneath them, and caked the wheels of his handcart. Even with all this warm weather this track had not fully dried out. He smiled grimly to himself. Feet of clay? Wasn't that something he had heard once? Most likely from a priest. He frowned again, and put down the handles of the cart, letting it rest on the track for a moment while he attempted to compose himself. Looking down he saw that his hands were shaking. When he balled one into a fist and clasped it in the other, his grip felt weak.

A horse and rider suddenly appeared from behind him.

Despite the galloping and snorting of the animal, Ned had not been aware of their approach. They seemed to him almost conjured from the warm summer breeze. They rode close by – too close for safety - splashing Ned with filthy puddle water as they passed. Ned gasped in surprise, and staggered backwards, his legs nearly failing him, forcing him to lean on the cart to support himself.

The rider had reached and entered the gate before Ned had mustered the courage to pick up the cart handles and continue onward. It was only another thirty or so yards to the gate, but with each step he had to struggle against the urge to turn the cart around and head back down the track into the safety of the busy streets and alleyways of the town.

All you have to do right now is walk up to those damned gates, and announce your arrival, Ned told himself. *After that, you go through and do what you came to do. The door. A day's work at most. Then you can leave this place. The door. You have to get it done. That's all there is to it. Then you can leave.*

Another rider passed him. This one, however, shouted a warning, and gave Ned a much wider birth than the previous one, looking Ned in the face, and nodding a greeting as he went by. Any other day and Ned might have returned the nod. Not today. Today, he only stopped and watched, blank-faced, as this second rider slowed his animal's pace and trotted blithely through the gate. Simple as that. The most everyday thing in the world. And yet, to Ned it weighed more heavily with every step; made somehow worse by the fact that, if asked, he could not have said why. Yes, what happened with the girl had been unsettling at the time – even downright frightening when the angry crowd had gathered about him – but, as William the tiler had said just after, it had only been an unfortunate misunderstanding, and it was in the past. No harm was done, and the same thing would not happen again. It could not. Even if the nervous young woman were to be in exactly the same spot in exactly the same jumpy frame of mind as before, Ned would know now to announce his presence before he did anything else. So why on earth was he still so damned uneasy about it all? It made no sense, and Ned knew it. Unfortunately, that knowledge made no difference to how he felt. Something was going to happen if he was not careful. Or if even if he was. Something awful, something he could not put a name to, waited for him in that place. It had seen him, marked him out, and now it was waiting for his return.

Ah, what nonsense! What fucking nonsense! A child's nightmare of ghosts and hobgoblins. What was he doing allowing himself to think like this, let alone giving any credence to those thoughts? When he had been a child he had suffered from nightmares. His night terrors would sometimes carry on into the daylight hours. He would be frightened of a creature he had convinced himself lived in some place or other – in a well, perhaps, or up a tree - and be unable to venture near that spot. When this happened, his mother had this thing she used to say that helped him see sense back then, and could still help him now. After all, didn't he feel just like that frightened child he had once been? "If it is real, little Neddy," his mother would ask him, "don't you think you ought to go warn our neighbours, maybe even the whole town?" Meaning, of course, that if you would not tell them because they would think you a fool for believing such a thing, then, deep down, you already knew it was not real. His response to his mother's question was, invariably, a sniff, followed by a vigorous shake of his head.

He hadn't thought of those conversations with his mother in years. What would she say if she were here right now? What would be the equivalent question? Easy, really. If he believed there was danger lurking in the new chapel, why would he not go and warn the good sisters? Or Allard, the gatekeeper, waiting at the gatehouse, and watching Ned's snail-like approach at that very moment? Or was that Swire up there? Ned's eyes were not what they once were. What difference did it make? Swire or Allard – whichever was on duty - why not grab him by the sleeve, insist he accompany Ned to the still doorless chapel, and get him to look inside? Make him see whatever sprite awaited anyone who set foot in the place? Because there was no sprite, that was why. None at all. Ned simply had the shakes because he had had a bad time of it there recently. He was still a bit raw, that was all. He was only human. He was bound to be reminded of it if he returned so soon to the spot where it all took place. And that really was all it was, unwanted reminders. Nothing more.

Ned sighed, shaking his head at his own foolishness, and then increased his pace. Soon he found himself passing under the stone arch of the Abbey gates. Swire, recognising him, and knowing already what his business there was, waved him through without comment. Ned now chuckled to himself at the very idea of his being able to make someone as oafish and stubborn as Swire do anything he did not want to do.

As Ned entered the Abbey grounds Swire called after him in his thick voice, "No interfering with any of the sisters this time, huh?" and then laughed heartily at his own joke.

Ned pretended to laugh at this too, but did not turn back lest the big man see the anger in his eyes, and read in them the curses he would have directed at him had he felt safe to do so.

It was not long before Ned's route took him around the side of the refectory building, beyond which lay the cloister – an area he, like most of the townsfolk, had only a vague idea about. Then, at right angles to the refectory, he went along the side of the dormitory building and, once past this, he was below the walls of the west end of the great Abbey Church itself. Rounding the corner, he walked along the south side of the building to where the south transept stuck out like a great stone promontory. As he rounded this, Ned's heart began to race, and he had a cold, fluttering feeling in the pit of his stomach. *Fool,* he told himself. *Stop it. Stop it, right now, or you'll never be trusted with work again. Then where will you and the family be?* He began to worry his legs would fail him again. As if coming to his rescue, he heard in his head, his mother's voice once more, "Don't you think you ought to go warn the neighbours?" Little Neddy and the adult Ned, both shook their heads emphatically. "Well, then…?" said his mother.

"Well, then…?" repeated Ned, startling himself with the sound of his own voice. He glanced around anxiously to see if he had been overheard. He already had a reputation for being at the centre of trouble in this place – albeit not trouble of his own making. He did not want to add being muddle-headed to that reputation. Thankfully, the only person who seemed to have noticed him at all from among the sisters and abbey servants he saw going about their business around him was a young lad who glanced up at Ned with look of surprise on his face, then ran off in the direction of William the Tiler and his assistant. Both men were stood looking down at a raised area in the ground that Ned assumed must be the tile kiln he had heard about, although he only had a passing knowledge of the process. Almost at that same moment, William looked up, presumably having heard the boy's running footsteps. In doing so, he noticed Ned, and raised a hand in greeting. Ned returned the gesture, reassured by the ordinariness of the greeting, and the air of calm normality it projected. William was working on the chapel, just as Ned was. He was going about the work of his own particular craft, just as Ned was. William gave no sign of being troubled by hobgoblins or any such creature. Why should Ned be?

******

"You alright there, young Alf?" asked Will.

Alf's eyes were bright with excitement about something. Enough excitement, in fact, for him to overcome his usual reticence, and talk about it. He did what he usually did when he wanted to talk, but feared his stammer would interfere. He took a deep breath. Still the words would not come.

"Well, boy?" demanded Silas. "We have things to do. Spit it out or swallow it back and keep it to yourself. Which'll it be?"

Will shot the old man an angry glance. Silas was generally more patient with Alf's speech problems, and he certainly knew better than to goad the boy; it only made things worse. The more anxious Alf became, the more his tongue tripped over the words he wanted it to form. It was Silas's hangover that was making him short tempered.

"Is it urgent, Alf?" asked Will. The boy looked confused. Will tried again. "I mean, do we need to know right now? Will it hurt to wait?" The boy shook his head. "Good. Then I tell you what. Why don't you get on with things here, and you can tell me later when the words come. How does that sound?" The boy nodded, still embarrassed, but calmer than he was. "Good," said Will. "Now, fetch me a jug of that water will you. There's a good lad."

When Alf had run off, Will turned to Silas, ready to admonish the old man. Silas spoke before he had the chance. "I know what you will tell me. And you are right. It's my head…"

"It's your greediness for ale. The boy cannot help his tongue. Your head…now that's your own doing. So maybe you should act like you suffer the same problem as Alf for a bit, huh?"

It was Silas who now looked confused. "Do what?"

"Say nothing for a while," explained Will, whose own head was hurting. Not from excess of alcohol, but from worry. Ingrith had sent a servant with word that she would not be joining them straight away that morning. She had something she wished him to see, but the Abbess must see it first. Which could only mean her design for the tile was complete. Glad as he was at the prospect of getting things moving again with the work, Will could not help worrying about what he might be asked to produce. If the Abbess liked Ingrith's idea, she would insist it be reproduced as accurately as possible. Whilst

Ingrith had seemed to understand his explanation about the limitations of the process when it came to images, there was always the chance that she had let herself get carried away and come up with something of which the Abbess would approve, but that Will could not reproduce. It was that possibility that was worrying him now.

It wasn't only that, though. Will found he also did not want to disappoint the girl.

******

Ned had been proud when he was chosen from the carpenters in the town to create the door for the new chapel. It had been expected that Abbess Rhoswen and the Sisters would bring in some outsider whose reputation for such work was known to them. As it turned out, that was not what they wanted. To his surprise, Ned had been called to a face to face interview with the Reverend Mother, and it was at that interview she had made her wishes known. Saint Merwinna, she told him, was a humble woman, but of very strong will. It was fitting, therefore, that her chapel, as much as possible should echo this in all things. Unfortunately, that was not be, she had said rather cryptically. However, where the door was concerned, she said, it could be achieved. What was required was nothing elaborate. What was required was a well-made, but simple door of strong local oak. Exactly the sort of thing that Ned knew he did well. Even so, he had taken extra care with this particular commission. After all, done well and it would serve him in both this world and the next. If it pleased the Abbess, he might see more work heading his way from the Abbey – and it was well known the Church had the money to pay. If it pleased the saint…well, his time in purgatory might be made a little shorter for it. Ned could think of no great sins in his life which would require expiation, but the priests made it plain that no one was without sin of some kind.

As the small chapel drew near, Ned said, "Well, then?" to himself once again, and pushed the handcart so it was only a few feet from the doorway. Then he undid the bindings and pulled away the sacking that covered the door. Looking down at his own work he smiled, and then ran his hand over the wood. It *was* good work. No doubt about it. All that was required were the few minor adjustments that were always needed for such tasks, and then the door could be hung.

The oak was heavy wood, but it would not be a problem. Ned was experienced in lifting and manoeuvring large wooden objects like the door. Nevertheless, it took all of his strength to swing it around off the handcart, and then lift it over to the front of chapel, where he propped it against the wall while he set about removing a makeshift cover of old boarding that had been placed over the doorway. The boarding had not been there on his last visit, and Ned could not help wandering if somehow it had been prompted by what took place between him and that overexcited young nun. Although what difference it would have made, he could not understand. In order for her to have been inside the chapel, she would still have had to remove it, and that would have made for exactly the same circumstances as before, and the possibility of the same thing happening. Then again, it would at least serve as a reminder that the chapel was still under construction and not somewhere to wander inside at leisure. Yes, he could see the sense of it now. If you were prepared to make the effort to take down the boarding on entering, and then replace it when your task inside was complete, you must have some incentive, some good reason, to venture inside in the first place.

Despite the anxiety being once again at the chapel caused him, Ned could not help but smile when he saw the rough-and-ready quality of the crude door, clearly improvised by someone with only the barest of carpentry skills. But then that was why people like Ned were paid for what they were able to do, wasn't it? Thank heavens for the incompetence of others, or there would be no work for the competent. That said, he still winced and cursed when, setting the boarding to one side, a large splinter entered the flesh at the base of his left palm. He couldn't remember the last time he got a splinter. In his trade rough edges were smoothed out, not left to injure the next poor soul who was unlucky enough to take hold of them. He lifted his palm to his mouth and used his teeth to nibble at the splinter, without success. The damn thing had broken off beneath the surface. He would look at it later. It would probably take the careful application of a bradawl to dig it out. There was one in the box of carpentry tools he had with him. He rubbed absentmindedly at the palm with his other hand as he stood back to look at the entrance, comparing it to the door set against the wall nearby. At first glance, his experienced eye told him the match looked good. Now to find out for certain. He walked over, heaved up the door – wincing again as the weight of it squeezed at the splinter in his palm – and manhandled it into place.

He had set the frame in place already, and the door and frame matched well, as far as Ned could see. Maybe a small amount could be shaved off one side where they were a little tight. The question now was: should he take the plane to the door or the frame? Easier to replace part of the frame than the door, should he accidently over-plane the area. The frame it would be then.

Quarter of an hour later, having worked the plane at the point where he judged the wood was a touch close-fitting, Ned once again set the door into the frame. He stood back. It looked good from the outside. But, like it or not, he would need to see what it was like from the inside. For a moment he considered trusting to his skills, and leaving it at that. Why bother going inside at all if, as it so obviously was, the thing was a good fit on the outside? It must follow that it looked good inside as well. The one followed on from the other, did it not?

No, it didn't. Ned knew better than that. Fitting well was

one thing. Looking just right was another. A door might swing to and fro with ease and sit happily in its frame, and still appear awkward. If the gap between door and frame was not the same thickness all along it spoiled the look of the thing. There was nothing for it; he would have to go inside. And that would be tricky without help. He had not considered that part. How good was the light in there? He would need a flame. And he could not hold a flame and the door in place at the same time. He needed extra hands. He looked about, saw William Tiler.

"You're lucky Will could spare me," Silas told Ned, as they walked back to the chapel, a few minutes later. "And that that old servant had a candle he would let you have the use of. Lucky, that's what you are. He might not have been free with his candle, you know. Or might not have had one."

Ned would have preferred it if William had come himself. Instead he had offered this old fool who seemed to derive great pleasure from stating the obvious, and stating it more than once. Still, he looked strong, and that was all Ned really needed – someone to hold the door in place while he looked over the join from the inside.

"You know what to do?" he asked as he stepped inside the chapel, candle in hand.

"Which way up does it go?" asked Silas.

Ned had been about to reply when he saw the facetious look on the old man's face. He dearly wanted to tell him to stop being such a damned fool, but reminded himself that the man was doing him a favour. So he simply smiled as if he were amused, and then beckoned for Silas to put the door in place. Silas did as he was asked, and Ned watched from the cool gloom inside the chapel as the gap between door and frame narrowed, shutting out more and more of the Abbey grounds and the summer sky. His heart beat faster, and he struggled to supress a rising panic; glad of the candle, even though its glow made the surrounding shadows beyond seem even deeper and blacker by contrast. A moment before the thing closed up fully, he realised Silas was saying something to him.

"What was that?" Ned asked.

"I said," said an amused sounding Silas. "When you're done in there, knock, and I'll open the door for you." He was clearly enjoying himself. Ned wondered if the fellow sensed how nervous he was, and was playing on this. He couldn't be, could he? *Why* would he? It must be his way, that was all. He was probably like this by nature. Ned knew the sort, and had never much enjoyed their company. Why William employed such a man was a mystery. All the same, he would have to stand Silas the cost of a few ales for his help. It was what William would expect.

As the door slotted into place Ned suddenly had the urge to put his shoulder to it, knock it aside, and escape from the confinement of the chapel. He fought the feeling back – if for no other reason than he could not stomach the thought of the laughter that would come from the old man outside if he were to do it. He took a deep, heaving breath, and raised the candle. *Get it done and get out*, he told himself. *Nothing simpler.*

Ned's left hand was held at his side, the palm, still throbbing from the splinter, rubbing distractedly against his thigh. In his right hand he held the candle. He raised his arm, so the candlelight fell on the area where the top of the door met the lintel beam. He ran the light along, grunted with satisfaction. The join there was good. He ran the light down the sides, left then right. Both were good – straight and even in width. He sighed with relief. He could get out of this place.

Something flitted past his face. Most likely a moth or a fly. A big one though, from the waft of its wings. Possibly a bat, then? After all, it would make sense in a place like this. Not quite big enough for that, though. Whatever it was, it came close again and Ned brushed it aside as he called out, "All done in here, old man." The door did not move. "All done in here, I say." Still the door did not move. Ned sighed again, only this time not with relief but with frustration. Obviously, the old fool outside was having his little game. His little jest. "Come on now, open up." Angry, but at least believing he understood now, Ned raised his hand and knocked on the oak. "You see," he shouted through the wood, "I'm knocking... as you said I should. Now, will you *please* let me out of here?" The door remained in place. Ned grunted in exasperation, and said to himself, "No fucking ale for you, you old devil!" He knocked again, harder this time. Still the door stayed in place. "Very well, if it's what you wish, old man," said Ned, all his patience gone, and shoved at the wood.

To his consternation the door did not seem to move at all. Not at all. The old man had looked strong, but not *that* strong. He must have put something against the door! Ned's anger was swiftly being replaced by alarm. He shoved at the door a second time, with the same results. "Enough!" he shouted. "Let me out of here!"

This time, Ned took a pace back, and then threw himself at the door, slamming his shoulder against it as hard as he could. The jolt as he made contact with the oak - immovable as ever - knocked the candle from his hand, the weak flame extinguished before it even hit the earth.

******

Outside in the sunlight, Silas wondered what was keeping the stout little carpenter. The humourless fellow had evidently been in a hurry to get the job done, and yet he was taking his precious time about it. After another minute or two Silas began to wonder if he was alright.

"Everything as it should be in there, carpenter?" he called.

When there was no response, Silas considered pulling the door away, but thought better of it. Perhaps the man was in the middle of some delicate adjustment. He did not want to pull the door out of position and spoil the man's work. He'd give it a few moments more.

******

With the candlelight gone, Ned found himself in almost complete darkness, which made no sense. Shouldn't there be some additional light from the small window? Too late Ned guessed that that too must have been boarded up like the doorway. He had not thought to check before he entered. Wait a moment…Yes, that was right…it had already been boarded up before, hadn't it? That was why the nun had been so frightened. She, like Ned, had been enveloped in total darkness when the doorway was closed. But the window opening would provide a way out. Silas would not have thought to block that too. How could he? It was too far up to roll anything against it. It would simply be a matter of Ned knocking away whatever boarding there was in place. It shouldn't be too difficult. He placed his hands against the wall, and began to feel his way around towards the window – all the while cursing Silas for his stupidity and spitefulness.

Even on a hot day like this one the stone was cool to the touch; almost oddly so. Still, not too far now. Another couple of feet and he should be there.

******

Silas was getting peeved. What the hell was taking the carpenter so long? Delicate adjustment or not, the man should have the decency to respond to his calls, and let him know how much longer he thought he was likely to be. Silas came to a decision. The man might well become angry. Who cared? Silas worked for William, not him. Gingerly, he took his hands away from on the door. To his surprise, instead of falling, it seemed to stay in place without being held. Well, what of it? The man was perfectly capable of pushing it aside when he wanted to leave.

Silas turned to walk away, and then thought better of it. He could not so easily abandon a task he had been set. He stepped up to the door and knocked.

"Hello?"

Nothing.

"You alright in there, man?"

Nothing.

Silas knocked much harder - so hard the vibration must surely cause the door to fall. And yet it stayed in place. Worried now, Silas forced his fingertips into the gap between frame and door, and then tugged as best he could. It would not come. He tried again with the same result. He stepped back and looked at the door, still standing in place.

"How in hell…?" he muttered.

A thought occurred to him. The man must have tools on his cart. He hurried over to the handcart, found a long file of some sort, took it back to the door, and attempted to lever the door away from the frame. The metal file snapped.

Silas banged once more on the door.

"I'll get help, wait there."

There were one or two people nearer, but Silas's first instinct was to call to Will.

On first hearing his name called, Will looked up, and then held out his hands and shook his head in a *'what's the matter?'* gesture. Then, when Silas called again, he must have recognized the matter was an urgent one because he began to run over. Confused, and uncertain what to do, Alf remained where he was for a moment or two, and then followed - his much younger legs making it no problem at all for him to catch up with his master. He could easily have overtaken him, in fact, but something in the tone of Silas's calls made Alf hang back. Whatever it was that was happening, Alf instinctively knew he did not want to be there without Will being there with him.

"What is it?" Will asked between breaths as he drew close to Silas, and slowed to a halt.

"Somethin' is not right in there," replied the old man, gesturing towards the chapel.

"Not right? What do you mean?"

"Somethin' is not right. I can't get in, and he's not saying anything back when I call to him."

Uncertain what to make of this, Will said, "Maybe he's busy?" He knew as soon as the words came out it was not sufficient to explain what Silas had said.

"I can't get in," repeated Silas. "And he don't say anythin' when I shout to him. You try for yourself if you think I'm tellin' a tale."

"Of course I don't," replied Will. Even so, he walked up to the door - which he assumed was merely propped in place while the carpenter did whatever it was he needed to do inside – and knocked. "You alright inside there, Ned?" There was silence, so Will knocked again, much harder. "I said are you alright in there?"

"You see now?" said Silas.

"He must have fallen ill…been taken with a fit or something like that," said Will.

"Why can't I get in then? The door is only leaning there. I was holding it for him. I wondered if he had fallen against it, but that wouldn't work to hold it like it is. Try it. Go on."

Will pushed. The door did not move. He leaned his shoulder against it, and pushed. Still it would not move. He frowned. "Perhaps he propped it somehow from inside. Maybe carpenters have a way…I don't know..." He stepped back, studied the chapel while he thought. It was then that the obvious occurred to him. "The window…Ah, how could I forget that? There's the window."

Silas looked up, saw where Will was pointing. "Damn it," he said, embarrassed not have thought of it himself.

Will strode over and peered into the darkness beyond the gap in the wall. "Ned? Ned, you ill? You hurt or something?" Will squinted into the darkness for signs of movement. He could only see the grey stone of the opposite wall. If Ned had collapsed, he would be on the floor, and none of it was visible from this angle. Will turned to Alf. "Come here lad. If I lift you, you can climb inside."

Alf looked frightened, took a step back.

"There's nothing to be scared of. The man in there needs our help, that's all. All I'm asking is that you jump down and move whatever it is that is stopping the door from opening. Nothing more than that. Will you do it?" *Whatever it is, or whoever,* thought Will, and briefly considered not sending the boy. He ought to climb in himself; the window was easily big enough. But Alf now had a determined look about him that Will did not want to crush. It would be good for the boy. "You'll do it then?"

Alf nodded.

"Good! Good lad!" said Will.

******

Ned could make no sense of it. The window just didn't seem to be where he knew it should be. He had run his hands up and down the length of the wall – twice now – and still not located the gap in the stonework. He was sobbing with frustration and a mounting sense of panic. Perhaps he had lost his sense of direction? Perhaps it was not this wall? But it *was*. It *had* to be. The window was in the same wall as the door, and that was the wall he was facing. He knew it was because he could feel the door to his left. Oh God, had they bricked the window in for some reason? Why, though? Why would they do that?

Without being aware that he was doing it, Ned began to pace in circles as his mind raced, trying to make sense of what was happening. Then it came to him: there was another window! The one into the church! He only had to find it.

It was then that he stepped off the edge, and into nothing.

He screamed in terror as he plunged down through the darkness, his arms and legs thrashing wildly in the air, his terrified cries echoing off the walls of whatever pit had swallowed him until, after what seemed like minutes, he hit the bottom.

To his relief – and astonishment – he did not seem badly hurt. A little shaken, a little bruised, but none of the snapping of bone and excruciating agony he had been dreading as he plummeted downward – assuming, that was, he even survived the fall.

Where was he, though? Had he stepped into a well? Or an abandoned and long forgotten cellar? Something that had been hidden all these years, and finally uncovered by the disturbance of the ground caused by the recent building work? Wherever he was, he needed to find a way out.

He sat up. Still in complete darkness, he checked himself over more thoroughly for signs of any injuries. He had none. It was a miracle. A genuine miracle. He had a thought: Saint Merwinna. Had she intervened on his behalf? He had heard stories of such things. When he was finally rescued, the people that came for him would never believe it. He could hardly believe it himself. And yet here he was. He had stepped off a precipice, fallen from some great height into an abyss, and yet he had not a single serious injury to speak of. Despite of himself, Ned laughed. He felt a little calmer. His miraculous escape had helped quell the panic that had come close to overwhelming him only moments early. He was able to think more clearly now. He would not be stuck in here forever. That old man…what was his name?… Silas…He would raise the alarm sooner or later. All Ned need do was sit tight. He laughed again. What else was he going to do? Blessed Saint Merwinna. He lifted his head to offer up a prayer of thanks. It was as he opened his mouth that the first of the earth landed upon him. A trickle at first. Probably something he had dislodged when he fell. Then more. Handfuls of dry dirt. Then more still. Heavy lumps of the stuff, intermingled with stones of ever-increasing size. Ned's first few screams echoed off walls somewhere out there in the surrounding darkness until, gradually, they began to be stifled by the dirt and grit that filled his mouth as he was slowly buried alive.

The immense pressure of the weight of so much earth on top of him was excruciating. It crushed his body, clamping him in place, making it impossible for him to move. He could not even heave his chest to gasp as dirt filled his mouth, and denied him the air he needed to live.

Eventually, all Ned knew was panic and pain. His entire being was centred on those two sensations. He was utterly alone, and dying down here, in a darkness so absolute that he feared not even God could find him.

Despite the near insanity to which such torment brought him, Ned managed a single, clear, utterly terrifying thought: was he dying or was he already beyond that? Was this, in fact, the Hell the men of God spoke so much about in their preaching? Which would mean this would never be over. *Never* be over. The thought tormented him as much as any of his physical agonies. An eternity of this, of enduring the unendurable. Suffering without end.

His mouth now so crammed and straining with earth, he could no longer scream, in his mind he prayed, pleaded - a red hot flame in the otherwise absolute darkness of his existence - *Please let it end. Please. Amen. Please. Amen. Please. Amen. Please. Amen. Please....*

******

"What's that, boy? What d'ya mean, he's not in there?" shouted Silas, incredulously.

Will scowled at Silas; put a finger to his lips. "Don't worry about that now, Alf," he called in through the window. "Get to the door and see if you can shift whatever is holding it fast. Don't worry if you can't. If I have to, I'll crawl in and help you with it. Give it a try, eh?"

Will saw Silas look at the narrow window, and then back

at Will's broad shoulders. Seeing the expression of doubt on the old man's face, Will added, "Or maybe Silas will, if I can't fit." Silas's mouth fell open at that suggestion, although he knew better than to object.

Before Will could say any more, the oak door Ned had set in place simply dropped forward onto the ground, revealing the boy.

"What the…? But…" said Silas.

Will stepped forward. He looked first at Alf standing in the open doorway, shielding his eyes against the light, and then he looked down at the door at the boy's feet.

"What did you do, boy?" he asked.

Alf shrugged, raised his hands palm outward and made a pushing motion.

"Nothing else?" asked Will. "Just…" he copied the gesture Alf had made.

Alf nodded his head, and then pointed back inside. Remembering Ned, Will stepped swiftly past him. Behind him he heard Alf say, "N…n…not…th…there!"

"Of course he's bloody there!" said Silas, and stepped past Alf to join Will inside the chapel. The light from the doorway was enough to reveal the truth of what Alf was saying. Ned the carpenter was not inside. Both men turned about, unable to believe the evidence of their own eyes.

"It's not right," said Silas under his breath. "Not right." Confused, he lurched back outside.

Behind him, Will called, "Wait! Silas. Get back in here! I've found him. Sweet Jesus, I've found him! He *is* here. He *is*!"

Silas glanced at Alf. The look of apprehension on the boy's face matched the uneasy feeling rising in his own chest. Stepping back inside, Silas found Will on his knees scrabbling at the dirt on the floor, tugging at something.

"It was sticking out…" he said without looking up. I only found it because I caught it with my foot.

Silas looked down and saw to his astonishment that Will was pulling at a man's hand, sticking up out of the earth and rubble of the chapel floor.

"Help me!" shouted Will.

Silas knelt and joined him as he scrabbled away the earth to reveal Ned the carpenter buried only one or two inches under the surface.

"How did he get *there*?" asked Silas.

"How in Hell would I know?" growled Will.

"Do you think he's alive?"

"I don't know. I don't know. Stop asking questions, and fucking dig, old man!"

******

CHAPTER 9

Rhoswen knew that Sir Geoffrey de Longe had no particular wish to hear the truth. No more than he did any of the speculation or outright lies that people might offer him concerning the recent death of Sister Euphemia. True of false, that was irrelevant to Sir Geoffrey de Longe. Expediency was what mattered to men like him. What he needed to put together was an acceptable explanation. An explanation he could comfortably give to the Sheriff if it became necessary. Sometimes the truth provided such an explanation. Then again, sometimes the truth could not be found, or the explanation it provided when it was proved to be anything but expedient or comfortable. Rhoswen knew from past experience that, as long as the final explanation arrived at was plausible enough to be believed and politic enough not to cause trouble, it would suffice. She watched the man as he crouched to look more closely at the bloodstains in the ambulatory where, over a week ago now, Sister Euphemia had been killed.

Over a week ago. The man had a duty. Where had he been all this time? Word had been sent to the Deputy Sheriff immediately, but only today had the man and his underling - a big man Sir Geoffrey addressed as Dicken - ridden through the Abbey gate and demanded an immediate audience with the Abbess.

"Here, you say?" asked Sir Geoffrey, indicating the spot at his feet.

"Quite obviously, yes. You can see the bloodstains for yourself, can you not? We've kept them covered until now, but there they are." Rhoswen flicked her hand in the general direction of the stains, careful to give the impression that they were of no real importance beyond the evidence they offered of the site of poor Sister Euphemia's killing. What she believed they had subsequently revealed to her about the wishes of Saint Merwinna regarding her chapel was of no concern of this brutish man, and probably beyond his faculties to appreciate. Whereas he might have sufficient wits to serve as Deputy to the Sheriff of Hampshire, and resolve matters such as the murder of a nun of no real name or consequence in a manner that suited the Sheriff's altogether temporal purposes, Rhoswen very much doubted he could grasp something as transcendent and divine as the interpretation of the saint's message.

Sir Geoffrey glanced up at Dicken who was standing only a few feet behind him. It seemed to Rhoswen that the two men exchanged amused smiles. She told herself she must conceal her temper; she must not allow them the pleasure of knowing how observing their attitude affected her.

Turning his face to Rhoswen, Sir Geoffrey asked, "You did not think to wash this away?"

"I thought you would wish to see it," replied Rhoswen. "It might assist you in reaching your conclusion…"

Sir Geoffrey gave a slight nod. "Indeed." He studied the bloodstains a moment more before asking, "There were two other members of your order with her when this took place. Yet they saw nothing of her assailant. How is that possible, I wonder?"

"No, only one was in here when it happened: Sister Winifred. The other… young Sister Marigold… arrived shortly afterward…It was over by then," replied Rhoswen.

"One, then. However, you have still not provided an answer to my question."

Rhoswen frowned. "Which was?"

Sir Geoffrey yawned as if he were bored, and more than a little frustrated. Rhoswen knew that in reality he was enjoying himself. The Sheriff was up in London, had been this past month. Sir Geoffrey, as his deputy, was enjoying the extra authority this absence afforded him. He repeated his question slowly, almost as if he believed she were simple-minded. "How is it possible they…she… saw nothing of the assailant? It will not have been dark; I see there are candles enough in this place to light my way to Winchester on a moonless night. So… I ask again… how was the attacker able to go unseen?"

"Sister Winifred…it is she who was in here…was not in the ambulatory at the time. All the candles in the world cannot light the way through solid stone pillars and walls."

Sir Geoffrey smiled coldly. "That I will grant you. However, unless whoever it was is still in here with us…" He glanced around in mock fear, "… they must have made their escape at some point, don't you think? Not enough pillars to hide the entire way to the doors, now are there? Hidden in the ambulatory or not. Besides, according to what you have told me, there were two sisters by then. Therefore two sets of eyes to have seen…well…nothing, you say."

"It could be done," insisted Rhoswen, unsure, even as she spoke, if it could.

Sir Geoffrey looked curious. "Oh? *How* could it be?"

"If one were to duck… and hide…it might be possible to remain beyond the view of another."

"Even if they were aware of your presence?"

"Even then…conceivably."

Sir Geoffrey reached forward and traced the outline of the stain with his fingers. Rhoswen openly grimaced, for it felt to her as if he were touching a holy relic. Immediately she wished she had had more control.

"My doing this bothers you, Reverend Mother?" asked Sir Geoffrey.

"Sister Euphemia was someone I had known for many years. That stain you touch…is…"

"A stain," said Sir Geoffrey dismissively, and stood up. "I wish to speak with the sister who was in here when it happened…Sister…?"

"Winifred. I know it will do no good my telling you that she has not fully recovered from that night. Speak with her if you must. She will tell you very little… and none of it of consequence."

"Not fully recovered, you say? She was injured? I was not aware of this."

"She was not injured bodily. The balance of her mind…it is… shaken."

"She is made mad, then?"

"Shaken."

"Where is she now, this madwoman?"

"The infirmary."

"Yes, I suppose she would be. Take us there."

"She may be walking in the grounds. If so, she may be difficult to locate speedily."

"Take me there," demanded Sir Geoffrey. Guessing Rhoswen was about to raise the same objection once more, he added, "Bring her to me if she is not there."

******

Rhoswen stared down at the lifeless body of the carpenter on the table. She had arrived at the infirmary with Sir Geoffrey and Dicken - taking them to talk with Sister Winifred - when she saw Sister Helewise supervising the laying of the man's body onto the table. Sir Geoffrey had barely glanced at it; he probably assumed it was just another sick nobody in the Abbey hospital being laid out by Abbey servants. But Rhoswen recognised the men carrying the body as Will and Silas, and this had made her curious. She decided that, as soon as she could, she would come back to find out whom it was, and what had happened. That had been sooner than she had thought because, despite Rhoswen's objections – perhaps, in part, because of them - Sir Geoffrey had insisted on speaking with Sister Winifred without the Abbess being present. He had agreed that one of the other sisters could sit with them, but not Rhoswen. So, not wanted by Sir Geoffrey, she had hurried back to find out who it was that Will and Silas had brought in. Sister Helewise was using a cloth to clear dirt from the poor man's distorted face. When it was clean, she looked up, saw Rhoswen standing there, gave a slight nod of her head, and stepped away so the Abbess might better see.

"I believe I know this man," said Rhoswen. "Not well, but I know him. He was engaged to make the door was he not?" She looked over at William Tiler. The man said nothing. "Master Tiler," she said, "he was engaged to build the door for Saint Merwinna's Chapel, is that not correct?"

Will had been absorbed in watching the earth being cleared from Ned's face. He could not understand how the man had come to be buried. Nor could he understand how so shallow a covering could have been sufficient to smother the life from him. He looked up when he heard his name. "Pardon me, Abbess Rhoswen, I did not…"

"This man was to build our door?"

"Oh…yes…he was. That is to say…he did. For the door is built. I understood him to be making any final adjustments. That is why he was at the Abbey today." Will looked at the man lying there in front of him. "It is a fine door. The man was a good carpenter. I cannot understand how he is now dead."

"You cannot?" asked Rhoswen. "That is a pity. It was my hope that you could explain this to me."

"That I cannot, Reverend Mother. How a man can lose his life from lack of air when he is covered by only a few spadesful of earth …. Why he would not sit up…shake himself free of it when that was all it would have taken…I cannot say. Nor can I say how he got that way in the first place."

Sister Helewise was frowning. "Given your description of how he was when you found him, I fear the mystery we are confronted with may be far greater than that, Master Tiler. It is possible this man did not die from suffocation. He may have been deprived of air…indeed he shows some signs of it… but I am not certain it was the eventual cause of his death."

"Oh…?" asked Rhoswen. She glowered at Will for a moment, wondering if he had been deliberately lying to her. She saw immediately from his bewildered expression that he had not been. The man had apparently spoken what he believed was the truth.

"This poor man appears to me to have been crushed to death," explained Sister Helewise. She spoke as if she could not quite believe what she was telling them. "Many of his bones are broken. Some of them completely shattered. His ribs are all smashed. His jaw splintered. When you brought him to me William, I assumed there had been some terrible collapse."

"No, sister," said Will. "Not the chapel. It still stands. All of it."

Silas, standing at Will's side, added, "T'was as if a dog or fox or some such had scrabbled a bit of earth over him. Like to hide a catch for later. No more than that."

Both Abbess Rhoswen and Sister Helewise looked from Silas to Will. But if the Tiler felt his assistant's description crude or inaccurate, he did not say so.

Before any of them spoke again, Rhoswen heard the unwelcome voice of Sir Geoffrey from the other side of the room.

"A waste of our time, Dicken. We might as well ask for the story from one of the cats that roam this place." He laughed at his own joke. "They might have seen something while keeping down the mice. Ah, Reverend Mother."

"Sir Geoffrey," replied Rhoswen. "Your interview was not a success?"

"It was not. It was barely an interview. The woman is mad. She saw nothing, and was terrified by what she saw. She witnessed everything, and can describe none of it." As he spoke, Sir Geoffrey noticed the corpse of the carpenter. "What have we here?" A thought struck him, and he took a step back, placed a gauntleted hand over his mouth. "Not diseased, I hope?"

Rhoswen fought back the impulse to say *yes, the plague took him* or claim that the remains of the man lying before them were those of a leper. Instead, she said, "The man was a carpenter. He met with an accident. It is tragic."

Sir Geoffrey nodded, and said, "Tragic," although with no real attempt at sincerity. He turned away, and was about to leave, when Dicken took his arm and held him back. While Sir Geoffrey had been speaking to the Abbess, Dicken explained, he himself had been watching the others. Dicken was a man with experience in such things and, to his mind, they looked uneasy. Sir Geoffrey looked a little perplexed to begin with, but evidently respected his man's judgement because he did not object when Dicken began to question them.

Hand on the hilt of his sword, Dicken stepped up to Silas and stood looking down at him without speaking for a few moments. Silas knew better than to maintain eye contact with such a man, and looked down at the floor. Eventually Dicken said, "You look troubled, old man. What is the cause of it?"

Silas also knew better than to lie. "The manner of this man's end. T'was odd, sir."

"*Odd?*" echoed Sir Geoffrey, stepping alongside Dicken, and looking into Silas's face. "How so?"

Silas coughed, and shuffled his feet. "Well, you know…"

"No, I *don't* know. That's why I'm asking *you*, man. How can I know until you tell me?" Sir Geoffrey stepped even closer to Silas, and prodded him painfully in the chest. "Spit it out, fellow. Spit it out!"

The close scrutiny of someone like Sir Geoffrey only served to fluster the old man even more. "It was not like a death should be," he said. "That's right, Will, ain't it?"

Will gave Silas the faintest of nods; it was not for them to conceal anything. Dicken spotted this, and he turned to Will instead. "Let us save time. *Will*, is it? Why don't *you* tell it to Sir Geoffrey?"

"I shall, sir. Only it is not so easy to understand." Noting the impatience on the faces of Sir Geoffrey and Dicken, Will added hastily, "I only say that so you will know that I cannot account for what happened." Both Dicken and Sir Geoffrey continued to look impatient. "That said, I will gladly tell what I know," said Will, hurriedly.

"*Gladly*?" mocked Dicken. He turned briefly to Sir Geoffrey. The two of them exchanged smirks. "He's glad," said Dicken.

"I am pleased to hear it," said Sir Geoffrey. Looking again at Will, he said, "Now, for the love of all that is holy, go on with your tale. The day grows ever warmer and, if I am not mistaken, the bowels of the dead man failed him when he died. He will soon be of more interest to the flies than he is to me. So get on with it."

Will explained what had happened, and how they had found Ned inside the chapel. When he was finished, Sir Geoffrey asked, "Why was he nervous, this carpenter?"

"I beg your pardon, sir?" asked Will.

"At the start of your tale, you said the man was nervous. He was hanging a door not riding into battle. Why on earth should he be nervous?"

"On account of what happened before, with Ingrith…"

"Ingrith? We have Ingrith to consider now. Who is she?"

To Will, hearing himself say Ingrith's name out loud to these people had felt somehow like an indiscretion. Hearing it repeated back by Sir Geoffrey, the Sheriff of Hampshire's deputy, was worse; it changed that feeling to one of betrayal. "It was none of the girl's doing what happened," he said. "She had a bit of a shock, poor thing, that's all. She was unwilling for them to take him away after it happened. Said it wasn't his fault. Made a point of it, she did."

Sir Geoffrey cocked his head. "Is that so? I am confused. Did you not just now tell me it was *not* her fault? 'None of her doing', I believe you said."

For a moment Will did not understand the question. He

knew he was being toyed with, but was uncertain what he should say. "It… wasn't…it…"

Sir Geoffrey indicated the lifeless body of the carpenter lying on the table between them. "Then why would she say it was not this man's fault either? Explain that to me. If *he* was not, if *she* was not, then who *was* to blame, hmmm. And for *what*, exactly?"

"Nobody. It was neither, as I understand it," offered the Abbess, having noted Will's confusion. "It was a misunderstanding. The girl…Ingrith… was praying in our new chapel. This man…a carpenter… as William explained…he was engaged to build and fit the new door. She was taken by surprise by his sudden arrival as he went about that task. Nothing more than that."

The deputy sheriff deliberately narrowed his eyes to emphasise the fact that he was pondering what she had told him. "Nobody's fault, you say? I wonder at that." A trace of a smile now appeared on his lips. It was not very different from the smirk he had exchanged with Dicken only moments earlier. The Abbess knew immediately what it meant.

"Nobody's fault," she emphasised, already knowing it was too late. He had found the explanation for which he searched.

"It has been my experience that in such things it is almost never *nobody's* fault," said Sir Geoffrey. "Not this kind of thing…And by that, I mean where men and women are involved. There is always someone behind the 'misunderstanding', as you choose to describe it; someone who understands only too well." He raised his eyebrows expectantly, as if he were waiting – hoping, even – for Rhoswen to contradict him, but she knew better than to argue, and remained silent. When he saw that she would say nothing, Sir Geoffrey filled the silence himself. "So, then, no confusion here that I can see. None whatsoever. Your carpenter made an attempt on the poor girl's virtue, and was, thank the Lord, interrupted before he could carry out his reprehensible intentions. You may object. You may say he had no prior reputation for such behaviour. Let me assure you that such is quite often the case. It may be that the carpenter was a good man up until that moment. But it may also be that never before had such temptation been put before him. And then he, all of a sudden, finds himself…a man in his middle years…alone with this girl. This…young…virginal... girl. And well…he is…*was*…a man with the tastes and urges of a man." Sir Geoffrey turned to Will. "This fellow here tells me the girl is blameless. I wonder, is that true? She may not have wanted or expected such an attack. Yet she might have prevented it. Might she not have anticipated such a thing had she but thought through her actions? If she had had a care, this man might not be lying here before us, his soul on its way to damnation."

"I do not understand you," said Rhoswen, compelled to break her silence.

"Surely it is simple," said Sir Geoffrey, in pretend surprise. "Opportunity presented itself. He was tested. He failed the test. Then, overcome with remorse, he goes back to the scene of his shame and takes his own life."

"By throwing himself on the floor, and then smothering himself with earth until he is crushed to death by it?" said Sister Helewise. "Absurd! You distort the facts to fit your own expedient version of them. No man…even one consumed by guilt as you claim…could possibly have…"

"Sister! Enough!" warned Rhoswen. "You forget yourself."

Sir Geoffrey nodded. "Thank you for that, Reverend Mother. Your good sister here did forget her place, I think. If you had not done so, I myself would have been obliged to remind her of it…and less gently than you have done. However, it may be that I *am* a trifle guilty of oversimplifying things. Though not in the manner suggested by this impudent and ill-mannered crone." He pursed his lips for a few seconds before he went on. "You see, I do consider there is more to tell here. That is because, having given it thought, I am now of the opinion that this man was not overcome by remorse at one assault, but at two. He was guilty of another, far more serious, attack. An attack with a deadly and tragic outcome."

Rhoswen nodded. Not in agreement with Sir Geoffrey, but in resignation at what she knew was to come.

"The reason I was called here," continued Sir Geoffrey, "was to inquire into the violent death of your Sister Euphemia. A woman of God murdered in the house of God. A more heinous crime I cannot easily conceive. A crime for which there are no suspects and no witnesses. At least no useful witnesses. Yet now, by God's will, we have been provided with our explanation."

"Have we?" asked Sister Helewise, sardonically, and received a surreptitious warning pinch on the arm from Rhoswen, who was standing next to her.

Either Sir Geoffrey did not pick up on any of this, or he chose to ignore it. "We have," he replied. "The explanation lies dead before us. Your young Ingrith had a fortunate escape. For this man had already brutally murdered one of your order."

"Your explanation for the death of our Sister Euphemia will be that this man was guilty of her murder," said Rhoswen in a flat tone. It had not been put as a question. Sir Geoffrey answered it, nonetheless.

"It will be. After which he then killed himself. There..." He snapped his fingers, although the gauntlet he wore muffled any sound it might have made. "Your troubles here are at an end. Your frightened sisters may walk this place in safety once more."

"And the unusual manner of his death?" asked Rhoswen.

"His suicide," corrected Sir Geoffrey. "It was unusual...peculiar...that much I will grant you. However, the peculiarity of it is a mere detail. The way in which he chose to end his miserable life, although hard for us to know how he achieved it, is not important. Men will do extraordinary things when the mind is fevered. And this man's mind we can assume was tormented by guilt. In a moment of clarity he saw what he had done…what he was capable of doing again…and chose, God be praised, to put an end to it all. A single moral act in an otherwise immoral life. That is what matters here, the fact that he did kill himself, and he and his evil ways will haunt this Abbey no more."

Rhoswen remained unconvinced. "Suicide is a crime against God… there are steps we must take. I would wish to be certain before taking them because of the danger to what may be an innocent man's soul. You know as well as I that, if it was suicide, then…"

"It was," interrupted Sir Geoffrey, impatiently.

"It was not!" insisted Sister Helewise, no longer able to remain silent on the matter, in spite of the warnings she had received. "You play with a man's very soul!"

Sir Geoffrey looked away, shook his head, and then, turning back, he slapped the old nun so hard she fell to the floor. When both Will and Rhoswen moved forward to help her up, Sir Geoffrey raised a hand to stop them. "No, you will let her remain where she is for a while. It may help to remind her to hold her tongue in future." He glanced down at Sister Helewise who had struggled to her knees, and was wiping blood away from her mouth with the back of her hand. "Anything you wish to say to me now, sister?"

Rhoswen glanced anxiously at the old woman, whose eyes now shone with tears; as much, Rhoswen suspected, from anger as from pain and shock. To Rhoswen's relief, Sister Helewise shook her head.

"Are you absolutely sure?" asked Sir Geoffrey. "Nothing you wish to add? Nothing you think I should know?" Sister Helewise shook her head again, then looked away. Sir Geoffrey smiled. "Good. Now, as I was saying, it *was* suicide…" His tone softened before he added, "But can we not be generous today, hmm?"

"I do not follow your meaning," said Rhoswen.

"This man…he had family?" asked Sir Geoffrey.

"In all probability …" Rhoswen turned to Will. "Did he ever speak of them to you, William?"

"I did not know him that well, Reverend Mother," said Will.

"He did," said Sister Helewise, through swollen and bloodied lips. "I have treated their ailments in the past."

Rhoswen was afraid Sir Geoffrey would hit Sister Helewise again, or worse. Instead, he ignored her and, feigning an exaggerated beneficence, said to Rhoswen. "Well then, Reverend Mother, would you add to his family's shame and grief by stripping them of any possessions that belonged to him? I don't believe any of us wish for that to happen. Oh, no, no, no. And yet, if we pursue the law on such things to its very letter, then we must strip this man's relatives of all possessions that can be attributed to him. His wretched children would inherit nothing but his shame. Self-murder is, after all, a crime against the Crown as well as God Almighty. The Crown has the right to confiscate all the deceased's property. Do you wish this business dragged out into the light so you can examine it? So you can be sure? What good can come of that? No, no, no. If it bothers you, you must decide what to do to ease your own mind on the matter, of course. But be assured, if you examine things publicly, if you do not agree with my findings here, I will see to it that his family is ruined."

"I am simply saying I think it possible he is not a suicide!" protested Rhoswen.

"That may well be your finding. But if I am forced to continue to look at all that has happened here because of a refusal on your part to let things rest, I will have no other choice than to make it known that I myself *do* believe him to have taken his own life. I will then have to take the appropriate action. Do you see what I am saying?" Rhoswen said nothing, only lowered her head. "Good. Then we understand each other," said Sir Geoffrey. "You find a crossroads and bury him there in un-consecrated ground as a suicide or, if you must, give him a burial in consecrated ground as a soul worthy of consideration on judgement day. Either way, it matters not to me. Only, whatever you do, do it quietly... discreetly. Abide by that and, as far as I am concerned, the matter is over with." Without waiting for a response, he turned to Dicken. "Come. Let us be gone from this stinking corpse. Nothing more is required of us here. We have business in Alresford. We can be there by tomorrow morning if we ride out now."

As both men were leaving, Dicken stopped and studied the face of the corpse for a moment. He looked up at Will. "This man have a handcart?"

"A handcart? Yes, he did," replied Will, puzzled by the question.

Dicken nodded. "Thought so. Rode past him coming in, if I am not mistaken. Didn't look much of a dangerous type standing out there on the track...no killer...not a little fat fellow such as this." He smiled - first to himself, and then, less sincerely, at them all. "Then again, who can tell who has it in him to kill, hmm? Who can tell?" His smile vanished abruptly. "None of *you* people, I think."

******

CHAPTER 10

Ingrith smiled, in spite of herself. She could not help the pride that swelled in her. She patted the folded piece of vellum, and then lifted it, holding it against her chest. The design was good; she knew it was. She looked forward to the opportunity to show it to Abbess Rhoswen and, as much - maybe more - to showing it to Will. He, more than anyone, must appreciate the skill, the artistry it had required. The Abbess would simply attribute the success of the thing to God and... Ingrith took a breath. To God. That was right. The Abbess would be right. If Ingrith had any kind of gift, it was a gift that had been given to her by God. She must remember that. Humility, that was the correct way. She could be pleased with the design, yes: pleased at what God had given her the gift to do, and, more importantly, humbled by such a gift.

Oh, but it would be good to show Will. He would smile when he saw it. He would understand straightaway. It might take some explaining to the Abbess. She was a clever woman, but she was not an artisan with the awareness of such things that came with being one. Ingrith stepped out from the small cubicle in the cloister that had been allotted to her while she worked on the design for the tile, and hurried along the passage until she reached a turning into another, much shorter, passage to a door that opened onto the Abbey grounds outside. Once through that door, she hurried along the side of the refectory, turned the corner past the west end of the great Abbey Church and stopped. She had expected to see Will across by the kiln at this time of day. He was not there. She could only see the boy, Alfred. He was sitting on the end of a cart, swinging his legs and gazing about himself absent-mindedly. If Will saw him looking so idle, thought Ingrith, he might fetch the boy a clout around the ear. She walked over.

"Hello, young Alfred," she said as she drew near. Alf, who had not noticed her approaching, looked up, startled. Ingrith smiled. "Well now, you know what the apostle Paul says about idle hands!" As soon as the words came out of her mouth, she realised that the boy probably had no idea what idleness meant, let alone what Paul had to say about it. As if to confirm her thoughts, Alf shook his head, but he did not look down, as she knew he might if spoken to by most adults. Ingrith felt a tightening of her heart at this display of trust. "Where is your master," she asked. "Where is William?"

Alf lifted an arm and pointed back in the direction she had come.

"Oh, the chapel. He is inside St Merwinna's Chapel?" Of course, thought Ingrith. She should have thought to look there first. To her surprise, Alf shook his head.

"He's not in there?"

Alf shook his head once more.

"Where, then?"

Alf pointed again. Ingrith tried hard to follow his gesture; there were several buildings roughly in that direction that he might mean.

"I'm sorry, Alfred, I do not understand. Would you tell me?" she asked, then added, "or take me, if you do not wish to speak."

Alf shook his head at the latter suggestion and pointed at the ground.

"You have to stay here?" asked Ingrith.

Alf nodded.

"Then I'm afraid I must ask once more that you tell me."

Now Alf did look down at his feet. They had stopped swinging.

"I will not laugh at your struggle. I certainly will not scold you, if that is what you worry about. The opposite is true in fact. I will be grateful for your trust in me."

Alf did not move for a moment, and then, slowly he lifted his head. He still did not look at Ingrith. "F...f...fir..." he struggled.

"Font?" said Ingrith without thinking, and immediately appreciated how ridiculous the suggestion was.

Alf stopped for a minute as if composing himself. "F...f..." he began again. Ingrith struggled to think of any building in the Abbey complex that began with an F. Then Alf managed to say, "*Firmary!*"

Ingrith smiled. "Ah, the infirmary. You mean the infirmary?"

Alf nodded, pleased. And relieved.

A thought struck Ingrith. "Is your master sick or injured?"

"No," said Alf, without apparent difficulty.

"Silas, then?" asked Ingrith.

"No."

"Why then is he there?"

"D...d...dead man," said Alf.

"Dead? Who is dead?"

Alf attempted to speak again. Unfortunately, Ingrith's anxiety had infected him, and he began to struggle. "C...c...ca..." He gave up the attempt and, instead, mimed some actions. They were easily recognisable as sawing and hammering.

"You mean the carpenter?"

Alf nodded.

"He's *dead?*"

Alf nodded again.

It did not take long to cross the stretch of ground between where she had spoken with Alf and the infirmary. In confirmation of what the boy had told her, Ingrith saw a body she easily recognised as that of the man who had unintentionally startled her only a few days before. Neither Will nor Silas was in sight. One of the sisters helping out in the infirmary explained that Will had agreed to accompany Sister Helewise into the town. They were going to the home of the carpenter in order to break the tragic news to his family. As for Silas, as far as the sister knew, he had been told to go back to work, and should have been with the boy. The mystery of his whereabouts was explained as Ingrith was leaving the infirmary and spotted the old man exiting one of the servants' latrine huts, making no effort to conceal the fact that he was adjusting his hose having recently removed them to facilitate emptying his bowels.

******

Rhoswen sat alone in her receiving room. She had moved her chair so that she now faced the painting depicting Saint Merwinna, and she gazed up at the image as she struggled to bring some kind of order to the confusion of thoughts running through her mind.

Sister Euphemia was at peace now. That must be what really mattered. It was true that – despite Sir Geoffrey's doubtful claims to the contrary - the mystery of her killing remained unsolved, but that was in the past. What was done was done, and Sister Euphemia's time of suffering was at an end. In that respect, if no other, the dead woman was blessed. Sir Geoffrey had said that to kill someone in the house of God was a terrible sin and, despite the fact that Rhoswen was all too aware that it had been said more for effect than through any real conviction on the man's part, it remained true. However, if one were to be the victim of such a dreadful crime, what better place than a church for God to witness your fate? Of course, nobody would want to die like that, but at least there was the comfort of the certainty that He saw all. He knew.

The problem remained, nonetheless. Who had really killed Sister Euphemia, and were they still at large - maybe even preparing to kill again? Had they already done so? Had they also been responsible for the death of the carpenter? Was he, in fact, not the perpetrator of a brutal and murderous crime, as he was being characterised by Sir Geoffrey and the dreadful Dicken, but the victim of one? Which would mean there might still be a danger to the sisters - still alive and lying in wait out there somewhere right now. Nevertheless, there was the undeniable convenience of the solution Sir Geoffrey had decided upon. Blame the carpenter, and there was no unsolved mystery to cast a shadow over the building of the new chapel. The two things – the chapel and the deaths - would be considered completely unrelated by any who knew of them. Even though, as Rhoswen herself knew, there *were* related. Inextricably so, in fact. Had not her own change of mind on the matter of the chapel been brought about by a message from the saint? And had not the medium for that message been the very blood spilled in the killing of Sister Euphemia? That was as much of a mystery as anything else. Why had the saint used what would otherwise have been a terrible and tragic event - one with no redeeming aspects to it whatsoever - as the means to deliver her message and convey her wishes? Was it possible that Sister Euphemia's death was an integral part of it all; a part of the saint's design? If so, the woman really was blessed. She had been chosen for what could almost be considered a martyr's death. The kind of death that assured a place in heaven, if any could. Rhoswen bowed her head and raised her hands, intending to pray, to give thanks to God and Saint Merwinna.

She hesitated. She was uncertain which aspects of all that had taken place she should be giving thanks for. After all, people had died. Should she, as an alternative, simply pray for Sister Euphemia's innocent soul or the, more than likely, equally innocent soul of that of the poor maligned carpenter? She tried again to pray. Failed again. Instead, she put her hands over her face, and began to cry into them in a way she had not done for many years; not since she was a child. This wonderful thing – the message from the saint; her blessing for the chapel; the kind of thing Rhoswen had hoped for all of her life – was somehow sullied, mired in the mystery surrounding two innocent deaths. Rhoswen knew it. She also knew that she would have to keep that knowledge to herself and live with any consequences of having done so if she wanted to see the saint's chapel completed. Even to the extent of burying the carpenter in unhallowed ground, thereby condemning his soul to eternal purgatory? Could she do that, despite the distinct possibility – particularly according to what Sister Helewise said - that his death had not been suicide? Because, if Sir Geoffrey's version of events were to be given out as the accurate one, that was what she would have to do in order to give that version the appearance of truthfulness. Yes, she would do it. For now, at least, she must. But she vowed to have the carpenter secretly moved to a better resting place in the future when things had quietened down a little. As for what the poor man's family must endure in the meantime, there was little she could do. That was a sacrifice that must be made, even if it were an unjust and unknowing one. Perhaps there would be a reward for them also when the time came that they too met their maker?

After a while, Rhoswen's chest stopped heaving, and she looked up once again at the painting. Its lines and shapes were distorted by the liquid in her eyes. She sniffed, then wiped away the last of the tears, and was able to see it more clearly. Perhaps she, like Merwinna, was being tested? The path the faithful were required to walk was not meant to be an easy path, and the choices it required of you were not necessarily straightforward ones. After all, that was the nature of faith, was it not? Rhoswen would pray after all. Not merely to give thanks. She must also ask for guidance and, more than that, the strength to keep the secret with which the Lord had chosen to burden her.

******

"How'd they take it?" asked Silas when he saw Will approach later that afternoon.

"They danced around like it was the first day of May," snapped Will.

Scowling, Silas said nothing more and returned to packing away the tools.

Will turned to Alf. "Nobody came to steal anything while I was gone did they?" Alf shook his head. "Good lad," said Will, ruffling the boy's hair. Then, feeling a touch guilty for having snapped at the old man he said. "Watching that Helewise telling the carpenter's family he was gone near broke my heart. And I tell you this Silas, whatever that Sir Geoffrey has to say about the matter, I don't believe that Ned did self-murder, do you?"

"No I do not!" agreed Silas unnecessarily emphatically, pleased to be speaking once more. "That said, I could not tell you what *did* happen in that chapel. One moment he's inside measuring up, the next he's numbered among the dead…. Dirt all over him there may have been, but not enough to smother a mouse, let alone crush a full-grown man. It gives me the shivers, Will. Somethin' not right about it. A fool could tell you that."

Will suppressed the urge to respond by saying that a fool just had. He had known it was inevitable Silas would pick up on the mysteriousness of the carpenter's death, and resigned himself to the fact that it would be a subject of speculation for the old man for some time to come. Will knew he himself would not be able to forget about it easily either. Nor could he explain it. Perhaps the Abbess – a clever and educated woman – would be able to do so when she had had more time to think on the matter. Will could never ask her, of course, but she might discuss it among the sisters, so Ingrith might learn what was said and pass it on to him. Then again, Ingrith had had more than her fair share of frights linked to that chapel and Ned the carpenter, and might not want to talk about it. He resolved to hold his tongue on the matter and to make sure Silas did the same when Ingrith was present.

Will felt a tugging at his sleeve. Alf wanted to say something.

"What is it, lad?" he asked. "Take your time. You can do it. What have I said about relaxing, remember? You are always better when you don't think about it."

"Ingrith..c... came."

"Oh, did she say what she wanted?"

Alf shook his head.

"I hope it was because she's got a pattern for the tile," said Silas. "Why it has to be her to do it, I'll never know." He saw Will glower. "I know, I know, the Abbess wants it that way. But a woman's view on the matter...well, it can't be right, now can it? Still, if it has to be that girl, then the sooner the better, I say."

"So do I," agreed Will. "So do I. Idle hands, hmm, Alf?" To Will's surprise, Alf looked as if he had something to add. "What is it boy?" he asked, curious as to what it might be.

"P..P..Postle Paul," said Alfred proudly.

"Whatever you say, lad," said Will, with a perplexed shake of his head. "Whatever you say."

******

Shortly after first light the following day Will, Silas, and Alf left their lodgings in the town and returned to the Abbey. Will was already fretting; there really was very little left for them to do until Ingrith had a tile design they could use. They had built the kiln, and the clay was as ready as it would ever be. He supposed they could make a start on preparing the chapel floor if they had to. It was a bit too soon for that for Will's liking, but if the work ran out, the money ran out. He was bound by agreement to complete this job, and it could easily start to cost him money, rather than make it for him, if he were forced to linger while the girl and the Abbess fussed over what the design should be. He had some coins put aside, but hoped he would not have to use any of them. So, when

Ingrith stepped out in front of them as they passed through the Abbey gates, his hope was that the broad smile she had upon her face meant she had the news he hoped for.

"Well?" asked Will the moment he saw her.

"And a fine morning to you too, master Tiler," replied Ingrith, still smiling.

Will saw she held something behind her back. "Well...?" he said again, reaching forward, finding that – despite his better judgement – a smile was also forming on his own lips. Ingrith raised her eyebrows. Will sighed good-naturedly. "Very well. *Good morning*, Ingrith. Now, let me see, would you please."

Will held out his hand, but Ingrith took a step backward shaking her head. For an uncomfortable moment Will was reminded of the way some of the tavern girls tempted their customers. He felt ashamed of the thought and pushed it aside.

"Good morning Silas, good morning Alfred," said Ingrith, her teasing tone also suggesting things to Will of which he found himself ashamed.

Will turned to the old man and the boy. "Better wish her a good morning or we'll never see what she hides behind her back," said Will.

"Mornin' girl," said Silas, scratching his backside as he did so.

Ingrith turned to Alf. "And you, Alfred?"

Alf reddened, took a deep breath, but struggled to say anything.

"It comes and goes with him," explained Will. "Because you made a point of asking for it, he had time to think about it, and it's thinking on it that chokes him up."

"Never mind," said Ingrith. Clearly sorry to have caused the boy any distress, she put an arm around his shoulders as the group walked over towards the kiln where they had left Will's cart the previous evening – assured by the Abbey servants that its contents would be safe within the Abbey grounds. With the other arm Ingrith had had handed Will a rolled-up sheet of vellum. To her frustration, he seemed to be deliberately holding back from unfolding it until they reached the cart, even though she knew the temptation to do so must be great. She realised he was paying her back for her own teasing.

As they neared the cart, Alf ran ahead, startling a small band of rooks that had gathered just beyond it, picking out the worms in the earth disturbed by the digging of the kiln. Once there, the boy began unrigging the covering of the cart and lifting out the tools.

"Hold there a moment, Alf," said Will. Alf stopped, looked back, puzzled. It was clear to Will that the boy had not understood the significance of Ingrith's early appearance or the folded vellum she had passed to him. He held it up. "Don't you want to see what it is we shall be making?"

Alf's eyes grew wide with interest, and he nodded.

Will had a sudden worry. "The Abbess has seen this?"

"She has," replied Ingrith.

"So it has her approval?" asked Will.

"It does."

"That is good."

Ingrith watched as Will squatted and began to unfold the vellum on the grass at his feet.

"'Tis' a big piece for a single tile, girl," observed Silas, stating something that had already occurred to Will.

"For a single tile it would be," said Ingrith, her words confirming Will's suspicion only moments before what he saw spread out before him did the same.

"Well now, ain't that something," said Silas.

Alf came and stood at Will's shoulder. "W...? W...?" he stammered.

"It's called a mosaic," said Will in reply. "Lots of tiles used to make a single, bigger image in this fashion...it's called a mosaic. See how each one is different but makes up a part of the whole picture... like a stone in a wall?" He looked up at

Ingrith. "It's a wonder, girl!" he said, "Truly, it is." He reached out and began tracing the lines inked into the surface.

Ingrith had divided the image up into squares, each one representing a tile. Around the edge of the image there were many blank squares. These were simply there to represent those tiles necessary to cover the full area of the chapel floor. At the image's centre, however, were around a hundred individual tiles – Will had not yet counted - each containing its own unique set of lines and blocks of solid ink that, when put together, formed a representation of the image of St Merwinna in the Abbess's room. It was not an exact reproduction, however. Ingrith had - either instinctively or, perhaps, consciously aware of the limitations of the process – reduced some of the more complex elements of the original in such a way that they could be reproduced in the form of inlaid tiles. The combination of the lines, and the shapes they created – some empty, some filled in - had a satisfying balance to them. Gone was the uncomfortable comeliness of the original image, now replaced by a harmony and order that, while it still represented the saint, conveyed a sense of piety that was much more fitting whilst, at the same time, managing, if anything, to be more arresting than the original painting. Little wonder then that the Abbess had approved.

"It's a wonder!" Will said again.

"That it is," agreed Silas.

Ingrith blushed, pleased by their reaction. "Thank you," she said.

Alf, who had not, until then, taken his eyes from the vellum, looked up at her. "Wun...da." he said carefully, and then looked away shyly.

A few more minutes passed, during which time the two men and the boy continued to study the vellum, making approving noises or pointing out some or other detail that had caught their eye. Eventually, Will looked over at Ingrith. To his surprise, a slight frown now wrinkled her brow.

Anticipating her question, he said, "Oh, yes, it *can* be made. It will be difficult to get it right, mind you. And it will take time. There are many different pieces." He looked directly at Ingrith. "Does your Abbess understand that? To make this…it will require a great deal of time and work. It's unavoidable if we are to get it right."

"That is understood Master Tiler," said a voice behind him.

Will turned, saw Abbess Rhoswen approaching them.

"I knew Ingrith would be eager to show her work to you." She turned to Ingrith. "Forgive me, daughter, I followed you." To Will she said, "It *can* be made, then?"

"As I explained to Ingrith just now, it can, but it will take…"

"Time," said Rhoswen, a little impatiently. "I heard what you said. You may take the time. You have my blessing."

"I would ask something else of you," said Will, awkwardly. "Go on."

"This design…it is intricate…"

"I can see that."

"I would ask that Ingrith is given permission to work on it. These rough hands of mine possess the skills of my trade. This though…this is beyond them. The marking out of the pattern, I mean. I can transfer it across…that I can do…I have the hands for that. But this girl has the eyes, if you follow me. Maybe it would be better if…"

Rhoswen raised a hand to silence Will, and she herself fell silent as she considered the request. Ingrith watched her intently. She had hoped Will would ask that she be allowed to do more than simply observe. Now the suggestion had been made, she wanted it more than ever. It seemed to her only fair. After all, it was her work Will would be reproducing. She tried not to appear too eager when the Abbess looked over at her, however. She knew it would be better if she were seen to be in control of her emotions regarding the matter.

Rhoswen studied her. "Daughter, what do *you* say to William's request. Does it seem a good idea to you?"

Ingrith kept her voice as calm and considered as she could. "Well, I must say…on consideration…it does seem to be quite a good suggestion to me."

"Yes…I thought it might," said Rhoswen. "Very well. You may assist Master Tiler here as he requires. Mind you behave in a way that does not compromise your status here. While he is here, William merely *serves* the Abbey. You, on the other hand, *represent* it. Keep that always in mind, Ingrith. *Always.* You represent it. So take care. I will be watching."

"Thank you, Reverend Mother," said Ingrith.

"Yes, thank you," echoed Will. "I am most grateful."

"Grateful. Yet, you will not be reducing your fee, I think. Despite part of the work being carried out by someone from within the Abbey community."

William hoped the small woman was not serious, and gave no reply. To his surprise, the Abbess addressed her next remark to Alf. "What do you think, boy? Should your master here lower his fees?"

Alf said nothing.

Rhoswen smiled. "A good response. You are wise for your lack of years." She spoke now to Ingrith. "As before, you are excused your usual duties for the daylight hours only. Prayers after dark you must still attend with the rest of the sisters." Ingrith showed she understood with a slight incline of her head. "Good," said Rhoswen, and then turned and left them.

"Do you really think it is good?" Ingrith asked Will when she was sure the Abbess was out of earshot.

"That I do," he replied. "I also think you have made my task difficult for me." When Ingrith looked worried, he added. "Don't misunderstand me. I intend to meet the challenge. If I can do this…as well as it deserves to be done, that is…then it may well be the best piece of work I ever do."

Ingrith felt the colour in her cheeks. At the same moment, Will turned away and appeared to busy himself with some small task that may or may not have needed attending to. At first, she assumed it was to save her embarrassment, then it occurred to her it may have been to save his own. After a minute or two he turned back.

Almost at the top of his voice, it seemed to Ingrith, Will said, "Well, girl, I think we need to get on with things, don't you?" Ingrith nodded her agreement, wondering why Will had asked the question quite so loudly; he was only a few feet from her. However, when she heard what he said next, the reason for the increase in volume became clear. "I tell you, Silas and young Alf have had less than their share of labours lately, it seems to me. The sooner we have something to get them busy making and setting in place, the sooner I will not feel I am paying them a day's wage for simply lazing around. And the less time the rogue will have to spend in the tavern. I don't think Alf visits taverns as yet, but the time will soon come, hmm, Alf?""

Ingrith heard a grunt of displeasure from over where Silas stood, and a sniffing gurgling from Alf's direction that she realised was a giggle. It occurred to her that this was the first time she had ever heard the boy really laugh. She already knew from what she had witnessed of them working together that Will was a good master who had the boy's best interest at heart – man and boy seemed genuinely fond of each other. What then, she wondered, had happened to make the child as withdrawn and sombre as he so evidently was? There were many things in this harsh world that crushed the spirit; what was Alfred's story? If the opportunity presented itself, and she judged him in a mood to respond, she might ask Will. Without meaning to, she had been staring at the boy. He must have spotted it, because he quickly stopped laughing and turned away, as if he thought she would scold him for it.

"Well…?"

It was Will. He must have asked her something.

"I'm sorry," she said, "what is it?"

Will had a troubled look upon his face. To her dismay,

Ingrith saw him look from her to Alf. The frown he wore deepened, and there was a question on his face when he looked back at her.

"I think I upset him," she said, almost in a whisper, so the boy would not hear. "He was laughing…and then he stopped when he saw me watching. I meant nothing by it."

"Of course you didn't. What could you mean by it?" Will was talking loudly again. "Don't you fret, girl. He's a good lad, but what goes on inside his head…let's just say it's not always easy to know. So don't you worry. You didn't upset him, he upset himself."

"I'm not sure I understand," said Ingrith.

"No, I don't suppose you do. Don't worry. He likes you. Don't you, lad?" Alf had his back to them, but something in the way he held himself – a tightness of the shoulders – made it clear he was listening. "If you have upset him," Will went on, "he'll come around soon. He doesn't hold a grudge. Not like Silas here. He never forgets and never forgives. Unless it's a job I ask him to do. He forgets that soon enough."

Silas grunted a response.

"What was that?" asked Will.

Silas turned and faced them. "I said, not everything a man like you says is worth remembering. Now, hadn't you and the girl better start preparing the stamps? I feel the tavern calling."

"The tavern, or one of the women who frequent it?" asked Will.

Silas opened his mouth as if to reply, and then he glanced at Ingrith, and must have thought better of saying whatever it was he had intended to say in front of her. Instead he said, "Blocks won't carve themselves, William." After that, he went to the cart and came back with an armful of wooden blocks which he handed, almost ceremoniously, to Will. "There, now," he said, and walked away.

Will turned to Ingrith. "He's right. So where is best for you to do this?"

"What is it you require of me?" asked Ingrith.

Will handed her one the blocks. Ingrith turned it about in her hands. She saw that it was not one, but two blocks of wood. The larger piece was roughly hewn, a small plank of wood of a type she did not recognise, about two inches thick cut into a square of about ten inches by ten. Fixed to it, at the centre, was a smaller piece of a wood. This second piece was only a little larger than a tile and made of a wood she recognised as oak. It had also been cut into a square, but with far more care than the larger piece; the square was precise, and perfect, and had been planed so that the outward face was smooth and even.

"The stamps?" she guessed.

"That's right," confirmed Will. "We're going to cut your designs into them. That is, I'm going to cut them following the lines you are going to draw for me."

"I see." Ingrith studied the stamp some more. Will saw she looked puzzled.

"What is it?" he asked.

"This smaller piece…the oak…it represents the tile?"

"How do you mean?"

"It is the stamp? The part that is pressed into the clay?"

"That's it."

"It's just that it seems a bit too large to me. I do not say I am a good judge of such things. You know your trade. Only I set out mine so they were around what I judged to be the size of a tile. This is…well…it seems a little bigger than that. Bigger than mine, I mean."

Will grinned. "That's right. You do have a good eye. It *is* bigger. There is a good reason for it. I should have thought to tell you. It didn't occur to me. For that I am sorry. You will have to recreate your images a bit larger when you set them onto the wood."

"What is it?"

"What is what?"

"The reason. What is the reason they are larger?"

"Shrinkage in the kiln. Anything you place in that heat will come out about one part of ten smaller than when it went in."

"Oh, I see."

"There is more you need to understand," said Will. "We have to be patient...persistent. It is not a precise thing. Unfortunately, some tiles may need pressing and firing more than once. They do not always shrink at the same rate. Or maybe they crack. Differences in the clay, in the temperature outside…things like that…things that we cannot control can mean we have to make more than one batch before we get what we are after. Like I said, sometimes they just crack in there. But that is a problem for me and Silas. You need only draw the designs once. The stamp when its cut can be used over and over, provided care is taken with it."

"Oh, no," said Ingrith. "I want to be involved at every stage. "I want to see it all through."

"Like a mother with a child," said Silas, who had been listening.

"If you wish," said Ingrith.

"You'd better get birthin' then, girl," said Silas, and immediately wished he had not when he saw Will's face. Will then grabbed the tools and materials they would need for the task, handed some of them to Ingrith, and told her to follow him. As they walked away, Will cast one last angry glance at an already sheepish, although not, Will suspected, entirely repentant Silas.

It was only then that it occurred to Will he did not know where he was heading. Perhaps it would have been better to stay by the cart, except that there was the look of an impending summer shower about the sky, and the work required a relatively dry atmosphere. When it came to firing the tiles, providing they were robustly enough made, the kilns could burn through all but the heaviest of downpours. The charcoaling of designs onto the wooden stamps prior to carving, on the other hand, needed to be done in the dry, if the lines were to remain clear and precise, and not wash away no sooner than they were drawn. Besides, he could not ask this slightly built girl to sit in the rain and work. Still, the question remained: where did he imagine he was leading them?

"The cloister," said Ingrith suddenly, as if she had read his thoughts. "That is where I created them in the first place. Why not there? It will be perfect. I have a place set aside for my work. Abbess Rhoswen saw to it."

Will did not like the idea. The cloister was not a place for such as him. "I cannot go in there, girl," he protested.

Ingrith looked confused, and slightly amused. "Why ever not?"

"You know full well why not. I am not a man of the church. It is not a place for the likes of me."

"It is ideal for our purposes."

"That Abbess of yours would never agree to it. You might do the work there on your own... if you believe you understand what is required..."

"No, it must be done with you there," insisted Ingrith. "What I mean is, I would much prefer it if you oversaw what I was doing. I have already made one mistake because I did not know better... the size of the design, I mean. There may be more such things neither you nor I can foresee. If it will put your mind at ease, I will secure Abbess Rhoswen's approval beforehand...or when she is available. She may be too busy to interrupt at present."

"Good. I cannot come there until you have it, mind."

Ingrith looked frustrated.

"Oh, William. Can you not take the small chance that she might be a bit cross, and begin work before we have secured the permission of Abbess Rhoswen? It's permission I know she will give. She is as keen as I that..."

"No, I cannot" said Will, speaking over her. "Not where my work...my livelihood... and that of the old man and the boy... are concerned, I can't."

Will had stressed the word livelihood, and Ingrith felt a pang of shame that she may not have looked at things sufficiently from Will's perspective. She was about to express her regret when Will spoke again.

"Nor should you risk getting on the wrong side of that woman," he said. "It would not be the first time, now would it?" Will saw the hurt come into Ingrith's eyes and wished he had not mentioned her previous problems at Althurst. It occurred to him that he did not really know what they had been. He had assumed they were something relatively trivial that would soon be forgotten. He did not know, nor could he imagine, what sort of problems these women faced. They lived lives of relative ease as far as he could tell. Always fed, never without shelter, protected from violence by the laws of the land, and only the lightest of work to occupy them - what problems could they possibly face compared to those faced by the ordinary people in the town beyond the Abbey walls, and the countryside beyond the walls of the town? There was the lack of menfolk, yes, but given some of the behaviour of men towards women Will had witnessed in his time, that might not seem that much of a loss to many living within these walls. Yet, what did he really know? For all he knew the subject of her problems could be far more painful to this young woman than he could possibly understand. Unfortunately, it was too late to take back what he had said. Besides, there was wisdom in the warning for all it might have hurt her feelings. If she had upset the Abbess, and if it had been a serious issue, it would be best if she trod a careful path in her dealings with the woman. Ingrith was excited by the involvement she had been allowed to have in relation to the design and manufacture of the tiles, he could see that, and he could not deny he found it endearing, even motivating; being around her had seemed to cause some of her enthusiasm had rub off on him. But she was in danger of letting that enthusiasm get the better of her. Even the death of Ned, which had disturbed her as much as anyone, did not seem to be enough to dampen her enthusiasm. Like the Abbess, Ingrith truly seemed to believe she was doing God's bidding. Not in the manner that he himself always had - by using the skills he had been gifted with in order to create work that would honour that gift - but directly, in response to a specific message. Although Will wasn't sure he really understood what that meant, that in itself didn't matter; these were holy women, and he would trust their judgement on such things. What mattered was the recklessness he was coming to see it had engendered in Ingrith. He needed to temporize with her, get her to calm down a little. Maybe later he would say he was sorry for what he had said. Right now, however, to do so would only weaken his position. Before he knew what he had done, he had lifted a hand and put it on her shoulder. He was so surprised by his own actions that whatever it was he had intended to say to accompany the gesture left his head.

Ingrith glanced at the hand, but made no effort to remove it. "You really will not begin work in the cloister without Abbess Rhoswen's permission?" she asked.

Will withdrew his hand. "I can't. I've stated my position, and I mean it. Although I do not wish to upset you. I know you are keen to get on with things. Is there nowhere else the work could be done?"

Ingrith shrugged. "There is, I suppose. There are storerooms…sheds… none of them so fitted to it, though"

Will had worked in far worse conditions than sheds. All the same, he could tell from the lack of certainty in Ingrith's voice that she had not, and would not want to. "They would suit me fine. If you still wish it to be the cloister, you must talk to the Abbess. The sooner you get that little woman's agreement to it, the sooner we can begin."

"Oh, as you wish. If it is something you really insist upon, it seems I have no choice in the matter."

"On this, no you do not. Hurry along, hmm?"

"I shall find her now…if I can, that is… and secure her permission. I will make it clear you insisted we have permission. I would not have you compromised." She smiled then. "Although I do not think I will tell her you referred to her as *that little woman*."

"Best not," said Will, with a slight smile himself.

"You will wait here?" Ingrith indicated a stack of barrels outside the entrance to the undercroft. "Sitting on those may be more comfortable than leaning against the wall. I cannot say how long I may be."

"I will be fine here."

"If it appears I will be a very long time before I am able to speak with the Reverend Mother, I will return and let you know. And then we will do as you wish."

"As I wish?"

"Find a shed or a stable in which to work."

"I do not mind where we work, so long as it has a roof to prevent the rain." Will held out his hand, and looked to the sky, "which I believe will soon be upon us. Oh…and that we are not alone. We must be in full view of the sisters or the servants. And, if it is someplace where we need someone's permission to be, that we have that permission."

Ingrith did not say anything in reply. She shook her head and rolled her eyes in an 'of course' gesture, and then turned and walked away.

******

Will had waited so long now he was beginning to think about going in search of Ingrith, but there were any number of places she might be – many of which would not be open to him – so it would, more than likely, be a fruitless search. Better to stay where he was. The rain he had predicted had arrived, so Will had taken shelter in the entrance to the undercroft. Every few minutes he had to step aside for one of the Abbey servants as they went about their business; most of whom, Will felt, made it clear from their expressions that they thought he ought to take himself elsewhere and be about his own. If the Cellaress herself had thought fit to tell him to move on, he would have obeyed. Any comment from the servants, however, would have been met with either stony silence or perhaps harsh words, depending on how Will saw fit. In the end, not one of them spoke a word to him, and Will began to wonder if even their supposed critical looks were simply in his imagination; more to do with his own awkwardness at being there, than any opinions on the part of the people who passed him.

When, at last, Ingrith returned, she was not alone. Walking a few paces behind her, clearly struggling to match her pace, was one of the sisters. The woman was small. Not much taller than the Abbess, in fact, but much older. When the difference in age was considered, and the fact that Ingrith was clearly in a hurry, the old woman had done well to keep up at all. She had barely come to a halt next to Ingrith when the younger woman gestured towards her, and said, by way of introduction, "William, I would like you to meet Sister Alice. She is to…in the words of the Abbess…be her eyes on me, as mine where once hers on you."

"Sister," said Will, and bowed. Sister Alice responded with a slight incline of her head. Had it really been disdainful, or was this Will's imagination again?

The unspoken part of what Ingrith had said about this old woman was that she would actually be Abbess Rhoswen's eyes on them both – Will as well as Ingrith - as a safeguard against improper behaviour. Will had expected, in fact hoped for, such an arrangement, but now the woman stood before him, he felt a resentment begin to rise. He wondered at the reason for it. Ingrith was no great beauty, but she was attractive – at least Will found her to be - he could not deny it. But he was not aware of harbouring any less than respectable desires, let alone actual intentions, where she was concerned. In fairness he knew he was probably not even suspected of such intentions. The arrangement had been made because it was the correct thing to do. It protected them both from unfounded speculation. So why was he troubled by the presence of the old nun? A conspiratorial glance of shared impatience with the situation from Ingrith provided all the answer he needed; it was the fact that he did enjoy Ingrith's company, and the unexpected frankness with which she talked to him. Having this old woman there was bound to curb that frankness.

"That's' the bad part," said Ingrith, then realised how that sounded. Turning to Sister Alice, she said, "It seems such a shame to have to impose upon your time like this."

Sister Alice remained stony faced, but did not argue the explanation, weak as it so obviously was.

"I take it that the Abbess has agreed to my working with you in the cloister?" asked Will.

Ingrith gave him a questioning look. "She has. Why did you assume it?"

"You said there was a bad part. In my experience things spoken of like that have a good part to them as well." Will lifted up a block of wood he held in his hands. "So, shall we get on with things? These stamps will not make themselves."

******

CHAPTER 11

Merwinna, 1171

It was dawn. In the Abbey Church Father Jerome was leading the nuns of Althurst in the liturgy for Matins. Inside her cell Merwinna, as best she could, was also following the rites, pressed up against the small opening in her cell wall that looked out onto the choir of the church, and put there for that purpose. She still did her best to take part in all the divine offices, although it was becoming increasingly difficult, exhausted and distracted as she was by the activities of Garrick. Or was it the demon? Or were they the same? She shook her head, trying to clear it and give full attention to the words spoken by Father Jerome. She had even missed communion on some occasions, always prompting Father Jerome to enquire later if she was unwell. Always she answered yes, she was, because she could not reveal the truth. It felt wrong, almost sinful, to lie to a priest, but she had no choice. Given her reasons for doing so Merwinna believed she would receive God's forgiveness.

In the faint light of dawn that came through her other small window - the one onto the outside world, in the opposite wall - Merwinna could see her breath. She had hung sacking over the gap to keep out the chill. Unfortunately, this also kept out the light, which she enjoyed in the mornings. So, as she had this morning, she often pushed the sacking to one side to allow her to delight in the start of the new day. She could never quite see the sun at this time because it rose too far round - at the east end of the church – but she could still see the light from its rays as they fell like a blessing from God upon the tops of the buildings across from her cell. A renewed day; renewed strength. All being well.

Winter had seemed to come around very quickly. She had entered her cell in the spring. Summer and autumn had come and gone, and now winter had arrived, bringing with it frost that, if she was not careful to close all the gaps in the walls, found its way inside the cell and settled on her covers as she slept. She wondered how it would be when the first snows arrived. They could not be far off now. If she was honest with herself, back when she had first received the anchorite's calling, she had not considered the cold. Perhaps she thought the intensity of her fervour alone would keep her warm. When it came, the cold had been a shock to her. As an ordinary nun she had endured many a harsh winter at Althurst, but alone in this small space, three of its walls facing the outside, the cold seemed far more piercing than it ever had on those chilly mornings as part of the Abbey community. She shivered, pulling her worn habit more closely about herself. She did not want to, but she would have to give in and ask Father Jerome for some more blankets.

"Blankets? Such weakness of spirit for one such as you claim to be. Oh dear. Where is your faith when you need to be warm?"

Merwinna's eyes closed as she fought back hopelessness and summoned the strength for the struggle she knew must ensue. "Go away!" she hissed. To her chagrin she shivered again.

"You need warming up, I see. Something to keep off the chill. If faith can do anything, surely it can do that? I've heard others make such claims for it. Why not you, Merwinna? Why not you? I wonder at it, I really do."

"Oh, you will not break me with your nonsense, monster!" hissed Merwinna.

"Maybe so, but I *could* keep you warm. You might think you would be warmer with more garments. I can show you a different way. Take off what you have on, and I know a fine way to keep us both warm. Ha! Look what I have for you here…"

She would not turn and look. "If you are cold, why not go back to the flames from which you come?" she asked.

"And where you yourself belong, Merwinna. As you well know."

Merwinna kept her face resolutely towards the opening onto the church. It seemed to her that the only air that she could breathe came from inside there. The air inside her cell was poisoned by the presence of the beast. "No, I do not. I do not know what you mean!"

"Can that be true? Have you really forgotten so soon? Could a person ever truly forget something like that? We both know very well that they could not...that *you* have not. It is with you every waking moment, and it fills your dreams when you sleep. The smell of your guilt pervades the air in here worse than does the reek of the piss and shit in that filthy bucket of yours. That is what you find so hard to breathe. What stifles you, Merwinna, is your own guilt. Denial will no more help you breathe more clearly than will the stale air from your precious church. Your prayers do not rise up with the incense they burn through there; they sink, weighed down by their own hypocrisy!"

"I will not hear you, Garrick! I do not know how it is you are able to enter this place of God...what demon it is assists you in your tormenting me... but I will not hear you."

"Brave words. Brave words. Then again, they are your only weapons, are they not? Words. Able to defeat only other words. What of the physical...the palpable?"

Merwinna gasped as she felt fingers grip the back of her neck. She pulled away. The fingers came again, gripping more tightly this time, the long nails biting painfully into her flesh. Then an arm snaked around her waist, squeezing, and then pulling so hard that, despite her attempts to resist, she was wrenched violently around to face back into the gloom of the cell. The beast – its fingers gripping her tightly by the throat now - stood in front of the other small window, blocking any daylight, so that the only light was that which came through the opening into the church and the candles that burned beyond. This weak candlelight from over her shoulder fell upon an expanse of something that might have been flesh - a broad chest, so covered with thick, matted hair it was more animal than man – or might simply have been darkness itself, made solid in some way she could not understand. Garrick made a noise as if taking in a deep breath. Merwinna was aware of the darkness expanding in front of her as his chest rose, and then she heard the low whistle, and felt the rush of warm air as a foul breath was blown past her and into the church beyond. She heard the startled cries from inside when, as one, all the candles in there went out. Then she herself began to scream; so loudly, and with such distress that the cries from inside the church ceased as the people in there listened in alarm to the noises coming from the anchoress's cell.

******

CHAPTER 12

Althurst Abbey – 1307

Sister Marigold did not need to hurry this time. She had been awake and ready to prepare the church for the Matins service long before the hour arrived. The Abbess had not yet appointed a new sacrist since the death of Sister Euphemia, and it was generally assumed it would be some time before she did. This was partly because it would not be respectful to do it quite so soon after the unfortunate loss of the previous holder of the role, and partly because there was no longer an obvious successor. In their whispered speculation, all the sisters agreed that, ordinarily, it would have been proper for the role to go to Sister Winifred. She, however, seemed unlikely ever to fully recover her wits, so filling the role would take some thought on the part of the Reverend Mother. For the time being, Sister Emma had been assigned the duties of the sacrist. She was usually only a succentrix – one of the assistants to the sacrist – like Sister Marigold, and was by no means certain to inherit the role permanently.

Whoever was finally chosen, Sister Marigold knew it would not be herself. She had no illusions about that. But she might still rise a little further as roles were reassigned. To that end, and despite her still shaky nerves, she had resolved to get back to her duties as soon as she possibly could, and do them to the best of her abilities. Sister Helewise had been doubtful; as had the Abbess. In the end, however, Sister Marigold had been able to convince both women that what she needed most was a return to her previous routine. And that meant a return to her duties, which had been easy enough until tonight – the first time she would be back in the church at the same hour as Sister Euphemia had met her end.

The flame of the taper Sister Marigold was using to light the candles shook. This time, not because she was hurrying, but because, to her great annoyance, she found that her hand was shaking. If Sister Emma saw it, she might report back to the Abbess that she was not yet sufficiently recovered, so Sister Marigold clasped her other hand around the wrist of the one in which she held the flame and pulled her elbows into her sides in an effort to steady the flame. It helped a little, although she would still have to avoid giving Sister Emma any opportunity to watch her too closely.

She found she was holding her breath as she rounded the ambulatory near to the spot where Sister Euphemia's body had been discovered. It still puzzled her why more of an effort had not been made to clean away the bloodstains. She had heard that Abbess Rhoswen repeatedly dismissed any suggestions that the area be further scrubbed as being disrespectful to the dead woman's memory, but in Sister Marigold's view it seemed far more disrespectful – even shameful – to leave that horrible patch of discoloured stone unattended to; merely covering it with piece of cloth – however grand - was not enough. Not to mention the traces of blood sprayed on the walls that had not been covered at all. Sister Marigold shuddered as she drew near them. This was no shrine; it was merely a grim reminder. It was as if the most important thing about the woman's life – the thing she would be most remembered for, if the Abbess had her way – was the dreadful way it had been ended. Still, whatever the Reverend Mother's reasons were for acting as she was, Sister Marigold knew they would not be swayed by her own humble opinion on the matter. Perhaps if the woman had been there that terrible night when it had happened, and had felt for herself the atmosphere of evil and menace there had been, she might be more inclined to be rid of such a stark reminder of what had taken place here.

Sister Marigold exhaled with relief as she rounded a corner so that the stains were no longer in view. She even allowed herself a half-smile of satisfaction as she saw how the interior of the building was beginning to glow with the candles she had lit. Sister Emma was busying herself over by the doorway that led to the dormitory. She was overly attentive sometimes - every detail had to be perfect, so she checked and re-checked - but then she was new to the role and clearly anxious that it be carried out correctly. Better that than she be careless and neglectful.

"Better that than have her skin flayed from her body."

Sister Marigold gasped, and spun around. What she saw caused her to drop her candle, and run from the building, knocking a startled Sister Emma aside as she went.

******

"What is it, daughter?" asked Rhoswen. "What was it frightened you so?" Rhoswen turned from Sister Marigold to look at Sister Helewise.

The Infirmaress shook her head. "I doubt she even hears you, Reverend Mother. Nor does she see, if her eyes are any indication. She sees what you and I cannot." Sister Helewise paused before adding, "And I think we should count ourselves fortunate for that." She reached forward and touched Sister Marigold's cheek. "Poor child."

"You mean whatever it was frightened her... she sees it still?" asked Rhoswen.

"I do. It is no mystery. It is my belief that the poor child saw...and still does see... our dear Sister Euphemia." Sister Helewise closed her eyes as if she too saw what Sister Marigold saw.

"Sister Euphemia?" Rhoswen asked anxiously.

Sister Helewise opened her eyes again. She lifted a reassuring hand. "Not an apparition. Nothing of that sort. I believe she sees what she saw before. Or imagined she saw. I have come across this in the past... with men whose minds were damaged by battle. Events stay with them...return afresh... as if they had only just now happened. Their ghosts exist only in their minds. But they are no less disturbing for that." Sister Helewise looked down, absentmindedly picked at some loose skin next to one of her fingernails. "I blame myself. I should not have allowed the girl to return to her duties so soon. She may always be troubled in this way. It may never leave her entirely.'"

"You mean *I* should not have allowed it," corrected Rhoswen.

"No, Reverend Mother, that is not what I mean. I myself was as convinced by her claims to recovery as was anybody. As Infirmaress I, of all people, should have known better. I should have seen beyond them. Instead, I allowed her to convince me otherwise. I ignored the signs...And now..."

Rhoswen bent forward and once again looked into the younger woman's frightened eyes - eyes that did not seem to see her at all. "Will she ever return to us?"

Sister Helewise shrugged. "That I cannot tell you. What I can say is that she should not stay here in this place, with its reminders at every turn."

"Yes, you are quite right. I will have her moved. Sister Winifred, too. They can both go to the priory at Ellisfield. It is a small one. It will quiet there. Peaceful. Prioress Marjory is a good woman. She shall have the care of them until such time as..."

Rhoswen left the sentence unfinished. Neither she nor Sister Helewise had believed Sister Winifred would ever be herself again. Sister Marigold, however, had been thought to show every sign of making a full recovery. All she needed was to put enough of a distance of time between herself and that terrible night, and she would surely have regained her health and peace of mind. Now, however, the girl before her appeared lost in whatever place her mind had wandered to, and unlikely to return from there. Rhoswen felt the feeling of unease she had been struggling to supress these last few days threatening to return at a greater strength than before. Adding to that unease was now a measure of guilt. Rhoswen knew that she was sending the women away as much for her own benefit as theirs. With the two of them gone, it would be easier to carry on as if life in Althurst Abbey were normal. More than that: as if Althurst Abbey were blessed.

Was that so wrong? The message from Saint Merwinna, and the chapel in her honour; these *were* blessings. How could such things not be? What had to be faced was the fact that with these blessings came a test. The deaths, the broken minds of two of the sisters; these were trials to be endured. The saint had chosen this time, and these people to make her wishes known; those chosen were simply being asked to prove their worthiness for that choice. For Rhoswen in particular, as leader of the community at Althurst, it was a time to examine the nature and strength of her own faith. She was determined it would not be found wanting.

******

Will was already in the cloister working with Ingrith, so did not see the two nuns leaving for Ellisfield Priory early the following morning. He learned about it later from Silas, who had seen them being led away in a cart, and had asked one of the kitchen servants what was going on.

"Their minds are gone," said Silas. "So frightened were they by what they saw when the old nun was done to death that their minds cracked and broke like dropped clay pots. You only had to look at 'em to know the truth of it. Just sat there they was...not talking or anything. I think the younger one was cryin'."

"Like dropped clay pots? What in the world are you prattling on about, you daft old fool?" asked Will, tired of Silas's fondness for stories about the events in the Abbey. If anything, Will himself was already made uncomfortable by what he knew, and did not share Silas's, seemingly endless, enthusiasm for talking about it all.

"I'm only telling you what I was told," insisted an offended Silas.

"Well, I'm sure the clay pots part was your own addition. Now, if you are done with telling your tales, can you and Alf get on with filling the moulds? We'll soon have enough stamps cut to make it worth firing the first batch."

This piece of news was enough to move Silas's attention away from events at the Abbey. "Tell me again why we need so many different designs...I still can't understand it. It's not such a big area of floor. We've covered much bigger with only three of four."

"It's a mosaic, remember. You saw the image Ingrith made on the vellum, didn't you? And how it was made up of many different squares? How each one of them needs a tile?" At his own mention of Ingrith, Will was struck by the thought that it was odd that she had not thought to mention the news about the two sisters being sent away. She was not a gossip in the way Silas was, but it was surely significant enough for her to have mentioned it, if only in passing. Not for the first time, Will wondered if Ingrith did not share some of the Abbess's growing obsession with the chapel - even to the point where she did not seem much interested in anything else. He was then struck by a second and, he knew, inappropriate thought. Was her friendliness towards him solely due to her interest in the tiled floor they were creating? He enjoyed the girl's company. He had hoped she enjoyed his. He shook off the thought. What did it matter? He realised then that Silas was talking to him. "What?"

Silas looked angry. "You're not even listenin' to me now! I said I know what a fuckin' mosaic is! You know damn well I do! What I don't understand is why make something so grand for what is only a small place."

Will tried to keep his temper, hoping Silas's wish for an argument would fade if he did not rise to it. "It's what they want," he said calmly.

"I know that. But *why* do they want it?"

"I don't know, Silas. It's not really my business, and I really don't care all that much. You shouldn't either. You know how these holy types can get over their shrines and such," replied Will, attempting now to divert Silas's anger away from himself and onto the Abbess and the sisters. "The place is important to the people here for some reason. Like I say, I don't care, and neither should you. What you should care about…be glad about… is it creates paying work for us. All I can tell you is it means something more important than that to these nuns."

"Does it now? I remember you told me before how the Good Mother don't even want the damned thing built. T'was all that fat bishop's doin', you said. You're tellin' me now her mind is changed on the matter?"

"I am. For some reason it's become important to her. Besides, why complain when it will pay better? More coins for you to put aside for that indulgence of yours, eh?"

"Don't you make jokes about that," said Silas.

"I'm not," said Will, a little disingenuously. "I'm only telling you how I see things."

Will normally knew better than to make light of the subject of Silas's indulgence. At some point, somewhere on one of their previous jobs, the old man claimed he had been told by a priest there that past sins could be atoned for, and salvation from eternal damnation granted, in return for money. Despite Will telling him he was not sure that was quite how it worked, ever since then Silas had begun saving his few coins – when he did not drink them away – for payment to a Pardoner, the church official whose role it was to sell such indulgences. Will had no idea how much such a thing would cost, but his guess was that it was likely to be far more than a man of Silas's limited means could ever hope to scrape together in his lifetime, even if he were not a drinker. The other thing Will did not know – because, for all his gossip, it was the one thing Silas would never reveal – was the nature of the particular sin that so worried him. Will was mulling over whether he should apologise to Silas for bringing the subject up, when Ingrith returned. She had been given temporary permission to miss most of the services held in the hours of daylight, and excused her normal duties, but today, for some reason – perhaps to explain the reason for the removal of the two sisters – the Abbess had sent a message that she and Sister Alice must attend a specially convened gathering in the chapter house. Another mystery to Will, and another subject he could not ask about.

Sister Alice, as ever, stood a few feet back. Ingrith came right up to Will, smiled, and said, "I am released once more, as you see." Beyond Ingrith, Will had noticed Sister Alice frown, and he sensed that Ingrith might have spoken out of turn. Seeing that Will was at a loss as to how he should respond, Ingrith glanced briefly over her shoulder at the other woman, and then turned back to Will, adding, "All is well. Shall we get back to work then?"

Will's eyes narrowed slightly. He was still uncertain. "If you are free…"

Ingrith's expression made it clear she was growing uncharacteristically irritated. "Master Tiler, can we *please* return to our work. It is what you are engaged here to do, is it not?"

Almost immediately, she regretted how she had spoken. She reached forward and touched Will gently upon the sleeve. "Forgive me. I find interruptions such as the one I have just now endured very frustrating. You must, by now, be aware how important our work on the design is to Abbess Rhoswen." She lowered her voice so Sister Alice could not hear, and added, "and to me."

Behind Ingrith, Sister Alice cleared her throat. Ingrith rolled her eyes so Will could see, and then she turned to face the nun. For a moment Will worried Ingrith would say something she might later regret. Thankfully, when she spoke, her voice was calm and placatory. "You, also, must forgive me, Sister Alice. I forgot myself, and you are right to reproach me."

"I said nothing," said Sister Alice.

"Your meaning was clear, nonetheless. And you are quite correct," said Ingrith. "If you are satisfied…and *only* if you are satisfied… I would like to return to my work in the cloister with Master Tiler here. And with you, too, of course. I am grateful for your patience and guidance."

This was the second time in a matter of minutes that Ingrith had referred to Will by the title 'Master Tiler.' The first had been unkindly employed to put him in his place and make him uncomfortable; the second had been part of Ingrith's attempt to appease Sister Alice. Both had had the former effect as far as Will was concerned.

In a clumsy display of play-acting, and all too obviously enjoying the fact that it was she who had the final say over the matter, Sister Alice took far longer than she needed to reach her decision before responding to Ingrith. "Very well," she said at last, when the unnecessary deliberations were apparently at an end. "You may go to the cloister. I judge it seemly. Remember though, without my presence it would not be."

Ingrith gave a slight bow to demonstrate her obedience. As before, her voice was calm and conciliatory when she said, "Then do, please, lead the way, sister." However, from where he stood, Will could see how tightly Ingrith clenched the fingers of the hands held at her sides. Such pretence, it seemed, came hard to the young woman. But, Will thought to himself with some amusement, if the smug smile Sister Alice was now so unsuccessfully struggling to supress in reaction to Ingrith's apparent deference was anything to go by, Ingrith was the better at it of the two women by far.

******

CHAPTER 13

Merwinna, 1171

Father Jerome felt sick. Worse than that; he was also beginning to feel a little afraid. He did not want to hear any more of Merwinna's lurid and disturbing confession. Not another word. He wanted to turn from the gap in the stone that gave onto her cell and run from the church. But what would happen to her if he did? What would happen to *him*? How could he face God if he had abandoned one of His most devoted – and tormented - servants? Instead, the priest turned and leaned his back against the cold stones of the wall to one side of the opening, fearful that, if he did not, his trembling legs might fail to support his weight.

He had known for some time that something was wrong with the girl, but this was far worse than he had imagined. *Far* worse. He sensed her waiting in the shadows beyond for him to say something, to offer advice or comfort, but what could he possibly say? Eventually - almost as if it were someone else's words giving voice to someone else's thoughts – he heard himself say, "Do you not think…I mean to say…could you not…well… leave your cell?"

"And abandon what I have achieved?!" exclaimed Merwinna, her voice reverberating from inside her cell. "Never!"

"Daughter, you should not let your pride…"

"*Pride!* How *dare* you accuse me of that? I am *His* instrument. It is *His* will I follow, not my own. *He* commands me."

Father Jerome questioned for a moment exactly which 'he' the girl meant. She could not have fallen that far, surely? "God will forgive," he whispered, and then, realising she would not have heard, he repeated, "God will forgive. He will forgive all your failings. You have done more than anyone could have expected. More than anyone would have the right to expect."

"You are wrong Father. *He*, He has the right. Do you really understand so little? Can you really be so blind as to what is happening… here… in this very church? Are you really so deceived?"

"Deceived? By whom, my child?"

"Is it not plain?"

"Plain? No…no it is not. I cannot tell…"

"By *Garrick*, Father. By *Garrick!* He has always wished to know me… always coveted my body…"

"I hear what you say, Sister Merwinna, only I think perhaps…"

"He wants to know me. Know my flesh. He craves it, yearns for it. To that end, he has bargained with Satan himself. My flesh for his sinner's soul. He has made covenant with the Evil One that he may have his desires fulfilled. How else has he been able to come and go from my cell unhindered by stone walls, unseen by the eyes of all but me? *How* Father? Tell me that? How? It is with the Devil he has traded. His soul for the taste and feel of my flesh. My pure flesh. Oh, how I have had to fight with him these past months."

When Merwinna had told him about what she referred to as her 'battles' with evil, Father Jerome had thought the girl was run mad by too much time alone with only her own thoughts. Even now he prayed it was that alone made her say the things she said. And yet it was difficult not to fear there may be some real evil at work in the way she had brought Garrick into her stories of those battles. Exactly where that evil resided, he was not yet certain. He feared it may be in her own heart. He had no choice now but to confront her with what he knew she must already know.

"Garrick the potter is *dead*, my child. You know that."

Father Jerome had expected confusion, denial, or even remonstration at what he had told her. The cry he heard from inside the cell was one of joy and relief.

"God be praised! Then I am free of him. When? How?"

"My child?"

"How has he died? At someone's hand? Has the Good Lord guided someone's hand to save me? Or has He seen fit to strike down Garrick with disease, and free me from him in that way? Oh, joy is mine whatever the cause of it. Joy is mine!"

"Merwinna, you already know the cause," replied Jerome, shocked and confused by her reaction.

"I tell you I do not," insisted Merwinna. "How could I? You are the first to bring me this glad news, Father. Oh, and I am most grateful to you for it."

Not for the first time since they had begun speaking, Father Jerome made the sign of the cross. The girl sounded genuine. But it could not be possible for her to have forgotten so soon. Before he could say anything, Merwinna continued, "Oh, I understand your silence. You are shocked at one such as myself showing such pleasure...yes, pleasure... I will not deny it...at the death of another. Yet, surely, with what I have told you, you can understand why?"

What she had told him? To the priest, Merwinna's stories of repeated visits from some sort of demon - a demon she had chosen to believe was Garrick – and of its unholy and unnatural behaviour to towards her had filled him with nothing but fear and disgust. There was surely nothing reassuring or deserving of celebration in the fact that the real Garrick was dead.

"Child," he asked, as evenly as he could manage, "how am I to understand when Garrick has been dead these two years past. You, of all people, know that. You *must* know that. He drowned in the river."

"He is drowned, then?"

"Yes. But I don't understand the need for your questions. You know all this already, Merwinna. Some say he fell, others that he killed himself for shame of the accusations that you yourself had made against him…Accusations that may or may not have been true."

When she spoke next, Merwinna's voice was petulant, confused. "Why would you say such a thing, Father?"

"Oh, I do not doubt the truth of the accusations you made. I myself never did. Not like some. I have never for a moment doubted your claims…" Even as he said this, part of the priest wondered if it was true. He knew he had wanted to believe them. Had he *made* himself believe?

Inside her cell, her thoughts becoming disordered, Merwinna put her hands to her head, and walked around in a small circle before putting her mouth to the hole in the wall once more. "I do not know of what you speak! I do not understand your reply! I asked why you would say he has been dead for two years when he cannot have been. I did *not* ask whether you believed my accusations against him." Frustrated, she walked around in another circle, then said, "Garrick is not dead, Father Jerome. He has been in *here*…with *me*…So how can he be? It is he who has been the source of my torments. I have endured them as best I am able. As I know I must. For it is God's test of my worthiness. Yet now you tell me it cannot be so. Do you doubt my word, Father? Is that it?"

Father Jerome hesitated.

"Well, *do* you?" asked Merwinna.

"Child, I do not know how to answer that question."

"You have trouble answering questions, it seems. Well, it is simple enough: Do you or do you not believe what I have told you?"

Father Jerome thought for a moment. "I believe that you are tormented. I do believe that much. I have the evidence of my own ears. I have heard your cries. What I am not able to say with any certainty is the source of your torments. I only know that Garrick has been dead these past two years now. His body returns to dust in the ground, and his soul…his soul, we may hope, has been gathered unto…"

"His soul, indeed! He is *not* dead, Father! He is not…Ah, but wait…" Merwinna's tone became suddenly milder, enquiring. "He succumbed to self-murder you say?"

"Some said so, yes."

"'*Some*'…what does that mean?"

"Only that it was suggested by some people at the time."

"By some. Not all, then?"

"A number thought it might have been an accident. However, as I say, there were some in town who claimed it was suicide. They said it was shame at your own accusations against him that did it…drove him to do it, I mean." The priest cleared his throat. "You should feel no guilt; it was his own choice."

"To commit the unforgivable sin of taking his own life." Merwinna huffed. "And why should I feel any guilt about that?"

"You wish to hear? Though it goes against you?"

"Against me?" Merwinna was puzzled. "I do," she insisted. "I have a right to hear."

Father Jerome rubbed his hands together as he considered how best to explain.

"Tell me, Father," said Merwinna when he had not spoken for nearly a minute.

"Because…," he said after nearly another minute had passed. "Because, my daughter, there were those in town… and, it pains me to add, here in the Abbey too…a small number… who believed you were…"

Inside her cell, Merwinna's eyebrows rose; she had guessed what it was they believed. "Untruthful? That I was lying?"

"Mistaken. That you were mistaken. That perchance some terrible misunderstanding existed between you and the unhappy young man, and it was that which led him to do what he eventually did. If that was so, you need not blame yourself."

"Be assured, Father, I do not!"

Even though he knew Merwinna could not see him, Father Jerome held out his palms in an appeasing gesture. "That is well. Besides, he may not even have done it. It was icy that night, so he may well have slipped. We do not know. No one, save the Lord Himself, knows."

Father Jerome didn't add that there were also some who were strongly of the opinion that it was her feelings of guilt at having made false accusations of sexual assault against the potter, and his resulting suicide, that were in some way behind Merwinna's later decision to adopt the anchorite life. She was hiding from the truth inside the walls of her cell, they said. It was, in fact, she, who had propositioned Garrick, not the other way around. Why, they asked, would a young man as handsome as he, and with a pretty wife to match, risk everything for Merwinna? True, she was comely, but not more so than his wife. A wife that he had always shown every sign of loving very dearly.

"Only the Lord knows," repeated Father Jerome, with a shake of his head, and crossing himself. He was becoming ever more unnerved and confused by the circles their conversation was going in. He could not discern what aspects of what he had told Merwinna she accepted and what she denied. Nor was he any longer certain what he himself understood to be the truth.

"Or the Devil!" shouted Merwinna. "Or the Devil!"

The priest's hand came up and made the sign of the cross yet again. "Have a care what you say in this house of God! It may be that Garrick did himself to death. It may be that his soul knows no rest. We cannot know, you nor I. And it is not for us to speculate!"

"Oh, Father, Father. If what you say is true...and I still do not know if I should believe it...but if it is, then he resides in Hell as surely as I stand here in my cell, and you stand out there, no doubt making the sign of the cross over and over in your puzzlement and trepidation."

"Why is it that you are so resolute in your belief that he is in Hell?" asked Father Jerome. "Might it no be possible that…"

"No, Father, nothing else is possible."

"But why?"

"Because it is plain. If Garrick really is dead, and has not made his covenant with Satan in this life, then he has made it in the next. Suicides go to Hell. And it is there where he has bargained with the Devil. A blackened and tainted soul for my pure one. Whether the wicked man is living or dead, there is no difference as far as I am concerned. Either way, his only purpose is to torment me. Whether he strolls up from the stinking streets of the town, or flies up like a bat from the pits of Hell itself, it makes no difference. It is always Satan who shows him the way…allows him to gain entry into my cell…to visit his wickedness upon me…Satan allows it…*Satan!*"

"Daughter, I…"

"Oh, but I am strong. Strong enough to rebuff all he can send my way. For he is damned, whereas I am worthy. He is weak where I am strong. Can you not see, Father? I am worthy! I am worthy! I am worthy! Oh, pray with me, Father. Give thanks for the test God has put before me, and for the strength with which he has endowed me that I might demonstrate my worthiness. Will you not pray with me, Father? Pray with me! Pray with me! Pray with me!"

At first, Jerome was uncertain, still afraid. His nausea had increased, and he felt dizzy as the girl's passionate - almost desperate - pleas echoed around the church, the words bouncing off the stone, and soon finding their way inside his head, filling it, making it impossible to fix his thoughts on anything else. He staggered away from the opening, turned, and held on to a nearby pillar for support. He closed his eyes as the girl kept repeating the same thing, over and over - "Pray with me! Pray with me!" - until, finally, he felt his head might actually split open as it vibrated with the phrase. He put his hands over his ears, pressed his forehead to the cold stone blocks of the pillar, rubbing it back and forth, wincing in pain as the rough surface scrapped his skin, and yet glad of the distraction.

Then, gradually, he began to feel his fear leaving him as the words, and the certainty and passion behind them, took hold. It was as if a soft, warm blanket had been gently dropped down on him, wrapping itself around him, making him feel safe, and reassuring him that all would be well. All would be well. All would be well. He felt no anguish. No fear. Nothing now, apart from great elation. The force, the repetition, of the words was no longer distressing. Instead, it soothed him, a balm to all his troubles. Those words; they were an invitation to join the girl in that state where all was joy, and sorrow was unknown. He fell to his knees, raised his arms in praise. "Yes, my child," he cried. "Yes. Yes. I shall pray with you! I *shall* pray!"

Father Jerome had always made certain the church was empty of other people when he took Merwinna's confession. He felt it was only right that she should enjoy the same privacy as anyone else during the sacrament and, as she had to speak to him via the small opening between her cell and the church, that privacy was not possible with others inside the building who might overhear. So, as was usual, he was alone with her on that day. The only witness on the day the saint disappeared.

******

CHAPTER 14

Althurst Abbey – 1307

Alf was growing impatient. The first batch of tiles had been formed from the heap of seasoned clay, and then stamped with Ingrith's designs. At present, they were all stacked up in a large wooden frame Will and Silas had built in the corner of a small shed on the Abbey grounds to which Will had been granted temporary access. The tiles had been placed there in order that they might dry a little. It was an absolutely necessary stage before they could be glazed and placed in the kiln for firing, and Alf understood that, but still he was impatient. He could hardly wait to see how they appeared once they had been fired. Will didn't often make tiles this way anymore, and since Alf had been with him, he had only seen it done twice before. Even then it had never been to create anything as complex as the image Ingrith and the Abbess had asked Will to produce.

Alf enjoyed all of the process, but the part he liked best of all was the opening of the kiln. It was almost like magic, seeing the final product being removed from the still warm belly of the kiln. Like bread from an oven, Will had told him once. But a feast for the eyes, not the belly. When it came out – and providing nothing had gone wrong during firing, as it so easily could - the brown clay would be a much darker, almost reddish, brown. The pattern created where the white clay was poured into the indentations created by the wooden stamps Will had made would be a golden yellow. Frustratingly for Alf, that would not happen for days yet. Will insisted that the tiles had to dry sufficiently well to be fired, and that meant they must reach a hard and leathery texture, rather than being soft to touch, like they were now. Only then would a lead glaze be added before they were stacked in the kiln and fired. Alf glanced over at the shed and sighed. Soon, he hoped, and they would be stacking the tiles into the top chamber of the kiln.

Firing the tiles was almost as exciting as the final opening of the kiln. It would go on for days and days – sometimes nearly a week. For all of that time the furnace chamber that had been formed by the trench that had been dug must be continually fed with fuel to maintain the temperature in the kiln above. While Will had been working with Ingrith on the tiles, Alf had accompanied Silas on several trips to a nearby forest that was part of the Abbey lands, in order to collect cartloads of brushwood for this purpose. More trips might yet be needed, depending on how things went. Manning the stoke-holes, and judging when best to add more twigs or possibly a small branch, was a day and night operation. It was as important that the heat be constant as it was it be high. Silas and Will would take it in turns to man the kiln, one sleeping while the other kept a constant watch.

"Not long, I'm told."

Alf turned and saw Ingrith standing there. He had the feeling she may have been watching him for some time. He felt his face growing hot. She walked over, followed a few paces back by the old nun, Sister Alice. Alf did not like Sister Alice, so he was glad when Ingrith turned and told the old nun to leave them.

"Do you see William Tiler here, sister?" asked Ingrith with an unnecessarily dramatic sweep of her hand. "In fact, do you see *anyone* save for this child and me?"

Sister Alice glanced at Alf. She shrugged. It looked to Alf as if the old woman were about to speak, but Ingrith spoke over her. "No, you do not. Only this boy, then. A child. I do not think the situation requires your oversight, do you?"

Again, Sister Alice shrugged, looking as if she might say something given time to compose her thoughts. Again Ingrith spoke over her.

"No, you do not. You cannot possibly. So, please leave us. I suggest you go find something else to occupy your time.

Perhaps find Will…William. Alfred and I will join you when we are done. Go. Leave us."

The tone of command in her own voice had surprised Ingrith; she was, after all, merely a novice. Sister Alice was clearly even more surprised but, making no attempt at a reply, she simply turned and left.

"I saw you looking over at where the tiles are stacked in the shed," Ingrith said to Alf. "Shall we go take a look? What do you say?"

Alf shook his head. He had been told he must not go into the shed without Will or Silas. Will had been very clear on that point, and Alf would not disobey the instruction, even if he thought it a little unjust. After all, he knew better than to touch the tiles. He did not need Will or Silas there to remind him. Nevertheless, he would not disobey.

"Why not?" asked Ingrith. "Don't you want so see how the tiles are getting on? We could just take a peek." Suddenly, Ingrith understood. "You're not allowed, is that it?"

Alf nodded.

"I am here, remember. You will be with me. That makes it acceptable, doesn't it?" Alf still looked unconvinced. Ingrith was about to tease him about being too afraid to break one of Will's rules, even with her permission, when she thought better of it. Instead she said, "I admire your loyalty and obedience, young Alfred. I wish I were as steadfast." Alf frowned. He had not understood. "What I mean to say," explained Ingrith, "is that Will would be proud of how you follow his instructions. You have done well."

Alf allowed himself a smile, then was taken aback when Ingrith stepped forward and whispered in his ear.

"Listen, I have an idea."

The fact that she was whispering suggested it was not necessarily something that everyone would approve of, and Alf's first instinct was to step back. But he was curious, so he stayed put. She drew closer so that, when she spoke again, he felt her warm breath on his ear.

"You will have seen the vellum with the images I created? Of course you have." Alf appeared to think for a moment, but said nothing, neither a yes nor a no. It was possible the boy simply didn't understand, but Ingrith thought that unlikely. She suspected he was just a little overwhelmed, so she stepped back - giving him more space - and then slowly asked her question again to give him time to recover. "The vellum… with my pictures on it?… Will and I used what was on it as the basis for the images now on the tiles… He cut the stamps to match what was on it." This time, Alf nodded. "Well, how would you like to see the painting itself? The one my images are based upon?"

When Alf's eye's widened, Ingrith smiled.

The design for the tiles had struck Alf as wondrous, but he was aware that the image it depicted had been based on a painting somewhere in the Abbess's keeping. The prospect of his actually seeing the painting itself was beyond anything he could have expected. Beyond even the novelty of having someone like Ingrith whispering to him. The problem was that Alf knew the picture of which she spoke was housed in the building where the Abbess resided. If Will were to find out Alf had been inside there without proper approval, he would be very angry, and Alf could not imagine how approval for a boy like himself to venture inside those walls could ever be obtained. His hand rose to his head and he began stroking the scar at his temple.

Ingrith had seen the doubt flash in his eyes. She said in a voice that was a deliberate mix of matter of fact and light-hearted, "Oh, don't worry, Alfred. It is not for Will to say who can and cannot go there. He does not have authority over the comings and goings in the Abbey buildings, now does he? Moreover, you will only be acting on my say. You yourself cannot, in any way, get into any trouble for this."

Alf's hand left his temple. He used it now to point at Ingrith.

For a moment Ingrith did not understand. Then, touched

by the boy's concern when she at last realised what it was he was asking, she said, "Oh…no…nor can I. I cannot get into trouble either."

Alf still looked doubtful.

"What is it now? Tell me," said Ingrith, careful that it did not sound impatient.

Alf took a deep breath. Ingrith knew him well enough by now to know that this meant he was about to speak. It always moved her when he felt relaxed enough in her presence to make the attempt. "R…R… R…" stammered Alf.

Ingrith did not understand until Alf held out his hand, palm down, lifted it to roughly the level of her head, and then brought it back down to just above her waist. She suppressed a giggle when she understood the boy was trying to describe the short stature of Abbess Rhoswen. "The Reverend Mother!" she said, before remembering Will had said it was better to let the boy say things if he could, rather than say them for him. But her saying it first seemed to have relaxed Alf enough to repeat it.

"Reverend Mother," he said. "H…h…her r…r…room."

"Yes, it is. However, I have permission to enter. She has given me that permission." Whether this actually extended to include taking in a boy like Alf, Ingrith did not really know. What she did know was that Abbess Rhoswen was away from Althurst for the day, so as long as she was careful that they were not seen, taking Alf to see the painting of Merwinna should be safe.

From the tight hold she kept on his arm, and the furtive way she glanced about them as she steered him towards the Abbess's rooms, Alf quickly sensed that Ingrith had been far from truthful when she had assured him that it was fine for her to take him to see the painting. But he had become so taken with the prospect of seeing it that he was prepared to take the risk. He also knew that, if they were discovered, and it did prove to be against the Reverend Mother's wishes, it would be Ingrith rather than him who took the blame. He was, after all, being guided by what Ingrith had told him; even if he did suspect it was not wholly true. However, when, having listened to see if anyone was inside, Ingrith began to open the door to the Abbess's receiving room, Alf surprised himself as well as Ingrith when he reached out to stop her.

"No," he said firmly.

"It's fine," said Ingrith. "I promise you will not get into any trouble."

"N..not me. *You*," said Alf.

Ingrith touched Alf's cheek. "Bless you, Alfred. Really, it's safe."

She opened the door, and stepped inside. When she turned around, she saw that Alf had not moved. He remained where he was, beyond the doorway, in the other room. "Oh, Alfred, really. I told you, it's safe. It really is. I have the Reverend Mother's consent." She took his hand, gently pulling him towards her. For a moment Alf considered resisting, then changed his mind when he caught sight of what lay beyond the table at the far side of the room. He could not remove his gaze from the painting. As he stepped inside the room, his eyes remained fixed on the image on the wall in front of him.

"You see?" asked Ingrith. "You see now how the image Will...and you, of course...are helping me to create with your tiles is similar to this, and yet different at the same time?"

Alf saw immediately what Ingrith meant. The image the painter had created on the wall before him was, undeniably, the same as that of the woman the tiles would depict when they were assembled on the floor of Saint Merwinna's chapel. And yet, at the same time, the two were not the same. The depiction of the Saint before him now was far more detailed and, as far as Alf was concerned, far more striking. He understood immediately that this was largely because it was far more colourful. The artist had not been forced to rely on the limited, two colour palette that the use of tiles imposed.

Whoever it was had painted this had been able to use colour to enhance details - separating out one area from another, drawing the eye to one aspect of the picture by making those around it recede in a way that a tile-based image would never allow. Alf had thought the image Ingrith had made was wondrous. This was even more magnificent.

He realised Ingrith was talking to him. She had leaned in towards him and was pointing at something. "You see? Alfred, do you see?"

Alf looked toward the area Ingrith seemed to want him to study. It appeared to be a fold in the saint's gown. "Well?" she asked. Alf frowned, looked uneasy. Realising he had not been listening, Ingrith smiled patiently. "It alright. I was just saying how the changes in how dark or light the colour is…sometimes gradual, sometimes deliberately sudden… have been used to indicate the fall of light upon the saint…the shadows it creates…Do you see? There, the fold in Merwinna's gown. Can you imagine reaching out and touching it? If you moved it this way or that, the shadow would increase or decrease in size depending on how much light was permitted to fall upon it.

Alf looked at the saint's gown, then down at the folds in the habit Ingrith was wearing.

"That's right," she said, obviously pleased. "Well done, that's exactly it. Watch…" Ingrith bent forward, lifted the hem of her habit up into the light that shone in from the high window, so that it spread across the surface of the outstretched material. Then she withdrew it, and the light was replaced by shadow, in which the material appeared darker. "The painter has created exactly that effect. Isn't it wonderful?"

Alf nodded and smiled. He looked up at the picture, and then back down again at Ingrith's gown. He was pleased with himself, enjoying the fact that he understood. He was also glad to have pleased Ingrith. She was kind; he liked her.

Alf looked up at the picture again. This time he did not

look back at Ingrith. Something seemed to be different about the picture now, and, for some reason, wrong. In his understanding of what the painter had achieved – particularly in Ingrith's demonstration of it – Alf had been vaguely aware of some other aspect of things; something waiting to be similarly understood, at the back of his mind. Now it had become clear, and he didn't quite know what to make of it. He wasn't sure he liked it. It was as if by uncovering that layer, he had become aware of yet another one below it which he still did not understand. And it was all about layers wasn't it? As he had turned from Ingrith, and looked once more at the representation of the fabric covering the figure of saint, he had suddenly grasped that implicit in that representation was the fact of the figure beneath the fabric, of the woman's body beneath the gown – concealed by its folds and, at the same time revealed by them. He wished he could do what Ingrith had talked about. He wished he could touch the material. More than that, he wished he could push against it until it made contact with the woman beneath. It would be good to touch her, to feel her warmth, and to trace the line of the curves suggested by the way the cloth fell. He didn't really know why he wanted to touch it so much. It confused him, made him feel good and bad at the same time. Excited and ashamed. He knew men were supposed to like women. The idea was not new to him. They were supposed to want to lay down with them or something like that. Silas quite often made comments about some woman he saw. Comments about how she made him feel, and what he wished he could do with her. Usually, Will would glare at Silas when he said those things. Sometimes he would shake his head and then nod in Alf's direction, letting Silas know he should not say them in front of the boy. Alf had never been sure if this was simply because Will judged him too young to hear, or if it was because of Alf's mother, and what had happened to her. Alf didn't know all of what had happened, but he knew the men who killed his mother had not done it because they especially disliked her or wanted her dead, so much as because they wanted something from her and in the taking of it they had needed to kill her. The tone in which Silas made his comments did not seem murderous to Alf, and yet it did not always seem that Silas particularly liked the woman in question, only how she made him feel. There were other times when the way he said what he said was almost as if he blamed the woman for how she made him feel, and was angry at her because of it. Which could not be fair, could it? What was especially odd was that, usually, the comments were made regarding a woman Silas could not possibly know well enough to like or dislike. She might only be some woman who passed by them while they were working. Even the women Silas visited on the occasions when they were in the towns where such women lived did not seem to be people Silas would count among his friends. Whoever they were, Will never visited those women. But even he would, once in a while, pass a comment on a woman's appearance if he thought Alf was out of earshot. Will's comments, however, always seemed kinder, more complimentary in nature. But even they were still only the result of how the woman looked rather than any tenderness of feeling towards her personally.

And now he, Alf, had a sense of wanting to be near this woman in the picture – not even a real person - for how her image alone made him feel, rather than any sense of who she was: a saint, a woman Alf knew enough to know he should hold in the highest regard due to her nearness to God. A word suddenly entered Alf's head. *Virgin.* He had heard it used about such women in the past, and knew it meant something special, something to be respected. After all, wasn't the mother of God called The Virgin? The Blessed Virgin. So it must be something good. On the other hand, Alf had once heard Silas remark that such women were of no use to a man when it was cold outside. Alf remembered even Will had allowed himself to chuckle a little at that, but had stopped when he caught Alf watching him.

"Alfred?" he heard Ingrith say beside him. "You seem discomforted all of a sudden. Are you unwell?"

Ingrith. Right beside him. Alf began to wonder about *her* figure. It was not quite as curvy as that of the woman in the picture in front of him, not quite as enticing. Then again, it was not painted on stone, it was real. It was there. In the room. Right next to him. Alf forced himself to stop. He didn't understand what he was feeling, and he was beginning to be troubled by it. Besides, he liked Ingrith. She was friendly towards him, and kind, so how could she be one of the women Silas talked so unkindly about, and seemed to want something from? Careful to look only at her face, he said to Ingrith, "W…w…want to go."

"So soon. There is time to study her more if you desire it."

Although part of Alf did, he shook his head. "Na. W…Will…"

"Oh, yes. Yes, of course," said Ingrith. "You are worried he will be beginning to wonder where you have got to. Don't worry, I'll explain you were with me. Seeing this…understanding how it is the starting point for the work you are embarked upon…I think you will find your Will glad that I showed you." As they were leaving, Ingrith added, "You are fond of William, aren't you."

"Yes."

"He seems to me a good master."

"Yes."

As Ingrith reached back to close the door of the receiving room, Alf allowed himself one more look at the picture. As he had just now when he spoke to Ingrith, he looked only at Saint Merwinna's face.

Alf stumbled back with a cry.

"What is it?" asked Ingrith, startled. Alf made no attempt to reply. Ingrith looked at the boy's face. It was pale. She lifted a hand to his forehead, found it to be warm and clammy. "Oh, Alfred, you know I do believe you are unwell. You show signs of a fever. Come, I will take you to see Sister

Helewise. Don't worry, for she will make you well again."
Ingrith forced a smile, "We have a jest here in Althurst that
she could cure a cat of its curiosity."

Alf did not resist or object. He allowed Ingrith to lead him
to the infirmary. He didn't take in his surroundings as they
went. All he saw was the brief image he had seen through the
doorway to the Abbess's receiving room just before Ingrith
had closed the door: The face of Saint Merwinna, turning to
look directly at him. Turning as if she were come to life up
there on the wall behind the Abbess's chair. Her eyes blazing
with an intensity that made Alf feel she could see into his
head and read his thoughts. She knew exactly what he had
been thinking. She knew his thoughts had been of the flesh
beneath the fabric. The woman, not the saint. Even now,
with Sister Helewise studying him with concern, and Ingrith
at her side explaining her fears that the boy was unwell, all
Alf saw still were those eyes, accusing him of wanting
something he did not fully understand while, at the same
time, tempting him with that same thing.

******

"Hello, Alf, lad," said Will. "You taken a bit of a turn, have
you?" He knelt down beside the bed. "Gave Ingrith a bit of
fright, she tells me. Still, the old nun over there," Will
gestured towards Sister Helewise, who was tending to an old
man in a bed at the far end of the room, "she says it's nothing
to worry about. More than likely it was just something to do
with you growing. Your body adjusting to the changes that
are going on inside you. Good news really. You're getting
bigger. Which means stronger. Which means I can get more
work out of you." Will had hoped to amuse the boy with this
last comment. On seeing him frown slightly, he added hastily,
"Not that you don't do enough as it is." Will got to his feet.
Looking down at Alf he said, "Well, never you mind. Me and
Silas can get on with the firing for a bit without you, until

you're ready."

At mention of the firing, Alf's eyes widened. He threw aside the blanket that covered him and swung his legs over the side of the bed. He made to stand up, but felt dizzy and staggered forward. Will caught him and lifted him back onto the bed, at the same time silently cursing himself for bringing up the subject of the firing. He should have known the boy would not want to miss it. "Now you wait," he said. "Not until Sister Helewise says you are fit for it. She tells me you haven't got a fever or anything bad like that, so it won't be long."

Alf made to rise again. Will bent forward and put a restraining hand on the boy's chest.

"Be still boy! Don't make me cross now. It won't be until tomorrow that we light the fires. Who knows, you may be up by then. Well enough to watch, even if you can't help." Will smiled. "I should take it out of your wages. Still I won't be paying for your room and board in the town for a day or so...the nuns will take care of that while you're in here...so we'll call it even, huh? Mind you, I reckon you got the better part of the bargain. Food here looks a damn sight better than down at the Inn. Now, you lie back and rest. Even if you miss the start, we'll be on that kiln day and night for the best part of a week. You're bound to be up and about for some of it. Whatever happens, you'll be there to see the tiles come out."

Alf opened his mouth and struggled to say something. Being unwell made his difficulties with speech worse. Luckily for Alf, Will seemed to know what it was he was trying to say.

"I promise. If I have to lift you up and carry you out of here, I'll do it. Whatever happens, I'll be certain to make sure you are there when we open the kiln. But you'll be up and about days before that anyway. Right then, you rest up here for the time being."

Despite all Will had said, Alf looked as if he might still

attempt to sit up. Will narrowed his eyes suspiciously. "Don't," he warned, with a wag of his finger. "I won't hear of you coming to help until I get the word from Sister Helewise that you're fit for it. You're no good to me sick. I want you well. There's an end to it. You may as well make the most of it." Will glanced around himself. "Worse places to be," he said. Then added with a chuckle, "If you don't mind the smell of all the sick people, that is." Will made a face, leaned in and whispered. "All the rank farts!" This time the boy did smile. "Mind you, right now, that includes you, young Alf. Sick I mean, not windy. So, like I say, you make the most of it. Get yourself fully better. Then you can join Silas and me at the kiln. Only then. Good and well, that's how I want you. The more you rest, the sooner that will be. You should think of resting as a task. Like a job I have set you to do. So mind you do it well. Do you see what I'm telling you?"

In answer, Alf did as he often did, and as Will knew he would. He nodded.

Will said, "Another task for you...and me...and only when you are well again, mind you...is to work on your speaking a bit more. I know you try, but we need to get more from you. I wonder your head doesn't roll straight off your shoulders; you nod it and shake it so much. Well, that's not something for now. When the chapel is done...when we're not so busy. Next place, next job perhaps."

As Will knew he would be, the boy looked anxious at the suggestion. He nodded again, but only slightly.

"Good lad," said Will. "I'll leave you in the care of the sisters for now. I'll be back later. Oh, and Silas said to say he will look in on you at some point. And I'll wager Ingrith will too."

Left alone, Alf lay back and stared at the ceiling above him. He tried to look past it at the events that had led him to be where he was now: in bed in the infirmary. But all he saw before him was wooden timbers, and dusty cobwebs stretched between the rafters – and beyond them, only shadows. He closed his eyes to see if that way would be more successful, and tried harder still to remember. Why was he here in this place of sickness that smelled so badly? What had happened to him before they brought him here? Still nothing definite came to him; only faint recollections of dizziness, the ground seeming to slide out from under him, of falling. Then of being caught, carried, and of being watched. *Watched?* Had that been by the women here in the infirmary? Was that what he was remembering? Had they watched over him while he was asleep? He tried to picture who it was whose eyes had been fixed so intently upon him. No, it was not the sisters, it had been someone else. And, whoever they were, they had not watched him, they had looked *at* him. Stared *at* him. Almost *into* him. Someone whom he had been looking at, had then looked back. Alf had a brief image of eyes. Beautiful eyes looking directing into his own. Eyes that wanted him to…what? The image faded. Alf struggled to find it again, nearly had it for a moment, and then lost it once more.

Across the room, Sister Helewise, on hearing what she thought was a slight whimper from the tiler's boy in the bed near the doorway, turned and glanced in his direction. To her old eyes he seemed asleep. *Bad dreams*, she thought. *If they get too bad, I will wake him. Not yet, though. He needs all the rest he can get.* She looked back down at the patient she was tending.

Alf had lost the image of the eyes, but in that last, brief recollection there had been a sense of something else. Something bad that now made him glad he could not fully remember. He rolled on his side, drew his knees up to his chest, and pulled the blanket tightly over his shoulder. Instead of trying to remember, now he hoped that whatever it was would not come back. Would *never* come back. He didn't fully understand, and he didn't want to. He only knew that it would be bad if whatever it was came back. He pulled the blanket further up, afraid of any eyes that might be watching him right now that he didn't know about. Maybe from the shadows overhead.

Sister Helewise heard the boy whimper again. This time she did not look around. *Only more bad dreams*, she thought.

******

Will went straight from the infirmary to the shed where the tiles where stacked. The weather had been warm, and the tiles were already sufficiently dry to allow them to be fired. He and Silas had been on their way there with a handcart in which to carry the tiles to the kiln when Ingrith had come to find him with the news that Alf was unwell. Although she had assured him that the boy was in no danger, and comfortable for the time being, Will had wanted to see for himself, and headed straight for the infirmary. He had expected Ingrith to return with him, and was surprised when she made no move to follow. On his return from the infirmary he found she was still with Silas, but they had now been joined by Sister Alice. The old nun was the only one who did not seem to wear a guilty expression. The reason for Silas's unease at Will's approach was easy enough to understand; the old man had begun the task of unloading the tiles from the racks and into the handcart without Will being in attendance, as Silas knew Will would have wanted. It was a delicate operation and one that Will would have insisted upon supervising – if not carrying out entirely on his own. And it was easy enough to guess that Silas's decision to ignore Will's wishes had been prompted by the presence of Ingrith, and Silas's desire not to appear overly under Will's thumb. Why Ingrith looked so guilty it was not so easy to understand. She could not know Will's requirements regarding the tiles. If she had, she would, more than likely, have made certain Silas followed them. It occurred to Will that it might have something to do with Alf, and why she had not returned with Will to see the boy in the infirmary. He was thinking how best to broach the subject – he would deal with Silas later –

when Ingrith brought it up herself.

"I'm sorry, Will. It was my doing?"

Will looked puzzled. "What was? The boy? Don't be so foolish, girl. He fell ill. People do. You cannot be to blame."

"Oh, but I can. I *am*."

"Nonsense. Speak no more of it," Will said, very aware of both Silas and Sister Alice listening.

"No, I must tell you what happened."

"There is no need of it. Sister Helewise has already told me what happened. The boy took a bit of a turn…dizzy and not himself. Nothing more than that. Could be something to do with his age, she thinks. First signs of manhood, if you see what I mean. Growing up not taking place as smoothly as it might. Bewildering for him…for his body… so to speak." Will had the sense of what he meant to say, but found he was struggling to put it into words that would not be indelicate. Again he was aware of Silas listening, preparing a mocking comment for later, so he decided it was best to expand no more on that particular explanation. "Or, most likely, it was nothing more unusual than a bit of bad meat. Whatever it is, it's nothing serious. And nothing *you* could have caused." As he said this, it occurred to Will that, if it were, as Sister Helewise suggested, all part of Alf growing up, then being around Ingrith might well have confused the boy. "Or it might be the heat. Hot weather can do that. I've seen it in others. So, you see, it could be my fault for working him too hard."

"I took him to see the painting," said Ingrith flatly, as if this confession explained everything. "It was I who did that. No one else."

"The *painting*?" asked Will, confused.

"In the Abbess's room. Saint Merwinna. The one we're using for our design. I took Alf there to see it. It was there he took ill."

Behind her, Sister Alice gasped, but this, Will knew, was only at the apparent nerve Ingrith had shown in going into the Abbess's receiving room without permission or invitation. It was nothing to do with any concern the nun might have had on behalf of young Alf. Irritated by the old woman and her attitude, he said to Ingrith, pointedly, "Well, you have permission to be there. Abbess Rhoswen well understands the need for you to have admittance in order to create the design for the tiles." Beyond Ingrith, Will thought he saw a look of disappointment cross the old nun's face. He hoped he had.

"Oh…possibly…However, the design is complete," objected Ingrith. "I do not think I…"

"You have *permission*," insisted Will, a little frustrated that Ingrith herself was undermining his defence of her right to enter the Abbess's room. This time he was careful not to look at Sister Alice; her reaction would only irritate him further.

"I do…and I don't…Either way, it is not what I meant," protested Ingrith.

"What did you mean, then? I am confused."

Silas, who had been stroking his whiskery chin, studying the scene with more and more interest, looked as if he might be about to make a comment there and then, not save it for later. Will gave him a look that told him not to say it, whatever it was.

"It was the picture," said Ingrith. "I thought he would be interested to see it, you see. He seems so fascinated by all of this...all we are doing here. I have seen how he studies my design. I thought he would enjoy seeing what lay behind the idea…the inspiration for it."

"Well, I'm sure he did," said Will, still confused as to the significance of what Ingrith was telling him.

"Yes, only it's so very grand."

Will tilted his head to one side, obviously unable to grasp whatever point it was that Ingrith was attempting to make. "It is an impressive piece of work, I grant you. What of it?"

"He is but a common boy." Whether it did or didn't, Ingrith thought she saw Will's expression darken. "I mean no offence. I am fond of Alf. I like him very much. That said, his background *is* that of a common boy."

"What of it?"

Will's slightly cold repetition of the same phrase meant Ingrith was certain now she had offended him. She wrung her hands and groaned at her inability to explain. "What I'm trying to say is that I fear such a sight may have overwhelmed him. It was immediately after I had shown him that he took ill. He seemed unable to takes his eyes of her...Saint Merwinna...up there on the Reverend Mother's wall...Even as I helped him out of the room, he was pulling away from me, straining back, trying to see the painting. That is what was drawing his attention. I have no doubt of it."

Ingrith was surprised to see that what Will was supressing was not anger, but what seemed to be a laugh. She followed his eyes as he looked over at Silas who was also trying, with less success, to do the same. Her relief that Will was not angry was mixed with confusion as to what these men could possibly find amusing about her story. Behind her she heard Sister Alice tut. Ingrith did not know, nor did she care, which particular aspect of what was happening had now provoked the old woman's disapproval.

"Forgive us, Ingrith, please," said Will. "Do not be offended, I beg you. It is good of you to worry for the lad. It is, truly it is. We are grateful. It is only that your guilty feelings are misplaced"

"The picture...for him...a boy of his background... to be confronted with something like that...It could be overwhelming. You did not see his reaction, Will."

"Ingrith, girl, this is what we do," Will gestured toward the tiles in the handcart and on the racks. "We make tiles. And tiles are not a poor man's luxury. Only the purses of the wealthy can run to such things. The church has wealth enough. Most of our work is in the houses of God. And our trade means we travel, so this is not the first Abbey that the boy has seen. I'll warrant he has seen inside as many as you yourself have...more, maybe. He has seen paintings and carvings and buildings as magnificent as many a rich man's child will ever get to see. He may not know his letters like the children in the Abbey school here, but his head has plenty to fill it. So don't trouble yourself with unnecessary guilt." Will stopped for a moment, studied Ingrith. "Is that why you would not come with me to the infirmary?" Ingrith gave a single nod. "Foolishness again. When I said you would almost certainly visit him, it seemed to give him cheer. Whatever is wrong with him, the boy will not hold you to account for it. In fact your Sister Helewise is of the opinion that he doesn't really remember anything much of what happened anyway. When I spoke with him, his only worry was that he might miss the firing. Nothing more than that. He just wants to get out in time for the firing, and is not enjoying being made to lie still."

Ingrith was still not entirely convinced that Alf's bout of sickness had not had something to do with the picture. There was some truth in what Will said. The difficulty was that Will had not seen the way the boy looked at the image of the saint before and during his attack. "I will visit him when we are done with our labours for the day," she said. Will gave her a look she did not understand. "What is it?" she asked.

"I'm sorry, I do not think you can be of help right now. Loading the kiln takes care and..."

"I am as capable as you are of being careful," insisted Ingrith. "More so."

"I was going to say care and skill. There is more to it than a gentle touch. You need to know how to set them so they fire properly." Anticipating how Ingrith might respond, Will went on, "Yes, I suppose Silas and I could teach you...if there was time. And I am sure you would learn it well... as you have learned the other parts of our trade. But, all being well, we shall not have to do this again, so where then would be the need of teaching you? And if it does not go well, time will be against us, and there will be even less opportunity for you to learn."

"Can I watch, at least?"

"I would rather you went and saw the boy," Will said, his tone more short-tempered than he had intended. He was worried about Alf, and really did believe a visit from Ingrith might cheer the boy up. On the other hand he was also worried about the firing of the tiles. It had been a while since he had had to do it on site like this, and he was concerned that he might have lost the aptitude. On such occasions he needed to concentrate; trying to remember all his father had taught him about the process. While he usually enjoyed Ingrith's company, and her interest in his trade was flattering, she was also a distraction, and one he worried he could ill afford right now. There was also the uncomfortable truth that he didn't want her to see him make a mistake. He wanted to be able to open the kiln with her present and see her excited and impressed by how well the tiles had turned out. He had been confident of his abilities during every other stage of their creation, but even the best tile maker could fall foul of the ups and downs of the firing process. Many aspects of it would be beyond his control, no matter how much attention he paid - particularly the temperature. Getting that right and maintaining it was not easy, and relied as much on luck as on judgment and experience.

"I will go and see Alfred," said Ingrith. "I want to, and plan to. Honestly, I do. I am as worried about him as you are. You know that. I still feel responsible…at least somewhat…no matter what you say. Only I do want to see how this part is done first. I don't mean that to sound selfish. It may be the only opportunity I have. Besides, more than anything, Sister Helewise told me Alfred will need to rest. I would go to him straight away if I thought that my immediate appearance would make a real difference to his healing. In truth, it will not. I will watch for a time, and then go to him. I need not see the whole of the kiln being filled. Once I see how it is done, I will visit the boy." She turned to Sister Alice.

"You will not need to accompany me when I do. The boy presents no threat to my virtue."

Sister Alice tutted.

The work to load the kiln had been underway for little more than an hour when Ingrith noticed that Sister Alice had fallen asleep. As ever, completely uninterested in the business of making the tiles, she had placed herself as far away from it as she possibly could while still being close enough to maintain her watch over Ingrith. She had sat down with her back against a nearby stack of hay and, through a combination of the effects of the heat of the late afternoon sun and her own boredom, had drifted off to sleep. Unlike the old woman, Ingrith was fascinated by the work, and had watched intently, studying how Will and Silas handled the tiles. She followed their movements as they stacked them above the furnace chamber while, at the same time, they shaped the kiln walls around them.

Will looked up at Ingrith, following her gaze to where the old nun slept.

"She'll slump over any moment," he said. "Sure to wake up then."

Taking Will's hint, Ingrith went over to Sister Alice and gently propped her up using a bundle of hay and some old sacks.

"That should help her stay asleep longer."

"She's bound to guess it was you who placed that there, and why," warned Will.

"If she complains, she'll have to admit to the fact that she has failed in her duty." Ingrith imitated one of Sister Alice's disapproving tuts. "She fell asleep while under strict instructions from the Abbess to observe me at all times when I am about the work on the tiles."

"When you are with me and Silas," corrected Will.

"Well, yes. Still, in some ways I pity her. She is not interested in this work, and she old. Is it really any wonder she cannot keep herself awake? It must be a struggle for her.

I understand the feeling. I myself struggle at times during some of the services we must endure."

Appreciating Ingrith had admitted to something she possibly should not have, and that she might regret it, Will turned, and began shifting more of the tiles.

Silas was not so sensitive. "Boring, is they?" he asked. "There was me thinking they was all mystery and magic for you nuns and monks and suchlike. Not like the ones we normal folk has to put up with."

"Oh, no I did not mean to imply…"

"Not that I'm complaining. The priest has his job same as I do. The word of God needs to be heard. Only I thought you nuns and monks would have somethin' a bit more special, that's all. Specially those ones you do at night. All the light I seen coming from the windows of Romsey Abbey one time we was there." Silas raised his hands as if in wonder at some great spectacle. "I reckon they must have had…oh…I don't know… a thousand candles burnin' away in that place, all the light there was comin' out of it. I tell you, it might have been night-time where I was stood standin' outside, but it was like daytime inside there, judging by the glow I seen comin' out of that place. Those candles must have been a sight to see."

"Not a thousand of them though, surely?" said Ingrith, very aware that Sister Alice might wake up at any moment, and therefore keen to change the direction of the conversation.

In fact, now she studied the sleeping nun, Ingrith was not sure the old woman was not above actually pretending to be asleep in order to discover what she might overhear. Not for the first time, Ingrith felt a flush of irritation. The old woman's role could, and *should,* as far as Ingrith was concerned, be seen as that of protecting her – helping her guard against any accusations of improper behaviour that might be unfairly levelled at her. The reality was different. The reality was that all Sister Alice seemed intent on doing was the exact opposite. She seemed to Ingrith to go out of her way to put the worst interpretation on almost everything she witnessed. Anything Ingrith said or did that Sister Alice considered even a tiny bit unsuitable – which essentially meant anything at all out of the ordinary and, therefore, almost all the activity associated with Will and creating the tiles – was met with a huff or a tut or a shake of her suspicious old head. Also, no doubt, these were then followed by a great deal of gleeful anticipation of feeding back the details of the perceived transgression to Abbess Rhoswen. Even something as inconsequential as the fact that Ingrith had not only allowed, but encouraged, Will to address her by her first name without proceeding it with a respectful 'Mistress' had surely been disapprovingly noted. Although, it had to be said that, so far, the Reverend Mother had not as yet confronted Ingrith over the great list of lapses and indiscretions that Sister Alice gave the distinct impression of compiling against her. Perhaps Ingrith was wrong about Sister Alice? Although this hardly seemed likely. Probably the truth of it was that the Reverend Mother, a sensible and fair-minded woman, listened patiently to all the old nun told her, said she was grateful for the care she had taken, and then dismissed the information as unfair or irrelevant. Or – and Ingrith felt a wrench of anxiety at the thought – Abbess Rhoswen was allowing Ingrith to complete her work with Will before she confronted her with Sister Alice's spiteful and inaccurate list in its entirety. But that, too, seemed unlikely.

It both bewildered and irritated Ingrith that Sister Alice, for all her apparent lack of interest in the work, and irritation at having to accompany Ingrith at every stage of it was, in truth, enjoying herself. And for what Ingrith considered entirely the wrong reasons. Instead of relishing, as Ingrith did, this once in a lifetime chance to observe the creation of something as wonderful as the floor of the saint's chapel, the poisonous old woman was seeing it only as an opportunity to revel in having power over another human being. Hardly charitable, and definitely not fair.

As she watched, Ingrith was amused to see a thin line of drool escaping from Sister Alice's lips. It stretched and, finally, broke, landing in her lap. Ingrith was also relieved because the woman would hardly wish to add this little detail to her dissembling, so she must genuinely be asleep. When she turned back to Will and Silas, she realised Silas was in the middle of answering her question about the number of candles burning in Romsey Abbey.

"Well, maybe not quite so many," Silas conceded. Then, reluctant to give up on his claim entirely and, therefore, diminish the effect of his story, he added, "However many there was, it was enough to light the place up like daytime in the dead of the night. 'Well, look at that,' I said to myself when I saw it, 'that must cost more than I earn in a whole year to do that.' I said it to Will too, didn't I, Will?"

Will looked up. "Did you? If you did, I don't recall it. Then you say so many things."

Silas responded with a grunt.

"To tell the truth," continued Will, "I don't recall the lights being quite so bright, either. And I must have been there if you said that to me."

"Don't mind him," Silas said to Ingrith. "He's ill-tempered because this…" Silas nodded toward the kiln, "is where the tiles work or don't work, that's all. Makes him argumentative. He won't take it out on you, so he takes it out on poor old me. When he gets like this he wouldn't admit to a dagger stuck in his chest if it was me pointed out it had been put there. It's the tiles on his mind, see?"

Will had to concede, if only to himself, that he was anxious about the success or failure of the firing process, and he knew too, that it made him ill-tempered. However, having the fact of it pointed out to him only served to make him worse. Alf being unwell did not help his mood either. "Well, we don't get paid for making a second batch if these should fail. Same pay, twice the work, twice the materials. You should be worried about that too, old man. You would be if you understood."

"I am, I don't show it in an ill-temper, that's all. And I *do* understand. You know I do," protested Silas. To Ingrith he said, "He knows he won't find better'n me at the job. I was workin' on kilns with his father when he was the same age as young Alf."

"Then it is even more of a wonder that you don't know more than you do!" snapped Will.

Silas grunted, and then gave Will a dark look, but must have decided, for the moment, to give up the argument because he fell silent and returned to placing tiles in the kiln.

After a while, Ingrith asked, "Is there really nothing I can do?"

Although the question had been directed at Will, Silas was unable to resist saying something. Over his shoulder, without looking at either of them, he said, "You could fetch that dagger I mentioned, girl…stick it in Will, see if I was not right."

Ignoring Silas, Ingrith said to Will. "I think I have watched enough. I understand now how you are stacking them. Please, might I not try?"

"Best not," Will said. He indicated the now empty hand-cart, and then pointed at the stacked kiln. "Besides, we are done with this part. That was the last load from the shed. The next part you'll find interesting to watch, though. We'll be finishing off building up the sides and putting on the top…using earth and old tiles."

"To watch. Once more I am permitted only to watch?"

"For the best, I'm afraid. We can't afford any mistakes at this stage."

"I promise I would be careful," she said.

"I don't doubt you would. Like I have already said, it is not your care that concerns me. It would be your skill that was lacking. I would have to watch your every action. If one part of the kiln is not built correctly, then all of it is wrong.

No, I'm sorry, Ingrith, but Silas speaks the truth. I *am* worried about the firing."

"And about the boy."

"That too," conceded Will. "All of it does go to making me ill-tempered. I should not want to lose that temper with you. As for Silas…well, he is used to it. If I say a harsh word to him once in a while, his old hide is tough. Not much gets through. You are not as he is. You do not have his thick skin. You, I might upset. I would not want that."

Without thinking, Will had lifted his hand, and placed it upon Ingrith's shoulder, surprising them both. It was only the gentlest of touches, but Ingrith quickly withdrew a pace so that his hand fell away.

"Forgive me," said Will immediately, looking down at his hand as if it belonged to someone else. "I do not know why I allowed myself to…I only meant…"

Ingrith leaned forward, whispering hurriedly. "I am not offended, Will. It is only that Sister Alice…You have observed how the woman sees the worst version of everything. Her interpretation would not be a kind one. To her a drop of rain is always a storm. If she had been awake…" Then, having satisfied herself that Sister Alice remained asleep, Ingrith reached forward, took Will's hand in her own. The hand was rough, as of course it would be on such a man. Ingrith did not know why she had not expected it to be. "I am grateful for your concern. For your friendship. It is has been…" Ingrith searched for the right words, settled on, "heartening to me."

It was now Will's turn to look around anxiously. He glanced at Silas, aware that it was not only the eyes of the old nun that were capable of interpreting things in ways that would not be kind. Thankfully, the old man was sulking, and had his back to them. Ingrith followed his gaze. She smiled, but let go of Will's hand, nonetheless. She did not, however, step back. Still in a hurried whisper, she said, "If there continues to be so little for me to do, Sister Alice may inform the Reverend Mother that I have no more role here."

"It was my understanding that Abbess Rhoswen wanted you to oversee everything connected with the chapel floor."

"So she does, yet I fear she may feel that, once the tiles are made, my presence is less necessary."

Will did not want the girl to be taken off the task. "Has she said as much?"

"In truth, no. It is only that if I am seen to be simply standing by…my hands idle…her opinion may change." She looked rueful. "Not that any of the sisters will be missing me about the place in my usual duties…Some perhaps…"

Will considered for a moment. "Tomorrow, once we light the kiln, you can take a turn or two at stoking the fires. Alf always enjoys that part. I have been meaning to teach more…" There followed an awkward silence when both Ingrith and Will understood that he had, albeit unintentionally, offered her a task that was fit for the boy to carry out.

"A child's task?"

"A child who knows I will not look kindly if the fire burns too low or too high. Alf is no ordinary lad when it comes to this sort of thing. He has a feel for the work that is not given to many."

"You think he may be as good as you one day, then?"

"Better," replied Will without hesitation.

"*Much* better," added Silas, giving both Will and Ingrith a slight start. Thankfully, any worries they had about what he might have overheard where quickly dispelled by the slightly bored expression on his face that made it clear he had not heard anything to rouse his interest. He spat out some phlegm, and then said, "Don't worry lass, I'll show you how to do the stoking. It will be good to have another pair of hands at it. Especially if the boy's still not up to it. It's a day and night job. Oh, and it is a safe wager as to who will be made to do the watching at night."

"Aye, that will be you," agreed Will.

"Suppose you do it for a change?" grumbled Silas.

"Fine, let's suppose I were to do it. Suppose I was sleeping in the day, as I would surely need to. Then suppose the Abbess wanted a word. Or even the Bishop. You never know; he could arrive at any time. Suppose that," said Will. "Would you want to deal with them? Well?"

Silas's only reply was another of his grunts.

"I thought not," said Will. "I would just a well send the boy! You're only real concern is that night work keeps you from the tavern. You mind you keep a clear head now!" Will knew the last part was unfair. Silas had rarely been too drunk to work when the task was one that required a watchful eye or a steady hand. He was not the craftsman Will was, but he prided himself on being good at the parts he could carry out.

"I'll do my share," protested Silas.

"And I mine," replied Will. "And when he's fit, I'll have Alf sit up with you. He can share the night duty. He'll enjoy that."

Silas nodded, smiled. He was pleased. "Good. He will be better company than you."

"None of your ghost stories, though. I want his mind on the work, not glancing around at shadows because you've gone and put the fear of I don't know what into the boy."

******

CHAPTER 15

Compline was over. As was her practice, Rhoswen thanked the priest, Father Thomas, and then she and Thomas stood to one side and watched as the sisters filed out of the church. Most of them were on their way to the dormitory for the night. One or two were headed to other duties they had yet to perform despite the lateness of the hour. At the end of this column of women were the novices and, as usual, Ingrith took up the very rear of this small group. She was the oldest of the novices by several years and, if things went as intended, she was soon to take holy orders. Next in age was Maud who was a few years younger, but would take orders at the same time as Ingrith, having joined the community at Althurst from a younger age. The other girls were much younger, still only children, some quite new to the Abbey. Rhoswen smiled at Maud as she passed. She liked Maud. She was a little slow-witted, but she was a kind girl and always diligent about any task she was given. She was unlikely ever to rise to any great status or take any lead role in the world of the Abbey, but she had already become a much-liked and steadfast member of the community, and she would no doubt always continue to be.

Then there was Ingrith. A young woman whom Rhoswen had mixed feelings about. She could be likeable enough when she chose to be, but that was the problem. Rhoswen could not help suspecting there were times when Ingrith went out of her way *not* to be likeable. It was hard to define. Whereas some of the nuns could be difficult, even disagreeable, despite their best efforts not to be so; Ingrith, Rhoswen suspected, was perfectly capable of fulfilling her role at Althurst more than competently and as affably as any woman there. She was among the more intelligent of the community and could, unlike dear, sweet Maud, expect to rise within it if she so chose. And yet, for reasons Rhoswen could not comprehend, Ingrith seemed almost to go out of her way to disobey the rules, or neglect her duties. This had never quite been to the point where Rhoswen had thought it best that Ingrith should leave the Abbey and pursue a different course in life. It had come close, but always Rhoswen held back from that final step, convinced that there was something worth nurturing in the girl, something that would be of benefit to both Ingrith and the Abbey if only it were to be discovered. The design for the floor of the chapel dedicated to St Merwinna had seemed to fulfil something of that role. Despite the frequent and, to Rhoswen's mind, petty complaints from Sister Alice, Ingrith had applied herself to the work with more enthusiasm than Rhoswen could ever recall having seen from the girl for any previous task allotted to her. Of course the work was a novelty. The problem would come when the floor was completed, and Ingrith was no longer called upon to contribute to its creation. What then? Rhoswen, guided by St Merwinna herself, had seen something in Ingrith, and the design she produced for tiles had more than confirmed it. But what then? Returning to her mundane duties once again might make her worse than before; it might drive her to do something Rhoswen could not ignore or forgive this time. If that were to happen, it would seem so unjust for Ingrith to have been chosen for a role, and then for that very role to, ultimately, be the cause of her undoing. Surely Merwinna would not desert this young woman having used her to enact her will? But what, then, of Sister Euphemia? Had she not paid a far greater price so that the saint's will would be known? What was the hardship of the boredom Ingrith would feel when she no longer had the work on the tiles to make life more exciting for her when compared to Sister Euphemia's sacrifice? And then there were Sister Marigold and Sister Winifred. Those two women were not ever going be as they once had been. It seemed Saint Merwinna had expected sacrifices from a great many in order that her chapel be completed. Were there to be more? Was

Ingrith's, in fact, one of the least of them. *Then what of me?* thought Rhoswen. *What must I give?*

"Are you unwell, Reverend Mother?" asked Father Thomas at Rhoswen's side. "You look somewhat drawn…and a little pale I think."

"Unwell? No, you are mistaken," replied Rhoswen, immediately regretting the slightly indignant tone of voice she had permitted herself to employ to the old priest. "You must forgive me Father, I am a little distracted by my thoughts, nothing more."

"Ah," said Father Thomas, his tone irritating Rhoswen further by seeming to indicate a degree of understanding she knew he could not possibly possess. "Abbey business is ever a trial."

"Yes," she replied flatly. Father Thomas nodded sagely, said nothing. Rhoswen felt she could happily slap the silly old man's face. "It occurs to me that I have something I must attend to. Goodnight to you, Father," she said, and then departed. She had the feeling of eyes upon her as she walked away, and assumed they were those of the tiresome priest.

Following after the column of sisters, Rhoswen increased her pace until she came up behind the small band of novices at their rear.

"Ingrith, please stay a moment. I would have a word with you."

Recognising the Abbess's voice, Ingrith stopped and turned around. As she did so, she caught a sympathetic glance from Maud. Sympathetic, but also curious. The Abbess had evidently seen it as well. "Get to the dormitory, the rest of you. What I have to say is between myself and Ingrith." Seeing the anxiety on Maud's face, Rhoswen added, "Sleep well," in what she hoped was a kinder voice.

Ingrith said nothing. She knew what subject was about to be raised.

"Ingrith, I have heard about the tiler's boy's illness."

That would not normally bother you, thought Ingrith. "Yes,

Reverend Mother. It was unfortunate. The good news is he is recovering well. He is young and strong for his age…an otherwise healthy child."

"A stammerer, though," said Rhoswen, shocked by her own unkindness. From the look on Ingrith's face, Rhoswen could tell she felt the same.

"That aside," said Ingrith, "Alfred…that is his name… is very healthy. Generally, I mean. I believe William sees to it that he is well fed and cared for. His illness, such as it was, was brief and…"

"Avoidable," said Rhoswen. "For a child as healthy as you are at pains to claim, it would seem the illness was unusual. And *avoidable*."

"Avoidable, Reverend Mother?"

"From what I hear, the boy was overwhelmed. Had you not seen fit to bring him into my receiving room…"

"You hear this from Sister Alice. That is a woman who has no love for me. For my part I do not…" Ingrith put a hand over her mouth.

"Yes, it is well that you stop there," warned Rhoswen. "Tell me, daughter, what on earth did you think you were doing taking him there? I have given you a temporary permission to enter my receiving room. Temporary, and for you alone… …No one else was included…Well, perhaps your Master Tiler also, if the work makes it absolutely necessary. Certainly not for some lowly born child who had no more business there than the sheep from our fields."

"Was not Christ himself lowly born? The son of a carpenter?" Ingrith saw the flaw in her crude defence the moment she spoke it, and Rhoswen wasted no time pointing it out.

"Christ was the son of God! The son of *God*! How dare you use such an argument with me? How *dare* you? I had planned only a gentle reprimand for your actions in allowing the boy into my rooms, and to give warning against further similar behaviour. I was even at pains to ensure it was out of the hearing of the other sisters. Now I find I must begin to consider the possibility of a more severe punishment." Rhoswen paused, waiting for the girl to speak in her defence.

Ingrith's immediate fear was that she would be taken off the work on the floor. She considered pleading that this not be done, but changed her mind. It might put the idea into the Abbess's head when it had not previously been there. She also knew that there was little she could really say that would make a difference if such a decision were to have been made. "Whatever you see fit, Reverend Mother. My argument was unworthy. I hope in time you will forgive me."

A moment went by while Rhoswen scrutinised the young woman in front of her, after which she no longer appeared to be quite so angry. "Tell me, why *did* you take the boy into my receiving room, Ingrith? I have been at a loss to make sense of it. What was your purpose? Sister Alice …and yes, it *was* she who told me…she could not provide an answer to that question when I asked it of her."

Relieved at the apparent change in the Abbess's mood, although still uncertain, Ingrith replied carefully, "I intended no mischief by it, Reverend Mother."

"Daughter, I never thought that. However, that was not my question to you. I asked what was your purpose in doing what you did?"

"I wished the boy to see the painting of our saint. I hoped he would enjoy seeing it," she explained, and then corrected herself, "No, enjoy is not the right word. He has a calling of sorts…the tiles…they are his entire life. I hoped that he would learn from it."

"Learn?"

"From seeing the painting that has been the starting point from which our floor …"

Rhoswen raised her eyebrows. Ingrith knew that it was her use of the word *our* that had been the cause. For the second time she put a hand to her mouth. The Abbess gestured for her to continue.

"He has played a part in the creation of the tiles that are based upon it. And if you could only observe for yourself how closely and with what enthusiasm he follows the work William does…. William works him hard, and still the boy applies himself harder than ever he is bidden. I believe… though I do not know the details… that his beginnings were difficult. And yet, with William's help, he seeks to find his way in life."

"I see," said Rhoswen; a signal that Ingrith had said enough, and should say no more.

Ingrith waited, her eyes to the floor.

"There will be no punishment this time, my daughter. *This* time. Your intentions in this instance were not unworthy. As for your actions, they were… ill-advised. So, I will not punish you beyond this reprimand. Although, should any of the sisters question you about this, it might be prudent to have them believe I was more severe than I am being. And you may…you *should*…see fit to offer up prayers on the matter. I fear you lack guidance. We here at Althurst provide what we can. There is a greater source from whom you might seek it."

"Yes, Reverend Mother. I am sorry to have…"

Rhoswen shook her head. "Go now, daughter."

If God wills it, that may be all the protection I can offer you, child, thought Rhoswen, as she watched Ingrith hurry off into the darkness of the corridor. *Merwinna will have her chapel, however much I may regret the cost.*

******

Alf was torn. He desperately wanted to get up out of bed. He wanted to go and join Will and the others at the kiln. Will had said they would be lighting the fires in the morning, and Alf badly wanted to be there for that. Though his eyes were closed, he could sense by the change in the light that reached him through the lids that night had passed, and morning had arrived. The problem was opening his eyes. Just as he was able to sense the change in the light from day to night, he was also able to sense that there was someone standing over him. If he moved his head from side to side – something he did very slowly so whoever it was would not know he was aware of them – Alf could see a change in the quality of the light where they blocked the view. He had become aware of them quite quickly from the moment he awoke. In fact, he had a feeling that he had known they were there even before he was awake. His sleep had been crowded with dreams. Not all of them were nightmares; some had been good. There had been ones much like those he often had where his mother was alive again. Although he didn't remember her face, he always knew it was his mother when she came to him in his dreams. Just as he knew it was her voice - often singing to him, sometimes talking; always soothing. Then a man had come to take his mother away from him. Alf wasn't sure whether she had wanted to go with the man or not. It hurt to think that she might leave him. He cried out to her, but she was gone, and he was alone and lost in some high-ceilinged building. There were pillars and high windows. It might have been the Abbey Church at Althurst; Alf could not have said for certain. It was too dark, and he was too confused. Then someone had reached out from behind a pillar and taken him by the hand. He looked up to see who it was; he couldn't be sure. It was woman. It was not his mother, though. From the darkness at the far end of the building he heard Will telling him that his mother was gone and that she was never coming back. Will sounded sad. Alf tried again to see who the woman was who held his hand. He felt almost certain now it was Ingrith. He was standing next to her, holding her hand, and looking up at the painting in Abbess Rhoswen's room. Then the woman in the painting seemed to have gone. A blank space remained on the stone wall where she ought to have been. Next to him, Ingrith began to laugh. At the same time something flitted in front of his face. He used his free hand to brush it away. It would not go. It kept coming back, flitting against his face. He wanted to use both hands to brush at it, but Ingrith would not let go of his other hand. By now she was squeezing so tightly it had begun to hurt. Alf pulled away as hard as he could. Still she held him. He was surprised at how strong she was. The more he tugged, the tighter she held. And the more she laughed.

"You let go of me!" he yelled. Even in his dream he was surprised by the absence of his stammer. "You let go of me, you *hell-bitch*!" he shouted, using an insult he had heard Silas use on many an occasion "Let go, let go, let go!" Another of Silas's words came to him. "Let go, *whore*, or I will fucking kick you!" He struck out with his foot. Hit nothing. He tried again. Still nothing. And still the woman laughed. No matter how hard he tried, he could not seem to land a kick with his foot or a blow with his free hand. In their struggles they had moved nearer to the window. Aware that he could see her better now, he looked up. It was not Ingrith. The woman from the painting looked down at him, her painted eyes wide as she laughed and laughed and laughed. Then she was gone, and Alf was all alone in the high-ceilinged building he had been in before. Then he was not alone. Somewhere in the shadows, someone was watching him. He ran forward to escape their gaze, but they followed - always just out of sight, but always there – a deeper shadow than the shadows in which they hid.

His eyes still tightly shut, Alf rolled over, away from where he still sensed the watching presence.

This time they were not content to simply watch. They reached forward from behind a pillar and grasped his shoulder. Alf yelled.

"Hey now!" said Silas, "don't you fret so boy." Silas shook Alf gently. "Wake up, lad. You been having some bad dreams it seems to me."

Alf opened his eyes, looked up into the grinning face of

the old man, sitting on the edge of the bed.

"S…Silas?"

"Now who else would it be? Tell me that." A look of amusement crossed Silas's weathered old face, wrinkling it even more than usual. "Maybe you thought I was the person you was shoutin' at in your sleep? I tell you now; I never did hear you say such words before." He chuckled, and gestured over his shoulder. "I hope none of these here nuns caught any of it. Bless me, boy; you curse as bad as a blacksmith hitting his thumb! Or, come to think of it, as bad as me!" Silas chuckled again. "Mind you, you said 'em well enough. None of your trippin' over the words like you normally does. Proves you can say 'em if you ain't worryin' over it so much. Will is right about that." Silas winked. "Maybe you should curse more often, eh? Think on that."

Relieved to be fully awake, and to find himself in the reassuring presence of Silas, Alf giggled; albeit sheepishly.

Alf's giggling came to an abrupt halt when he became aware of a dark form appearing over Silas's shoulder. He held his breath.

Pleased to see the boy more relaxed, Silas had continued to chuckle. He stopped, however, when he saw how Alf had become suddenly anxious. Then Alf breathed out when he saw it was only Sister Helewise.

"I heard you men laughing," said the Infirmaress. "I am sorry to see my appearance put an end to it."

"I think you gave the boy a fright," replied Silas, giving Alf a puzzled look.

"Well, I am sorry for that. It is good to hear a child's laughter in this place of sickness. Good, moreover, because it signals the beginning of your recovery, young man."

Silas looked up at the Infirmaress. "Does this mean he can join me and Will…Master Tiler, that is…at the kilns? I know he'll be wantin' to, sister." Silas prodded Alf's shoulder, "Wont you boy?"

Alf nodded vehemently.

"See that?" asked Silas.

"I see it," agreed Sister Helewise. "However, you will recall I said the *beginning* of his recovery. He looks well enough lying there, I grant you. Well enough to work is another matter entirely. I do not want all our good ministrations ruined by him throwing himself into his labours before time."

Silas looked as puzzled as the boy.

"What I mean is that he may make himself sick once more if he gets back to work too quickly."

"Well, I never heard the like," said Silas.

"Whatever do you mean, man?" asked Sister Helewise.

"'Tis' a soft and easy world you find yourself in here, young Alf." Silas kneaded the mattress beneath himself as if in illustration of his point. "Well enough to laugh is well enough to work where I come from. You sisters, though…you would have the boy here eatin' honey and sleepin' the day through, it seems to me."

"Honey?" said Sister Helewise, a little bewildered. "I do not recall having made any mention of *honey*. I said the boy would benefit from further rest, and ought not to leave his bed just yet. That is all."

"He can rest just as well outside with Will and me," said Silas.

"Ridiculous," replied Sister Helewise.

Silas pointed at Alf's already anxious face. "Look at him, sister. He'll do nothing but fret all day if you don't allow it. He wants to attend the setting of the fire. He has his heart set on it. Anyone can see that. Will…Master Tiler…sent me to fetch him."

Sister Helewise lifted her hands in mock surprise. "So your Master Tiler is skilled in more than one art, is he?"

"What's that?"

"Am I to understand he knows the craft of healing in addition to that of tiling?" As she spoke Sister Helewise saw the disappointment on Alf's face. To the boy she said, "You really want to go back to work? In spite of the fact that I can arrange for you to remain here for a day or so more, where no task will be required of you? No work, only rest."

"Y…y…yes," said Alf.

"If he goes to the trouble of saying it, he means it," said Silas.

"He means it," echoed Sister Helewise. "Why?"

"It costs the boy a lot to open that mouth of his. He risked it now because he enjoys the work…The firing of a kiln such as we have made, more than anything maybe. It's not something he has seen often. He wanted you to know that."

"It could overtax him."

"You have mistaken my meaning, sister. Will did not intend for young Alf here to get back to work until he has the strength for it. There is some masters who would. Not Will. He thought the boy would want to join us at the kiln…to watch, you see? Only that."

"And you want this?" Sister Helewise asked Alf.

"Y…yes."

"Very much?"

"Yes."

Sister Helewise beamed. "You speak so eloquently, Alfred, how am I to refuse you? You have charmed me. You may have your wish."

Grinning, Alf swung his legs out of the bed and stood up.

"Easy now, Alf," warned Silas.

Alf swayed, unsteady for a second or two until Silas took him by the shoulders.

"You see, boy, how you must be careful," warned Sister Helewise. "Don't make me regret my decision. Now you, old man, what name do you go by?"

Silas looked at her suspiciously. "Silas is my name."

"Well, Silas, I want your promise that you will watch him for any signs of his condition worsening. He is not to do any work whatsoever until I give my full approval. I shall come and check on him now and then. Only at such a time as I think him up to it will I say he can work. And you, young man," she reached out and gently lifted Alf by the chin, so he was looking directly at her, "do we have a bargain? If I agree to let you go with your friends will you, in return, undertake to perform no labours for them until I judge you fit to do so, and you have received my full and unconditional approval…and heard it with your own ears? It is not to come from anyone else purporting to speak on my behalf, is that understood? From my lips only. Do you agree to my terms? I will not…"

"Oh, he agrees to whatever it is you asks of him," interrupted Silas. "We both do, if it means he can come back with me. Ain't that right, Alf?"

Alf, frowning, looked from Sister Helewise to Silas, and then back again. He sensed that the old man's words, however well intentioned, might somehow of have made things worse rather than better. If the expression on the nun's face was anything to go by, it was definitely the former.

"I'm sorry to say that is not good enough," said Sister Helewise, frustrated by Silas's interruption, but more frustrated with herself for using language she should have known such a boy would not be capable of understanding; particularly when it was plain that Silas did not understand either. "So, young man, I believe you do not understand what it is I am asking of you?" The boy looked down at the ground. "There is no need to hang your head so. It was not a test. You are in no trouble. I am not angry. Let me attempt to explain in a way that is easier to comprehend… understand, I mean." Sister Helewise spoke slowly now. "I ask that you agree to do no work…no work at all… until I tell you that you are well enough." She took one of Alf's hands in her own. "Is that clearer? Do you understand me now and, as importantly, do you agree?"

This woman in the clothing of a nun holding his hand was an uncomfortable reminder of the bad dreams Alf would as soon forget, but he was careful to hide his discomfort from her. "Yes," he replied, without stammering.

******

Sister Alice saw them coming first. "I believe that is the boy," she said. It was a mere statement of fact; there was no hint of pleasure or surprise in her voice. Ingrith was surprised to hear her say even that much.

"Oh, I see it is our young Lazarus, come back to us at last," said Ingrith, smiling as Silas and Alf drew near.

Will looked up from his work. "How are you, boy?"

"Well, the lad's no leper," protested Silas. "Lazarus... callin' the boy by a leper's name... I ask you now..."

Ingrith waved her hands dismissively in front of her, stepped towards Alf and took him by the shoulders. "Oh no. It was not my intention to imply he was unclean. I only meant that, like Lazarus in the good book, he is back from the dead." Ingrith looked pained at her own words. "Oh dear. I am sorry, Alf. Perhaps it *was* a bad jest to have made."

Alf appeared more confused than offended.

"Perhaps," agreed Will. "Still, at least it gave you a chance to say you were sorry to someone. You have not done that since..." Will made a pretence of calculating something on his fingers. "Oh, since the sun rose this morning, by my reckoning. We do know how much you like to say you are sorry." Ingrith blushed. "Either way, don't worry," Will told her. "Alf took no offence, did you boy." Will ruffled Alf's hair. The boy pushed his hand away, but smiled as he did so. "And nobody worries what Silas thinks anyway," added Will.

"No, they don't," agreed Silas. "They ought to, but they don't. Callin' the boy by a leper's name..."

"She told you it's not what she meant," said Will.

Ingrith was about to apologise again. Instead she decided to try to explain. "Simon was the leper...When our lord came to Bethany..." she stopped when she saw Will shaking his head and casting his eyes in the direction of Sister Alice in gentle warning.

"And there's me thinking that sister in the infirmary was hard to make sense of," said Silas.

Only now did Ingrith see that Sister Alice had stood up from the stack of barrels where she chose to spend most of her time these days. The old nun walked slowly forward, arms folded inside the sleeves of her habit, stopped a few paces away from them, and then began to speak in a tone that suggested she had already prepared what she was saying. "I don't believe…and I am sure the Reverend Mother would share my belief…as would any *good* Christian…"

The emphasis on the word 'good' had been unsubtle. Will shook his head when the old nun chose to repeat the phrase.

"Any good Christian…would find anything amusing in the miracles of our Lord Jesus Christ. Nor would they…" Seeing Ingrith open her mouth as if she might protest, Sister Alice raised her voice, "Nor would they…" the old woman faltered, her eyes searching the space in front of her as if trying to remember something; thereby increasing the impression that the speech had already been prepared. "Nor would they find anything amusing in the subjects of death or the dreadful affliction of leprosy. If you doubt the terrible nature of the affliction, Ingrith, perhaps you should visit the poor wretches who reside at the colony in Cliddesden, hmm?"

Ingrith, her face red, took a single, measured step towards the old woman. Her voice quavered as she said, "Sister Alice, I am sure you know that I have been there. We *all* visit at one time or another to offer what comfort we can. It is part of the duty of *every* member of this community. I would no more mock them for their sufferings than I would…oh…I don't know…"

"The girl was not meaning lepers when she spoke of Saint Lazarus," said Will. "She made that plain. It was Silas here spoke of lepers… and that was not in jest, as I recall. Ingrith was only attempting to put us straight on the story. You must forgive us for not being as good Christians as we might. It is our lack of learning that leads us to make such mistakes. I thank you for the benefit of yours, sister, I do. Please do let us know if we stray from the path of what is fitting and proper in the future. It is a kindness on your part, I know that, and am grateful for it. We all are…Silas, the boy… and me."

Sister Alice looked uncertain. She was not fool enough not to spot the omissions in Will's version of things, but his gamble had been that she could not be sure whether they had been deliberate or not. And Will hoped his attempt at misdirection would be further reinforced by his show of gratitude; the spiteful old nun could not enjoy that gratitude if she chose to deny his version. In the end she merely nodded - unwilling to commit herself by saying anything that would seem to agree with Will's interpretation of the reasons for her intervention, but equally unwilling to deny it. She hovered where she was for a few seconds more, and then returned to sit upon the barrels. Once there, she could bask in the gratitude of these simple, humble men in the same way she had been basking in the morning sunlight. However, Will knew there was every chance she had not entirely abandoned the idea that she might yet inform Abbess Rhoswen of this further lapse by the proud and presumptuous novice.

Ingrith mouthed her thanks to Will who, in return, shrugged to indicate he was not at all sure if his strategy had worked. Ingrith had the same doubts. She knew the vindictive old nun would still find unkind things to say about her to Abbess Rhoswen, no matter what Will, Ingrith herself, or anybody, might do to dissuade her. There could be no doubting that she had done so already. However, the fact that Ingrith had been allowed to continue with her work on the tiles, despite what Sister Alice might have already said, must mean the Abbess saw the old nun's spitefulness for what it was, and considered the chapel worth tolerating whatever minor – and Ingrith hoped they *were* minor – offenses Ingrith might be guilty of committing. She was, after all, still only a novice and, for once, that might be to her advantage because less would be expected of her. There might be slips in discipline that she could make that would not be tolerated from one of the sisters. But that advantage only worked so far. If she ever wanted to take holy orders, Ingrith could not afford too many more mistakes; she already had a reputation at Althurst for being troublesome. For a moment Ingrith wondered if she was being foolish in disregarding the comments Sister Alice made. Maybe the old woman had been set to watch over her for more than the sake of appearances. Maybe she was genuinely a safeguard whose comments Ingrith would be mistaken to ignore. But if that were true, what did it say about the Reverend Mother's having, as Ingrith suspected, ignored what the old woman had reported back to her already? Was it possible Ingrith's future at the Abbey was being sacrificed by Abbess Rhoswen for the sake of the chapel? Ingrith froze in place for a moment before dismissing the idea as being unworthy, disrespectful to Abbess Rhoswen. The Reverend Mother was a fair and generous woman. A woman of God who knew right from wrong. Ingrith would not believe her capable of such duplicity.

"You alright girl?"

Ingrith looked up. It had been Silas who asked the question. He, Will, and Alf were all looking at her, clearly amused. "You daydreaming?" asked Silas.

"No I was…" Ingrith glanced nervously at Sister Alice.

"Don't worry yourself. She's asleep again," said Silas. It was true. The old woman had once again fallen foul of the summer heat, and had dozed off.

"So, let's not disturb her, eh?" said Will. Turning to Alf who, true to his agreement with Sister Helewise, had done nothing but sit and watch the final preparations being made to the kiln, he said, "Well now, we are about ready to set the flame to the kindling. You want to do it, lad? Fetch me that flint, and I'll show you where to place it."

Alf looked eager, and rose to his feet.

"Steady now," warned Silas. "Mind you don't get dizzy again."

This seemed to remind Alf of something that made him look doubtful.

"What is it?" asked Will.

"The boy's not supposed to work, remember? That Helewise made him promise her," explained Silas.

"Ah, I see now," said Will. After as second, he said. "Alf, do you *want* to light it?"

Alf, as Will knew he would, nodded.

"And will it be fun?"

Alf nodded again.

"Well, then," said Will, "it can't be work then, can it? The woman didn't say you can't have fun, now did she?"

No one was fully convinced by Will's argument. Perhaps Alf least of all. Even so, under Will's careful instruction, he set the flame to the kindling in the stoke hole.

"That'll do it," said Will, when the flames finally took hold. He took Alf by the shoulders and gently steered him away from the kiln. "Time for you to rest now, Alf. I'll let you do more when the old Infirmaress says you can. Not before, mind. You made a bargain with her, and I aim to see you keep your side of it. You won't sleep until your body gives out on you, I know that much. All the same, you go sit over there." Will pointed towards the barrels where Sister Alice now sat with her head bowed forward, the sound of snoring clearly audible. Alf looked at the old woman and shook his head. "Where then?" asked Will. Alf looked around, pointed to the handcart. "You can't sleep on that. It's not a bed for boys who should know better. How would that look if the Abbess were to appear?"

"No worse than Sister Alice, snoring to wake the dead," whispered Ingrith under her breath, so only Will could hear her. Louder, she said, "Alf, why not bring some of the old straw from the barn over there? An armful or two. You can set yourself down on that." To Will, she said, "If anyone asks, we can say it's needed as fuel for the kilns." Then to Alf, "Don't worry; I will watch you when you go. If I see anyone trouble you, I will come over and explain to them. It will only be servants. They will do as I tell them. Besides, we will not need much. It will not be missed."

"Good," said Will. "What are you waiting for? Off you go now, boy." Alf began to run. "Walk!" shouted Will. "You are unwell, remember." As the boy half walked half trotted away, Will said, "He is not well, you only have to look at him, pale and unsteady on his feet. Yet he behaves like he is a spring lamb in the meadow."

"I should have gone with him," said Ingrith.

"No, there was no need. We can watch his progress from where we are," said Will.

"True, he'll be back with the straw for his nest in no time," said Silas.

"No making fun of him now," warned Will. "And you know what I would say to you right now, old man."

Silas looked to the sky, snorted in resignation. "Yes, I do."

"Which is…?"

Silas straightened his back, put one hand on his hip, raised the forefinger of the other hand and shook it in front of him when he spoke, as if he were issuing commands. "Go get some sleep, Silas. I need you wakeful for the night, Silas. Don't spend the time you should be resting in the tavern instead, Silas. Dance around the maypole, Silas."

"Good, I'm glad to hear you know what is wanted of you. And yes, don't spend too much time in the tavern."

Silas, who had already turned and begun making his way towards the Abbey gatehouse, did not look back. He waved his hand above his head in acknowledgement and continued walking.

Ingrith looked up at Will. "He won't, will he? Get drunk, I mean."

"Oh, he will," said Will. "Only not so drunk as to be no

good. Silas wants this batch to work as much as any of us here. Despite how he may behave, he takes pride in the results of his labours. I would not have a man working for me who did not."

Ingrith nodded. "Of course."

They stood side by side, and watched as the flames beneath the kiln spread, and the fuel inside began to hiss and crackle.

"What do we do now?" asked Ingrith.

"We hope the tiles don't crack," said Will. Ingrith gave a half laugh, more in grim acknowledgment than amusement. Will added, "And you might want to offer up a prayer."

Ingrith looked up at Will. "*I* might? Why not you, Will? Why not you?"

"Oh, trust me, I shall. I do every day. In this particular case, though, I do think He will listen to you more than He will me."

"Why should that be?"

In answer, Will looked her up and down, then down at himself.

"You mean I am a nun...or nearly so...and you a mere craftsman?" said Ingrith, adding quickly, "In His eyes, I mean," and felt she might only have made things worse.

"Something like that, yes."

"I don't think that is how it works."

"Oh, why not? It should be that way, it seems to me. Just as I am the more skilled at making tiles, so should you and the sisters here be at offering up prayers. It's what you do, isn't it? If your prayers are no better than mine...no more likely to reach God's ears... then why are there such places as this? No, without question He will listen to you over me. Like I say, it is right that He should."

"I don't think it works like that either," said Ingrith, aware of the inadequacy of that as an answer, but unwilling to attempt a better one for fear that, if she tried, she might only succeed in making things more difficult for herself.

Will seemed to sense her discomfort and did not pursue the matter. Together they watched the glow from the stoke hole grow more intense as the flames inside grew more fierce. After a while Ingrith asked, "What else? Prayer aside, that is…What else can we do?"

"What we *are* doing: watch. If the flames get too low we stoke it, if they get too high we make sure not to feed it until it dies back…maybe even rake some of it out if need be."

"How will we know? How do you judge what level of flame is right?"

Will shrugged. "It is like you and your prayers…Some things are difficult to explain."

"Experience, I suppose," said Ingrith.

"Not as much as I would like. Not these days when most tiles are no longer made on site. Something like that, though. More a feeling…not quite a guess…a feeling. My father used to say the flames needed to be a bit angry."

"Angry?"

"Never have them calm, he said. They shouldn't be content, always complaining. Not raging, though. They need to be on the verge of leaping out of the kiln and biting you…but not quite. It's the '*not quite*' bit that takes the judgement. And like with any fire, you need to watch it doesn't get away from you."

"Even inside there?"

"One good spark making its way over to the straw in that barn…"

"Yes, I can imagine."

At that point Alf arrived back with an armful of straw. He lifted it as if to ask what he should do with it.

"Set it down, boy. Then set your arse on top of it," said Will. "Oh, begging your pardon, Ingrith." Ingrith waved the matter away. "I know you'll be wanting to watch what's going on, young Alf," said Will, "but don't get so close as a spark might set off that straw. The ground hereabouts is dry. Everything is dry come to that. Keep a bit of a distance, hmm?" Alf took a few paces back and held the straw out, looking to Will for agreement. "One more step back," Will told him. "There, that's it. That's the very spot. Perfect. Can you see from there, though?" Alf sat down on the straw, craned his neck, and shook his head. "Very well, one pace forward. We don't want you getting a bad neck on top of everything else." Will adopted a mock-serious tone, and held up a single finger, much as Silas had a few moments before. "Only one pace, mind." Alf did as he was instructed. "How's it now?" asked Will. Alf nodded. "Good, boy," said Will. "You still look uncomfortable sitting up like that. Wait now, I've an idea. Stay where you are." Will went over to where Sister Alice was still snoring, and pulled out one of the empty barrels. More to himself than to Ingrith or Alf he said, "left out like this these are set to rot. A waste of good barrels." Then he carried the barrel over to where Alf was sitting, and placed it behind him. "There boy, you can sit up with your back against it. Less effort that way." Alf shuffled himself backwards until his back met the wood of the barrel. "Better?" asked Will." Alf smiled.

Will grunted in satisfaction and then walked back to stand next to Ingrith.

*****

CHAPTER 16

Merwinna, 1171

Father Jerome's account of the disappearance of Merwinna had been vague and confused even when he first came to tell it. The tale very quickly became exaggerated and embellished through his own telling and retelling, and then even more so through that of others, as it was passed down second, and then third hand. And so on through the years. Within a relatively short time there were sufficient miraculous elements included within the narrative – interpretations as divine of what was already mysterious - to merit calls for her canonisation, and within fifty years Merwinna had become *Saint* Merwinna.

As Father Jerome himself first told it, the anchoress had fallen quiet in the middle of making confession. He was careful always to miss out some of the more lurid and uncomfortable detail of what it was Merwinna had actually been confessing to, and the fact of her – and his – almost feverish prayers only moments before she fell silent. At first, he had assumed she was merely collecting her thoughts, he said, and so he had waited for her to continue at her own pace and in her own time. When some few minutes more had passed, the priest had cleared his throat as a gentle reminder, if one were needed, that he was present outside her cell, and waiting for her to continue. Still no answer came, and as the time stretched on Father Jerome had begun to feel uneasy. No amount of prompting on his part would elicit any kind of response from within. Eventually, he had raised his voice to a shout, but still there was no reply. Even if Merwinna, exhausted by her long battles with the evil she believed was tasking her, had fallen asleep, it was not possible she would sleep through his calls to her. It was possible the young woman had become so immersed in her own religious reverie that she had simply shut out the external world. She was capable of quite extreme and deeply felt devotions it was true. But so deep that repeated shouting would not rouse her from them? It seemed unlikely.

Father Jerome began to pace up and down the church. At one point a nun entered, and he surprised himself, and her, by shouting at her to leave. In due course, he returned to the hole in the wall and spoke Merwinna's name. Nothing. He spoke it again. Still nothing. He began to shout it, as he had before, calling out that she must respond or he would assume she had fallen ill, and he must therefore take the action necessary to see that she was attended to. He knew that this last statement would cause her to respond if she were simply ignoring him. She would insist that such a thing was directly against what had been agreed when first she entered her cell. Had not the Bishop himself read the order of the dead on the day she was first confined? As an anchoress she was no longer to be considered part of the world beyond the stone walls of her cell, and no longer subject to the same cares and concerns. Her body was simply a vessel within which her soul waited to be gathered unto God – a cell of flesh housed inside a cell of stone. If it failed her, so be it. In fact, Jerome was sure, she would welcome it because it meant the time of transition was at hand. But there were other concerns that were not hers alone. What if she were to be carrying the plague, or had contracted leprosy? What then? She may welcome the death that those things carried with them; the rest of the community at Althurst would not. The congregation would not welcome the idea of worshipping only feet away from a person with such an affliction. It was not known exactly how such things were contracted and carried from person to person; it was known that close proximity was ill-advised. The stone wall would offer little comfort, even if the hole in it were to be bricked up.

Father Jerome had stopped pacing for a moment, a

thought having occurred to him. He glanced in the direction of the hole in the wall. Perhaps the girl had only fainted, as young women were prone to do. Of course, of course. Fainted. Why had he not thought of it before? It would explain why his shouting had had no effect. The girl would come to in her own good time. That said, it would be good to be sure. He looked around for something to stand on, saw an old stool the nuns used in order to light the more difficult to reach candles. He carried it over to the wall. Standing on it, he leaned forward and called into the opening of the cell. Again there was no reply. He took a deep breath, nervously looking about himself as if he were a thief breaking into a building where he had no business to be. Then he slowly pushed aside the sacking that hung there. It was an almost unforgivable breach of the agreement between himself and Merwinna, but then, if she were unconscious, she would never know. If she were not, she would surely yell out in anger at him before he had pulled it all the way across. Just to be certain, he called out one more time, explaining what it was he was doing, and why he was doing it. He had not expected a reply, and he got none. By now he had pulled the sacking all the way across. He took another deep breath and leaned inward, peering inside. He had expected it to be dark, and it was. Darker than he had expected, in fact, and his eyes needed time to adjust. All he could make out was what he thought was the end of a very rudimentary bed, and a stool – not unlike the one he himself now stood upon – at its foot. He had also expected it to smell. After all, the girl slept, ate, defecated, and urinated in the place. He had pinched his nose with the fingers of one hand against the odours he expected to emanate from inside, but something – a large fly perhaps – flew out at him from the darkness beyond and bounced off his face, causing him to wobble slightly on the stool upon which he stood, and forcing him to grasp with both hands at the ledge of the opening in order to steady himself. In doing so, he had released his nostrils. The smell that reached them was more shocking to him than any ordure or other bodily filth could ever have given off. It was shocking because it was unexpected, and wholly inexplicable. He would later describe it as being like the combined aroma of a thousand of the sweetest scented flowers imaginable, all of them warmed by the summer sun. It was so strong it was impossible it had always been there; he and the congregation must surely have smelled it before if it had. The intensity and freshness of the smell convinced him that it was new, that whatever had given rise to it had taken place only moments before. The question was what on earth *could* have given rise to it? What could Merwinna have inside the cell with her to create such a wave of fragrance, and of such concentration and sweetness? Perfume, was that it? Oils of some sort? It was not the smell of any of the sacramental oils. Was she using a liniment with which Father Jerome was unfamiliar to ease some disorder – an embrocation of some sort for rubbing on her body to relieve some pain or other? But such an oil, so richly and exotically perfumed as this one, could only come from the very best of merchants, perhaps even from over the sea. It would surely cost a small fortune. How on earth could Merwinna have come by it, let alone have the wealth to purchase it. A gift then? Unlikely; it was not like her to accept gifts, nor to purchase such luxury, even if she had the means to do so. Whatever the source, the aroma of it was wonderful, intoxicating.

Only now did Father Jerome realise he had no idea how long he had been standing there contemplating the fragrance. It seemed to him that the light of the sun through the tall windows behind him had shifted its position quite significantly. Had he really been there for so long?

With a shudder, he remembered why he was there, upon the stool.

"Merwinna?" he called, hastily. "Is all well with you. It is I, Father Jerome. Please, you must forgive me this intrusion. I was concerned for your welfare. I was…" It might have been something in the way his own voice had echoed back to him, or the absolute stillness of the shadows beyond. Whatever the reason, Father Jerome had the strongest feeling that there was no one inside the cell. No one who would answer him no matter how often he might call her name. Merwinna had gone. But he did not say exactly that to the Abbey servants he ordered to help him break down the wall. He made up a story about Merwinna needing assistance after having fallen and injured herself.

Not wanting to create unnecessary damage inside the church, Father Jerome directed the men to swing their hammers and pickaxes against the outside walls of the cell. Despite their lack of enthusiasm for the task, Big Peter the mason and his men had done their job well when they had walled Merwinna up inside; it took the better part of an hour before the smallest of breaches was created in the wall by the men now trying to break it down. When, at last, enough of the wall had come down that the priest could enter, he found to his astonishment that his instinct had been correct; there was no sign of Merwinna to be found. No search was necessary; the room was so small. All that remained, apart from her simple furniture, were her few earthly possessions: worn and ragged clothes, a bible, a book of hours, some eating utensils, and a half-full chamber pot. The sweet fragrance Jerome had smelled previously was gone, replaced by the sort of base and unpleasant odours one would have expected from a room where someone had lived such an enclosed life.

The story of Merwinna's mysterious disappearance gave rise to much speculation. A few sought to explain it as a deception. The woman, they said, had obviously lacked the strength of will or the faith necessary for the role she had chosen for herself. So, having given up the life of an anchoress, she had simply left her cell. It would be no difficult thing – particularly with the connivance of the sisters and the priest involved - to have the wall broken down and then rebuilt; the stones put back in place to allow her escape to appear somehow miraculous. It would save her and, more importantly, the Abbey the embarrassment of being forced to admit that their much-vaunted holy anchoress was nothing but a weak-willed girl, her calling nothing but a delusion misguidedly encouraged by the nuns of the Abbey. Perhaps, some said, Merwinna had lost her reason, driven insane by the pressure of the prolonged confinement for which she was not suited? Tales began to be told of a mysterious madwoman spotted living in the countryside thereabouts. A woman who might well be Merwinna, now unable to bear any walls around her, and so choosing to live wild among the open spaces of field and forest.

However, these stories, and those who spread them represented only a small minority. Most people believed, as had been claimed, that Merwinna, her earthly life having reached its end, had been taken up to heaven. Not only her soul, but also her mortal remains. A second Assumption. Like that of the Virgin Mary herself. What better, what more fitting, end to the life of one whose final days had been ones of such complete devotion? This was the view encouraged by the Abbey, and it soon gave rise to a cult of Merwinna. *Saint* Merwinna, as she was later to become.

******

CHAPTER 17

Althurst Abbey – 1307

A s she promised, Sister Helewise came out to check on Alf's wellbeing around mid-afternoon of the day the kiln was first lit. The boy was recovering, she told Will, but warned against him being permitted to overtax himself. When asked by Sister Helewise if he would not be more comfortable back in the infirmary, Alf had shaken his head and pointed at the kiln. The Infirmaress had known better than to press her point, and conceded to Will that, despite the risk of him becoming tired, Alf seemed to profit from being out with what she called his 'work companions and their work'. The benefits, for the moment at least, outweighed the dangers. However, by late afternoon Alf's determination to remain awake had failed him, and he slept, curled up on his heap of straw, his cap clutched tightly in his hands.

"Should we carry him back inside?" asked Ingrith.

Will considered the suggestion. "Not yet. He'll be upset if he wakes to find there is still sun in the sky and we have taken him away from here. Besides, when the time comes, I think I'll take him back to the inn where we are lodging. I don't think he likes the infirmary."

"Better off with his 'work companions' you mean?" asked Ingrith

"I think so, don't you?" replied Will. "Mind you, if he stays out like that in this high sun without his head covered, he'll regret it. I'd better go put his cap back on. I tell him time and again that the sun can burn the back of the neck so it hurts, but you know how boys are about such things.

"You care for that boy as if he were your own son," observed Ingrith quietly when Will joined her again at the kiln.

"Well, he's not, if that's what you are asking."

"I wasn't. I never thought…"

"Although I will admit I am fond of the boy," said Will, almost defensively, as if his affection for Alf were a weakness.

"He is easy to like," said Ingrith.

"Aye, that he is. Silas is fond of him too, although the old man would not admit it as readily as I have. In answer to your question…"

"A question I have not asked."

"In answer to your question. What young Alf is…*was*…is the son of a friend of mine."

"Was?"

"The man died. His wife too, poor woman."

"He is still their son for all that. "

"That he is. Only they are not around to be his parents, are they? The age he is now it is right that he should be apprenticed to someone, working wherever that apprenticeship takes him. Thing is, it was to have been to his father, Ralph, my friend, that he was apprenticed. He was a mason, was Ralph. A good one, too. Alf would have been apprentice to his own father, not to me, had things been different. Had they been as they should have been. Oh, I don't regret taking the boy on. He's proved good at the work. And... well…" Will pointed to the sleeping boy. "You only have to look at him now to see how much he takes to it. It's almost all he cares about. More than even I do sometimes, it seems to me. Too much, maybe."

"What happened. To his parents, I mean. How is it he came to be apprenticed to you and not his father? Ralph, I think you said?"

"Yes, Ralph. Good fellow he was. He and poor Lizzy. Good people. Not deserving of what happened. Who would be? It's not a very nice story." Will looked at Ingrith. Her expression showed she wanted him to continue. "They lived in Winchester…I was raised not far from there. I knew Ralph and Lizzy from when they were young. They always had eyes for each other. No surprise to anyone when they married. Lizzy was always a pretty girl. She made a handsome woman." Will looked down, scuffed the ground with his foot. "You'd think that would be a good thing. But she paid the price for it. Why she should have to go through what she did…" Will finally looked back up at Ingrith. She had already guessed what he was about to tell her. "She was raped and then she was murdered and the boy saw all of it." Will had spat out the words rapidly, one after another, as if they tasted bitter in his mouth. "Then, whoever did it, hit the boy for good measure. Hit him hard. Hard enough to kill him. More than likely it's what they intended. Only, God be praised, it didn't."

Ingrith looked over at where Alf still slept. "The scar on his head?"

"That's it. It was believed he must have witnessed it all. The rape, the murder. The killers must have wanted to kill him too so he could not tell. They must have believed they had done it with the one blow because they didn't finish the task. A mercy we should be grateful for, I suppose. The joke of it was, when he came round, he could remember nothing and could utter not a word. So they did what they were trying to do…silence him for good…anyway. He speaks these days, after a fashion, but he still remembers nothing of what happened. Another mercy, I suppose. Although it does not bring his mother back. Or his father."

"His father too? The father was murdered too?"

"Oh, not with their bare hands. More with their deeds, if you take my meaning. Ralph could not bear it, you see. He died within the year."

"Suicide?" said Ingrith, shocked, but wishing she had kept shock out of her voice.

"Oh, no," said Will, brushing the idea away with his hand. "Ralph would never…he was a God-fearing man. And he would never have willingly abandoned his boy…particularly at such a time…when he needed his father more than ever before. It was his heart they think. It gave out on him. Bad luck they said. A weak heart…nothing could be done about it, they said. A blind man could see it was the grief that killed him. The strain of it all. Anyway, the boy was left on his own in the world. His father had been my friend, so I took him on. I'm glad to have him, as I say. I only wish I had come by him differently."

"He was lucky…That his father had such a friend, I mean."

"I can't help thinking it was the only bit of luck he ever had."

"He still does not remember?"

"We should be grateful for that for his sake. Although it meant that he wasn't able to point the finger at who did it. Whoever it was got away without the punishment they deserved. They were lucky is all I can say." Will smiled grimly. "In the next life they will not be so. I hope they burn."

Ingrith studied Will for a moment. His eyes watched something in the past that he was not telling her. "You speak almost as if you *did* know who they were, Will?"

Will looked awkward. "No."

"What troubles you, then? I see that something does."

Will looked over at Alf when he spoke. "There was some talk of men from the sea having been around the place. Sailors, up from Southampton or Portsmouth. His father and I tried to find them."

"And did you?"

"No, thank God. What was in our hearts that day…in mine…I am ashamed of it. Even now. If God sees into our hearts, what he saw in mine He will remember when my time comes to be judged. I cannot forget it, nor will He. If we *had* found them…caught up with them…guilty or not…I know we would have killed them." He turned to face Ingrith. "God help me. She was not even my wife, and yet I would have gladly killed those men in revenge for the pain I saw in my friend's eyes that day. I had murder in my heart.

Real...vengeful... murder. I would have done it, I know I would. I would have killed them."

"Or they might have killed you instead! Have you not considered that? Besides..."

Will turned his head slightly, looking at her now with eyes narrowed, uncertain. "Besides what?"

For some reason, Ingrith had had a sudden urge to ask where Will's own son was that day. How old he had been...could he possibly have...but she quickly dismissed it as groundless and contemptible. Instead she said, "I understand your feelings, Will, believe me. That said, have a care not to let revenge enter your heart in such a way ever again...or the boy's heart for that matter. God will punish the men who sinned against his mother. That is the correct way. It is not for us to do it." It was what she knew she should say. It was what any good priest would have told Will, and possibly already had. That did not prevent it from sounding hollow on her own lips. They seemed weak, unhelpful words.

"If He sees, He saw all, and will punish my own sins that day," said Will.

"You are right. He *does* see, Will. And He does not forget." She took his hands, held them in her own – gently at first, and then gripping them more firmly when she spoke, emphasising her words. "But some...those who truly repent...as I believe you do...if the evil that was in their hearts has been vanquished...them He forgives. I am sure of it. He forgives, Will. Your sin...the murder in your heart..." She lifted his hands to his chest. "It is gone, is it not?"

"I hope so," said Will. "I have the rage in me still, but..."

"You would not act upon it?"

Will considered this. "No, I believe I would not."

"You trust in God?"

"I have no choice but to trust in God. And I do. Only..." Will paused. Ingrith said nothing, waited for him to speak. "Ralph was my friend. My good friend. They both were...Ralph and Lizzy. Lizzy was good to my daughter. She helped her with the things I could not when she was without a mother. For those men, whoever they may have been, to have…"

"Will," warned Ingrith gently. "The anger…is it still so quick to rise in you?"

"Only when I look at the boy," said Will. "Only for a moment. It passes soon enough."

"Good," said Ingrith. "It is good that it passes."

Behind them they heard Sister Alice cough. How long had the old woman been awake?

"She could not have heard, our voices were low so as not to wake the boy," said Ingrith.

"Not so low they did not wake the dragon. She may have seen," said Will.

"Seen?"

"Our hands… in each other's."

Ingrith looked down at her hands, now free of Will's. She remembered taking his in her own. She did not know when she had released them. Had it been only at that moment when the suspicious old nun had made her presence know, or had been earlier? "I was guiding you. Christian fellowship, nothing more. Curse that woman and her unkind interpretations. Let her think what she will. It is her concern alone; it is not mine. For my part, I do not care what she chooses to make of it."

"Well, you should," said Will, firmly. "We *both* should. My work here is my livelihood. I cannot afford to damage my reputation if I am to find the same work elsewhere when this is done. Word of such things travels. A man may starve if he has no work. As for you…you should not put your future here at stake."

"The Abbess will not listen to the woman. She will understand."

"As it suits her to," said Will. To Ingrith's surprise he turned and walked over to where Sister Alice was sitting, now rubbing her eyes and stretching after having slept. As he drew near, he held his hands out in front of him. From the old woman's expression, she was as surprised by Will's actions as was Ingrith. "Pardon me for startling you. I would ask your advice, sister," said Will.

Sister Alice looked up at Will with unconcealed mistrust and, thought Ingrith, more than a hint of contempt. "You wish for my advice?"

Will turned his head back in Ingrith's direction. "I don't know if you heard, Sister Alice?" Ingrith winced at the question, and the gamble Will was taking. "Only the girl there has been of no help. None at all. I had hoped you would prove more knowledgeable."

The old woman looked up at him, half suspicious, half flattered. "What is it you would you ask of me?"

Will turned his hands, looked down at his palms as if searching for something in them, and then turned them back to face her. "Is it true what they say about the future being in the hands? Sister Ingrith says there is nothing to see there…that it is nothing but foolish superstition. If that is so, why do I hear so many tales of it being done…futures told that way? Could not our futures be put there by God Himself…to be read by those as have the understanding…those God has given the gift to do it? She was at great pains to deny it. 'Look, Master Tiler' she said, 'nothing but callouses and scars'." He looked again at his hands. "Is she right, sister?"

Sister Alice huffed. "For once I have to say the girl *is* right. News has reached the Church of such practices… and they have been condemned for what they are: witchcraft from the East." Will shook his head, pretending not to understand. "I speak of the crusades, man," said Sister Alice, acting as if she were impatient, when quite obviously enjoying the opportunity offered to show off her learning. "Moorish devilry, brought back from the east by men who should know better. It was not only disease those ships carried with them upon their return."

"Yes," agreed Ingrith, silently asking God for forgiveness for the lies in which she was now colluding. "I told him all such divination is best avoided."

"Not so, daughter. There are ways it can be done correctly. Have you not heard of the Sortes Biblicae, girl?"

Will, who was not sure he had heard the expression before, was equally sure that Ingrith would have done.

Ingrith bowed her head slightly when she said, "No, I regret I have not. Please enlighten me. I would be most grateful if you would."

Will almost smiled.

Sister Alice did smile. She said, "Really? I am surprised to hear it. I have always been led to believe you had much learning. Was I misled, I wonder?" Without waiting for a reply, she set her hands upon her lap, and then continued in a voice that reminded Ingrith of a child attempting to sound mature when giving instruction to younger child. "Sortes Biblicae is the word of God as taken directly from the Bible itself."

Ingrith frowned. "But this is not new; is not the Bible the only true source of His word?"

"You misunderstand me. Of course, that is so. Of course, it is. What I am attempting to explain to you is that individual words…words chosen from pages opened at random… can answer specific questions. It is from them a message is taken." Sister Alice thought for a moment. "It is more in the way of instruction than prediction. Our futures can be guided by God, not foretold. Is it not related by Saint Augustine that he found the true path when he heard a voice chanting 'Tolle lege', take up and read?"

"Ah, yes… Paul's letter to the Romans was it not?" asked Ingrith. Will glanced at her, gave a slight shake of the head. "Or am I wrong, I am sure I must be," she corrected herself. "I do not have the benefit of your…"

"Yes," said Sister Alice, disappointed. "Yes, it was." Her role as instructor now undermined, her face hardened. "Well, in future I would counsel against such questions, Master Tiler. Save them for your priest. Ingrith…for she is not yet *Sister* Ingrith…can ill afford to be seen in such deep conversation with one such as yourself, let alone holding his hands in hers, whatever the reason may have been. I give thanks that I was able to understand the cause. Another person witnessing such behaviour might be less able to do so… and a far less charitable interpretation reached."

Ingrith inclined her head. "It is why the Abbess saw fit to have *you* accompany me while I work with Master William, and I am grateful for your guidance. However, we must, perforce, discuss the work we undertake here," said Ingrith. "The Abbess herself has also…"

Sister Alice waved her hand impatiently. "Yes, yes. That, I suppose, is true. It must inevitably be talked of. Nothing else, mind you. Nothing else. I have a duty to see to such things."

Ingrith nodded. Looking about her she saw that Will had already returned to watching the kiln. She gave another slight bow of her head to the older woman, and went over to Will – careful this time to stand a little further off from him than she had previously.

"You tell tales well, girl," he whispered. "Silas could learn something from you."

Ingrith grinned. "Not half so well as you do yourself, Master Tiler," she replied. "I wonder you have not become a minstrel, or gone into the priesthood. With such skill at stories you would no doubt prosper."

"Oh? Do priests have to tell lies, then?"

"You know that is not what I meant. I myself will have to confess even the small deception I have just now been party to." She looked thoughtful. "Although it may have to be couched in terms that are not too specific if we are to avoid further trouble."

"You do not trust the priest here?" asked Will.

"I trust him. He is a good man. I trust him to act in what he believes is the best interest of the Church… As he should.

That may not always be the same as my best interest."

Will appeared to consider something, and then grunted - more to himself than to Ingrith. She had assumed this was in response to what she had said until he grunted again, and then walked over to the pile of fuel, gathered up an armful of the smaller logs there, and carried them back. He then crouched down and began feeding them, one by one, into the stoke hole.

The scent of the burning wood was carried up on the breeze. It was pleasant, and for some reason reminded Ingrith of earlier times before she had come to Althurst. She felt a momentary sorrow, a longing for something she could not quite name.

Will stood up, dusted off his hands. "There, that'll do it for a while. Nearly let it get too low. We will have to watch that. We must be more careful."

******

With the painting of Saint Merwinna behind her, Rhoswen sat back in her chair, put her fingers to her temples, and let out a slow, measured breath as she attempted to rub away the dull ache that had settled there. The last of that morning's business was complete. The last of what had seemed an almost endless procession of visitors had finally departed. She gave brief thought to offering up a prayer that she be spared any more such mornings for quite some time to come, but knew in her heart that such a request was unworthy, and far too petty to warrant the Good Lord's attention. Instead she gave thanks that the business was complete and the outcomes, so it seemed, satisfactory to all parties involved. After all, there had been times today, it was true, when the people to whom she played host in her receiving room were people with problems that they genuinely could not have resolved without her ruling or advice. The Cellaress had the permission she asked for to buy more wine; the Master of the

Abbey Lands now had the freedom he had requested to purchase more sheep and to sell off some of the cattle at his own discretion; and poor, distraught, Sister Maud now had the permission she had begged to visit her dying mother in Alton. Those were genuine cases where the word of the Abbess of Althurst was a necessary requirement before things could proceed any further. That said, there had also been a good number of visitors whose particular issues had had no real need of her involvement whatsoever. They could just as easily have been resolved without recourse to the Reverend Mother's ruling – or *time* - had those involved been only a bit more ready to think for themselves for once. There were, of course, days when Rhoswen had visitors with no problems to be resolved at all whom she, nonetheless, made time to see. These were the people of such importance in the land – bishops, barons, other abbesses, even the King once, long ago – that custom dictated must receive the time and respect due to them. There had been none of those today.

Rhoswen looked down at her feet, which barely touched the floor when she sat in the unnecessarily grand, and *high,* chair a previous incumbent had seen fit to have made. During periods of self- doubt, this chair had seemed the physical embodiment of her inner feelings. What was it Bishop Baldwin had once been heard to say? *'A small woman in a role too large for her.'* Although it had not been said in her hearing, it had reached her ears, nonetheless. She was reasonably certain the Bishop had meant it to. Doubtless he had said it on more than once occasion, just to be sure. In all likelihood, he still said it. But it did not serve its purpose. It had been meant to undermine her confidence. Instead, at such times when she felt in danger of being overwhelmed by the role of Abbess and all the responsibilities that came with it, she had often thought back to those words and used her determination to prove Baldwin – a fat man in role that could barely accommodate his ambition – wrong as the spur to keep her on course.

As if in defiance of all it stood for, Rhoswen swung her feet back and forth, and smiled to herself. There, now. Was that not more pleasant than having large thighs squeezed uncomfortably between creaking armrests, and the embarrassing requirement for a stool to ease the discomfort of fat legs and ankles swollen with gout?

She allowed herself to close her eyes for a moment, and soon slept. She awoke when she felt the sensation of something having moved behind her – the slightest stirring of the air at her neck. Then something flew past her face. Probably one of the summer insects up from the river. They often made their way up here from the town, particularly when the sun was as high and hot as it was today. It came again. She brushed it away, but could not quite see it. There was movement behind her once more – a feeling that something far too large to be any insect was now standing at her back. She flinched a little as a hand closed over her shoulder, but almost as quickly she relaxed, certain now – although she could not have said why – that, whoever it was, they meant her no harm. Following on from this feeling of certainty that she was safe came a glorious certainty that she also now knew who it was that stood behind her.

"Your head…it pains you?" asked Merwinna.

"Oh… no…well…yes …Yes, a little…" Even in this small matter Rhoswen felt she must not, *could* not tell the saint anything but the truth.

"Let me," said Merwinna.

The Saint's touch was like no balm Rhoswen had ever encountered. The pain behind her eyes that had been threatening to send her to the infirmary now vanished completely, replaced by a sense of well-being that made the Abbess want to cry with happiness. Between gasps, she asked, "Why…? Why is it…?"

"Why is it that I come to you?"

"Yes," said Rhoswen, a touch ashamed at the lack of faith implied by the question at such a time. As if in confirmation of this, she felt a momentary hardening of the saint's grip and a brief flaring of the pain in her head. "Please…forgive me. It is not for me to…"

The grip eased, and the head-pain went once more. "No, Abbess Rhoswen of Althurst, it is you must forgive me," said Merwinna. "It is only right that you should have such questions, for how else are you to learn? But surely you understand that it is our Lord's will that I come to you, not my own. The Lord's will. As are all things, now and henceforth. I am come here from another place... returned to this world I once knew and forsook…that I may instruct you in all it is He would have you do."

"Your chapel!" said Rhoswen, confused as to how she could not have understood this sooner.

"The chapel," confirmed Merwinna softly, the smile in her voice unmistakable.

"Of course. Oh, wonderment…Oh, joy. To be so instructed…I cannot express…to be your instrument…"

"*His* instrument. The Lord's instrument…The *Lord's*," corrected Merwinna. "I, as do you, do only His bidding."

"*His bidding*," echoed Rhoswen, delighting in the words, her arms clamped to her chest in pleasure. "*His instrument*. Please tell me, what is it?"

"What is *what?*"

The slight hint of irritation in the saint's voice, and the brief tremor of fear she felt upon sensing it both surprised and confused Rhoswen. "His bidding?" she asked gingerly.

"Ah, that. In time, Rhoswen. In time. Forgive me if I have frightened you. I too am impatient for things to progress. For now, His bidding… it is…your preparedness. He would have your preparedness. And something else…there is one other important thing."

"Anything."

"Your silence."

"My silence?"

"You are to tell no one of this."

"But…" protested Rhoswen.

"Have a care, Rhoswen, Abbess of Althurst, that you do not let your own sense of pride guide you when only His word should."

Rhoswen felt a rush of shame so strong it was as if all her failings and weaknesses were exposed before the whole world. She thought she might be sick, so strong was the disgust she felt at herself. "I am unworthy!" she cried, and would have fallen from her chair, had not the saint's saving arm come around her, and held her in place.

"That you feel such shame right now is the very proof of your worthiness," whispered Merwinna into her ear. "You *are* worthy. You *are* chosen. Believe that, and you will not fail in this."

"Oh, I am blessed," cried Rhoswen. She had a sudden urge to see the saint who had, so far, remained at her back. She attempted to turn her head.

"Not yet," replied Merwinna. The fingers that had soothed Rhoswen's pain now held her head so she could not turn it. "Not yet. Soon."

Merwinna was gone.

The supporting arm of the saint removed, Rhoswen did now fall from the chair, jarring her knees, and rolling onto her back. She felt faint, and the pain in her head had doubled now that it was no longer soothed by the saint's gentle touch. Oh, but what was such pain when it was so easily outweighed by the joy she felt in her heart? She managed to rise to her knees, and then, clutching at the chair, attempted to stand. She was still too giddy, and was forced to sit back down on the floor. From this position she could, at least, look up at the painting of the saint on the wall above her. The image was blurred and swam until she wiped away the tears of joy from her eyes, allowing her to see more clearly. Painted from the life, they said. Painted from the life, indeed. She shook her head and laughed. Oh, if only they knew, if only they knew.

CHAPTER 18

Alf was not sure how long he had slept. Without opening his eyes, he was still able to sense it had grown dark - the sensation backed up by the fact that he could no longer hear the birds in the trees. It was late. How late? A worrying thought suddenly occurred to him: perhaps he was no longer outside, perhaps he had suffered another attack and been taken back to the infirmary? He recalled lying there with his eyes closed in exactly this way. He quickly opened them. All he could see was darkness above him – infirmary ceiling or the night sky, he could not yet tell - so he rolled onto his side, and was immediately relieved to see the unmistakable shape of Silas, silhouetted against the glow from the stoke hole. He was still outside. As if to confirm the fact, a faint breeze brushed his face. Alf smiled to himself. Will must have decided to let him remain outside with the kiln.

After a while, Silas bent forward, and the glow surrounding him increased in intensity for a moment as the fire flared around the fuel he must have added.

Alf rolled back and looked at the sky. This time he was able to quite clearly make out a few stars through the thin layer of cloud. His mouth was dry. Without thinking, he cleared his throat, and then coughed a little.

"Sounds to me like you're awake, Alf boy?" said Silas, without turning around. "I can hear you scratchin' about behind me. Unless that's a hedgehog or a fox or some such? But I never heard tell of a hedgehog coughing before now, or a fox that cleared its throat. So, I'm guessin' that's you, Alf." The old man bent forward, picked something up, and came over. In his hand he held a clay bottle. "That Sister Helewise said you'd be wantin' this when you woke up. Sounds to me like she was right." He handed Alf the bottle.

"Water…Go on, take it now."

Alf took the bottle and drank greedily, spilling some down his front, and gasping when he finally took the bottle away from his lips.

"She *was* right," laughed Silas. "Here now, let me take that. You hungry?"

Alf nodded.

"I got some bread and cheese over by the kiln. You comin' over or you stayin' put?"

Alf gestured that he wanted to go over by the kiln.

"Only if you're steady on your feet, mind. I got to watch the flames. I can't be carrying you back to the bed in the 'firmary. You well enough for this?"

Alf nodded that he was.

"You're not gonna fall?"

Alf shook his head.

"You certain now?"

Alf nodded in answer, although he was not altogether sure that it was true. Silas must have guessed this because, when Alf began to walk, the old man put his arm around him in support, and did not remove it until they were safely at the kiln. "There now, sit yourself down there, boy. Not too close, mind. It gets hot as hellfire up close. We never get to do this in winter when the heat would be welcome. Only in the summer when the nights are already warm like this."

Silas was right. It was hot. Even at nearly six feet away where Alf was now sitting. But Alf didn't mind. He enjoyed the feeling of the warmth on his face as he watched the flames. Once or twice he edged a little closer, but as soon as Silas spotted this, he made the boy sit further back once more. "Now how would I explain it to Will if I allowed you to catch fire?" he asked. "You be careful now, you hear me? If you are, I might let you have a turn at feedin' it. Will said you are not to do any work until you are fully rested. Well, you slept like the dead most of the afternoon, so you must be pretty well rested by now, huh? Besides, I reckon you want to feed the fire, and a person can't be said to be fully workin' if he is enjoyin' the thing he's doin', now can he?"

Eager to have a turn, Alf reached for a piece of wood from the pile, and moved with it towards the stoke hole.

Silas grabbed his wrist. "Not yet boy! You should know better than that. Only when I tell you that you can, understand? The moment has to be right. See the colour of them flames there? That almost white yellow dancin' with the orange? Golden like. Well, when that starts to fall away, then you can put some on. Not before. It can have too much as well as too little." Silas tapped the side of his head. "Use these too. The ears can tell you that as well as the eyes if you know what you're listenin' for. Right now, it's grumblin'…hear that?"

Alf leaned in, listened. He smiled when he heard what Silas meant.

"Well," continued Silas having seen the boy's smile. "That's good. It wants to stay grumblin' like that. Keep it just a little bit cross. Only a little bit, mind you. You go puttin' too much in and it starts to roar with anger…like a great bear at the fair…and then you know you've put on too much. Understand? Like me with old Will. You know the way he's always a bit annoyed at me…things I say and do that bother him…but I never get him roaring with anger do I? Do the same with this. Keep it cross, but needing your help, and you'll be fine."

Alf nodded. And then, worried that this might not be the correct response, shook his head. Either way, Silas seemed satisfied.

"Good. Now, sit with me and watch a while. By my reckonin' the time will soon be right to put in that log you have in your hand there. Not yet, mind. In a while. You watch and tell me when you think it's like I said…the grumble fadin' and the flame less golden."

Alf sat gazing at the circle of fire in front of him, trying to judge when what he saw and heard there matched Silas's description of the point at which it should be fed. Once or twice he looked up at the face of old man sitting next to him, hoping to read it for clues but, apart from a small grin indicating that he knew he was being watched, Silas kept his face free from any expression that might offer a clue - the lines there showing a deep black within the orange-gold glow of his skin in the light of the flames. Alf knew Silas would not let the kiln become too cool. If the time came when it needed to be stoked or fed, Silas would tell him, but Alf wanted to spot it first if he could.

Alf missed it the first time, and Silas fed the fire himself before the boy had a chance to do it. The second time, however, Alf nudged Silas when he judged the moment to have arrived. The old man nodded solemnly and gestured for Alf to put in his piece of wood. "Mind you use the tongs. Arm's length now…that fire's a hell-bitch in a cave …It'll take your eyebrows off and worse if you get too close…even for a moment. And use the rag to rap around your hands."

Alf did as he was told, and then watched as the flames grew. It didn't seem quite enough. He turned questioningly to Silas, who nodded and gestured towards the nearby pile. "That's right, a bit more wood. Not much…a small bit more…good…"

By his third attempt, Alf had judged both time and amount perfectly without any prompting required from Silas.

"By God, boy," the old man said, patting Alf on the back. "Took me much longer than that to learn to get it right. It's a tricky business. One time I know beyond any question I was the one responsible for ruinin' a batch. You can never know for sure how they would've come out, of course. On this occasion, though, it were my doin'. No doubt about it. Will, he was damned angry, I could tell he were. He couldn't speak to me for a whole day for fear he would say somethin' he would later wish he hadn't. Even now I still worry I'll make a mistake. You now…well you seem to have the eye for it already."

Alf looked pleased at first, and the he looked anxious.

"Hey, now…" said Silas. "What's the worry? Oh, now, don't you worry yourself, I won't be expectin' you to do it on your own. Not yet. That *would* make Will angry. I doubt he could hold his tongue over *that!*" He patted Alf on the back again. "You and me…we will watch together. Two sets of eyes on the job instead of one, eh?"

Another hour passed, during which time Silas noticed Alf began to yawn quite frequently.

"What say you fetch more of that water from the butt, eh?" suggested Silas. "Some to drink, some to splash over our faces. We got a while to go before the sun comes up and Will shows his face. Mind you, if you feel you wanna get some sleep, I won't be holdin' it against you. In fact, better that you should if you wanna watch a while with Will too. How about it? You wanna sleep some?"

Alf shook his head.

"Maybe a short while, eh? Looks to me like you won't have any choice soon. You'll close those eyes afore you can open 'em soon. If you wanna watch with Will later, you need to get some sleep now. As for me, I'm more used to this sort of work. Done it before. Besides, I plan to go straight to the Inn, and my bed there, the very moment Will appears."

******

This time, Alf knew exactly where he was when he awoke. Even if he had not, the breeze had changed so he could smell the kiln from where he lay. It was still dark when he opened his eyes, and there was not yet the faintest trace of the coming day that would have shown as a soft glow rising towards the east, beyond the great tower of the Abbey. He looked over towards the kiln. He could not see Silas as he had before when he awoke, but he knew the old man could not be far away. Alf smiled to himself. Silas was probably off pissing somewhere again. Will was forever teasing him about his frequent need to relieve himself. And Silas was forever responding that while Will might be his master, nature was his mistress, and she punished harshly if you did not obey her particular commands. Often adding after this that Will would be an old man himself one day, and he should keep that in mind the next time he felt the need to comment.

Apart from Silas, there was something else missing, only Alf could not quite think what it was right now. Still a bit sleepy, he closed his eyes again.

Whether or not he had actually slept, Alf could not tell. He heard a soft footfall on the grass right next to him. Strange that he had not heard Silas approaching before then.

The hand that touched his face was soft and small. Not the large, calloused hands of Silas or of Will. A woman's hand. And a woman whose labours were not physical – or if they were, they were not hard on the hands. Ingrith, then? Or the old nun from the infirmary? No, Alf already knew it would be neither of them he would see leaning over him when he opened his eyes. If he didn't open them, perhaps she would go away? But he did anyway. He couldn't seem to help himself.

Although he could not see her clearly yet, he could tell he had been right. This woman was not Ingrith. And nor was it Sister Helewise. It was dark, but he knew who she was.

Or *had* been.

Alf felt his heart beat faster as the woman from the painting leaned in closer. He thought she would smell of stone and damp, but she smelled of flowers, warm and sweet, comforting. She smiled, and all fear of her left him. The face looking at him – half flesh and blood, half stone and pigment – seemed kind. Yet there was something in her manner towards him that was almost reproachful, as if he had forgotten something of which she was gently reminding him.

The kiln! He had not seen the light from the kiln. It was that that had been missing. Where was Silas? Why had he allowed it to burn so low? They could not have finished the

firing so soon, could they? A stupid thought. Of course, they
had not. It would take days, and he could not have slept for
days. Could he? If he had, why, then, would they leave him
alone out here like this. A new fear gripped him. Had Will
and Silas abandoned him here? Simply packed up the cart and
left him? The emptiness of abandonment was something Alf
feared more than most people. He began to panic, tears
formed in his eyes. Then the woman touched his cheek again
and shook her head in reassurance. No, Will would never do
such a cruel thing. Once more, all fear left him. It simply
drained away at this woman's touch.

The mild reproach in her expression remained, however.
The hand that had touched his cheek now pointed towards
the kiln.

"It has gone out," said Alf, his voice free of any stammer.

The full reds lips – lips Alf suddenly ached to touch –
parted, spoke. "All is not lost, child. There is still heat enough
inside to rekindle the flames if you are quick to feed it,
Alfred."

"You know my name," said Alf, flattered.

The lips smiled. "Of course, I do, my sweet boy. I know
all about you."

"Did Will tell you?"

"Will? Oh, no. But you must hurry to the kiln now. Be
quick! Go!"

Eager to do anything this woman asked of him, Alf threw
aside the rough blanket that he guessed someone – most
likely it was Silas, wherever he was - must have put over him,
despite the warmth of the night, and stood up.

"That's right, Alf. Good boy. Hurry now!"

Alf ran in the direction of the kiln. Despite what the
woman had told him, he could see no trace of a glow there
as he approached. There was absolutely nothing to suggest
any heat remained beyond the darkness of the stoke hole.
Drawing near, he squatted down, peered inside, and saw only
a darkness deeper than the surrounding night. In that

blackness even the faintest of embers would surely show as a point of light. He turned enquiringly to the woman. A little impatiently, she gestured him forward. "Inside, reach inside, and you will soon discover a spot where there is still warmth enough…You have my word…You have only to reach inside, and there you will find the heat source you seek."

Something made Alf cautious, in spite of the complete darkness and the lack of warmth from inside. If the woman was correct, he might still hurt his fingers if they were to come into contact the embers she promised were within. He searched about for the tongs.

Behind him the woman hissed, "What are you waiting for *now*? First you tell me there is no heat at all. Now you waste my time while you look for protection for which you will have no need. Do it, boy. Do it! I grow weary of this." In a more friendly tone, she added, "You want me to be pleased with you, don't you?" She gave him a smile, and Alf returned it. Still with his face towards the woman, he then did as he was told.

"No, no, no! Mother of God, boy! What are you doing?" Alf recognized the voice of Silas. Beyond the still smiling woman he caught a brief glimpse of the old man running out of the darkness towards him.

Then the woman had vanished. There was only Silas, still running towards him, the look of horror and disbelief that contorted his features becoming clearer as he drew close to the bright glow from the flames roaring inside the stoke hole.

Alf turned around and looked at where he had placed his arm.

Allard, the gatekeeper on duty that night, would say later that the screams of pain before the boy passed out were the worst thing he could ever remember having heard.

******

Apart from the Abbess, who had her own separate house in

the Abbey grounds, Sister Helewise was the only one of the sisters permitted to sleep apart from the other nuns. She had a small cell attached to the infirmary, and it was there she rested when she was not on duty or at prayer. She was a light sleeper at the best of times, and was awake even before Sister Evelyn, the nun on duty in the infirmary that night, burst into her chamber. Only tonight it was not Sister Helewise's usual difficulty sleeping that had woken her. Something else had troubled her. She had sensed – or was it heard? – something was wrong, and had sat upright in bed, calling out from a still only half-awake state, "What is it? What has happened?"

By the time Sister Evelyn had entered the cell, the old woman was already up out of bed and fully clothed.

Sister Helewise would normally have scolded the younger nun for entering unannounced and without permission, but even in the candlelight, unsteady in Sister Evelyn's shaking hand, Sister Helewise could see she looked pale and anxious. "Sister? What has…?"

"You must come now, Sister Helewise. Please, you must come at once. The poor child…his injury…it is beyond my skill. I do not know…"

It was evident the young nun was on the verge of hysteria, and Sister Helewise felt an uncomfortable frisson of Sister Evelyn's panic herself. Thankfully, she was experienced enough to recognise the danger it posed. So, with a conscious effort to steady herself, she raised a reassuring hand, and said, "Calm yourself, sister. Now, take me to him, and tell me what has happened as we go." It seemed to have the desired effect. Sister Evelyn gave the impression of being a bit less agitated. She bowed very slightly as if the command had come from someone much more senior than the Infirmaress.

"Yes, sister. Of course. This way…Please hurry." The candle flame still shook in Sister Evelyn's hand, but her voice was steadier.

"The child is here, then? Inside?" asked Sister Helewise.

"He is."

"He makes no sound. He is unconscious?"

"He is. It is a mercy. They brought him in, and I had them carry him to one of the beds. Oh, he is terribly burned…" Some of Sister Evelyn's composure slipped as she said the last part.

Stepping out from her cell, Sister Helewise saw there was no need for Sister Evelyn to guide her. The boy had been placed on the bed nearest the infirmary entrance. The nearby door still hung open to the night where whoever had carried him in must have knocked it aside in their haste. The fact that no one had taken the trouble to close again it told her a lot about the seriousness of the injury before she had even seen it. That, and the smell of burned flesh that now reached her.

Despite a bright torch burning in a sconce above the bed, the face of the child was obscured by two figures standing over him with their backs to her. As she drew near, they both turned. In the torchlight she saw Allard the gatekeeper, and an old man she recognised as the assistant to William Tiler.

"It is the tiler's boy, young Alfred, then," she said, even before she could see the child for herself.

"I believe that is his name," confirmed Sister Evelyn.

At almost the same time Silas said, "Please sister, you have to help him."

She hurried over, pushed past the two men. Beyond them, kneeling next to the bed, was Willow, one of the infirmary servants, not much older than the boy on the bed beside her. She was bent forward over the boy's right side, her elbow moving back and forth – presumably as she applied something to his injury.

"His arm?" asked Sister Helewise, pulling the girl aside, and then recoiling a little at what she saw. "Oh, dear God!" It was only the briefest of reactions - a slight hesitation before she took hold of herself – but it was enough to make her feel ashamed. She had never before seen a burn quite so bad. The lower arm was reduced to a few remnants of charred pulp hanging from blackened sticks of bone, completely unrecognisable as the child's limb it had once been. Above the elbow more of the flesh remained, although most of the skin there had blistered and curled away.

Beside the bed was a bowl of water that Willow had been using to sooth the burns. Sister Helewise took the cloth from the girl's hands and wiped it gently over what remained of the arm. "Fetch me fresh," she said, indicating the water. As Willow hurried away, Sister Helewise turned to Silas. "Who did this to him?" she asked, convinced that such a prolonged exposure to fire could have been no accident, and could only have been deliberately done. Silas simply shook his head in reply. "I asked you a question, man!" demanded Sister Helewise. "*Who* did this to him?"

Silas shook his again, but this time spoke at the same time. "He did it himself," he said, almost as a question.

"*Himself?*" snapped Sister Helewise. "Don't be ridiculous, man. "How could he do it to himself? In what possible way could he…?"

"The kiln…for the tiles," said Silas, suddenly anxious that he was being blamed – perhaps even accused. "I went to take a…I was answering the call of nature. Only for a moment…I was gone only for a moment. The boy was asleep. When I came back… I couldn't believe what I was seein'."

"Which was?"

"Alf there…" Silas gestured towards the unconscious boy. "He was crouching by the kiln. Something about his manner was not right. I could tell…I can't say how exactly…can't explain it…but all the same, I could tell what the boy was thinkin' a doin'."

"Which *was?*" Sister Helewise was growing impatient.

"Reachin' inside! He should've known better than that. He did it anyway. I called out to stop him, but he did it anyway. Reached inside like he was drawin' water from a well. Why would he do such a thing, sister? Why would he? I can't figure it out!"

Any suspicion Sister Helewise had about what Silas was

telling her left her at the sight of the man's very real confusion and distress. She was at a loss to understand what he was telling her, nonetheless. "But so badly burned?" she asked. "Surely you are not telling me he held his arm in there for so long? He simply could *not* have. It is impossible. The heat…the pain…it would have been intolerable…unbearable, poor child. He would have been in agony, and withdrawn it as soon as he realised his mistake. He would have *had* to. Our nature compels us to remove ourselves from such things…things that would injure us so badly." A thought occurred to her. "Did he lose consciousness?"

Silas looked confused. "Did he what?"

"Did the pain make him pass out…faint away…Did he perhaps then slump forward… poor child…into the consuming fire?"

"No…that's what's so strange. He held it in there. It was only when I called out to him did he seem to feel the pain of it. He was screamin' to wake the dead when I got to him. Only then did the sleep take hold of him…and thank God it did."

"Aye," agreed Allard behind Silas. "Those cries… t'was a mercy when they ended."

Willow appeared with fresh water, and set it beside Sister Helewise who continued to bath the wounds as she addressed Allard. "And you, Gatekeeper. You saw all of this?"

"That I did not, sister. Not all. I saw the boy only after he had done it. His screams… I heard them first. So, I ran over… found this fellow cradling him in his arms. T'was then I said we must bring the child here to you."

"Can you help him, sister?" pleaded Silas. "He is only a boy. Can you help him?"

The look in Sister Helewise's eyes told Silas all he needed to know. "You can see for yourself the extent of the damage," she said softly. "The arm is lost, that much is certain." She heaved a sigh, and then added reluctantly, "I fear his young life must soon follow it."

"No, no. It is only his arm is ruined. The rest of him is unharmed," protested Silas.

Sister Helewise wished she could offer the old man some hope. All she had to offer was the truth as she saw it. "I'm sorry…with such a blow as his body has sustained…it is not so straightforward. If things were different than they are I would remove the arm straight away to prevent infection, but as things are, I fear it would only be more shock to his system. If he makes it through to tomorrow, perhaps there may be some hope. If so, I will take what remains of the arm… if I judge him strong enough."

******

Will had no doubt that Silas was well aware of what was required of him, and was more than capable of carrying it out. The old man knew how to watch and feed the flames almost as well as Will himself did, and would ensure the kiln was maintained at the right sort of temperature throughout the night. Knowing this, however, did not prevent Will from worrying how things were progressing in his absence or save him from a restless night. Nor did it prevent him from waking early and leaving for the Abbey even before the sun had fully risen. At the Abbey gates he gave his usual nod to the gatekeeper, only to be surprised, and slightly perplexed, by the expression on the man's face, and his failure to return the greeting. He was equally surprised, but not unhappy, when he passed through the gates and looked over in the direction of the Abbey, to see that Ingrith was already waiting with Silas next to the kiln. Ingrith. The presence of the girl always gladdened his heart. He knew it should not, but it did. He liked her. Was that so wrong? Liking someone? But that was not really a difficult question to answer, was it? Will already knew why it was wrong. It was because of who she was, and what she was. And, equally important, because of who and what he himself was not. Although the truth of it saddened him, it was unavoidable. He chided himself for his own foolishness. The whole world revolved around who you were or were not. This fact was made clear to you every minute of every day. Your labours, or lack of them, were dictated by who you were. Your friends, equally so. Craftsmen like himself were not permitted to be friends with young women like Ingrith. They never could be. After all, Will had never truly believed the Bishop was his friend. It was a convenient pretence, nothing more. Jovial greetings and quiet confidences notwithstanding, the Bishop would never truly count Will among his friends. He might have some slight affection for Will – and Will was reasonably sure he did – but that was not the same thing. You could have a favourite horse, but the animal was not a friend. In some ways Abbess Rhoswen should be given credit for being more honest. She, at least, had never made any pretence of being anything other than someone who valued Will for his usefulness to her in creating the floor of the chapel. Before that, when she had not been in favour of its construction, he had been no one to her. And when the chapel floor was finally completed to her satisfaction, he would be no one once again. Her approach was straightforward, almost comfortable; you knew where you stood.

And yet, for all he understood all this, Will could not help but feel there was something in the way Ingrith spoke to him that felt different, felt like the fondness of a real friend. Beyond her wish to see the floor she had designed made a reality by the skill he had in his hands, her comments and confidences to him were genuinely meant and without any hidden purpose, he was sure of it. He had never felt manipulated by her, or taken for granted. Her words were never the calculated, only seemingly informal and friendly, sharing of information for a particular purpose that the Bishop's often were. Nor were they the cold, hard statements of fact - with no pretence of affection - that the Abbess was prone to making.

How could he and Ingrith have worked so closely together to create something as significant as the floor of St Merwinna's chapel promised to be if there were not a genuine affection between them? Again Will reminded himself he was being foolish. His affection for the girl could be a cause of trouble for them both. It was the sort of thing easily misinterpreted by the uncharitable. In the world's eyes, men and women were never only friends. There was always that invisible something else in the space between them, daring them to cross it.

None of this altered the fact that he was glad to see her.

As he watched her, she turned, looked in his direction, saw him approaching. He raised a hand in greeting. Like the gatekeeper, she did not return the gesture. Instead, she said something Will could not make out to Silas, and then began to walk slowly towards him.

"Good morning to you, Ingrith," he said, as she drew near. He was about to say more when he saw that she had the same anxious expression on her face as had the gatekeeper. Much more so, in fact. He saw too, that she had recently been crying. He stopped walking, turned his head to one side and studied her for a moment before saying flatly, "What is it?"

Beyond Ingrith, Will could see that Silas was crouching by the kiln, watching them both, his eyes only occasionally looking towards the flames. Alf was nowhere in sight.

"What is it?" Will asked again.

"I didn't want to be the one, only Silas asked me to tell you," said Ingrith. "He said it would be better coming from me."

"What? What would be better?" Will glanced about. "And where is Alf?"

Ingrith let out a small cry, and then briefly turned her head away. The fingers of her hands which, up until then, she had been intertwining nervously, now formed into fists as she looked back at him and said, quietly but firmly. "Oh, Will,

I'm so sorry. Alf is dead." The last word trailed off into a sob, followed by the fresh tears that Ingrith could no longer hold back.

Unable to make sense of what he had been told, Will looked around for the boy. "No, he's not dead. Not young Alf. Why would you say such a thing? Where is he? I know he's not dead. He's off somewhere. Has to be…."

"It is as I have told you. He is dead."

Still Will could not accept her words. "No. Enough of this. Tell me. Truly. Come now, where is the boy?"

"Will, he *is* dead. He died in the night. Truly. I swear it. Why would I lie about such a thing? I am sad beyond words to have to tell you."

Will studied Ingrith, saw the almost sickly paleness of her face, the tears, and knew then that she spoke what she believed to be the truth. She must be wrong. "But he seemed on the mend when I left him. A little tired maybe…on the mend all the same. What happened? How is it you are now telling me he is dead?"

"Will, there was an accident. A dreadful accident."

Will walked past Ingrith towards Silas. "Old man, what is she telling me? What happened to the boy?"

"She speaks the truth, Will," said Silas reluctantly, standing up, his hands in front of him as if he believed he were about to be attacked. Will saw he had the same pale look as Ingrith. He saw too, to his discomfort and astonishment, that Silas also appeared to have been crying. "The boy died in the night, Will. He had a bad accident. Terrible it was. Terrible…"

"An accident? How? What can have happened? I left him asleep…or near to it…on the grass here. What possible danger was he in?" Even as he asked this Will knew where the danger lay. And his suspicions seemed confirmed when Silas's eyes strayed to the kiln for a second. But still it seemed incredible that the boy was dead. Kilns could give the unwary a nasty burn maybe – Will had suffered a few himself in his time – but he had never known one to kill.

Ingrith drew alongside Will, took his arm. "Come with me, Will. I will take you to where he is. His body, I mean. See him there, and you will know it is real. I'm so sorry, Will. Come with me. *Please*. Come… come…"

Will resisted at first, only giving in and allowing himself to be led away when he saw just how hard it was for Ingrith to keep her composure. His instinct then was to comfort her. The question was: comfort her about what? Alf was dead. That was what they were telling him, but it had not quite settled in his own mind as the truth that Silas and Ingrith seemed to have fully accepted it to be.

"*How* is he dead?" he finally asked, as Ingrith led him – as he had known she would - to the infirmary. "You said there had been an accident…?"

"He was badly hurt…burned. Despite what Silas has been saying, Alf must have stumbled…fallen forwards, put an arm out to steady himself. Poor Alf. His arm went inside…"

"Inside? Inside the kiln, you mean? How could it have? That makes no sense! No sense at all!"

"I know, I know, Will. We are of us all at a loss. That *is* what has happened, though. When you see him you will know it can have been nothing else. The terrible nature of his wounds…"

As they reached the door Will halted, stared at the ground in front of him. Once he had stepped inside and had seen for himself what he knew he must inevitably see, there would be no going back, no denying it. The boy would be dead, and there would be no room for any doubt or any hope, however faint, that a mistake had been made - that this was some other boy, and Alf was off somewhere else where he would eventually be found and returned in safety.

"Will," said Ingrith.

Will looked up at her. "What?"

"You must go inside. You know you must."

Will continued to hold back. "I cannot…"

Ingrith tried to take his hand, lead him inside. "All will be well, you must not worry."

The absurdity of Ingrith's last remark struck them both at the same time. Will looked up sharply and Ingrith let go of his hand, taking an involuntary step backwards when she saw his eyes flare with anger for a brief moment before becoming blank and unreadable, neither angry or sad. Her mouth opened slightly as she struggled to think of the words that would explain such an apparently insensitive comment, or sufficiently apologise for having made it. None came, and she wondered what difference it would it make to anything if they did. She closed her mouth, feeling foolish and awkward. Careful now to avoid meeting his eyes again, she motioned for Will to follow her into the darkness beyond the doorway. Still he did not move.

"Will, *please*," Ingrith said at last, and came and stood in front of him, forcing herself to look into his face. "Please," she said again. "You know you must."

Finally, Will took the last few steps that would lead him within the walls of the infirmary. Just inside the doorway, he seemed to freeze again. Before Ingrith could ask, he said, "The light...my eyes need time to get used to it...It was bright outside, it's dark in here."

"I understand," said Ingrith, not really believing his explanation. It was true it was dark in the infirmary compared to the summer morning outside, but her own eyes had needed very little time to adjust.

Almost a minute passed before Will moved again. Stepping into the centre of the room, he glanced around at the rows of beds.

"So, where is the boy?" he asked, the brusqueness of his tone causing Ingrith to grimace slightly.

"He is through here, Master Tiler," said Sister Helewise stepping out of the shadows. Having observed Will's difficulty bringing himself to enter she had stood back until she judged he was ready.

"Oh…Sister…" said Will, his bluntness gone, replaced by uncertainty. "Good morning to you…Where is…? I mean… I wish to ask…where is the boy?"

"You enquire after young Alfred," said Sister Helewise softly. "His body is here. If you will come with me…" She took Will by the hand, and gently led him towards a small chamber off the main room. Ingrith followed a few steps behind.

Alf was laid out on a trestle table at the centre of the room. Will, moaned slightly on first seeing him there, and then stepped up to the table. Ingrith joined Sister Helewise on the other side of the table. Both women watched in silence as Will looked over the boy's body. Ingrith saw his eyes dart to the ruined arm. He winced, as he took in what he saw there, and looked away, careful not to look in that direction again.

Will's hand reached out, then hovered indecisively. He looked up at the two women.

"You may touch him if you wish," said Sister Helewise. "It would not be improper."

Will reached forward, gently touched Alf's cheek, and then seemed to Ingrith to brush away stray hairs that may or may not have been there from the boy's forehead.

Will studied Alf's face. It seemed different somehow. It was not only that he was dead, there was something else. Will's eyebrows knitted, and Sister Helewise must have understood the confusion in his face because she said, "We washed him. Cleaned the body before burial." There was no hint of reproach in her voice, but still Will felt a sense of shame that the boy should have been so filthy whilst in his care. Of course most people – young boys in particular – carried their share of grime, only it should not have been to the extent that a washed face made him appear quite so different.

Perhaps reading his thoughts once more, Sister Helewise said, "He was not so very dirty beforehand. Unkempt as boys are wont to be, perhaps…Not so very dirty. No more than most. Less than many. It is because he is at peace now...the cares of this life no longer his… That is what changes him so."

Will hoped the old nun was right in what she said. He hoped Alf's cares were all gone. "Well then, young Alf," he said, his voice deceptively bluff, obviously forced. "It seems it is time for you and me to part company. Sooner than I would have wished for it." Will cleared his throat. "Well now, you listen to me. I've something to say to you I want you to hear. You were a damn good apprentice, boy. If you didn't already know it, I'm telling you now. You would have made a better tiler than I ever was if God had granted you the time. That was not His plan, it turns out. You will be joining your parents now. You be sure and wish them well from me. Oh, and you will not stammer in Heaven. So you make sure you speak to them at the top of your voice, eh." His eyes strayed down to the burnt remains of the arm, then back up to Alf's face. "They will do a better job of taking care of you than I have done, I reckon."

Ingrith began to take a step towards Will, but Sister Helewise rested a restraining hand on her forearm, and accompanied the gesture with a barely perceptible shake of the head. Reluctantly, Ingrith obeyed. At first, she assumed it was because Sister Helewise felt it necessary to give Will more time to compose himself. Then she understood. It was not about Will needing more time; it was about it being improper for someone like Ingrith to offer comfort to someone like him. The older woman had somehow sensed that the comfort Ingrith wished to offer Will was beyond that which, as a Christian, was plainly her duty to offer any man in his position, and was as much about her particular affection for this man, and the anguish she felt at seeing his grief.

Would that really have been so inappropriate? The Infirmaress appeared to think it would.

Ingrith felt an almost dizzying sense of disquiet. She felt

as if she were a step removed from all that was taking place immediately around her, and unable to properly judge what was right and what was not. As if in response to these feelings, Will turned and looked directly at her. She felt both him and Sister Helewise gazing at her. She swayed under their scrutiny. It took her a few seconds to realise Will was speaking, asking her a question.

"I'm sorry, Will. What is it?" she asked at last, her voice sounding to her like someone else's.

"How? I want the truth of it. How did this happen?"

Will's insistence had brought her back to her surroundings. "I only know what Silas has told me."

"Silas?" Now Will remembered something Ingrith had said to him earlier. "'*Despite what Silas has been saying.*' That's what you said. What did you mean by it?"

Ingrith shrugged as if it wasn't important, but Will remembered now how Silas had looked when he first saw him. He wondered now if he had he misread his behaviour. The expression on Silas's face; was it, in fact, guilt he had seen in the old man's features, not grief? He remembered now how Silas had stepped away as he approached, as if he had been expecting anger from him. Why would Silas think he would be angry? Unless...

Without explanation Will left the small chamber, strode through the infirmary, and out into the bright morning. Ingrith followed, struggling to keep up. His pace increased further until, by the time Silas looked up from the stoke hole and saw him approaching, he had broken into a run. Silas stood up, began to back away, but he backed into the cart, so Will was upon him before he could create any distance between them. Will raised a balled fist, swung his arm, and struck the old man a vicious blow to the side of the head. The blow had been clumsy and poorly aimed. Although Silas spun on his feet, and staggered, he did not fall. Determined to do better with his next blow, Will grabbed Silas by the scruff of his tunic, steadied him, and struck again. This time

Will knew he had done more damage. He felt the pain of the impact in his own knuckles as they landed against Silas's jaw, saw the old man's eyes roll back in his head, and felt the tug on his other hand - the hand which gripped the rough material of the tunic - as Silas slumped to the ground. Released from Will's grip, Silas rolled over against a wheel of the cart. Will had drawn back his foot ready to launch a kick when Ingrith reached them.

"No, Will! Stop! You must stop this!" she cried from behind him.

Will did stop what he was doing, only to turn on Ingrith instead, his face twisted by rage. "There you go again, telling me what it is I *must* do. Why did you not tell me I must *not* trust the boy into the care of this old fool, eh?" Will's yell was almost a sob when he added, "Why didn't you or anyone tell me that?"

"It was none of Silas's doing!" cried Ingrith. "Look at him, Will. Look what you have done!"

"Yes, and I am not done with him yet!"

Ingrith pushed Will aside and bent down to tend to Silas. Will stooped forward, put an arm about her waist, and pulled her away. "Leave me be," she screamed, hands clawing at the grass as she was dragged backwards. Once they were a few yards back, Will twisted around, leaned forward, and let her roll onto the ground behind him. Even in his rage, Ingrith sensed Will had been careful not to hurt her. It gave her courage. She pushed him aside again, ran ahead of him, and got to her knees in front of Silas. "Think what you are doing. It is your grief that makes you mad, Will. That is what's happening. Think! Why would Silas harm the boy?"

"I would never…" shouted Silas from behind her. He scrambled to his feet, grabbed at a shovel that lay in a heap of tools on the cart, and backed away with it held out defiantly in front of him. Will stepped past Ingrith, grabbed a second shovel, and faced Silas with it.

"Go ahead, old man, do your worst. Come on, swing that

thing if are going to!" shouted Will.

"Will...I...I don't..." Silas panted, blood and saliva spraying from his mouth as he spoke.

"Please stop this, I beg you," cried Ingrith. "Please... *Will*..."

Will turned to look at her once more, only this time the rage had drained from his face. He threw down the shovel, sank to his knees, his face in his hands. Ingrith went over to him, put her hands on his shoulders.

Only then did she notice the small group of onlookers that had gathered. She was relieved to see that it was only three of the Abbey servants: two middle aged women and much younger man. Thankfully, none of the sisters had been there to witness what had taken place, although there was little hope that the Abbess would not hear about it sooner or later.

"All is well here," Ingrith told them. "Be about your business, all of you." One woman picked up the bundle she had been carrying and walked away. But the other woman remained where she was, grabbing at the young man's arm, forcing him to stand his ground. She looked questioningly at Ingrith.

"Be off with you now," said Ingrith, mustering as much conviction and authority as she could. "I have told you; all is well here. Leave us. *Now!*"

The woman looked unsure, but this time she and the man did as they had been instructed. No doubt with the intention of telling everyone they encountered about what they had seen, thought Ingrith.

Will waited for them to go, and then looked up at Silas. "Why did you leave Alf alone for so long?"

Silas almost howled, "I didn't. I swear it. It's what I've been telling everyone. They won't believe me, though." Silas glanced accusingly at Ingrith. "None of them do. But I swear it. I *swear* it, Will. May God strike me down as I speak. I was only over there..." He pointed to the shed where the tiles had been housed prior to firing. "I just went to take a piss against the wall there. I was gone no time at all. The boy was sleepin'. I checked him before I went. I weren't gonna be long. I wouldn't leave the kiln for long, now would I?"

Will let his hands drop from his face. "I've seen his arm, Silas... what's left of it... I've *seen* it. The boy lying there dead, his arm all..." He closed his eyes against the memory. "That was not a bit of a bad burn from accidentally touching the thing. The arm is as good as gone...ruined. I've never seen anything..." He took a moment to collect himself, and then said, "It must have been *in* the flames... and for some time...long enough for that to happen." Will's head moved from side to side as he struggled to piece things together. "He'd been getting dizzy spells, hadn't he? He has to have fainted... or stumbled...maybe banged his head... then been lying there out of his senses for some time, his poor arm in the fire. It's the only way." Will looked directly at Silas. "So, why were you not there to pull him back from it if you were only where you say you were, eh? Pissing! God forgive you for not being there, old man." Will punched the ground. "And God forgive me for it, also!"

Silas threw down his shovel, took a step towards Will, his hands out in front of him. "Hear what I'm tellin' you, please, Will. Listen to what I say. He was not left to burn like you say he was. I would not let that happen. You know me. You know I wouldn't. Anyway, how could it happen like that? Even if he had done what you say...what they all say... fainted or some such...even if he fell forward like you all say...it couldn't have happened like that." Silas pointed at the kiln. "Look for yourself."

Ingrith, moved by the insistence in Silas's tone, stepped over to the kiln, and studied the position of the stoke hole. "He speaks the truth," she said.

Will looked at her, still caught between anger and confusion. "What?"

"He speaks the truth. Your anger is inappropriate. It is not possible for Alfred to have fallen with his arm inside. Look at the position of the hole, Will. Suppose he did faint and fall forward... the height of the hole...the angle...it couldn't have happened like they say. It's all wrong. Look for yourself. The arm could not come to rest in such a position. For it to happen, the arm would have to be held in there," she gasped, horrified by the implications of what she had said. "Oh, but who would do such an evil thing? Who would take a child and force him to endure such torment?"

Will looked back up at Silas who, a stricken look upon his face, was backing away again. Will waved him to a halt. "Not you, Silas. Not you. That much I do know. You were as fond of the boy as I was."

Silas looked relieved, and yet it seemed to both Will and Ingrith that there was something more he wanted to say, something that was troubling him. He gestured for them to draw near. Ingrith and Will exchanged glances, and then did as he asked.

"I have not been believed when I said the boy was not left long enough to have fallen and burned himself. There is more I could have said in my defence that for the boy's sake I have not told. Better for me to be thought an old fool who did not pay proper attention than for the boy to be thought ..." He stopped, seemed to consider something, a frown creasing his forehead. "I still do not know if I should tell it." He sighed heavily. "And I won't be believed if I do. Why should I be? Although I saw it with these old eyes, I do not know if I believe it myself."

"Tell us, nonetheless," said Ingrith softly.

"Why? You will not believe it," said Silas.

Ingrith looked at Will, urging him with her expression to encourage Silas to talk.

"Please, old friend," said Will.

"'Old friend' is it now?" said Silas with a huff. "Didn't feel that way when your fist was in my face."

"For that I am truly sorry," said Will bowing his head. "Forgive me, Silas...it's Alf... his death it..."

"And the girl there," interrupted Silas, pointing at Ingrith. "You should not have treated her so roughly!"

Will nodded. "I should not have. I ask forgiveness of you both. I do not know what I can do to make amends...I only..."

"Enough, Will. These are things for another time," said Ingrith. She turned to Silas. "Say what it is that you are not telling us. Who did it to him? For it is that you are afraid to reveal, is it not?"

Silas looked around to ensure they were not overheard. "It is. Though I'll wager not for the reasons you may be thinkin'of."

"So, who...?" said Will.

Silas looked uncertain.

"Who, Silas?" asked Ingrith

"I said there was not time enough for him to fall and have done that while I was away from the fire, didn't I? Well... there was time enough... if he..." Silas paused, then whispered so they could only just hear, "If he did it to himself." He looked from Will to Ingrith. When neither of them said anything he repeated what he had said, just as softly, but more slowly this time, stressing each syllable. "He did it to himself."

Will looked confused, sceptical. "Himself?"

"Aye, that's so."

"So what are you telling me? That he got up from his sleep while you were pissing, walked over and held his own arm in there? Held it there while it cooked like a leg of mutton on a spit?"

Silas hesitated. He knew how incredible it all sounded. He could only say what he knew had happened. He sighed heavily before saying, "Yes, Will, I am."

"*Why*? Why would he do it? Do you think me a fool, old man?"

"I don't *know* why," roared Silas. "If I had thought for a moment he would do such a thing I would never have left him alone even for the short time I did. He was asleep when I left him. I was only over there. I looked away for a second while I was about my business. Then, when I looked up, I could see him sitting by the kiln. He looked fine from where I was. That's why I didn't hurry. From where I was it looked like he was sittin' there tendin' the flames. He liked to do it...and he had the knack of it by then, see? So I let him get on with it. How could I know what he was really doin'? How could I dream he would do such a thing? How? When I did see, I shouted as loud I could for him to stop, but he seemed bewitched. He sat there with it..." Silas put his hand to his forehead. "With it held in the fire. Only when I drew near did he seem to see the folly of it. Then he screamed. Oh, God how he screamed, Will...It was terrible. The gatekeeper an' me we carried him to the 'firmary...I begged 'em, but they could do nothin' for him."

Incredible as his version of events was, neither Will nor Ingrith questioned Silas's belief in it; there was nothing for the old man to gain by telling such an implausible tale. Though she did not say so, Ingrith wondered if it was not perhaps something Silas had imagined – his mind still disturbed by whatever it was he had really witnessed that night, or his feelings of guilt at not being in time to save the boy. She decided she would suggest that to Will when she next had the opportunity.

The three of them stood in silence until Ingrith asked, "You said it was to protect the boy that you did not say this earlier. What did you mean by that?"

"He died," replied Silas, as if this were answer enough.

"What do you mean?" asked Ingrith.

"What he did killed him...put an end his own life," said Silas. "If that is what he *meant* to do by doin' it, then..."

"He would be counted a suicide," said Ingrith, completing the sentence.

"Aye," said Silas. "Suicide, that's it. And you know what they do with them. Buried so they won't get into Heaven. I wouldn't want that for the boy. How could he be deservin' of such treatment? No matter what he might have done to himself or how he might have died? Seems to me he was not in his right mind when he did it. Wrong to have him treated as one of those. Not right." Abruptly, as if he could stand to talk about it no longer, Silas changed the subject. "I better be gettin' back to tendin' the kiln." He sniffed, wiped a stray strand of bloody mucus from his nose, and then wiped the palm of his hand on his tunic. "The boy loved makin' the tiles. Especially the ones you come up with, girl. Aye, especially those. Would be wrong to let 'em spoil."

Will shook his head, "No, not you, old man." Silas looked worried, so Will added. "You go get rested. It's my turn to watch for now. Mind you get back in time for tonight's watch…you hear me?"

Silas nodded his understanding, and then turned to walk away towards the gatehouse and the town beyond. Will watched him for a minute. When he looked back, he saw Ingrith gazing down at the kiln, and he watched her for a few moments too. Eventually, sensing his scrutiny, she looked up, gesturing for him to join her.

"It really doesn't make sense…the idea that poor Alf fell. It would be impossible for his arm to stay in there, even if by some unlucky…and unlikely…. chance it went in there in the first place"

"You can't believe Silas's explanation?" asked Will. "That the boy stuck his own arm in there…?"

Ingrith's hand came up and began to rub at her own arm. "I confess it does seem unlikely. However, the suggestion that he fell does not serve as an explanation either."

"If he didn't fall…"

"Then it must be the other. Oh, it cannot be, can it?"

Will grunted incredulously. "Even if Alf did…and I can't imagine why he *would* do it…but let us suppose he *did* deliberately put his arm in there, he could not bear the pain. The strongest man could not. He would pass out, and fall back. I agree his falling forward and remaining there is not possible. The angle and the pull of the bodyweight works against it. I am at a loss, girl."

"You have not spoken of…" Ingrith hesitated, "…the other option."

"No, not that. Silas would not have done it. You don't believe that any more than I do."

"True, I do not. Which leaves someone else doing it. How though…without Silas seeing them? And why, in God's name…an innocent like Alf?"

While Ingrith spoke, Will had crouched down to feed the fire. He stayed where he was, gazing at the flames, as if hoping the explanation lay within. Suddenly, he stood up. This time his gaze went in the direction of the Abbey Church. It was clear that something had occurred to him. Something that he was struggling to accept.

"What is it?" asked Ingrith.

"Hmm?" Will looked at her as if noticing her there for the first time.

"Why were you looking at the church building?"

"I wasn't," said Will, bluntly.

"Then…? Wait…Where are you…?"

Will had begun striding towards the church. More specifically, Ingrith now saw, he was heading in the direction of the new chapel nestling in its walls. Ingrith caught up, did her best to stay alongside him, occasionally breaking into a half-run to keep up.

"We are going to Merwinna's chapel?" she asked.

"We are."

"Why? What is it you hope to find in there?"

"Find? I expect to *find* nothing. I just want to see if I…I don't know…maybe…*feel*…" The words died on his lips as if he lacked the conviction to say them out loud.

It didn't matter; Ingrith thought she now understood what was on his mind. "The carpenter…he died in a strange way too…You begin to think there is something not right about the chapel? Something, perhaps, malevolent...evil... within its walls?"

"I wouldn't go so far as to say that. Not yet. It's only that...I only know that..." Will struggled to put into words what he was feeling. "There have been two people dead in ways that defy explanation...Alf and, before him, Ned."

Ingrith stopped walking, pulled at Will's sleeve to halt him. "You believe Ned's death has some meaning? Something that ties it to that of our poor Alf?"

Even in this moment of such terrible sadness and foreboding, Will found himself gratified by Ingrith's unexpected use of the word *our* in connection with Alf. The feeling opened the door to other feelings about this young woman, but he knew now was not the time. He knew only too well there never really *would* be a time. Between him and this woman? How could there ever be? He studied her face a moment too long before he spoke again, and wondered if she noticed. Half-hoped that she did.

"Will..." she prompted. "Do you think there is a connection?"

Will blinked. "I do. Yes. It could be." He began striding towards the chapel again, Ingrith alongside him as he went. He glanced over at her, said, "Ned died alone in that place and, like Alf, in a manner that cannot be accounted for. There is surely something not right about it, I feel it now. Maybe I felt it before...just didn't think anything of it."

Soon they had reached the entrance to the chapel. Will stood on the threshold, looked back at Ingrith. "Both dead. And the only thing that they have in common is working on this place." He slapped the wooden lintel above his head. The lintel that Ned the carpenter had fixed in place.

"An accident of fate... a coincidence. Nothing more," said Ingrith. Will responded to her comment by pulling a face she could not quite interpret – half scornful, half hopeful. She looked into the darkness of the doorway, shuddered, despite herself. "There cannot be any relationship between the two events. How? And, if there was, why do you imagine you will find it inside here, Will?" She was aware of the lack of conviction in her own voice even as she spoke. For some reason, as far-fetched as it seemed, there appeared to her to be something in what Will was suggesting. It was almost as if something that should have been very obvious all along had been obscured by the thinnest of veils, and that veil was now pulled aside by Alf's death, revealing...What? It was there, even if she could not understand what it was, could not see the truth of things. Will was obviously experiencing something similar. She watched him as he stepped inside. She hesitated briefly, and then followed.

Inside the chapel, Will turned to her. His face was in shadow. He drew her near, leaning down so his mouth was by her ear. When he finally spoke, he kept his voice low, almost at a whisper. It was as if he believed there was something in there that might overhear if he were not careful. His words sounded hollow, distant - bouncing off the stone walls that enclosed them. "There are some places are wrong somehow. I've often heard of such things. I'm sure you must have too. It's a common enough tale. In my work you hear it all the time. This place is haunted, this place houses a darkness, a sadness, a whatever it may be...I have often heard it said of a place...It's nearly always nonsense...Nearly. But I have experienced it... a little... once before."

Ingrith lifted her head, looked directly at him, her eyes wide.

Will gathered his thoughts, then began, "A while back it was, when we were working on some steps leading up into a cloister walk in a monastery...In Devonshire it was...Axminster way... Silas and me...before Alf was with us..." Will paused for a moment after saying Alf's name. He breathed heavily, and then continued with his story. "Nothing quite like this... but the walk had a bad feeling. Turned out a young monk...younger even than you...had claimed he saw something there…The Devil, most likely. It's always the Virgin Mother in these tales if it's good, or the Devil if it's bad …" He sighed again. "Well, this time it was bad. Very bad. It was the Devil the young monk said he saw. I don't really know. Anyway, he lost his wits…bit like those two sisters of yours. He became like a madman, ran off. They searched everywhere. Nothing. Then they found him at last. He was in the cloister where it all started. One night, weeks later, they're all processing through on the way to some night prayer…what would that be? Compline is it?"

Ingrith nodded, wondering why it even mattered. "What had happened?"

"Wrists cut… blood covering everything… as if he had slashed them then run amok while he still had enough life in him, spraying the stuff everywhere. Things toppled over, pages of the holy books torn out, glass shattered. All of it running red with this young monk's blood. Turns out that that was why we ended up there…Silas and me. The Abbot decided rather than clear up, and make good, the best thing would be to rebuild the place entirely. Make a new cloister as if the one where it had happened had never existed." Will huffed through his nostrils. "That's the wealth of the Church at work for you. Anyway that's how I ended up there with Silas. New cloister, new tiles. Good money. Only thing was we neither of us liked the place. Couldn't say why. Just felt bad. Then we began to hear these stories. Mostly from the other craftsman. Sometimes from the Abbey servants. Never from the monks themselves. As you can imagine, they wanted it kept quiet… of course they did."

"What stories?" asked Ingrith.

"Only what you'd expect at first where that sort of thing had happened. People said they saw him…the young monk who died…usually when they were packing up for the day and the light was beginning to fade. And usually only for a moment. There, and not there. Well, it was not the first time I had been in places where they claimed to see ghosts. I didn't take any notice…Laughed it off, Silas and I did."

"Then you saw him?" guessed Ingrith.

"No, that's just it; we didn't. Not even a glimpse. Not once."

"I don't understand you."

"We…and we weren't the only ones…We *felt* him. There was something about that place didn't feel right. A coldness down your back…shivers…you know what I mean? Or a feeling in your stomach that something was not right. That was worse, if you ask me. The shivers you can get on a dark night traveling through a forest. A fox barking or an owl screeching or some such thing. But that uneasy feeling. Like waking up and thinking there was something out of order in the world. I didn't care for it."

"What happened?"

"Nothing. Nothing more than that. But I was glad to be gone from that place. I did my work as best as I could, then I went. Nothing happened there. What I'm saying is that it felt like it might any moment. And the feeling only came in the cloister."

"You're saying it was not the dead monk, though," said Ingrith, starting to understand.

Will shook his head solemnly. "Not the monk. Whatever he saw…whatever it was got to him… *that* is what it felt was dangerous. I wasn't ever worried I'd see him. It was what he saw I didn't want to have anything to do with." All the while he had been speaking, Will had kept his eyes fixed on Ingrith. Only now did he look about himself at the chapel. "I didn't think much of it at first. But now I can't really avoid it. This place…this chapel here…it has something about it the same as that monastery cloister in Devonshire. It's been growing, I think. The other place, it hit you the moment you walked inside…like walking into a heavy fall of rain…you follow me? Once you had felt it, you couldn't not feel it. Here it has been different…slow…like holding you hand in water that is slowly coming to the boil." Will looked back at her, and must have seen the unease on her face. He forced a smile. "Probably only a silly story. What with Alf…what happened to him…everything here has got me upset, and a bit muddle-headed I should think."

Ingrith didn't answer. She reached out and gently ran the tips of her fingers along the outlines of the newly placed stones in the section of wall nearest to her. The stones were cool. The warmth and light of the sun could not reach them here. Apart from the areas opposite the extremely costly stained-glass window that she knew was planned for the chapel, but not yet made, it never would. And there would not be much light even then; Abbess Rhoswen had insisted any new window must not be much more in size than the window that had been there originally, in Saint Merwinna's day. Not much light. But then was that not true for all buildings, from the smallest hovel to the largest castle? In all of them there were inevitably going to be at least some walls that were never directly touched by the light of the sun. It didn't mean they would never see daylight, only that it would not shine upon them directly. Why, then, did it seem such a different matter in this place? Why did it seem so profoundly sad? From the size of the boarded-up space in the wall where the window would be, there would be light enough. Not much light? She had been wrong; with the coloured glass, it would be a gloriously lit space on a summer's day, and there would be candles enough in such a chapel in the dark hours of winter. And yet, there it was again, the sadness. And something else…

Ingrith gasped.

"You feel that?" asked Will.

Ingrith covered her mouth with her hand, bent forward slightly, as if experiencing stomach pain. "God help us," she whispered through her fingers. Although the anxiety she felt had been only fleeting - a matter of seconds at most - while it lasted it had been almost overwhelming.

"I had not felt it so strongly before now," said Will. "Alf's death…Ned…the two deaths have been because of it. I know it to be true. I don't know how. There is something wrong in this place."

"Three deaths," corrected Ingrith. "We have been forgetting Sister Euphemia."

"The old nun who was slain in the church? Yes, I suppose so." Will pointed at the wall the small chapel shared with the vast church building beyond. The place where Sister Euphemia had been killed. "I suppose so," he repeated.

"I know it to be so," insisted Ingrith. She then told Will about Abbess Rhoswen's belief that there had been a sign received from St Merwinna herself, formed in the blood of the dead sacrist. Then she explained how the Abbess had convinced her that her own abilities had been bestowed so that she might contribute to the glory of the chapel.

Gradually, as she spoke, Ingrith saw Will's expression grow more and more dismayed while, at the same time, she herself became aware of a growing sense that what had previously seemed to her to be divine inspiration – the driving force behind her design for the tiles - now seemed a foolish and dangerous delusion. Worst of all was the worry that the boy, Alfred, might have in some way paid the price for it.

When she had finished explaining, and before Will could say anything in response, she insisted they both leave the chapel.

*****

CHAPTER 19

It was late. Rhoswen sat alone in her receiving room. It was where she most liked to be these days; the image of the saint always close by. And sometimes even…

A single candle burned on a candlestick at the centre of the great oak table in front of her. On such a large surface, far from brightening the otherwise dark room, the solitary flame gave off a lost, almost forlorn feel. Rhoswen had never really liked the table; it was too big, too ostentatious, exactly the sort of grand furniture the Bishop would enjoy having in his chambers. She steepled her fingers and held them under her chin in imitation of the gesture that fat man so often made. She giggled. The sound of it surprised her. It was the laugh of a child. Her own laugh, but from when she was a young girl, all those years ago, before all that had happened in her life. Before Althurst. She laughed again, harder this time. So hard that the candle flame fluttered in the draft of her breath for a few seconds, before settling back to a rigid vertical. After that, the only sound in the room, apart from her own breathing, was the occasional crackle or splutter from the melting wax. Rhoswen sat and watched the candle burn. She did not know for how long. She blinked, suddenly aware that the candle had reduced in length by several inches. How long had she been sitting there? Had she slept for a short while? It was possible; she was very tired these days. She shook herself awake, looked around the room, then back at the candle. She watched it burn for a few more minutes before she became aware of something beyond it. Peering deep into the shadows there, she saw only darkness at first. Then there was something darker, within the darkness. Something small was darting about in the air. She heard what might be the fluttering of wings. It might be taken for a trapped bird or, more likely, a bat. It was neither of those things.

Rhoswen smiled.

It came at her out of the darkness so quickly she had no time to see it clearly. She jerked her head back in surprise as it flitted about her face, but she had no fear of it, and she was still smiling as whatever it was darted swiftly back into the cover of darkness.

"Why the child?" asked Rhoswen, speaking into the black. There was no real protest in her voice, only a mild curiosity. She wondered why an innocent boy should have been required to give up his life, and why it should have to have been in so terrible a fashion. She did not question that there was good a reason, and harboured no secret doubts. She was merely curious.

From her place in the shadows Merwinna exhaled noisily, as if the question were nothing but a bore to her.

Rhoswen did not want to vex the saint, and would have asked no more about it if curiosity had not got the better of her. "I do not question. It is only that I cannot comprehend the purpose. From what I saw of the boy, he seemed to me to be entirely free of…"

"Enough!" snapped Merwinna. "Did not our lord Jesus call a little child unto himself, and set him in the midst of those equally uncomprehending disciples? Men like the self-satisfied and overstuffed Bishop Baldwin? Would you be counted among his kind?"

Rhoswen was puzzled. "You are telling me, then, that the child is in Heaven now? Is that what I am to understand?"

"Heaven or Hell! What of it?" shouted Merwinna, so loudly, and so angrily that Rhoswen slipped from her chair and onto her knees. At the same time, the candle was extinguished, plunging the room into complete darkness. "Where is your faith, Abbess Rhoswen? I am *telling* you nothing," hissed Merwinna into Rhoswen's ear. "It is not for you to know. If you are worthy, you will simply trust in the purpose. *Are* you worthy, Abbess Rhoswen?"

"Blessed, sainted lady, please forgive me," sobbed

Rhoswen. "You must know I meant no disrespect by my words. It was an unwise inquisitiveness on my part. Nothing more. It was never my intention to express doubt. Never, never. I swear it. I have none. I hope I am worthy. I try to be so. I pray that I am."

"Good. Then, there is nothing to forgive," said Merwinna in a pleasant sing-song voice. Rhoswen felt a light kiss on her cheek. *The lips of a saint* she told herself in wonder, *the very lips of a saint.*

There was silence for so long after that that Rhoswen began to wonder if the saint had left her.

"Am I alone? Are you there, my lady?" she whispered into the darkness.

There was silence for a moment longer, and then, "I am here, Abbess Rhoswen. I am *always* here."

Rhoswen reached out in the darkness, found the edge of the table and pulled herself up. As she groped around the surface of the table in search of the flint to relight the candle a soft hand caught her gently by the wrist.

"Are you so afraid of what resides within the shadows?"

"Afraid? Oh, no. I am not afraid. It is merely that I wish to see…"

"Your inquisitiveness again. But you have no need of candlelight to see what is God's will. His will *is* the light. Trust is that light. Faith is that light. Jesus cured the blind as a gesture for the unbelieving onlookers alone. Those he cured, those upon whom he laid his hands, at the very moment of their cure, had no more no need of their sight, for bestowed upon them was the gift of vision beyond all that is earthly. You ask me why the boy had to die. I tell you only that he had to. No more than that. And that must be enough. You did not question the death of Sister Euphemia, although you mourned her loss greatly, I know. As for the carpenter, I will not be told that you cared about that man's end. He was too old in years to have been without sin, and too low of birth to have mattered to the world. The loss of such a man was no loss at all. The boy, had he grown, would have been much the same. Take comfort in the knowledge that he had not the time for his sins to be great in number or magnitude."

"He *is* with God, then?"

"He may be, if he was deserving. That is something I cannot tell you. It is of no importance. There are things which must be attended to. The moment draws near when they will come to you."

"Who will come?"

"The tiler and the novice. They have had a small glimpse through the smoke. I was careless."

Rhoswen, having briefly considered saying that she did not understand what was meant by this, changed her mind.

"Faith, Rhoswen," said Merwinna, as if in answer to the unasked question. "That is what is required of you. You must do what is necessary when the time comes. For now, at least, we need them. Although we must watch them. Perhaps your decrepit Sister Alice may yet prove useful in the matter. Now there is a woman whose thoughts are ever ugly."

The candle on the table came back to life, its flame as tall and bright as before. The suddenness of it made Rhoswen gasp. No longer in darkness, she looked about the room. As she had expected, she was alone again.

******

How to convince the Abbess that the new chapel should not be completed, that was the problem that now faced them. She needed to be brought around to the idea that, far from being divinely sanctioned, the completion of the work could well be to some unholy purpose they could not yet foresee. The chances were she would reject all they attempted to tell her. And if Will were to simply refuse to continue, there were others in his trade who would be glad to complete the work in his place – not to mention the damage to his reputation it would cause. Abbess Rhoswen needed to believe what Will and Ingrith now believed. Even then, assuming they were successful in convincing the Abbess, there was still the problem of Bishop Baldwin. He had been able to force the start of work on the chapel back when Abbess Rhoswen had been set against it; it would not be difficult for him to do so again if she were to abandon her current enthusiasm for the project.

Neither Will nor Ingrith believed that just going to Rhoswen and confronting her with what they believed would be sufficient to change her mind. Without real proof, her fervor for the chapel would blind her to all they said, they knew that. So, until they were sure how to proceed, they agreed it was best to make a show of continuing with the work without the intention of ever bringing it to a conclusion. Will was uncomfortable with the idea, and not sure how long he could convincingly maintain the pretense. The one thing he could do, however, was to ensure the first batch of tiles in the kiln was a failure. This, at least, could be done without it appearing unusual or unexpected. After all, he had warned the Abbess it was a possibility. She, predictably, had said God would see to it that the tiles were successful first time round, but she would have to admit to the reality that things could, and did, go wrong with the firing process sometimes – the failed tiles would be evidence of the truth of it. A few subtle acts of sabotage should be sufficient to ruin the tiles. No one would be any the wiser.

Ingrith and Will had discussed it all after having returned from the chapel to watch over the kiln. There had been time enough before Sister Alice arrived to carry out her duty as Ingrith's chaperone. When she did, finally, appear, the old nun was angry. She had heard about the death of the tiler's apprentice and had assumed this would disrupt work for at least a day or two. It had not occurred to her that the kiln would still require watching. And even if it did, why was it necessary for Ingrith to be there? She still could not accept this was a necessity and, as ever, she was at pains to make her objections felt.

"We have been through this before. I will argue with you no longer," Ingrith snapped at her. Suddenly more infuriated by the pettiness of Sister Alice than she had ever been. "If you wish to object, go talk to the Reverend Mother about it. She will, no doubt, tell you that I have her approval as she, no doubt, did before when you, no doubt, raised the same objection before. Oh, and you might tell her of your tardiness this morning…Or will you leave that to me. I am disappointed by it, naturally. You are, after all, here to protect my honour. That is your role, is it not?"

"And if that involves protecting you from yourself?" asked Sister Alice, clearly pleased with her own response.

"Or from your ugly suspicions?" Ingrith replied, furiously. "What it is like for you living with a mind so full of mistrust and bitterness I cannot imagine. Go. Or stay if you must. I care not. Before you go, however, you might take a moment to ponder what sort of person it is that does not offer a single word of sympathy or regret upon the death of an innocent child. In fact, does not give the appearance of being concerned in the slightest. Not one word have you said on the matter other than how it has interfered with your day. Well…?"

Sister Alice took a step back as if she had received a blow. Then she lifted a finger and pointed it angrily at Ingrith. The arm lifting it shook with rage, and it was impossible for her to hold the finger steady. Ingrith glanced derisively at the finger before turning her back on it. This act of dismissal so offended Sister Alice that she to let out a cry of astonishment before shouting at Ingrith's back, "You are a novice. That much only. And not a good one by all accounts. No at all promising. You are elevated beyond your station temporarily with this…this…folly. Temporarily, mark you. You would do well to remember that. The time will come when this business is at an end and you will no longer have the Abbess's favour. Then you will answer for your behavior towards me. Until that time comes, you may be assured that I fully intend to stay. I will watch your every move, mark your every misstep."

For all of her show of indifference, Ingrith dearly wished the old woman would go away. She wished she could be left alone with Will. It was true there was no real need for Ingrith to be present while the kiln was tended - particularly now that the intention was to ensure the firing failed - but she had become strangely disconnected from the life she had previously known at Althurst. The prospect of going back to it after having worked with Will on the tiles had already begun to loom unpleasantly. The thought of her impending return to the never-ending cycle of small, tedious tasks, punctuated by prayer had been enough to make her want to cry. Now, with what she knew – or, at least sensed – about what was really happening, the thought of it seemed frightening. Out here there might just be some hope of combating whatever evil was taking root. Back within the confines of those stone walls, she was trapped like a woodcock in hunter's trap, fluttering helplessly until the unknown hands reached down and snapped its neck.

The rest of the day passed in silence. There was so much Ingrith wanted to discuss with Will, but with Sister Alice being so close at hand – and now, more than ever, determined not to fall asleep – there was no possibility of them safely do so.

At noon, Ingrith looked up and saw that the Abbess was walking towards them from the direction of the church. Ingrith cleared her throat to alert Will. As the Abbess approached, he stood up straight and bent his head. "Reverend Mother," he said. "Good day to you."

"I have come to say how saddened I was to hear about the boy."

Hearing this, Ingrith could not resist glancing reproachfully at Sister Alice whose own condolences had been sadly lacking. Disappointingly, the old nun refused to meet her eyes.

"Alf," said Will.

"That was his name was it?" said Rhoswen. "His accident….it is to be hoped he did not suffer much before the end."

Ingrith was astonished at the clumsiness and insensitivity of the remark. Either the Abbess had not bothered to enquire exactly how the boy had died, or she had not bothered to give much thought to her words. Whichever one, it was unforgivable. "Unfortunately, I think it likely he suffered a great deal!" she said before she could stop herself.

"Oh," replied Rhoswen. The shortness of her reply suggesting that she had at least realized her own tactlessness. "Oh… that is to be regretted."

"Yes, it is," said Ingrith.

"But he was not your son?" said Rhoswen, addressing Will.

Will frowned, confused by the question. "That he was not. He was…"

"Well, now," interrupted Rhoswen. "How are things? With the tiles, I mean. All is well, I trust?"

It was Will's turn to speak in haste. "Alf is dead," he said bluntly.

The Abbess's face flushed with anger. Although, to Ingrith's mind, it should have been with shame.

"Do not you dare reproach me, Master Tiler! Do not you dare it!" As she spoke, Rhoswen stepped up close to Will. The Abbess's lack of height set against a man of Will's size and strength ought to have made this gesture look ridiculous, but there was no denying the power the woman possessed to make things difficult for him if she chose. Nonetheless, Ingrith could not help imagining how satisfying it would be to see Will raise a fist and bring it down upon the Abbess's head, knocking the arrogant woman to the ground.

"I know the boy is dead," continued the Abbess. Saying

this appeared to have a softening effect on her. "I *do* know it," she said more calmly. "Have I not only this very moment expressed my deepest regret? I myself would not have wished him hurt." She looked away from Will, towards the church. "Be that as it may, the chapel must be built. Nothing changes that. Nothing, and no one. Not you nor I. You understand me? We are agreed upon that?"

"We are, Reverend Mother," said Will.

Rhoswen turned to Ingrith. "And you, daughter. You agree?"

Ingrith did answer at first. Her mind was still focused on what the Abbess had just said: She, Rhoswen, would not have wished it. Did this imply that someone else *had*? Merwinna. Wasn't it obvious? Merwinna. All of the Abbess's enthusiasm for the chapel stemmed from her belief that it was the will of the saint that it be built.

"Daughter, you agree, do you not?" pressed Rhoswen.

Ingrith now looked directly at the Abbess. "I do. I must," she said. She did not agree. What kind of saint wanted a child dead? Ingrith stared at the Abbess, searching for outward signs of the inner madness she suspected had taken hold.

******

Nobody was more surprised than Silas himself when he managed to return in good time to take over watching the kiln after sunset. He had not slept well. It was difficult enough anyway during the hours of daylight. Add to that the constant returning of his thoughts to the events leading up to Alf's death, and it began to seem near impossible. When sheer exhaustion eventually allowed him a few restless hours of slumber, he still felt no revitalising effect. He had awoken bleary-eyed and, if anything, more tired and miserable than before. From the height of the sun, he judged there was a good hour before he was due back at the Abbey. So, having given up on the idea of more sleep, before he knew it, Silas's steps had taken him to the entrance of the tavern down the street. If he drank at the inn where they were staying, there was a danger the landlord would make it known to Will. This tavern was safer.

If drink would not help him sort the disturbing jumble of thoughts in his head, Silas had hoped it might at least dull them enough to be ignored. Unfortunately for him, his conscience would not let him drink as much as he had originally intended. Before the shadows cast in the sunlight that made its way through the tavern's open doorway began to grow long, he had already stepped back outside into the daylight and begun to make his way up the hill to the Abbey gates.

Allard was on duty as gatekeeper again. Silas had hoped he would not be. Anything not to be reminded of what had happened. Perhaps Allard felt the same about Silas; his greeting was perfunctory at best. And he seemed uncomfortable meeting Silas's eye.

Silas was equally disappointed to see that the girl, Ingrith, was sitting with Will at the kiln. And with her present, inevitably, the old nun, Sister Alice was sitting on her pile of sacks not far away, the miserable old witch. Shouldn't they both be away to evening prayers or whatever it was these holy types did? He knew he ought to be grateful to Ingrith for defending him when Will had lost his temper that morning, and to a large degree he was, but the fewer people he had to have anything to do with right now the better as far as Silas was concerned. He had known that seeing Will was unavoidable, but he hoped their conversation would be limited to matters linked to the kiln.

The girl saw him approaching and waved. Immediately the disappointment he felt on seeing her there abated slightly. She was not half as bad as the rest of them in this damned place. Not so bad at all. He raised a hand and waved back. She must have told Will because he turned and looked in Silas's direction. He didn't wave, only nodded in greeting.

Silas did the same.

"You come before your time, old man," said Will standing up when Silas reached them. Although only an observation, it felt to Silas almost like an accusation – as if Will had known he had been to the tavern, that his being here on time was despite his intentions, not because of them. Will was standing close now. Was he smelling his breath for signs of drink?

"Aye, couldn't sleep," explained Silas, taking a step back.

"Aye," replied Will in a manner that implied he was not surprised. "Well, the fire is where it should be for now. I only this moment added fuel. Keep it like that and we should be fine. I'll see you in the morning."

Sister Alice was on her feet. "Then we may leave also. Come along, girl," she said to Ingrith. "You are not to be excused vespers. It is the order of the Reverend Mother."

"I know it is," snapped Ingrith. "I had no intention of disobeying it. I'm sorry if that disappoints you."

Sister Alice tutted.

Silas waited until all three, Will and the two women, had left before he took a seat before the kiln. The evening was still warm, despite a mild breeze having developed as the sun fell. He studied the flames for a while. Will had certainly got them at the correct sort of level right now, but Silas would have thought it would have required more fuel than appeared to have been used to have maintained that level throughout the day; the heap of wood nearby did not seem to have gone down as much as he would have expected. No matter. Will must have sent the girl for more. It would have to have been her now that Alf was not there to do it.

Alf. Silas's breath hitched in his chest. What had the boy thought he was doing? No, he would not think on it. He was not to blame. Not for that, at any rate. There was the other thing though, wasn't there? The thing nobody, not even Will, knew about. Silas was not new to guilt. He had lived with it all these years. It was funny really, when you thought about. For the first time in his life he had been considered responsible – if only through negligence – for someone else's death, and it really was not his fault. However, for the death that, beyond question, *had* been his fault he had never had to pay - never once even faced accusation. It was so long ago now he knew he never would. Not in this life, anyway. And even his fear of damnation in the next had lost some of its potency. You live with something like that long enough and it is bound to. There were times when he didn't quite believe it had happened, or if it had, it had been someone else who had done it.

Not for the first time, Silas found himself wondering what Will would think if he told him just why it was he saved what money he could for the sake of obtaining the indulgence the priest had once told him about – what the sin was for which he wished to be saved from punishment in purgatory. Will had laughed when he first found out, said whatever it was he wanted the indulgence for, there was no way Silas would ever put aside enough of the money Will paid him to obtain it. It was a wealthy man's privilege, and not for the likes of Silas, he said. Besides, the tavern keepers or whores would get their hands on all Silas's money long before he had enough, even if it were possible for him to save that much. Whenever the subject came up Will almost always laughed about it. When Will had once joked that, if the sin were mortal, no amount of money in the world could save him, Silas had hoped it was not true.

Silas grunted. Would Will still laugh if he were to know the truth? Would he laugh if Silas told him about how, long before Will was born, he had once killed a man - followed him out of a tavern in Winchester where they had got into an argument, the reason for which Silas could no longer remember, and stabbed him to death in a frenzied attack that left Silas covered, head to foot, in the dead man's blood? Silas could not even pretend to himself that it had been a spur of the moment action; he had followed man for miles into a winter night where the cold air had sobered him up sufficiently for him to consider what he was doing, and still he had continued to follow him out of the city until they were alone in the countryside. Once there, he had stabbed his victim over and over before throwing the body into the freezing water of the River Itchen. He himself had then been forced to wade into the same freezing water to get the blood from his clothes as best he could. He had spent the rest of the night shivering and feverish in the woods, but had survived and escaped even suspicion over the man's death, let alone any punishment. The man, whoever he had been, was a stranger, so it had been assumed he had simply moved on. Nobody in Winchester knew him or cared about his whereabouts. If there were other people elsewhere that did, Silas never heard of any.

Silas grunted again, tried to empty his thoughts of anything other than the task in hand – watching the kiln. He closed his eyes for a moment.

Silas gasped, sat upright. Had he fallen asleep? Must have. He hadn't slept well during the day, after all. The sky was fully dark now. At least an hour must have passed. He shivered, wrapping his arms about himself. Suddenly he was very cold. Freezing, in fact. As cold as that terrible night in the woods outside Winchester all those years ago. It made no sense to be so cold on a summer night like tonight. He must be coming down with something. A fever of some sort. Hurriedly he grabbed a handful of wood from the fuel pile, huddled closer to the kiln and, with shaking hands fed the wood into the stoke hole. He was still too cold. He looked around and then, on seeing a heap of sacks next to the barrels where Sister Alice often sat, he went over, grabbed a couple of empty ones, wrapped them around his shoulders, and then returned to his seat by the kiln. He must be careful not fall asleep again. If the fires went too low, the tiles might be ruined.

His eyes had begun to close again when he heard footsteps behind him. Silas looked around, saw no one at first. Then, from shadows stepped a small figure he recognized immediately. "Alf!" Silas cried out, bewildered. "You were dead, boy. You're not, then? You're all better?"

"I am, thank you Silas," said Alf in a clear, unfaltering voice that, even in his confusion, Silas noticed.

"I'm glad to hear it," said Silas.

"Yes, I'm very much better. So, you will be pleased to know, is John, here."

Silas was confused. "John? Who's John?" he asked. "I don't know any John in these parts." Only then did Silas see that Alf was holding someone's hand. A man, his face in the shadows. It struck Silas as odd that he should not have noticed this before now. "John…?" he asked, a knot of anxiety beginning to form in his chest.

"That would be me," said the man, leaning forward out of the shadows so Silas could see his face. The skin, which shone pale blue in the moonlight, was streaked down one side with darker patches, almost black, that glistened damply, and which could only be blood. Above them, where an eye should have been, was a pulpy mess.

Silas cried out in alarm, and fell back, eyes wide, gazing up fearfully into a face he recognized as belonging to the man he had killed all those years ago. Before now, Silas had almost forgotten what the man had looked like, but he knew this to be him as soon as he saw that face – its features those of a young man, much like Silas's had been on the night he had murdered him.

"John. That is my name. Did you not know that when you took the decision to end my life so many years ago? Was it not of importance to you as you stole from me the extra years of life you yourself have since enjoyed?"

"I'm truly sorry for what I done. You *have* to believe me!" cried Silas. "I have not enjoyed my years as I should. I've lived half a life. Guilt has tormented me all this time. I never meant no harm by it! Never!"

"*No harm?*" bellowed John, gesturing as he did so to the

ruined tissue in the socket where there should have been an eye. "You cruelly and deliberately take a man's life, and you mean no harm by it?"

"I'm sorry," pleaded Silas. "I was young…I had taken drink …I didn't know what I was doing."

"You were sober enough when you caught up with me."

"I was young…"

"As was I!" roared John.

Still holding John's hand, Alf tilted his head, looked up at him. "So Silas caused you to die also? Not burned, though." Alf raised the remains of his arm, looked at it sadly, and then accusingly at Silas.

"Wait…no...it was not my doing that *you* died, Alf!" protested Silas.

John silenced Silas with a scowl, and then smiled down at Alf - the expression out of place on his dead and damaged features. Alf smiled back, and John ruffled his hair affectionately.

"Oh no, Alf, not burned. Silas had a different fate in mind for me. Didn't I tell you? I was stabbed. Over and over." He pointed accusingly at Silas, who shrank from the gesture, one arm held up in front of him as if he could wave the truth away. "Stabbed to death. Murdered. A mortal sin," continued John. "One which no meagre indulgence could ever hope to redress. Are you truly so misinformed? Besides, such a thing was always beyond your means." John's dead brow furrowed in thought. "It would have made no difference if it were. Changed nothing. There can be no atonement for what you did. None. Do you not understand that? You are already numbered among the damned. All there is ahead of you is an eternity in the company of the legions of Hell. They have shown me the place they have picked out for you down there." John chuckled. It was more sneering than humorous. "I know what it is awaits you in the next life. Do you wish to know also? Would you know the details of the torments to come?"

"No, no!" sobbed Silas, now curled upon the ground, arms wrapped tightly around his head. "You can't…I didn't mean what I did…I was a fool, but I was only young. Hardly a man. Not much more than a boy…."

"You are no longer young, though, are you? Your body is wearing out. It begins to fail you. You have but a short time left. So short a time before Hell opens its gates to you for a time longer than ordinary imagining allows for."

Silas screamed. "Pleeeeeease!"

John and Alf watched impassively as Silas continued to squirm and plead, terrified, on the ground.

After a while Alf said, "Why beg so? There can be no escape for you, Silas." After that he fell silent, let the silence stretch.

And then John said, "Unless…"

"Unless?" asked Silas, looking over his arms.

******

When Will returned the next morning, he wondered if Silas was ill. The old man's face was pale and drawn, his eyes puffy, and surrounded by dark rings. He was stoking the kiln when Will arrived, but something about the fervent way he was going about it suggested that he may have neglected to do so earlier. Ordinarily, Will would have been dismayed by such inattentiveness to his work on Silas's part. However, as the intention was that the firing of the tiles should fail anyway, it didn't matter. Will was a little angry, nonetheless, because Silas was not aware that was the plan. But when Will opened his mouth to reprimand him, he found he had not the heart for it. Not today, and with everything that was happening.

Instead, he said, "Are you well, old man?"

"What's that?" asked Silas.

"I asked if you were well. To my eyes you look sickly."

Silas looked guilty, said, "I could say the same of you, Will. How is a man meant to look, after what happened to the boy?"

Will frowned, unconvinced. "Answer me. Are you sick?"

"No, nothin' wrong with me. Bit tired. That's all. I've been up all fuckin' night, haven't I?"

Been up all night drinking? wondered Will, but chose not to ask. *Maybe made your way back to the Inn when I was gone?* He nodded at the kiln. "Everything as it should be? No problems?"

"None. There's nothin' to worry about here," replied Silas, looking even more guilty.

Will looked about for any clues as to what might be troubling Silas. There were none. "Well," he said, with a heavy sigh, "you get yourself back to the Inn, then. Get some sleep. I'm here now."

"As you wish."

"Right then, I'll see you again at sundown. And Silas…"

"What is it?"

"Don't enjoy too much of the pleasure offered by the tavern, understand me?"

Although a look of anger passed across Silas's face as if he were about to protest, he only said, "I will not," and walked off.

Not long after that, Ingrith appeared. She was not alone. As well as Sister Alice who, as usual, walked a few paces behind, struggling to keep up with the much younger woman, Will saw that this morning Abbess Rhoswen was with them. Even at a distance he could see that Ingrith was anxious. As the small group drew near, Will did as he always did when the Abbess appeared; he bowed his head respectfully.

Rhoswen came to a halt directly in front of him, looking up into his face. Ingrith came and stood at her side.

"Good morning to you, Reverend Mother," said Will, careful not to look at Ingrith too much.

Ignoring his greeting entirely, Rhoswen said, "How long before the kiln is cool enough?"

"I beg your pardon, Reverend Mother?"

"It is not a difficult question, Master Tiler. I am asking you to tell me how much time must pass before it is safe to open the kiln…If you were to cease to feed it fuel…How long?"

"If I don't feed it, then perhaps a day…usually a day to be sure of it…The heat has a life of its own. It takes time for it to starve. That will not be necessary for a good few days more, though. The tiles…they will need more time before they are ready."

"Tomorrow morning at this same hour, you will open it."

"Reverend Mother, if we were to do that the tiles would not be fired as they should be. They will be ruined. We would have to begin again…start all over…" Despite himself, Will gave Ingrith a questioning look. She shook her head.

The Abbess had clearly seen this exchange of looks, as had Sister Alice.

"You see, Reverend Mother?" said Sister Alice, seizing the opportunity. "This illustrates exactly what I have… "

"The tiles will be unspoiled," said Rhoswen, ignoring Sister Alice, and talking over her. "They will be faultless…perfect. You need have no worries. I am assured of this. You are to stop feeding any more wood into that thing as of now, and you will open it as soon as it is safe to do so. Which, as you have assured me, will be this time tomorrow."

Will was stunned. "If that is your wish, then I shall do as I am asked…"

Rhoswen scowled. "It is not my wish, Master Tiler, it is my order. I am not asking you, or offering you a choice. You have said your piece…although you were not invited to do so…and I have heard it. Nevertheless, you will open the kiln…as ordered… this time tomorrow morning. I shall be here to observe. And you and I will both see then that I am perfectly correct. In spite of your insistence to the contrary, every tile will be perfect. There are greater hands at work here than your own. Your eyes will bear witness to that. Only yours and those of your assistant, mind you. Ingrith will no longer be available to help you. She has no further contribution to make."

Ingrith stepped towards the Abbess. "No, please, Reverend Mother."

"No, daughter! The tiles will be complete. That being so, your part is done. I deem it no longer necessary that you attend Master Tiler's every action. With the tiles made, the next step is to lay them. That is not a task for your hands. Your presence can add nothing to that process. As I have said, your part is done."

"Reverend Mother, you do not understand…" Ingrith cried.

"Oh? Is that so? Do I not?"

"No!" cried Ingrith, before she could stop herself.

When she spoke again, Rhoswen's voice was as low and controlled as Ingrith's had been high and passionate. "Have a care now, Ingrith. Have a care."

Before she had had time to reflect upon the wisdom of it, Ingrith had taken another step forward and opened her mouth to object further. Rhoswen glared at her, and she faltered.

"Do not speak another word, girl!" warned Rhoswen. "You assert that I do not understand. However, I do! I do very well! Let me say to you by way of a reply that I have been far from insensible to the stories of your behaviour that Sister Alice has relayed to me. That I have chosen to ignore them thus far is because of Merwinna's advice regarding your role in the completion of her chapel. That role is at an end. Bid your tiler a last farewell, and be gone from here. You need have no more dealings with him whatsoever. In fact, I forbid it. You continue to do so at your peril."

Ingrith's eyes grew wide.

"No more!" barked Rhoswen. "Be gone. Leave us."

Ingrith looked over at Will, her expression one of dismay. The way she looked at him told Will she hoped there was something he could say that would alter the Abbess's decision; some reason he could offer as to why she was still needed to work on the tiles. Much as he wished it were not so, Will knew there was nothing he could say that would not make matters worse. Even with the disadvantage of no longer having Alf, Silas and he were more than capable of finishing the work on their own. Any argument to the contrary would be weak, and would only serve to add weight to Sister Alice's accusations regarding the impropriety of Will and Ingrith working together. And, now he was faced with the prospect of not seeing Ingrith again, he knew in his heart that some aspects of what the bitter old nun claimed were true – at least on his part.

Ingrith must have understood this from his silence; he could see she was fighting back the urge to cry. She drew a long breath, steadied herself, and stood up straight. "Goodbye, Will," she said. Then, having shot a contemptuous look in the direction Sister Alice, added, "For all the shameful way in which others have chosen to view it, I have enjoyed our time working together. I have learned much."

Will lifted a hand. He wanted to reach out, touch her, but this small gesture of farewell was all that seemed safe. "Goodbye girl. And thank you for what you have done here. I think I've learned a lot too."

Ingrith would have said more if Abbess Rhoswen had not spoken over her.

"That is more than enough. Go. *Now!*"

Ingrith was only a few paces away when something seemed to occur to Rhoswen. Addressing Sister Alice, she said, "So, of course, you are no longer required here either, Sister Alice. If I am to believe what you have told me of your feelings on the matter, I imagine you will regret the ending of your involvement in all this somewhat less than our daughter Ingrith does. Is that not so?"

Sister Alice looked uncertain, said nothing.

Rhoswen went on, "And yet, I wonder…Have you, in fact, begun to revel somewhat in the opportunities for spite that have been afforded to you?" Sister Alice gasped now, but Rhoswen continued. "Yes, I think perhaps you have."

Sister Alice finally found her voice. "I have done only as I was instructed," she protested.

"Have you? Well, it is done. You, too, may leave us. I would speak with Master Tiler alone. Think on what I have said. Look into your heart. Pray for guidance. Confess. Perhaps the priest will be of help in your struggle."

Sister Alice glared back at Rhoswen, stunned by what she clearly considered a betrayal.

"Just go," said Rhoswen, bluntly.

The old nun seemed frozen to the spot, still staring back at her Abbess in shock. Finally, Rhoswen stepped forward, took her by the shoulders, and turned her to face the Abbey. In other circumstances it might have been comical to witness, but Will was almost as taken aback as was Sister Alice herself, who cried out in protest at this humiliating treatment.

"You pride yourself in doing as you are instructed," said Rhoswen. "Here is an opportunity. Do it now. Go!" With that, Rhoswen pushed Sister Alice so roughly that she stumbled, and would have fallen had Will not caught and steadied her.

Far from being grateful, being helped by a man she so despised was too much for Sister Alice. The old nun turned to Will and spat. "Take your coarse hands off me, William Tiler!" she hissed. "I am not your whore to be groped and squeezed! I am not your precious Ingrith."

Will stepped away, dumbfounded. He wanted to speak in defence of Ingrith, and might have done so, had the only words that came to him not been such that they would only make things worse for her, rather than better, if he were to give voice to them.

He was equally surprised to see that the Abbess was laughing. "No, indeed. You are nobody's whore, Sister Alice. That much is true. Now, go!" ordered Rhoswen again, still chuckling.

This time, Sister Alice needed no persuading. Will stood silently waiting, while Rhoswen watched her make her way slowly towards the main group of Abbey buildings. "She will pray to God," she said resignedly. "She may also talk to Father Thomas. And then? Then you can be sure she will interpret whatever guidance she receives from the old man...or even God... in such a way as to make her correct in her actions all along." She watched a little while longer before addressing Will, any trace of humour having left her face. "Now, to you William Tiler, I say this. Do not you dare fail me in this endeavour?"

"Reverend Mother?"

"You have but one task, and that is to lay the floor of Saint Merwinna's chapel. When that is completed to my satisfaction you may leave this place...Go where you will...Back to your fat Bishop Baldwin with sorry tales of my harsh treatment, if you so wish. I care not. But, mark you, before you leave, you will have completed our floor. It will be the best work you have done, you hear me? It is unlike anything you have ever been asked to do before... of far more significance... I can assure you of it. That being so, if I do not judge it to be your best work...if I am not pleased...or, worse still... if Merwinna informs me that she is not pleased, I will ensure you re-do what you have done until both she and I are satisfied with it. If you fail to do this, I will see to it that whatever reputation you have as a craftsman hereabouts is ruined forever. Now, remember, the kiln is to be opened tomorrow morning. I am aware of your objections, so you need not repeat them. It is to be done as I order; there is an end to it. Trust me on this if you wish, or do not trust me. Again, I care not. However you feel now, I believe...I *know*...you will be surprised by what is revealed to you in the morning. Then you may at last have some grasp of what it puzzles me you have not so far learned. That you are a blessed man to have been chosen for this task. When you open that kiln tomorrow, when you see what is there…despite your unasked for and disrespectful warnings to the contrary…then you may know that you are a man who should be grateful for what he has been tasked with, not ungrateful and mistrusting as I know you to be. No longer brazen and uncooperative… humble. More than anything else, grateful… for the blessing which Merwinna has seen fit to bestow upon you. Now, see to it that you do what you must in preparation for the opening of the kiln."

Throughout the Abbess's outburst Will had stood listening with his hands held at his sides, and his head bowed forward respectfully, as he knew he should. If she noticed the puzzled tilt of his head when she spoke for a second time of Merwinna's opinion - it was as if the woman believed the saint would actually be there to see the finished floor - the Abbess did not say anything. Will kept his eyes down even as he replied, not wishing to make eye contact with this woman whose grasp on reality he was beginning to doubt.

"There is nothing can be done at this moment. It is still too hot to touch right now, and set to stay that way for a good few hours to come. I will watch it until then. Is best to make sure the flames die evenly."

"Do as you see fit…for now. Oh, and if you repeat any of this conversation to anyone, I will see to it that you regret having done so. As you are well aware, it is within my power to see to it that far more than your reputation is destroyed if I so choose. While you may be prepared to accept ruination for yourself, I think we both know you would not see that old man who works for you starve." She smiled coldly. "And, as for my threat of destroyed reputations, there is also someone else upon whom I might choose to visit my displeasure that your care for, is there not?" The smile developed into an ugly chuckle. "Sister Alice *would* be pleased."

*****

CHAPTER 20

Ingrith bent forward, reached out a hand, and steadied herself against the wall of the cloister. She felt as if she might be sick or even faint. A dizzying nausea had set in soon after the Abbess had so cruelly denied her any further opportunity to work alongside Will. She had managed to walk as far as the cloister; now all her strength had deserted her.

Ingrith's unease had taken hold when Will had first discussed his own concerns about the chapel and the connections he believed it might have to the recent tragic events at Althurst Abbey. Now, after how Abbess Rhoswen had behaved towards her, and what she had said, that feeling had so increased in intensity that Ingrith felt as if the world itself were shifting, slipping away, replaced by one that looked much the same but where all the familiar sources of comfort or reassurance had been removed – replaced by shadows and uncertainty.

Two things troubled her more than anything else. The first of which, she had to admit to herself was nothing to do with anything mysterious or otherworldly. It was not difficult to recognise or to express; she wanted more time with Will. At first she had told herself it was the work on the tiles alone that she so enjoyed – the feeling of sheer joy at, for once in her time at Althurst, being involved with something where her input was not only valued; it was fundamental to the outcome. Now, however, she could no longer deny to herself that being around Will had played a big part in creating that feeling. Still, although her grief at the loss of contact with the source of that feeling, at the passing of that part of her life, was hard to bear, it was at least something she could understand. In fact, it was probably for the best that it ended sooner rather than later. She had always known it would. This way, at least, the bond of friendship she shared with Will would remain pure. She need not be ashamed of it and, eventually, could look back on that friendship and their time together with fondness, instead of the regret that would inevitably follow if it were to be allowed to develop into anything more. That could only end in disgrace and ruined lives. She did not even know with any certainty that Will felt anything like she did. None of this meant it did not hurt more than she had imagined it would. But it only hurt; it did not frighten her. What did, was the behaviour of Abbess Rhoswen.

Ingrith could identify the exact moment when her disquiet and suspicions about all that was happening had crystallised into fear and an absolute certainty that something was very wrong at Althurst Abbey. *'Merwinna's advice regarding your role in the completion of her chapel'.* Those had been Abbess Rhoswen's exact words. *'Merwinna's advice'.* This was not talk of some divine sign or obscure message – Ingrith's faith told her such things were possible – the Abbess had talked of a directly spoken communication between herself and the saint. It was no slip of the tongue; Abbess Rhoswen was too clever a woman for that. Her words, and their nuance, had been deliberately chosen. The Abbess had been proud to say them. There might be second thoughts later, but at the time she used those words, the Reverend Mother had been proud of what she was telling them. Her was meaning clear: she knew it to be the saint's wishes because the very saint herself had told her what they were. Actually *spoken* of them with her.

And what if Merwinna *had* spoken to Abbess Rhoswen? If it were only that, then there might even have been cause for celebration. It would be a true divine visitation. Such things were known to have happened before, weren't they? The difference was that divine visitations did not kill children. Whatever was happening here, it was far from divine. It was malevolent and dangerous. It was evil.

Ingrith closed her eyes and sank to the floor. What could

be done? She prayed to God for guidance. She needed to know what path she should take. She needed the clarity of thought she knew she was so desperately lacking.

"It's Ingrith, isn't it?"

Ingrith opened her eyes, and looked up. She already knew who it was that she would see there. She had recognised his voice. It was the voice she heard every day conducting services for the sisters at the Abbey.

"Yes, Father Thomas," she said, already wondering if this was some manner of answer to her prayers. She had given thought to talking to the priest, and this seemed to be the sign that she should.

"You are troubled, my daughter?"

Ingrith thought for a moment. She had always thought the old priest distant, aloof – it was why she had hesitated to talk to him. But now she thought there was – if not kindness – at least concern in his eyes. She glanced around, discovered they were not alone. At the far end of the cloister she saw four or five of the sisters, and one or two servants, all appearing to be busy with whatever task had caused them to be in the cloister in the first place. But their ears would be straining to catch anything she might say. If they were that interested in what was troubling her, Ingrith thought bitterly, they might already have come to her aid, not left it to Father Thomas.

"Daughter?" pressed the priest, gently.

"I find I am uneasy, Father. I have that which I would say to you, only it is of so strange and grievous a nature I find I hesitate to speak of it." She looked past him, at the others.

He seemed to understand. "The confessional may be the place. There the ears of others are excluded. It offers…"

"No, Father. It is not *my* actions of which I would speak."

The old priest frowned. "If someone else has transgressed, it may not be my place to…Discipline is the domain of the sisters. You must seek audience with Abbess Rhoswen…" He stopped speaking, noticing the expression of alarm on Ingrith's face. Almost whispering now, he asked incredulously, "It is about the *Abbess* that you wish to talk to me?"

Ingrith nodded.

Father Thomas looked uncomfortable. "Such matters are…difficult. Is it not possible you are being hasty? If she has been unfair or unkind, I beg you to consider that she is, nonetheless, a woman of God. Though you may have felt undeserving of some treatment you have received at her hands, I beg you to consider that she will have been acting in what she considered your best interest. I myself have always found her to be even-handed in such things." He forced a smile, held his hands out at his sides. "In a month, a week, or less…a day perhaps…it may seem as nothing to you. These small trials of abbey life…particularly to the life of a novice…they dwindle in significance with the years. I do not know the nature of the thing that is between you and the Reverend Mother…it may be best that it remain so… but I do ask you to consider that your own judgement in the matter is likely be strongly influenced by any sense of hurt or shame you are currently experiencing. Abbess Rhoswen is a woman of far more experience than you yourself are."

Before she replied, Ingrith got to her feet. She still found the need to use the wall to steady herself for a moment. Then, when she felt stable enough, she took Father Thomas by the arm and pulled him further along the cloister to where she felt certain they could not be overheard.

"Father, despite what you imagine, it is not for any treatment of me that I am so concerned."

"Daughter, please think before you…perhaps the Mistress of Novices…?"

"The Mistress of Novices is a well-meaning woman, and yet she is a fool for all that." Father Thomas's eyebrows rose. Before he could remonstrate, Ingrith continued, "Father, hear me, please! I have graver issues to raise with you than my own harsh treatment at the hands of anyone in this place. Things not for the Mistress of Novices. These are things that you, as a man of God, are best placed to address.

The old priest looked worried. It was evident that he had hoped to avoid being involved with something as mundane as the problems of a disaffected novice. Now here he was being confronted with something which promised to be much worse. He freed his arm from Ingrith's grip.

"Daughter, you yourself may believe the truth of what you say, however, I really cannot conceive of …."

Despite the dread that filled her, Ingrith found she still had room for anger. She did something now that she had never before done since arriving at Althurst: she used her nobility of birth. "Listen to me. My father is Baron Edgar of Basing. Ah, I see by your expression you have heard of him. He is also a good friend of Bishop Baldwin. Would you have me communicate my troubles to my father? And through him to the Bishop? Included in any such communication would be intelligences of the behaviour of others towards me, I can assure you! Those who sought to offer help…those who did not…?"

Father Thomas looked flustered. "I will do what I can." He lifted a finger. "But not, mark you, because I live in fear of the Bishop, or even your father. I will listen because your behaviour convinces me you go in real fear of something, and I would help if it is in my power. Although one might ask why, if, as you suggest, something is so badly wrong in this place…something that involves the Abbess herself…you have not considered it necessary to contact your father before now?"

"If there were time enough, I would have," replied Ingrith. "For all the good it might do. My father's skill is with the sword. Our enemy here is not susceptible to such things. It is to men of God such as yourself and…who can say? …the Bishop…that I must look for help. Will you hear me? Will you help?"

"Have I not said as much? For I think, in conscience, I must hear you," said Father Thomas. "Although, I make no promise to believe, for all I see you are in earnest. Nor can I promise to take action if I do." He gestured for her to come closer. "Now…tell me you tale, daughter."

As Ingrith told the old priest her story she began to appreciate quite how fanciful it must seem to him. She told it all the same, knowing that she must convince the man if she were to obtain his help. More than once he opened his mouth to ask a question or raise some objection. Each time, Ingrith ignored him, pressing on with her story until it was done.

When, at last, she had told him everything, she stood back, studied his face for a reaction. He did not look at her at first, and then his eyes came up, met her own.

"Well?" she asked.

"It is a fanciful tale you tell me."

"You do not believe it?"

"It is difficult…"

"You do not believe it. I cannot claim to be surprised by that. Please ask yourself this: why would I say such things if they were untrue?"

"People have their reasons. It is clear to me that there is ill feeling between you and the Abbess. Perhaps it is because you wish to discredit her…do her harm for the sake of the harm you feel she has done to you?"

"No, Father. No, it is not as you say."

Father Thomas considered for a moment, and then he reached forward, held Ingrith by the shoulders. He looked directly at her. "If I ask you a question, do you promise me you will answer it truthfully?"

"I will," said Ingrith, a little uneasy, already sensing what the question might be.

"William Tiler. You say the Abbess…or Sister Alice, at any rate…has accused you of harbouring inappropriate affections for this man? Answer me, daughter, does she have good grounds for such accusations? It she in the right?"

Ingrith looked away, drew in a long, unsteady breath. "She

is," she said softly. "But I have not…we…there has been no acting upon…"

Father Thomas gestured for her to be silent. "I will help you," he said firmly. Ingrith looked up at the old priest, perplexed. Father Thomas sighed. "To be truthful, I had expected you to deny your feelings. Instead of that, you have made me privy to something that might lead you into severe difficulty if I were to choose to use it against you. I had made no promises about what I would do with the knowledge. Moreover, you asked for none. You spoke the truth, regardless of the consequences. That leads me to believe you speak what you believe to be the truth about the rest of what you tell me…"

"Thank you, Father."

"I did not say I believe you. For I do not. It is important that you understand that. What I do believe is that what you have told me is your honest interpretation of events. Events that are beyond your understanding. It is my wish to help you see them more clearly in whatever way is open to me. Now, to that end, will you come with me to see the Abbess?"

Ingrith fought the urge to push the priest away. "No, no! She will only say what she wants you to believe. She will only tell you what you want to hear."

"I want only the truth."

"She will not give you that. She will dissemble…mislead you into thinking what she wants you to think."

"Oh, Ingrith, come now! I cannot believe you are in the right about that. I am sure you do Abbess Rhoswen a great disservice when you speak of her so. I am convinced she is an honest woman. What possible cause has she for falsehood?

Ingrith stamped her foot in frustration. "I do not *know*. I have already explained what I am able…It has something to do with what she believes about Saint Merwinna…about the chapel…"

"Then let us discover. There is a misunderstanding here.

Let us untangle the knots of confusion. Please…come with me, Ingrith. You know I will go alone if I must."

"Then you must go alone," said Ingrith, angry and disappointed. "I have sought your help, and you offer only interference. Have you not listened to anything I have said? It would be better you did nothing at all than you did that!"

"I have listened, my daughter. Now I am taking what action I think is best. I *have* listened."

"Only you do not believe me."

"It is a fanciful tale you tell. Nevertheless, I have made it plain that I do not think you lie. It is only that you…" Father Thomas struggled for the right word, said, "Misunderstand."

A thought occurred to Ingrith. "Very well, I ask only that you speak to Will first? Before you do anything else, please speak with Will."

Father Thomas turned his head slightly. "Will?"

"William Tiler. If you have spoken with him first, and you still wish to take this matter to Abbess Rhoswen, then I will accompany you. But you cannot speak on the matter with her until you have spoken with William. Do you agree to it?"

"If I do as you say, I have your absolute promise that you will accompany me to talk with the Abbess afterwards… if I so ask?"

"You have it," said Ingrith, emphatically, hoping Father Thomas could not read the lie in her eyes. She was glad he had only asked her to promise, and not to swear. She had no intention of speaking to Abbess Rhoswen, regardless of the outcome of the priest's talk with Will. She wanted as little to do with the woman as possible. While Ingrith did not know what motives lay behind the Reverend Mother's behaviour, it was clear that she would do anything she considered necessary to achieve them. If that included destroying the life of a novice, she would not hesitate, regardless of what that entailed.

******

CHAPTER 21

Will's eyes grew wide, and then narrowed, a look of confusion forming on his face. It was not possible. Given his deliberate neglect of the kiln, coupled with the Abbess's insistence that it be opened far too early, the tiles they found within should have been unusable. They should have been warped, cracked, uneven, and the glaze muddy at best. It did not require closer inspection to see straight away that none of these things were true. Carefully, Will reached down and took up one of the tiles. It was still very warm, but not so hot that it could not safely be held. He hefted it in his hand, feeling the weight, assessing the density. It was good. More than that, it was, as the Abbess had predicted, perfect. The image formed by the glaze was as even in density and as crisp in outline as any he had seen. He reached in with his free hand, picked out another. He held both tiles out in front of himself, comparing weight and shape. The shrinkage on the one matched that of the other exactly. He put one down, picked up another, once again comparing them, and finding the same result. These tiles would sit together almost seamlessly when laid. Another time this would have been a triumph and a wonder. This morning it only made him feel more uneasy than he did already.

He was only half aware of Silas next to him. The old man had been almost silent throughout the process of digging out the kiln, speaking only when necessary – Will still assumed this was grief and guilt over Alf. But even Silas spoke now. He, too, held tiles in his hands, making the same assessments as Will.

"How, Will? It ought not to be. It was too early to take them out. It ought not to be."

Will half-turned his head, saw the old man out of the corner of his eye. He said nothing in reply.

"It ought not to be," muttered Silas again.

"No, it ought not to be. Yet it is," said Abbess Rhoswen, who had been watching them from the moment they began to clear away the earth that covered the kiln. "It is. Now, William Tiler, what does that tell you? What do you have to say to me now? Nothing? No apology for having doubted my word, and the assurances I gave you. Not that I can claim any of the praise. That belongs entirely to Saint Merwinna. You should not have doubted the assurances she gave you."

"Gave me?"

"Through me," said Rhoswen as if it were the most normal and obvious of explanations. "I told you what she had told me, and you would have none of it. Do you still doubt, even now, with all the proof anyone could need held there in your own hands? What greater evidence could there be? You cannot now have any remaining doubts." Will shook his head. The gesture was ambiguous; Rhoswen knew that. She chose to take it as confirmation of his belief anyway. "Good. That is sufficient. Although that would be more appropriate."

Will did not understand. For the first time, he looked up from the tiles in his hands.

"What would be, Reverend Mother?"

"That."

Will looked in the direction indicated by Rhoswen's outstretched arm. He saw now that Silas had fallen to his knees, his hands clasped around the two tiles he had picked out of the kiln, holding them close to his chest. He was rocking back and forth muttering barely coherent prayers, presumably of praise and thanks. Will had been in church with Silas a thousand times, and never seen him like this before. It briefly crossed his mind that the Abbess might be right after all. Perhaps this was the miracle she believed it to be. Perhaps he, too, should be down on his knees, giving thanks, like Silas, for the marvel he had witnessed. The feeling passed quickly when he remembered Alf, Ned, and all that had happened. Miracles did not require violent death. Miracles did not leave a sickness in the pit of your stomach. But what else could he do for now other than go along with it? In what he hoped was a suitably reverential gesture, he got down onto his knees, made the sign of the cross, and bowed his head. He did not mumble and sigh like Silas; he could not bring himself to do that. Nor did he clutch the tiles he had been holding to his chest. He placed them to one side on the earth next to him, his eyes straying to them occasionally, as he wondered what had made them possible. Whatever it had been, the Abbess was wrong; it was not Saint Merwinna. The miracles of the saints were not created to serve their vanity.

To his astonishment, the next time he opened his eyes he discovered that the Abbess was on her knees beside him. Over Silas's noise he had not heard her approach. Her mouth was moving. He strained his ears to hear her words. All he was able to clearly make out was the single word, "*Merwinna*."

******

The daily meeting in the chapter house – a large, octagonal room attached to the side of the main church building - to hear the reading, and for the assignment of tasks for the day, had been delayed. This was almost unheard of. The Abbess, the sisters were informed, had something enormously important she must attend to before she could join them. Then, all would be explained. When, at last, they were called inside, the Abbess was waiting for them. Ingrith could tell from the way her eyes glowed, and the obvious struggle she was having to maintain her composure, that the woman was still in the thrall of whatever madness it was possessed her. Ingrith knew, too, that the news the Abbess was about to impart would, inevitably, be something to do with St Merwinna's chapel. Many of the nuns, sitting on the benches running the length of chapter house's high stone walls, were whispering to one another - speculating about what was going on. A few in the company attempted to shush their companions into silence, but to no avail; they had picked up on the Reverend Mother's air of excitement, and were now excited themselves. They did not see this as a symptom of the madness that Ingrith knew it to be. At last, the Abbess stood before them, her hands raised, gesturing them into silence.

"Daughters, today is a wondrous, wondrous day. A day you will never forget. Today a great miracle has occurred here in Althurst." She waited, letting this sink in before continuing, "You have all heard the stories of the marvellous miracles of healing that have happened here in the past… all of them linked to our blessed Saint Merwinna. Today a greater miracle…one that surpasses all that have gone beforehand…has taken place."

This announcement was greeted with great excitement. The room filled with gasps, more whispering, a few louder prayers, and cries of "Hallelujah." Ingrith wanted to shout at them. To tell them not to be so credulous and quick to believe whatever the Abbess told them. The expressions on their faces told her this would be futile. Better to hold her peace, and play along as best she could for the time being.

Then the Abbess's hands were raised again to silence them.

"We shall all, of course, give thanks in due course of time. For the present, though, you will remain silent that you may fully hear… and fully appreciate… the great news I have for you." Rhoswen waited a moment for the silence she had commanded. When it had at last settled, Ingrith saw the Abbess had begun weeping for joy as she said, "Our saint has spoken. *Our* saint." Here, Rhoswen paused again, to emphasis this point. Then she continued, "Merwinna has delivered a message that could be no clearer if she had whispered it into my very ear." Rhoswen paused yet again. This time, not for effect, but so she might collect herself. Her chest rose and fell as she inhaled deeply two or three times before speaking again. "In the past I made no secret of my objections to the building of a chapel on the site of Saint Merwinna's cell. Nor have I made a secret of my change of heart…that I now see things very differently. And so it is that I am now come before you… to explain…firstly the reasons for that change of heart…and then what a wonder it has given rise to. We have all of us…" Rhoswen's tone became more subdued, although it was clearly an effort for her to keep it that way. "We have all of us been greatly saddened by the recent loss of our dear Sister Euphemia. Some of you were made more than a little afraid by it too. Let me assure you now that you need not be saddened or afraid. Our late sister was *fortunate*." Rhoswen had stressed the last word. "By that I mean she was fortunate enough to be chosen for a great role…to be an instrument. She was already old, and would have had only a few years left to her…Years in which she would have become more and more infirm and of less and less use…to Althurst Abbey…to God. A state of affairs a woman such a Sister Euphemia would sorely lament. But, in place of that slow, sad decline, she was given a great gift. The gift of a purposeful death. I did not share this with you before today because I needed to be certain. Now I can tell you that her death was a sign. The blood she shed the means of a message that Merwinna wanted her chapel built! It was in this way my mind…my heart… came to be completely altered on the matter."

Ingrith glanced around at her companions. They were no longer as animated as they had been. Doubt and confusion showed on some of their faces. The Abbess must have been sensible of this because she said, "I understand your reservations. However, you must trust me when I tell you that it is so. It is hard to grasp, I understand that, believe me. I myself had my doubts. I entreat you, do not fail in your faith. Ask yourself this: what more fitting medium for a message from a saint than the very lifeblood of a devout and virtuous woman who had lived all her life in the service of

God? I say this because the blood that spilled on the spot where our beloved…and now, blessed…sister met her end formed a shape…a sign…The very shape of the painting of our saint that adorns the wall of my own receiving rooms. The exact image; no mere similarity. The *exact* image, I tell you. There could be no questioning it. It was there…there in the blood. I was witness to it." She clasped her hands together, shook her head in awe. "Oh, Merwinna chose the most precious of pigments. The *most* precious."

When some of the sisters begged to be allowed to see the stain for themselves, Ingrith noticed the Abbess frowned briefly. Perhaps she was determining if this request was because they still required proof, rather than due to the ecstatic frenzy she was so evidently attempting to instil in them. In the end, she must have satisfied herself that it was the latter, because she looked away, and then, a little too theatrically for Ingrith, put a hand to her head before explaining, "Alas, it has faded into nothing. I had the area covered…hidden. Only I and Sister Elisabeth… who was with me at the time… witnessed it." There were sighs of disappointment, and one or two envious glances cast in the direction of Sister Elisabeth, who looked down, but could not conceal her pride. "I would have shown it to you all when I judged you ready," continued Rhoswen. "I only regret that I cannot now do so. Do not be too disappointed, however. That was only a foretaste. A foretaste of the greater wonders to come…what I have witnessed this very morning…"

Ingrith again studied her companions' faces, gauging their reaction to this madness their Abbess was talking. To her consternation, she saw that they all now appeared to be convinced by it - swept up by this display of passion from the Reverend Mother - the fervour leaping from one to another like a flame. There were more prayers, more hallelujahs, and now some tears to match the Reverend Mother's. And all of this before the nature of the miracle had even been revealed.

The Abbess waited for the noise of the sisters to die down sufficiently for her voice to be heard, and then asked, "Would you know the miracle? Would you hear it from one who saw it first-hand?" Her question having received the sought after, and inevitable, cries of assent, she continued, "I had it from the man tasked with creating the tiles for Saint Merwinna's chapel that the firing...the somewhat involved process by which they would be made...rather like pots.... would on no account...not under any circumstance... be complete for some time to come. It would take *days*, he assured me. *Days* before they could be removed from the kiln where the clay of which they are made was in the process of undergoing that transformation necessary for the tiles to be formed. So it would be against all the governing rules of this world that they should be ready before then. But he...this simple craftsman... did not know what I knew. He had not been blessed with the message I had. A message from Merwinna herself, telling me that if the kiln were to be opened today, the tiles within would not only be ready for use, they would be perfect. Not a crack, not a blemish... And so they were...so they *were!*"

Rhoswen paused here for the nuns to take in what she was telling them, for the expected recurrence of their previous fervour. It did not come. No fresh cries of joy echoed from the vaulted ceiling above them, nobody fell to their knees or made the sign of the cross. Instead, she was greeted with a confused silence. One or two sisters - loyal to their Abbess, or embarrassed by the lack of response - clapped their hands or muttered half-hearted thanks, but the sense of disappointment was palpable.

Ingrith watched them all struggling to comprehend why such a thing should be given the name of miracle. Miracles were healings of the sick, partings of oceans, water into wine, not fortuitous outcomes of obscure processes. It made no sense to them. Only now did it strike Ingrith that, of all the women assembled in the chapter house, perhaps she was the only one, apart from the Abbess herself, who understood the impossibility of what had taken place. If it had, that was. But why would the Abbess lie? She would be found out the moment anyone asked to view the tiles. Ingrith looked back at the Abbess. The woman was visibly angry.

"I had expected some doubters. Some whose faith made them deny the hand of the saint in this. However, I confess myself disappointed in you all. *Very* disappointed. I wonder at your faith…is it there at all?" Her expression softened to one of patience – albeit strained patience. "Is it that you cannot see? That you do not understand?"

Ingrith was alarmed to see the Abbess's gaze come to rest upon her.

"Tell them, Ingrith. Tell them that this *is* a wonder. You, of all people in this chapter house, know the process. You know that the tiles could not, under normal conditions, have been ready for some time…And could never have been expected to be perfect….Not every one of them…Not perfect. And yet they are." She lifted her head, raising her chin, almost defiantly, addressing everyone, "I will show them to you all. Then you will see. Like Ingrith, you will know then that such a thing is not possible without the intervention of the divine. Ingrith knows this, and will confirm what I say."

Ingrith did know. What she was not so sure of was the nature of the intervention. She wished she could believe it was as the Abbess claimed. If only it were true. But Ingrith was now certain that whatever was taking place in connection with the chapel was not driven by anything good. Evil, too, had been known to intervene in the affairs of man. The Abbess was either blinded to this possibility, or she was knowingly acting as an agent of that evil. Either way, Ingrith knew she must be careful. The Abbess was looking at her expectantly.

"Tell them, Ingrith. Now is your chance, daughter, to make amends for your recent wayward behaviour. Join with me in convincing your fellow sisters of the truth of what I say."

Ingrith knew she had no choice right now other than to agree.

"Oh, indeed Reverend Mother. Such a development is inexplicable without the intervention of some supernatural hand." Noting a slight narrowing of the Abbess's eyes that might be suspicion at the ambiguity in what she had just said, Ingrith quickly corrected herself, choosing her words more carefully this time, and trying hard to project an appropriate sense of rapture as she said them. "Some… divine hand. And who else's would that be but the saint herself? Oh, there can be no doubting Merwinna is with us…none whatsoever."

Seemingly satisfied, Rhoswen nodded. "Well spoken, my daughter. Now, are there any among us who still entertain doubt? I will do all in my power to help you not to fail this test of faith. For I see now that it *is* a test. The obscure nature of our miracle…though it seemed not so to me…is Merwinna's way of challenging our faith. If it were easy…plain for all to see and understand…what need would we have of faith? And without faith, the Devil has his day."

"May we see the tiles, Reverend Mother?" asked Ingrith, unable to contain her curiosity, despite her increasing sense of dread. The design was, after all, hers. "May we have that privilege?"

Rhoswen smiled benignly, considered for a moment. "Not yet, I think. In due course, daughter, in due course. When they are in place, not before. There is work yet to be done." A trace of suspicion suddenly returned to her face. "But… as I have already made more than plain… none of it to be done by you, daughter."

******

The door made for the chapel by Ned the carpenter was now hanging in place. No new carpenter had been engaged, as far as Will knew, so presumably the task had been completed by one of the more able of the Abbey servants. Will pushed it open, feeling the change of temperature as he stepped out of the warmth of the sun and into the coolness of the chapel. On a day as hot as this one had turned out to be – the hottest of the year so far, if Will was any judge – the cool air should have been a welcome respite. Strange, then, that it was not. When it might have been refreshing, the chill was somehow uncomfortable. Will was not that surprised, however; the prospect of working in this place was not a welcome one. He shivered, only partly from the cold.

He turned to speak to Silas, only to discover the old man had not followed him inside. Will could see his shadow stretched across the ground beyond doorway where he still hovered outside. Will breathed out impatiently. Grabbing the doorframe with one hand, he leaned out, and used his free hand to beckon for Silas to join him. With obvious reluctance, Silas did as he was told. In fact, of late, he was doing everything with less energy and enthusiasm. That was perhaps to be expected, if he had the same feelings about what was going on as did Will – particularly about Alf's death. The problem was Silas refused to discuss anything other than the work. Even then, he limited himself to only the briefest of sentences – resorting, where possible, to simple nods and grunts. It was as if the man were trying to shield himself from the facts by focusing only on the task in hand, and even that only half-heartedly.

Once Silas had joined him inside, Will pointed at the floor. "It's going to take a bit more readying before we can lay the tiles." Silas only nodded in silent agreement. It made Will think of Alf. Trying to ignore the fresh wave of sadness that remembering the boy provoked, he cleared his throat, continued, "The job of levelling…not to find fault…only it has not been properly done…needs more work. I think I had expected…"

Will did not know what he had expected; he only knew

that he wanted to delay setting the tiles in place for as long as possible, and being exacting about the readiness of the chapel floor was the only way he could think of for the moment without it being too obvious what he was doing. The Abbess's so-called miracle had only served to further convince him that the task he was involved in was one from which no good would come. It was strange for the tiles to have turned out as they did, but something told Will that it was no miracle. The Abbess had been right to begin with, back when she believed the chapel was a mistake. Work on building it ought never to have been begun. Every step now taken towards its completion was a step towards a goal that would be best never reached. Something evil would result from it. That the Abbess now so fervently wished for its completion suggested to Will that something had occurred to make her no longer the woman she had been back when he first encountered her.

He crouched down, swept a hand over the surface of the chapel floor, searching for the humps and dips that would require levelling before the surface was ready to receive the tiles. There were plenty. Even if he had not been intentionally delaying the work, he would have had to do something about them. He looked up at Silas. "See what I mean?"

Silas scuffed the ground with his foot, shrugged.

Irritated, Will stood up. "Silas, this can't go on. I have to know why you are…"

Will stopped mid-sentence, his attention caught by the sudden change of light in the small chapel. Someone must be standing in the entrance. Will turned around. Although the man was in almost complete silhouette, it was obvious from his clothing that he was a priest. Most likely the one Will had seen about the Abbey grounds once or twice before. Ingrith had said his name was Father Thomas.

"You are William Tiler?"

"I am, Father. Can I help you?"

"I wish to talk with you, if I may? In private."

Reluctant in case this was more of the Abbess's doing, but knowing he was not in a position to refuse this request, Will said, "Would here do, Father?"

"It will be fine," replied the priest.

Without being told, Silas walked towards the doorway.

"Thank you," said the priest, stepping to one side to allow Silas to pass. When Silas was gone, the priest looked about himself. "This will be a fine chapel when it is complete."

Will said nothing.

"You do not agree?"

"The masons have done their work well enough. I can find no fault," said Will.

"Still, you do not agree?"

Emboldened by the priest's obvious discomfort, Will said, "What is it you want of me, Father. I have work I must complete if I am to avoid the displeasure of the Abbess. You wish to talk, then talk. Unless I am mistaken, your subject is not to be the craftsmanship on display here."

Will's lack of respect threw the priest. He appeared on the verge of admonishing Will for it, and then had a change of heart. "Very well, then," he said. "As you are so determined that I do so straight away, I will explain my purpose."

Will waited.

"My name is Father…"

"Thomas," said Will, impatiently completing the other man's sentence.

"You know my name?"

"I have learned it, yes."

"Really? May I know from whom?"

"Does it matter?"

"It might."

"I believe it was from Ingrith, the novice. It was she who spoke of you…I think."

As if mention of Ingrith's name were in some way a confirmation of something he had hoped were not true, the priest smiled wanly. "It is at her request I am here." Seeing

Will's expression soften on learning this, Father Thomas asked. "You will talk freely to me, then?"

"I will."

"She came to me...Ingrith, that is...with what I can only describe as a fantastic story. She claims that nothing short of devilry is afoot at Althurst. She claims that this chapel is at the heart of it. Of course, I set no store by the young woman's tale. She was in earnest, nonetheless. I could not doubt that. Whether she was correct was a different thing entirely. Naturally, I plan to put the problem before Abbess Rhoswen."

"You must not do that, Father!" insisted Will.

Surprised at the feeling in Will's voice, Father Thomas leaned back a little, studied him.

"Oh? Why is that?"

Will raised his hands, palms outward. "Forgive me, Father. But you must not. Ingrith speaks the truth. There is much that is wrong here, I am convinced of it."

"I see you, like Ingrith, are in earnest. You can, I am sure, understand that that fact alone does not convince me. Ingrith was as insistent as you that I should not raise the matter with the Reverend Mother. She got from me the agreement that I would talk with you first. If you fail to convince me otherwise, she said, she will accompany me when I talk with the Abbess."

Will's eyes grew wide. "To do so would mean her end. The Abbess intends her nothing but harm, Father. Even if I cannot get you to believe me, you must not hold her to her promise."

"Harm? What harm can she come to? Oh, I know about the boy. And Sister Euphemia. There was another...He was a..."

"Carpenter," said Will. "He had a name. Ned."

"Ned," echoed Father Thomas. "You will not convince me that Abbess Rhoswen had a hand in any of their deaths. It is impossible that she should have. She, like me, is a servant of God!"

Will grunted contemptuously. "And have you known no servant who served more than one master? Have you such faith in your kind? But I do not say Abbess Rhoswen killed anyone. She is in league...or bewitched...by whatever it was did."

"Where is your proof, man? Have a care when you make such an accusation. You may find yourself condemned for it."

"You have it the wrong way about, Father. I am condemned if I do not. Worse, I may be damned if I do not. Yet I find I am weak in the face of the challenge. Ingrith is stronger if she has promised to go with you to talk to that woman."

"Proof!" insisted Father Thomas.

"I can offer nothing you will not see differently if your mind is hard bent against it. But then, is it not faith that your kind insist is the cornerstone of the Christian life. I have that faith. Just as I have faith that there is evil in this place. Three people are dead. I do not know much of how your nun died, but I can tell you that both the boy and the carpenter died in ways that should not have been thinkable. A grown man crushed and starved of breath under a layer of little more than dust...On this very spot...in this very place... when all he had to do to save himself was stand up and walk outside. Then a boy...the most level-headed lad you could hope to meet...sticks his own arm into a fire as hot as damnation itself... and he holds it in there long enough to die from the damage done to him. If you had witnessed the result of either of these things you would wonder at the cause of it. I saw both."

"People can act against their natures...do things that you would not give credence to had you not seen. It happens. Madness takes hold of a person and..."

"Twice? Maybe three times? And all of them in some way or another linked with this cursed chapel? You wish to talk to me of people who do things you would not credit. How about an Abbess…a Reverend Mother…who dismisses the death of an innocent boy as easily as you or I might that of a rabbit for the pot? A chicken for a feast day. It meant nothing to her. The woman I met when I first came here was hard, proud. She had a heart for all that. You could see it. Where is that heart now, Father? Consumed by the need to complete this damned chapel because the saint herself has told her, that's where."

"The miracle of the tiles…" offered Father Thomas.

"You, a priest, know better than I that that is not in the way of a miracle. Black magic, devilry… maybe so. A miracle? I think not. Whoever heard of such a one as that? Kill a child, save the tiles? Do not talk as if you yourself have no doubts. You would not be here if that were true. You wish it were not so…that these things were not true…yet you feel it, Father. I know you do. You must. There is the proof you require. It is provided by your own instincts. They led you here to talk to me, did they not? If you do force Ingrith to go with you when you talk with Abbess Rhoswen, you look into the eyes of both women. You tell me then in which woman the truth lives and within which the madness burns."

Father Thomas put his hands to his ears, tufts of his grey hair sticking out between his fingers. "Enough of this. No more. I need time to consider. This is no proof."

"You have none either way, Father. You have only this…" Will put his hand to his heart.

Father Thomas turned to go, only to find his way blocked by the small figure of Abbess Rhoswen. He had no need to ask if she had overheard his conversation with Will; the anger in her face told him she had. He froze where he stood, waiting for her words of reproach. All she said was, "Out of my way, gullible priest."

To Father Thomas's astonishment, when he failed to move immediately, she kicked him in the shin. The old priest yelped in a mixture of pain and protest, and moved aside.

Rhoswen stormed over to Will. "You are forbidden to do it," she yelled. "Forbidden! Understand me?"

"No," said Will, standing his ground with difficulty, despite Rhoswen's lack of size. "I do not."

"What is it he must not do?" asked Father Thomas, nursing his shin.

Rhoswen glanced over her shoulder at the priest. "What?"

"I simply asked…"

"I heard you. What I don't know is why you think it your business. Get out…now!"

"Reverend Mother, I must speak with you…"

"I know what it is you would say. You are weak. You share this man's doubts. You are wrong. When you at last see, you will understand. For now, you can best serve Merwinna by doing as you are told. Now get out."

Father Thomas hesitated. For a brief moment it seemed he would object to the way the Abbess was talking to him. Then what resolve he might have had evidently failed him, and he backed away, stumbling out the door and into the daylight outside. He stood where he was, looking around indecisively for a few seconds. It was then that he saw Silas standing to one side of the doorway, evidently listening to the talk within. Father Thomas reflected for a moment, and then went and stood on the opposite side of the door.

Rhoswen had waited for the old priest to leave. Now he was gone, she turned back to Will.

"You want me to explain why I have come. Very well. I am here to tell you what Merwinna has told me."

"What *Saint Merwinna* has *told* you?" asked Will, as much for the benefit of Father Thomas, who he correctly guessed was listening outside.

Either Rhoswen did not hear the incredulity in Will's voice or she chose to ignore it. Her answer was matter of fact, almost casual. "Yes, she says you must cease your digging and scraping of the floor here. There is no need for it."

Will cocked his head. "What?" He could make no sense of

what he was hearing. It was an everyday – if absurd – order, regarding how he should proceed with the creation of the floor. And yet he was being told it was given at the behest of the saint herself - something the Abbess clearly believed.

Rhoswen grew impatient. "It is a simple enough instruction. You are to put an end to any work to level the ground."

"We have hardly begun, Reverend Mother. If we do not level things off, the tiles cannot be laid. They will not sit squarely. They will not…"

Rhoswen lifted her hands in despair. "Did you learn nothing from the miracle of the firing? The usual rules governing your methods have no place here. There is no need of them. If Merwinna tells me you must stop digging, then you must stop."

"The tiles will not take. If they set at all, they will set so they are irregular…," persisted Will, scuffing his foot across the uneven floor in illustration of his point. "It will be poor work."

"Oh man of distrust and disbelief!" hissed Rhoswen. "The work will be better than anything you have ever done before with your clumsy hands alone, for this time they will be guided. Why can you not see? Why do you persist in this doubting? The floor is ready as it is. The tiles will take. They will take, and they will lie in place perfectly. What is it prevents you from accepting the word of the saint?"

Will came to a decision. "Because this is not the holy place you claim it is. There is something wrong here, and I will not be part of it in the way you are. Whatever it is whispers in your ear, it is not Saint Merwinna."

With a howl of rage, Rhoswen slapped Will across the face. "How dare you!"

Will's hand quivered, rose slightly, as if he might return her violence. Then he took a steadying breath and said, "I will leave this place today. Whatever the cost."

As he stepped towards the doorway, Will half expected the

Abbess to block his way. Instead, she stood to one side and, as he was about to leave, asked, "What of the girl?"

Will stopped, his shoulders slumped. "Ingrith?"

"Yes, your beloved Ingrith. You and I both know you would not so easily leave her to her fate. I will make good on my threat to destroy her if you do. You think I will not, is that it? You think I will relent. Not so, man. Not so. You know I speak the truth. In your heart you know it. If your leaving this place were truly possible you would have already done so. No, you have no option but to do as I say. For her sake, if not your own."

"What is she to me?" Will bluffed. "You make too much of my liking for her. She is nothing to me."

"*Nothing* to you? Is that so?" Rhoswen's eyes grew wide with rage. "The pair of you make the beast behind my back. Behind the backs of all the sisters here. Mocking us. Betraying our trust with your sordid, ungodly behaviour. You and she sully the ground of this holy place with your base fornication. And now you tell me she is *nothing* to you? If that is so, it is her…Ingrith…you betray the most. You have corrupted that girl, and now you would abandon her…cast her aside? I do not believe it. I think…" Rhoswen's voice grew cruel, mocking, "I think you more than like her. You have deluded yourself that a man as lowborn as you are…a whore's bastard too, for all I know… has won her affections." She chuckled unkindly. "The affections of a high-born girl who you would hardly have dared look in the eye before you came to Althurst. As for her…I hardly know what she thinks she is doing." Rhoswen closed her eyes, shook her head long-sufferingly. "That she is filthy and lustful; that much is certain. That she deserves punishment for her behaviour is certain too." She opened her eyes again and glared at Will. "Now think on this, William Tiler. What form that punishment takes is for me to decide. I can make it little more than a straightforward penance if I choose. Something to be endured, recovered from, and put in her past. Or I can shame her outright...punish her to the point where she wishes for death. The entire thing is at my pleasure. You see that, don't you? Which way I choose depends wholly on you...on what you do now. Merwinna wants her chapel finished. She demands it be so. To that end, she wants the tiles laid. So you will do it. That is an end to it. I leave this place now on a visit I cannot avoid...more of your precious Bishop's interference...When I return tonight, I expect to find work on the floor has progressed...tiles having been laid. Who knows...you may even have completed it. Oh, I see the look on your face, William Tiler; do not trouble to tell me your objections once again. You will find it is possible, despite your assertions to the contrary. The saint will guide your hand...all shall be well." Rhoswen looked as if she were about to leave, then she paused. She leaned in to Will, almost confidentially. "I wonder, was she worth it? The little whore, I mean. Was the sating of your lust worth the price you now pay? You know Merwinna and I have laughed about it. Actually laughed. What fools you both have been, you and your novice. Rather than the brief gratification of the flesh, you could have shared in the glory to come. Instead..." She shook her head. "Such fools." Then she stepped out into the daylight. Looking up at Father Thomas, who still stood next to the entrance, she said, "As for you. I know you will do the right thing. Not because your faith is strong, as it should be. No, you will do it because your body is weak, that is why. Our tiler in there is strong in some regards; I will say that much for him. He has a misguided courage of a kind, also. Whereas you, my dear Father, lack even that." She spat contemptuously, and then walked away.

Inside the chapel, Will rubbed at his forehead with the heel of his palm as he studied the ground beneath his feet. It made no sense to attempt to lay tiles on an unprepared floor. You need not be a tiler to grasp that much. But then none of it made any sense to Will. Perhaps if he did as the Abbess wanted – made the damned floor - he could leave, and put this all behind him. Then that was the problem, wasn't it? The floor, the chapel, all of it – it was just that: damned. Truly damned. How could he take part in the building of something he felt was so cursed by God, and still hope to escape punishment? And yet how could he avoid doing so and still prevent Ingrith from facing the wrath of the Abbess for what he, Will, had refused to do. For the moment he had no choice. Unless he could discover what lay behind it all.

Behind it all, or should that be under...?

A thought had occurred to him. He crouched down, brushed his hand through the dust and grit as he done earlier when talking with Silas. Why would Merwinna – or whatever the Abbess believed was Merwinna – be so insistent that the ground not be interfered with? Why would it matter if the floor were to be made level? Another one of Abbess Rhoswen's miracles? *The tiles that lay flat on uneven ground.* Nonsense. Why then? Why be so adamant that the ground go undisturbed?

Outside, he found Father Thomas and Silas both standing in the sunlight. Silas was his usual silent self. The Father, now looking pale and anxious, was the first to speak.

"I see now that there is something in what you say," he said, looking over his shoulder as if he were worried the Abbess might still be there. "She is not herself. The Abbess Rhoswen I have grown to respect would never speak as she has done of a novice without good grounds to do so. Even then, the language she chose to use...it would not be so...."

"What of the Saint?" interrupted Will. "You believe the Abbess when she says she talks with her?"

The priest winced at the mention of it. "It is not for me to..."

"Do you believe her? Answer me, Father!" insisted Will.

Father Thomas's shoulders slumped. He could not look at Will when he said, "No, I do not."

Behind him, Silas surprised Will by whistling. It might

have been intended to convey some measure of mockery; Will could not be sure. He chose to ignore it.

"You were listening, Father, so you heard what she said in there. Why would she want the floor undisturbed? There has to be some reason for it."

"I myself hope that there is no reason for it whatsoever. None that would make any sense to you or me. That is the pity of it. What fevers burn in that poor woman's mind are beyond your or my comprehension. We cannot hope to understand. In truth, we should be grateful that we do not. To be like that…the poor woman is deserving of our sympathy."

"Poor woman?"

"Her mind is…"

Will groaned in frustration. "You still insist there is no evil here? You think it only the Reverend Mother's mind that is twisted? How can you be so sure that there is nothing that speaks to her? Something that is neither the saint nor her own broken mind that speaks to her…"

"Deceives her into thinking it is that which it is not?" asked Father Thomas. "It is too much to think on!"

"You have to. What of the deaths? Young Alf…"

For the first time, Father Thomas had turned to fully face Will. Will could see he was sweating profusely. "I don't know, William," said the priest, his voice tight and high. "I know you think as a man of God I should have the answers. I confess I do not. It might be as you say. Or it might be *you* that sees something that is not there. Have you considered *that*? Such proof you offer me is no proof at all. So, when you ask me if I am sure…one way or the other… I tell you no. No, I am not."

Silas whistled again. This time, Will shot him a look of reproach.

Father Thomas looked from Silas to Will. "I wish it were otherwise." He straightened up. "Now, tell me if I am mistaken, but I sense you have something to suggest,

William."

"That I do, Father. You are not mistaken. That floor…it is far too small a thing to be of importance in itself. Senseless for her to be so unbending on something so small, unless… it must be…" Will hesitated, then said, "What lies beneath it that she wants to prevent us discovering."

All three men were silent for a moment.

"So, what will you do?" asked Father Thomas, at last, already resigned to what the reply would be.

Will shrugged. "What I must, Father. I will dig it up. When she leaves for the day, I will dig it up. And I would ask that you…"

"Yes, yes," said Father Thomas, reluctantly. "I, too, will do what I must. The Abbess thinks me weak and a coward. I would prove her wrong in that. So, yes, I will be present when you do it. I pray God you are wrong, and that I am right. I understand my duty, nonetheless. Although there is one thing…"

"Yes?"

"The cost to Ingrith?" asked the priest. "You are not to tell me you do not care for her." Observing Will frown, he added, "Oh, I do not for a moment imagine what the Abbess says is true. Nothing like that has passed between you, of that I am sure. But nor do I believe there is no affection. Such unlikely bonds have formed in others before you; however inappropriate such a thing may be. However, that is a difficulty for your own consciences, not mine. I ask again, though, what of the cost to her if you do this thing?"

This time, it was Will who looked away. "She, like me, is already condemned, Father…perhaps even damned…if I do not do it. She may yet be saved from that if I do."

******

CHAPTER 22

Will had been heartened to see Ingrith was with Father Thomas when the priest appeared again later that day. He had watched Abbess Rhoswen and her companions ride out through the gatehouse on whatever business it was took her from Althurst for the day, and knew it was only a matter of time before the old priest returned. He wanted to be there to witness what, if anything, Will uncovered when he and Silas dug up the floor of the new chapel.

Although Will and Ingrith had exchanged nods and smiled, they shared no other greeting; the presence of the priest seemed to inhibit anything more.

"The girl insisted she accompany me," explained Father Thomas, noticing the exchange. "Though I was against it, she has a strong will." Before anything more could be said on the matter, he added, "Shall we begin? I want this business done with. If we find nothing...as I hope...the floor must be set as it was...and before Abbess Rhoswen returns. I do not know for certain when that will be."

"More than that," corrected Will. "The work of laying the tiles must appear to have begun at least."

"She travels by horse," said Ingrith. "And in company. Her journey must therefore be a long one."

"And the beast will carry her swiftly there, and just as swiftly back," said Father Thomas, impatiently. "We must make haste."

Will made no reply. He nodded to Silas, and the old man began the task of breaking the surface of the chapel floor with a pickaxe. There was not much space with the four of them in there. After only a few strikes, Silas said, "You hinder me. I can't swing without fear of hittin' one of ya. You'll have to get out while I do this."

"He is right," agreed Will. "It is not safe. Ingrith, you and the Father should step outside. Besides, someone should keep watch. I'm hoping any noise we make will be taken as part of the work of preparing the surface for the tiles. It would be well to have warning of anyone approaching all the same. I've stacked some of the tiles in here to help give the idea that that is what we are about. If you see someone, call out, and we will act as if we are laying them."

Reluctantly, Ingrith stepped out into the sun, accompanied by Father Thomas. They exchanged the occasional nervous glance, but spoke very little.

Inside the chapel, the surface of the floor was dry but not hard. It had a brittle crust that broke easily with each swing of the pickaxe, so it was not long before Will moved Silas aside and began digging with a spade. The work was hot, and after about an hour Will called out for Ingrith to fetch him and Silas some water. Ingrith did as she was asked. When she returned from the water butt, Father Thomas was nowhere in sight. She had a moment of panic when she thought something bad must have happened - perhaps they had been discovered – until she heard the voices of Will and the priest speaking in low tones coming from inside. She stepped inside herself, carrying the jug of water.

She did not notice Sister Alice watching her do so at a discreet distance.

Ingrith's eyes took time to adjust after the bright sunlight outside. Silas, she saw, was standing back against the wall. He had an odd look on his face, somewhere between fear and anger, as if he were experiencing both things at the same time and trying hard to conceal them both.

Father Thomas was in the middle of the chapel, leaning over Will, who had put his spade aside and was crouched down in the long ditch he had dug, using his bare hands to sweep away dirt from something nestled in the earth in front of him.

"What is it?" she asked. "What have you found?"

"Shhh, child!" said Father Thomas.

Ingrith stepped up beside the priest, following his gaze, her eyes getting more used to the lack of light. It was soon clear what Will's efforts were revealing. It was a skeleton. A skeleton that, from the look of it, had been under there for some time; the bones where brown, splintered, and disintegrating with age.

"How long do you think he's been down there?" she asked.

"*She*, more like," replied Will. "Judging from the size."

"How long dead?" asked Ingrith.

Will stood up, studied the bones at his feet. "I don't know. Could be years and years…Just look at her."

Father Thomas gasped, and then said in a half-whisper, "Merwinna!"

"*Merwinna?*" asked Ingrith. "But…"

"Who else could it be?" said Father Thomas reluctantly, almost bitterly. "There's been no one else…The shrine, and now the chapel. There's been no one else in this place all that time."

"If it is her, that would mean…" Ingrith let the sentence hang unfinished.

Father Thomas put his hands over his face. When he spoke, it was through his fingers. "No Assumption…No gathering up into Heaven, mortal remains and all."

"We don't know it's her," suggested Will.

"We don't know it isn't!" snapped Father Thomas. "Don't you understand? It casts a shadow over everything."

At first, Ingrith was surprised to find within herself some echo of the priest's distress. However, on reflection, she wondered why she should be surprised to feel that way? Although she might doubt the recent miracles that Abbess Rhoswen was claiming - attributing them to some other, more malign agency - she had never once questioned the story of the miraculous disappearance of Saint Merwinna. Her faith in the truth of it was at the heart of all she had done since coming to the Abbey. All that the good the sisters here hoped to achieve was grounded on the example of pure, unquestioning faith set by Saint Merwinna. If it had been a falsehood all along, then what else in this place might also be a lie? Could it be that, far from being a house of God, this was a place abandoned by Him? A place where the aims of the evil one had been a hidden part of the admixture of daily life for countless years, working towards some unknown harm, some evil, in the guise of working on behalf of the Lord?

"Wait! What's that?" asked Will, suddenly.

"What?" asked Ingrith.

"There, in the corner of the pit. There's something else. Another one...I don't know...Silas, get me a flame, I can't see well enough down there."

Father Thomas let his hands fall from his face. "Another? What on earth can that mean? Who could it *be*?"

Ignoring these questions, Will had jumped back down into the hole, and was using a trowel to scrape away at something concealed in the dirt. Whatever it was he was uncovering, it was hidden from view, within the shadows at the corner. Silas hurriedly lit a small stump of candle, passed it to Will, and just as hurriedly, stepped back, unwilling to look. Will grunted a thank you, set the candle on the earth, and then carried on scraping away at the dirt.

Unlike Silas, who sank back into the corner, Father Thomas and Ingrith both strained to see. After a minute or two, her curiosity getting the better of her, Ingrith climbed down into the pit with Will. She was about to squat down alongside him, when he yelled, dropped the trowel, and staggered back, wiping his hands on his tunic as if he had touched something unclean. In her effort to avoid him, Ingrith tripped and fell onto her side. She had scrabbled back to her feet, and was in the process of reaching into the corner when two strong hands grabbed her around the waist and pulled her back.

"Get away from there!" ordered Will, almost shouting. "You mustn't touch it!"

Ingrith had all but forgotten the earthenware jug of water she had been holding. It had fallen to the ground when she fell, and now its contents were pooling on the earth around the thing in the ground, before slowly sinking into the porous earth surrounding it. Where the water had splashed upon its face and forehead, the damp bone – for it was surely the skull of some long-dead creature – was glinting in the flickering light of the candle. Below the skull, Will had begun to uncover the beginnings of a ribcage, about the size of that of large dog or a wolf.

"Oh, God help us! Not that!" cried Ingrith. When Will and a wide-eyed Father Tomas looked questioningly at her, she asked them, "Can you not recognise it?"

"Some manner of demon…some manifestation of…" stuttered Father Thomas. "I know not what precisely…I can give it no name." His hands were shaking.

"I have a name for it!" cried Ingrith. "It is the Imp! The Althurst Imp!"

Will bent forward, reached for the candle, and held it over the thing in the ground. Like the priest's, his hands, too, were shaking. The movement of the shadows caused by the unsteadiness of his hold on the flame gave the unnerving impression that, whatever it was, it was changing its expression – its eyes widening and narrowing, its mouth a scowl one moment, a cold grin the next. Ingrith was right; it *was* the Imp. The creature rendered in stone, high on a pillar inside the church building. Will had admired its workmanship when he first came to this place - the remarkable skill of the carving, the care with which the stone had been shaped. But this version was not carved, nor was it stone. This was bone.

And it *was* the Imp. The skull had the exact same face shape, horns, and peculiarly twisted beak as the Althurst Imp. The one a mirror of the other.

As he watched, the mouth opened. Shadows again? Will held the flame as steady as he could. Not shadows; shadows could not produce such a perfect illusion of teeth – two rows of small needle-like points, all of them a brilliant white that contrasted with the faded brown of the jawbone in which they nestled. Then, in the dark holes of the eye sockets, Will saw what might have been the faint glow of eyes, dark and damp, with an iridescent sheen when caught in the light of the candle flame. The mouth had opened wider now. Beyond the teeth something serpent-like twitched in the hollow: a tongue. It opened wider still, and a high, hollow laugh filled the chapel.

Will leapt away, dropping the candle, which sizzled out in the damp earth where Ingrith had spilt the water. Behind him, above the laugh of the Imp, he heard Ingrith scream, and the priest cry out. Then, even as he struggled to make sense of what he was seeing, the thing had already returned to its previous, desiccated lifelessness. Even before the echoes of that hideous laugh had faded from the chapel walls, the mouth had closed, and the gleam in the eye sockets had shimmered, dulled, and then disappeared completely. Will stared down at the now lifeless thing in the earth. It *had* moved. He was sure of it. From their cries, and from the looks on their faces when he glanced up at them, it was plain that the others, too, had seen it. Only Silas looked unsurprised. Will wondered at this. Perhaps Silas had not been able to see from where he stood? That must be it. Then surely the laugh, and the cries of the others would have alerted him to something having taken place? But his face still had that same look of suppressed anger and fear it had worn earlier. From his reaction – or rather lack of it – one would think nothing extraordinary had just happened.

After a few seconds of stunned silence, during which an odd putrid smell, like rotting flesh, began rising in the chapel, Father Thomas was the first to move. "I have to leave," he said. "We all must." He put an arm around Ingrith, steering her towards the doorway. "Come away, child. Come away with me this instant!"

"Wait!" Ingrith struggled free of the priest's hold, and then reached out a hand, urgently beckoning for Will to join them. "He is right, Will. We must go. We have seen enough. If we make known what we saw... we must be believed." Will looked doubtful, so Ingrith added, "The good Father included... he will be believed, if not us...It will not be from you and me alone that the story comes..." She looked at Father Thomas for confirmation of this.

Impatient to leave, Father Thomas said hastily, "Yes, yes, be assured, I will say what I have seen here. Come away now!" Then, embarrassed by his own lack of dignity, he made an effort to regain his composure, and added in a calmer voice, "Forgive me. Yes, of course, this must be told. There is great evil here, and something must be done. The words of exorcism must be spoken. But, for now, come away. Please. All of you. We should not be in this place a moment more than is necessary."

Will nodded his agreement, and took Ingrith's hand, allowing her to pull him towards the door. They had all three turned to face the opening, only to find their way blocked by Silas. He was holding the pickaxe before himself like a weapon.

"What are you doing?" asked Will, coming to a stop.

"I'm sorry, Will. You have been a good friend and good master. I am sorry. I was given no choice."

"What do you mean? What are you...?"

Before Will could finish, Silas had reached behind himself and pulled the door closed, reducing the light in the already shadowy chapel by half again. Only the thin cracks between the wood of the still boarded up window provided any light now.

"Silas?" said Ingrith. "Let us pass. Please. Open the door."

"I'm sorry, girl. I got nothin' against you...I like you... but I can't do that."

Father Thomas was beginning to lose his struggle with fear. Close to panic he said, "Open it! Open it now! We have to leave this place. Didn't you see it? Can't you smell it?"

"I did, and I can. That's why I have to do what I am doin'."

"What if that thing comes back? You mean for us all to die in here," pleaded Father Thomas.

"Yes, if needs be. Don't have to be all, mind. Some. One, at least. It's what I have to do!"

"Oh, Silas. This thing…it has a hold on you, doesn't it?" said Ingrith. "Like it does Abbess Rhoswen…This is not you…Please ignore whatever it is it tells you. Please, I beg you, open the door." She took a tentative step forward.

Silas stamped his foot. "No more of that!" He shook the pickaxe in warning, despite Ingrith having already stepped back.

"Enough of this, Silas. Do as she tells you!" snapped Will. "Or I swear I will fucking make you!" When Silas made no attempt to open the door, Will moved angrily towards him. Silas raised the pickaxe and swiftly swung it in Will's direction. Will ducked back, the metal head of the tool missing him by only inches. "What the…? Silas!" he yelled, stumbling backwards into Ingrith's steadying hands. "Damn you, man! Damn you to Hell!"

"Hell, you say? Now that is just what I'm tryin' to escape by doin' this," said Silas, almost ruefully. "It says I must do it, or it is down there I go for sure. I can't have that, now can I?" There was a trace of real fear in Silas's voice.

"You will go there if you *do* do it," said Father Thomas. "I promise you that much. Murder is a sin. A *mortal* sin. Don't you know that?"

"That I do," replied Silas sadly. "For as things stand I am already damned. I have killed before, you see."

"What? When?" asked Will.

"As a younger man. Before you knew me, Will. I have been a damned man all this time. Every step I took after I did the deed was taken as a damned soul on his way to the flames. Can you imagine how it has been for me?"

"The indulgence," said Will.

"Aye, that's right. Like you always said, though, that was never gonna be within my grasp. And for a mortal sin what good would it do me? No, this is my one real chance to escape the end in store for me. I have to take it, you see that, don't you?"

"Your fate is decided by God alone!" insisted Father Thomas. "Nothing this… thing…this demon… has promised you will alter His judgement." The priest's voice was quavering with fear, but he seemed to draw strength from his faith as he spoke. Standing as tall as he could, his head held high, as if preaching, he said, "The outcome will be the same whatever you do, man. Do not, I beg you, add further sins to be weighed. Let us pass. This thing has deceived you, as I see now it has been deceiving Abbess Rhoswen."

Silas seemed to consider this. He lowered the axe, stepped back a little from the door as if he might be about to do as Father Thomas had asked. Then he cocked his head. It was as if he were listening to words only he could hear. He turned his head one way, then another, shook it vehemently as if in answer to a question, and then stood back in front of the door, the pickaxe held high once again, his legs braced.

"It has him once more," said Ingrith.

"Perchance," said Father Thomas, stepping forward. "Demon!" he shouted. "Demon, it is you I speak to now. Not this lost soul. Will you not answer me?"

"Have a care, Father," whispered Ingrith.

Father Thomas's head turned very slightly in her direction, and he nodded in silent acknowledgement of her warning. Then he continued forward. "Demon, hear me when I say this to you, *Vade retro sa….*"

Before Father Thomas could finish, Silas had swung the pickaxe sideways through the air in a ferocious arc that sent the metal spike through the old priest's upper arm, skewering it to his side, smashing through his ribs, and entering his chest. Father Thomas screamed, the scream being quickly replaced by coughs and gurgles as his lungs filled with blood that bubbled and spilled from his mouth, soaking into the front of his cassock, or splashing onto the ground.

The priest's legs gave way beneath him, the weight of his body when he fell wrenching the pickaxe free from Silas's hands. Both Ingrith and Will attempted to get to it before Silas, but the old man moved with a speed neither would have believed him capable of, twisting the pickaxe back out from the dying priest's body, tearing more of his flesh and splintering more of his bone in the process. A final strangled groan of anguish escaped from somewhere inside Father Thomas's throat before he rolled over onto his front, and lay still.

Silas stepped back, grunted triumphantly, and waved the blood-soaked pickaxe teasingly in front of them, splashing them with the blood that covered it. "You wish for this?" he sneered. "Why not take it from me. Go on!"

Will took a half-step forward, and then hesitated.

Silas waved the pickaxe at him. "Go on, take it!"

Will stopped dead. The voice Silas used now was not his own. There was no longer any trace of his familiar Hampshire dialect. It was a much deeper voice and, apart from a grating throatiness, free of any recognisable accent.

"Take it!" Silas said again. "Take it. I *want* you to."

Astonished, a cold knot of terror forming in his chest, Will looked questioningly at Ingrith. Even in the poor light of the chapel he could see her eyes where wide with fear.

"Keep back, Will. He speaks with the voice of a demon. The Imp dwells within him."

"I have never liked that name," said the thing inside Silas. "It is ignorant, and disrespectful. I suppose it must serve… until my true name can be spoken."

Will took another step back, stood alongside Ingrith. They were pressed against the far wall.

"What's this?" demanded Silas. "Where's your courage, man? Even the snivelling priest found his in the end. Not you, it seems. Not got it in you. Not even in front of your sweetheart here? Or should I say your whore?"

Will moved forward again, only to be driven back once more by a violent swing of the pickaxe.

"Oh, was I wrong?" scoffed Silas. "Some courage then…where the honour of your wanton is called into question. I pity your stupid honour. Fancy yourself a knight, do you? The noble Sir William rides to the rescue of his fair Lady Ingrith?" With that the thing began to sing a love song in a sweet voice that sounded for all the world like that of a young woman. Will quickly recognised the refrain as one his wife used to sing when they were first courting. After a moment more he realised with dismay and bewilderment that the voice he heard *was* that of his dead wife as a young woman. He covered his ears, unable to bear it.

Silas stopped singing, tilted his head, and held out a hand pleadingly. Still speaking in Will's wife's voice he said, "Why are you with that slut, Will my love? Why do you no longer keep me in your heart as you once did?"

"No, my love…I…I…" stammered Will.

"Why are you disloyal to my memory? How can you find it within you to betray me so? Betray me. Betray me. Betray me," the voice intoned, over and over.

Will began to feel dizzy. Tears filled his eyes, and he thought he would vomit. He bent forward, hands on his knees. It was then he felt Ingrith's grip on his arm. It broke the spell. "Enough of this, enough!" he howled at Silas, straightening up. "You are not she! You cannot be. She is dead. Long dead. These are not her words. I know not what you are, but whoever it is speaks from within that body, it is not the wife I knew. Nor are you the old man I have worked with all these years. Silas would never…"

"What? Confront you with your own sins? Tell me, then. Who am I that would?"

"You are a demon!" screamed Ingrith.

In the half-light it was difficult to make out Silas's expression. "Is that so? Undoubtedly it was what the priest thought. Much good it did him. Look at it…lying there…" Silas kicked the prone priest, who surprised them all by groaning. "Well, well, not quite dead after all," said Silas. He raised a foot and stamped down hard on Father Thomas's neck. It gave with a sickening snap. "Dead now, though, I think. Don't you?" Silas studied the corpse beneath his foot for a second or two before looking up. Although only in shadow, from the turn of his head, it seemed he was looking more at Ingrith than at Will. "Tell me, what good did all his years of serving God do for him in the end do you think? Not that much from where I am standing…on his neck."

"He is with Him now!" yelled Ingrith, her face wet with tears. "He is with God in a place *you* do not come from and will never see, monster!"

"Oh? And *you* will, will you? A debauched slut who aches for the depraved caresses of this low-born man? A tiler's novice? How does that serve God, I wonder…? The coming together of calloused hands and soft virginal flesh. If virginal it remains. Where in the requirements of your rule is that set down? I search the rubric in vain."

"Demon!" shouted Will, suddenly. Grabbing Ingrith by the wrist, he lunged forward, shouldered Silas out the way, and pulled her towards the door.

Instead of attempting to stop him, Silas merely laughed. "Too late, Master Tiler. Far too late."

Before they reached the door, it was opened from outside, and Abbess Rhoswen stepped into the chapel. At her shoulder stood Sir Geoffrey de Longe, and behind him, his man Dicken. Both men looked uneasy, and had their swords already drawn. Dicken stepped around Sir Geoffrey and put his blade to Will's throat, forcing him to step back, Ingrith still at his side, gripping his arm.

At the same time, Silas – now reverting to his familiar

Hampshire accent – fell to his knees, hands clasped together, snivelling and pleading. "Save me. Save your servant. Thank the Lord you have come, mighty sirs…Good Mother…they were sure to have slain me next had you not opened that door when you did."

"Next?" asked Sir Geoffrey, "Ah…" he added. The light from the open doorway fell upon the prone and blood-stained body of Father Thomas.

"I am proved right!" hissed Rhoswen, triumphantly. "You must believe me now, for here before you is the proof for which you asked. Our priest has been murdered. A priest! What greater sin than kill a servant of God? Did I not say when you arrived that there was devilry at this Abbey?"

Sir Geoffrey studied the scene before him, taking in Will, Ingrith, Silas, and the body of the priest.

He his words, when he spoke, were addressed to Rhoswen. "No, Reverend Mother, in point of fact, you did not. Not when I arrived. Let us be clear on this. Had your Sister Alice not approached us when she did, with her strange tales of something amiss in this chapel, would you even have mentioned it? I find I am inclined to think not. If you yourself already knew of a problem here, I can't help but wonder why you did not take steps sooner. You did not summon me. More to the point…given the nature of the problem… you did not seek help from others in your order? As it is, I myself am here in Althurst today by chance alone, on route to somewhere else. It is by chance alone that Dicken and I come upon this scene with you. Well, can you explain, Abbess Rhoswen? Can you?"

Rhoswen struggled to answer at first, and then grew impatient. "What difference does it make, Sir Geoffrey? The evil is here…*you* are here…it may be by divine providence that you are…Howsoever you come here, together we must act!"

"That's right, my lady," interrupted Silas, "These two, they have done your priest to death, poor man…And why?

Because he confronted them with their sin…shame to relate it…that is why. See for yourselves how his blood stains their clothing…their hands…and, oh, God save us…their very faces… They were about to have done the same for me when you entered. Without your timely arrival…with these good sirs… my blood, too, would be on their hands right now. T'is truly a mercy that you arrived when you did…another moment more and… well…" He gave a dramatic shake of his head, lost for words, and then suddenly looked up, a hand reaching imploringly towards Rhoswen. Her expression changed from one of triumph to one of unease as Silas continued, "My lady, will you not agree with me when I say this must be of Saint Merwinna's doin'? For t'is surely her intervention that had you come when you did, Good Mother? You… and these men."

Rhoswen did not reply. She looked from Silas to the bloodied body of the priest, and back again.

Sir Geoffrey's eyes had narrowed. "Saint Merwinna who intervenes is it? Tell me, old man, why she would save only you? A grizzled and lowborn craftsman …one of the plough horses of this world…and not this priest on the ground before us? A man of God."

"It..it is not for me to say…," said Silas. "I cannot tell you. Maybe the Good Mother here can explain…?"

Rhoswen continued to look uncomfortable. She still did not respond.

"Have you an answer for us, Reverend Mother?" asked Sir Geoffrey. "Why your Father…Thomas…was it? …why he lies dead before us, and not this tiler?"

"Not even that. Not a tiler. Only his assistant… if I remember rightly," added Dicken.

"So, less of a plough horse, more of a donkey," said Sir Geoffrey. He laughed, but it came across as forced, the normally arrogant man's unease quite evident. "So, Abbess Rhoswen. Have you an answer? I grow impatient for your reply."

Rhoswen demurred. "I am not certain…it is not for me to know such things."

"Is it not? Is that so?" asked Sir Geoffrey. He reached down a gauntleted hand, grabbed the still kneeling Silas by the scruff. "I am curious, old man. The Abbess…your *Good Mother*… insists she does not know. Whereas your words were that you *cannot* tell me. What am I to make of that, hmm? That you do not know. Or that you *do* know, but cannot tell me? You do see the difference? Might it, in fact, be that you *will* not tell me?"

"T'was but a manner of speakin'. I cannot because I do not," pleaded Silas. "I can not."

"Try!" roared Sir Geoffrey, releasing his grip, letting Silas fall back onto his behind. "What is it makes you so special, old man, that a saint saves you first, and only? *Your* life before that of a priest? Who are you to be so favoured? Oh, yes, I do believe there is evil at work here. Of that, there can be no question. I only question the source. There is blood on your clothing too. And these two…" he waved his sword in the direction of Ingrith and Will, "they seem frightened…only not so much of me, a Deputy Sheriff of all Hampshire…as of *you*, an old, old man. A man that I would gladly wager this fellow," he nodded at Will, "could easily knock to the ground if need be. And yet he, as much as the girl here, seemed to me to be most anxious to be free of you when this door was opened. Who are you? Answer me. I grow weary of this."

Silas stood, dusted himself down, wiped the tears and drool from his face with the back of his hand, and smiled. "Well… *Deputy Sheriff of all Hampshire*…I, too, grow weary. This game is at an end. It no longer amuses me."

"What has happened to your voice…I don't understand," said Sir Geoffrey, confused. Both he and Dicken raised their swords, and stood back.

"My voice? It troubles you? How then if I tell you my voice has not changed. It is as it has always been. However, if by that you mean the voice of this shell which, presently, I inhabit…That was the voice of a dead man you were listening to."

Sir Geoffrey's mouth fell open, and his jaw began to work up and down, soundlessly.

Silas stepped forward, his chest only inches from Sir Geoffrey's sword. "How is it you still fail to understand, Deputy Sheriff of all Hampshire? Perhaps a demonstration will help. How will you react, then, if I should do this?" Silas bent sideways, reached out a hand, and lifted the pickaxe from the floor. Sir Geoffrey and Dicken both braced for an attack. Instead, in one swift motion, Silas drove the point of the pickaxe into his own face, piercing one of his eyes.

Ingrith screamed.

Will yelled, "No, Silas…!"

The metal spike had been driven in so deep it should have killed him instantly, but Silas remained standing. With the pickaxe lodged in his face, he roared triumphantly, swaying his head from side to side so the axe handle swung to and fro like a pendulum. Then he laughed and, with a stomach-churning sucking sound, pulled the spike out. He held it up for a moment, gleefully studying it with his remaining eye. After that, he held the spike to his mouth, stuck out his tongue, and licked at the blood and gore that covered it.

"Holy Christ, save us," whispered Sir Geoffrey.

"Devil," yelled Rhoswen. "Devil, Devil, Devil!"

"Not him," said Silas, one side of his face now crimson and glistening with his own blood.

"What demon are you, then?" asked Rhoswen.

Silas spun around, leaned in towards her, running his tongue around his lips, tasting what he found there. Then, with a mouth red with his own blood, he said, "*I am Merwinna,*" in a voice Rhoswen recognised. "*I see from your face you know this voice. Is that not so?*"

"You are not she who spoke to me," protested Rhoswen, backing away. "You are not. You lie. You are a deceiver. An enchanter who would cloud my mind with your tricks. You are not Merwinna. You are not her, deceiver."

Silas nodded, stepping towards her again; closing the distance she was trying to create. "Yes, yes," he smiled. "I am what you say I am; a deceiver. And yet I *am* Merwinna. *Your* Merwinna, that is. The one you so wanted to communicate with. *Build a chapel in my name,* I commanded you. And you built it. *I have sent you a sign,* I told you. And you saw it. Saw it because you wanted to see it. You are your own deceiver, Abbess Rhoswen. A woman prepared to name the least of things a miracle because it suited her purposes. Perfect tiles, bah! That is no miracle! Little more than an oddity. An accident of chance could cause it. Or me, perhaps…hmm? And what are they anyway, these tiles of yours? Squares of baked shit, made to line the floor of a stone box. A hollow box…empty of anything worth praying to… built to honour the memory of some deluded girl who convinced herself she communed with God, rather than face the damage her lustful ways had done to a man she once loved who could not love her back. It was always there in her painted image for those who had eyes to see it. Not a saint, but a temptress… Soothing her own shame with her false faith. Hiding away behind walls of stone. Leaving the world beyond those walls to live with the damage she had caused. The least deserving winning all the admiration."

Rhoswen gasped. "Whose instrument have I been all this time?"

"Your *own*. Honour Merwinna well enough, and one day they might also honour you. Saint Rhoswen of Althurst. Vanity. I shit on your kind and their faith!"

"What door have I opened? Who have I allowed to enter?" asked Rhoswen.

"Reverend Mother, it is the Imp!" cried Ingrith. "See…here it lies!" She pointed to the horned skeleton in the ground.

"She speaks the truth," confirmed Silas. "The girl shows cleverness. I like her. I may even have her when all this is done with. What was it I called you, girl? Remind me. Whore? Slut? Tiler's novice? Why not continue to be all those things…for me? If I enjoy the feel of your fresh little cunt as much as I know William Tiler there hopes to, I may reward you for it."

"Never!" yelled Ingrith. "Never, never! You are a foul thing, and I reject you!"

"*Never*, you say? I think your Abbess here once said she would *never* allow this chapel to be built. Yet in it she now stands. I can be very persuasive." He looked at Rhoswen. Speaking again in the voice he had used for Merwinna, he said, "*Abbess Rhoswen, I choose you to be the bearer of my message.* Ha! Stupid woman! I chose *you* so you would build your precious chapel… build it on the very spot where I myself was once worshiped." He looked curious. "Can you understand that, I wonder? For eternities before your kind built their stone boxes in this place, other men and women of a different kind knelt in the open to worship *me*… in this very place. I will be worshipped that way again in time. Now I am released once more. Now I am dug up… thanks to this fellow and his assistant. *Oh, Rhoswen, don't let them dig up the floor,* I told you, and away you hurried with Merwinna's message. And so, their suspicions aroused… as I had fully intended them to be… they did just that; they dug up the floor. Exactly what you told them not to do. Dug up the floor. Dug up me. You see now? I have been the minstrel and you have all been my puppets. All working to free me." Silas spread his arms. "Here I am at last…. your Althurst Imp… returned in the flesh." He scowled. "Imp…such an ignominious title for one such as I, don't you think? Imp? Demon is far better. Yes, I like that much more. A way for you to know me. A term you and your kind will understand. Demon."

Rhoswen slumped back against the wall. "Oh, Saint Merwinna, what wrongs have I committed in your name? What evil have I set free?"

"Why not ask her?" said the Demon. "For once she *is* with you…truly so. She lies there in the dirt. Not taken up to heaven entire, after all. When I was done with her, I hid her there to give that impression. It would help keep this place sacred until I was ready. Didn't it work well? All those dull-witted and credulous pilgrims putting their desperate, ugly faces to the shit bucket hole to beg some relief from whatever torment your God thought to bestow upon them. All those desperate prayers. Some of the things that ailed them quite shameful. Itches between the legs. Cocks that dripped from too much dipping. You know, I even granted the occasion cure if it was within my power to do it. Straightened a twisted back here, soothed an aching tooth there. Small miracles only. Just enough to keep the legend alive. *My* legend, in the guise of that of your saint. *Mine*. I am gloating, I know. But answer me, do I not deserve it? My victory complete. Nothing you can do."

Ingrith's eyes strayed to the body of Father Thomas. "Reverend Mother, it fears the Vade Retro Satana. Father Thomas attempted to speak the words of exorcism, and he killed him before he could say them."

"Wily little bitch!" roared the Demon.

"Hold him," cried Rhoswen. "All of you… you must hold him… Do as I say, *now!*"

In the same moment, Dicken, with a practiced arm, used his sword to swipe the pickaxe from the Demon's grip. The Demon was momentarily distracted. It was long enough for Dicken and Sir Geoffrey to leap forward, taking Silas's struggling body by the arms.

"We have to help them, Will!" cried Ingrith, and she and Will joined the two men in the struggle to hold the Demon.

All the while, Silas's body twisted about as it attempted to kick and punch them. It roared in fury, spitting and snarling at them whenever they came close to its face.

"Whatever it is you would do, woman, do it fast!" said Sir Geoffrey, through gritted teeth. "He is strong! Time is against us. He will break free."

"What is it she will do?" asked Will.

As if in answer, Rhoswen said, "Hear the words set down by our order to repel all that is evil. The wisdom of Saint Benedict himself!"

"Say them, woman! Say them now!" shouted Sir Geoffrey. "It will break free when our strength fades."

"*Crux sacra sit mihi lux,*" said Rhoswen. "Let the Holy Cross be my light....Speak the words with me, Ingrith!"

The two women spoke the words together:

"*Non draco sit mihi dux* - Let not the dragon be my guide.

Vade retro Satana – Step back Satan.

Numquam suade mihi vana - Never tempt me with vain things.

Sunt mala quae libas - What you offer are evils.

Ipse…"

"It is gone!" said a breathless Sir Geoffrey, leaning back triumphantly.

Silas had fallen still, his dead weight pulling at their arms.

Will looked at Ingrith, "Is it?"

Ingrith shook her head. "I don't know."

"The words, they were not completed!" said Rhoswen. "They were not all spoken. The formula is not complete."

"It is gone from him, Reverend Mother. The man is dead," said Sir Geoffrey.

Rhoswen shook her head. "We must finish the rite. We must be certain."

"More certain than this?" said Dicken, and gripped Silas's dead face by the chin, lifting it so the empty eye socket looked directly at Rhoswen.

"Let the women finish if they will," said Sir Geoffrey with a sigh.

Rhoswen looked at Ingrith. "Say the final words with me, daughter. Let us continue. *Ipse…*"

Before Ingrith had had a chance to join in, earth and stones exploded up from the pit Will and Silas had dug, shooting violently into the air, hitting the vaulting above and showering back down upon them. In the midst of it all flapped what appeared to be a huge bat, the size of a large dog - the Demon, now in the form of the Imp. The bones were no longer desiccated and cracked, but encased in muscles, joined to them by living sinew. There was no skin. Instead the thing was covered all over with a slick film of a substance that resembled, in both colour and odor, the pus discharged from infected tissue; its very presence was nauseating. From its front hung two short, thin limbs ending in long, dagger-like claws. At its back were wings, the flesh on them stretched to a thin, translucent membrane. The wings and claws flapped and slashed wildly as the Imp thrashed around the chapel, bouncing off the stone of the walls and ceiling, forcing them all to cover their heads and duck.

Dicken attempted to cut it down - getting behind it, and slashing with his sword at its wings. The Demon roared, spun around, and slashed at him. For a moment Dicken simply stood there. Then he dropped his sword, put both hands to his stomach, and fell to his knees. A second later he was holding out his own intestines in his hands as they spilled out of the gash the Demon had slashed across his belly. His expression was more one of confusion than of pain. Ingrith, one hand over her face in horror, reached towards Dicken with the other. Despite all that was happening, for a brief moment, Will found himself wondering what she thought she could possibly do to help the man. The question was never answered; before Ingrith could reach him, the Demon had slashed again, and Dicken fell onto his side, and rolled over. The blood from his cut throat spraying up into the air and falling back onto his face and chest as he died.

Ingrith pulled her hand back.

"The words!" shouted Will to Rhoswen. "Finish them!"

Rhoswen nodded. "*Ipse venena bibas,*" she shouted. "*Ipse venena bibas!*"

"*Ipse venena bibas,*" joined in Ingrith. "You drink the poison yourself!"

Everything fell silent.

The Demon had ceased its thrashing, and had dropped into a crouch on the floor, its wings hanging limply from its shoulders, its head bowed forward. As they watched, its body began to glow as if it were burning from the inside. Then the pus-like substance that covered it began to steam and boil, giving of a smell that was unspeakable. Soon, splits and tears began to appear in the muscles, through which orange flames danced. An acrid, choking smoke began to fill the chapel, making them all retch and cough.

"The fires of Hell come to claim you!" cried Rhoswen, exultantly.

"Bitch!" howled the Demon, suddenly raising its head. "Holy… *fucking*… bitch!" With an effort, it lunged at Rhoswen. The Abbess of Althurst threw back her head and screamed as the dying Demon's red-hot wings wrapped about her, pulling her into a blistering, burning embrace.

"No!" cried Ingrith.

Will put his arm around Ingrith, using his own body, as best he could, to shield her from the ball of near-white flame that now raged around the knot of roasted flesh and charred bone that had previously been the Demon and the Abbess. Impossibly, it was growing in size and intensity, in spite of the fact that there was almost nothing in the way of fuel for it to feed upon contained within the chapel's stone walls. It appeared to be fed by some supernatural agency all of its own, burning ever more fiercely as the seconds passed. To his alarm, Will realized that he and Ingrith were trapped on the wrong side of it. The door was out of reach, the other side of its deadly heat. They were both coughing violently now. Surely, they would soon choke to death before the flames even reached them. He studied the ball of fire. They would have to jump or die. He tried to judge the distance.

As if sensing Will's thoughts, from the other side of the

flames, Sir Geoffrey shouted, "You will never clear it, man. Don't try it! Better to pass out than to burn!" Then he added, "I'm sorry," and left through the door.

"I think he's right," Will said, lifting Ingrith's face to his, resting his forehead against hers.

She pulled away, shaking her head. "No, Will. No, he can't be." She looked about urgently, then nudged him, and pointed. "What about that?"

Without thinking, Will kissed her on the cheek. "I have been a blind fool. Pass me that pickaxe."

It did not take long to break through the wood that boarded up the hole in the wall of the chapel that had once been the saint's window into the church. If the lintel had not given way years ago it would have been too small, and the surrounding stone too thick to break down in time for them to make their escape before they were overcome by the smoke. As it was, however, Will lifted Ingrith up, and she climbed through the space without difficulty. It took a bit more effort on Will's part but, with some assistance from Ingrith, he, too, eventually pulled himself to safety.

******

EPILOGUE

As was to be expected, Baron Edgar of Basing was much saddened on receiving the news of the death of his youngest daughter, Ingrith. Unfortunately, events elsewhere now occupied his time. The elderly King Edward had recently died, leaving his young - and not much admired - son in his place. And so it was that the Baron never did find the time, then or later, to visit the site of her grave. Nor did he ever see the blackened walls of the small chapel where she and a small band of men were said to have assisted Abbess Rhoswen in the struggle against a demon that would claim the lives of all but Sir Geoffrey de Longe, and some craftsman of no name. Truth to tell, Baron Edgar was never entirely certain that he believed the tale. He suspected it might be a well-intentioned, if somewhat fanciful, fiction that had been concocted by the nuns to ease the pain of his daughter dying so tragically in the fire. Or, perhaps, to free themselves of any blame for it? The Baron had never had much time for the vainglorious and self-serving Sir Geoffrey, so his account, when the Baron finally came to hear it, did nothing to lessen this suspicion.

After the fire, it was Sister Helewise who had been called upon to undertake the unpleasant task of attempting to make sense of what remained of those who had failed to escape the flames, in order that their bodies might receive proper burial. The sisters were particularly concerned that their Abbess be laid to rest with all the appropriate rites and ceremony. As she had expected, most of the corpses Sister Helewise found were too much damaged by the flames for any definitive identification to be made. It was a matter of trying, as best she could, to match what she found with the descriptions of who had been in there offered her by William Tiler and Sir Geoffrey, the only survivors.

In the centre of the chapel she found the ruined mass that must once have been Abbess Rhoswen. She was able to distinguish it as such through some small items of blackened jewellery that she tearfully identified as belonging to the Reverend Mother. From their height, and some partial scraps of clothing, the two men - the Sheriff's man Dicken, and the Tiler's assistant, Silas – were not too difficult to guess at. Finally, at the bottom of a shallow pit, Sister Helewise found a somewhat smaller skeleton. It was so badly burned it was little more than sticks of ash, but from its size she guessed it to be that of the young novice, Ingrith.

Nothing of the Imp was ever found.

******

Perhaps it was, as Ingrith wanted to believe, compassion for their obvious affection for one another, or perhaps it was, as Will was more inclined to believe, his sense of guilt at having abandoned them at the end. Whatever his reasons were, Sir Geoffrey went along with their request that Ingrith be said to have died in the fire.

Later that same year, when William Tiler returned to Romsey Abbey to lay the tiles for a floor in the house of the abbess there, the nuns were heartened to note that he was accompanied by his new, young bride. A pleasant, if quiet, young woman who one or two of the nuns could not help feeling they might have seen somewhere before. When asked if she had ever visited them on a previous occasion, the girl always shook her head and looked away.

******

For many years afterwards, the story of Abbess Rhoswen's vanquishing of the Althurst Imp was a much-celebrated account of good triumphing over evil. Particularly in the south of England where, for a short time, it even came to rival the famous tale of Saint Dunstan and the Devil. Unlike the latter story, however, Rhoswen's eventually faded from memory, and whatever records of it were set down were lost. Perhaps the monks of Glastonbury where simply more adept – or possessed fewer scruples – when it came to promoting the name of their abbey, than were the nuns of Althurst? Or maybe it was simply because Rhoswen had been a woman? Whatever the reason, by the time of the Dissolution and the final fall of Althurst Abbey – a little over two hundred years after the events - nothing remained of her story. And so, unlike the almost legendary Abbot Dunstan, Abbess Rhoswen never did receive the canonization some had once believed was her due.

******

Today, very little remains of Althurst Abbey. The occasional visitors to the ruin often remark upon the strange, demon-like carving that glares down at them from the top of one of the few pillars that still remain standing, and speculate about what it is intended to represent.

There are plans for a more thorough excavation of the site than has previously been attempted in the not too distant future.

ABOUT THE AUTHOR

Leo Black lives in London with his wife, cat, and too many guitars.

BY THE SAME AUTHOR

ELASTUN

In a time when violent death is an everyday occurrence, what manner of death is it that can still strike fear into the hearts of men who have themselves made a profession of killing?

England, in the year 1067. A year has passed since the Battle of Hastings, and the Norman Conquest is fully underway. When Orderic de Varaville, a low ranking Norman knight, looks into the unexplained disappearance of two of his men, he finds himself having to overcome the natural enmity between conquerors and conquered, and join forces with the inhabitants of the Saxon village of **Elastun** in their struggle against an **ancient evil** that has found its way into their valley.

Key to their chances of success is the knowledge of pagan rites possessed by Alditha, the young widow of a Saxon killed by the Normans at Hastings. She and Orderic must put aside their mutual dislike if anyone in the village is to survive what is coming.

Printed in Great Britain
by Amazon